TIME, FOR A CHANGE

ADAM ECCLES

Copyright © 2018 Adam Eccles

All rights reserved. This book or any portion thereof may not be reproduced or used in any manner whatsoever without the express written permission of the author except for the use of brief quotations in a book review.

This is a work of fiction. Names, characters, businesses, places, events, locales, and incidents are either the products of the author's imagination or used in a fictitious manner. Any resemblance to actual persons, living or dead, or actual events is purely coincidental.

Created with Vellum

For Robin & Willow

About the Author

Adam Eccles is a sarcastic, cynical, tech-nerd hermit, living in the west of Ireland for the last couple of decades, or so.

www.AdamEcclesBooks.com

▮ facebook.com/AdamEcclesWrites
▮ twitter.com/AdamEcclesBooks

Chapter One

FRIDAY 24TH AUGUST

A warm, wafting stench of body odour assaults my senses as someone walks behind me. A squawking, exaggerated laugh in my periphery. A dull constant throb of distant air conditioning, mingled in with a dozen phone calls, all competing for attention.

The random but frequent slam of a toilet door, followed by the artificially floral air-freshener scent, drifting over, heavy and mixed in with cheap bleach.

A middle-aged man struts past my line of sight, his hair cut like a twelve-year-old-boy, his shirt tucked into trousers, pulled up high, gesticulating as he argues with his Bluetooth headset. His face slug-like, his neck and chin blend into his body, his eyes mobile, poking out on stalks.

Welcome to work. Gainful employment and regular pay, in exchange for only your eternal soul and mental stability. A sensory circus in a dull and meaningless existence.

4:30 pm on a Friday and someone has scheduled a conference call, probably to satisfy their inflated ego. Twenty-seven people have dialled in. The call subject: lost to the mists of time, some kind of all-hands meeting. Absolutely no one cares what the point is anyway. They merely want their chance to raise their 'personal brand' or something equally vulgar. I can see the comments in the meeting chat: "Awesome deal!", "Nice work!", "Go, team!". None of them are sincere, none of them are congratulating, they only scream 'look at me, look how great I am'.

I'm at my desk, headset on, dialled into this pointless waste of my life, checking emails, filling in a tech-sheet, browsing the web, and logged into the local instant message system. I also have my phone in my hand, scrolling Twitter. I multi-task, therefore I am.

[16:35] Ward, Terry B:
This call is intensely boring.
Pissing with rain outside. Hope it clears up for the weekend.

[16:36] O'Brien, Ted:
Meant to be nice.

I open up my weather app. It duly insults me, and then presents a weekend outlook of pleasant weather, not too hot, not too cold. No rain, minimal wind. That's perfect for my needs.

[16:38] Ward, Terry B:
I still always find it amazing that tons and tons of water, and snow and stuff, can be just floating around up there in the sky.

[16:39] O'Brien, Ted:
Magic elves do it.

Ted is a programmer. He keeps me sane. They keep him shuttered away in some distant office. I haven't seen him for years. Doesn't matter, instant message is a direct link to someone's brain. You can tell an awful lot from a short string of text.

Someone on the conference call is talking about gold awards given to team members who did a fantastic job; I didn't get one.

[16:42] Ward, Terry B:
I thought so.
The same lads who do the rainbows?

[16:44] O'Brien, Ted:
Ya, different group within that group though.

Someone on the conference call is now reading out a list of silver awards given to team members who did a great job; I didn't get one of those either.

[16:46] Ward, Terry B:
Ah.
They know each other though?
Say 'Hi' as they walk the halls?

[16:51] O'Brien, Ted:
They know each other to see each other, but they wouldn't be very close.
More like acquaintances.

Someone on the call is now presenting a long list of bronze awards given to team members who did an okay job. Basically, they showed up to work every day and didn't murder anyone; Oddly, I didn't get one of those either. Last time I checked, no one died due to my project management skills. I've worked here for ten years, a decade of my life doing the same thankless tasks, nothing ever changes or improves, despite the constant meetings to discuss what went wrong and what can we do better next time.

It was exciting at the start, meeting new customers, coming up with innovative IT solutions for their specific needs, travelling around Europe, America, and even Asia, staying in expensive hotels, eating expensive food, shitting expensive shits, all on the company credit card. But now I am tired, bored, beaten down to a bitter core, forgotten by management and drifting slowly into obscurity. It could be time for a change. #YaThink?

I randomly post a tweet as an idea pops into my head.

Just came up with an invention for a device that would totally eliminate fart noises. #MillionEuroIdea

I send the tweet off into the world, not really sure why because rarely does anyone read them. I don't know how, but I have over a thousand 'followers'. I think most of them are bots or spam accounts or something. But still, I feel an idea written down is an idea saved. This type of random thought sometimes just appears in my head, I've learnt to mostly ignore them. Still worth saving sometimes because you never know what will happen.

. . .

Time, For a Change

Some days at work I'm busier than a one-armed man trying to masturbate in a shed full of angry bees. But today has dragged, the hours passing glacially, probably because I'm distracted with my weekend plans. I just want to get out of here and get this weekend over with.

> **[16:54] Ward, Terry B:**
> That's the problem in these big teams.
> If they worked together more - we might have more snow-bows.
> Which would be nice.
>
> **[16:54] O'Brien, Ted:**
> Ya, it would brighten up the day.
>
> **[16:54] Ward, Terry B:**
> Bring a bit of colour to the winter.

The call takes an ugly turn, handed over to the sales manager for Europe, explaining in a friendly tone, how each and every one of us must contribute to the whole team, by filling in new time management reports every week. Documenting every piss and shit-break we take and how long it takes to do it.

> **[16:55] Ward, Terry B:**
> You don't see many rainbows at night either.
> The Night Elves are a different team I'd say.
>
> **[16:56] O'Brien, Ted:**
> They repair shoes.
>
> **[16:56] Ward, Terry B:**

Nice sideline.

[16:56] O'Brien, Ted:
Totally different group.

[16:56] Ward, Terry B:
Different cost centre?

[16:57] O'Brien, Ted:
Yep, they get night-shift allowance though, extra pay.

I must have forgotten to set my chat status to 'Away', because another chat window pops open on my screen.

[16:59] Greene, Judith:
Hi Terry, have you got a second? Just wanted to ask about the procurement on those cards for DeltaWave.

Seriously? 4:59 on a Friday? No, I don't have a fucking second. I quickly close the chat window and change my status to 'Appear Offline'. I'd rather drown in a bucket of rat piss than talk to her now.

We at C.S.Tech are happy to take care of your custom IT installations, from scoping to lights on, we have you covered!

'Terrence B. Ward, Custom Project Manager'
That's what it says on my business cards. Cards that I never give to anyone.

Terry Brian Ward. My parents, Monty Python fans and a tiny bit cruel.

T.B. Ward - if I hear another joke about being consumed…

[16:59] Ward, Terry B:

> That's at least something for them.
> I don't though! So I'm outta here.
> Smell you later Ted.

[17:00] O'Brien, Ted:

> Smell you later Terry.

The call wraps up on time thankfully, and I've already prepared to leave on the dot of five. My laptop is in my bag, and I'm up and heading for the door quicker than a silent fart fills a meeting room after a canteen curry lunch. But I leave a small packet of salt on my chair to keep the slug-people away.

I've got things to organise after work, walking into town rather than driving home, I need to pick up a rental van for the weekend.

After a wet walk to the van rental place, I grab a takeaway pizza and drive home, wondering all the way if this weekend plan is going to be a pointless waste of time.

Chapter Two

SATURDAY 25TH AUGUST

I have plenty of time to think as I make the long drive to my dad's old workshop, taking it slowly in an unfamiliar vehicle. After nearly four years, the time has come to try and sort things out.

There have been many other opportunities I suppose, but, I wasn't ready. I'm still not ready, I may never be ready, but now is as good a time as any. Oh, and the bank wants to take the whole place back, and they won't wait any longer. So there's that.

The hedges by the road are blooming in fuchsia pink, montbretia orange, gorse yellow and some kind of purple thing I don't know. Reminds me of why the family decided on this remote location. No one will bother you down here in rural Ireland; the countryside is wild, the people are sparse, but the wind and rain can be brutal foes. You think: 'Ah, what can a bit of rain do? 'Tis only water…' But it eats at you, spots all over your glasses, trips you on muddy grass and permeates you to the core. Still, 'tis only water.

Time, For a Change

. . .

I left this morning super early, before any rational people were awake on a Saturday. The house was chilly, my electric toothbrush was still charging when I picked it up, that's how early it was! The roads are relatively empty, in fact, I don't think I've seen another vehicle for about twenty miles, sorry, thirty kilometres. Where am I going to put all the stuff?! I haven't thought that far ahead. Shed, I suppose. What am I actually going to do with the stuff? I have no idea right now, but one day it might come in useful.

My family keep telling me to throw it all away, but I can't. It isn't just useless junk and stuff; it's my memories. Every item has a story, and Dad carefully maintained and transported through many house moves, cared for, and instilled a sense of respect in me for this stuff, 'look after your tools, and they will look after you'.

As I get closer the memories become more vivid; the road is no longer just a road to drive on, it becomes a part of my life. I remember where it dips and you have to swerve over, a familiar wooden door falling off someone's shed - the paint peeling off. I know where there's a rusty train on a track to nowhere and a bench of metal trad players, forever in tune. I've been here many times, but over the last few years, I haven't been able to bring myself to visit. The landscape is always in flux with the seasons, but the basics never change. There's something eerily wild and barren about the place. Few trees can survive the relentless wind, so the fields are only broken by low hedges, thick with local stone. A few massive wind generators now complement the landscape. White vanes, fading down to green stalks like giant daisies.

They cast long and strange shadows, fill the air with energy. An imaginary harmonic drone flows from their blades as I watch them gently spin with mighty force.

I have to play some music to distract myself, so I fiddle with the controls on the van dashboard until some familiar noise blasts out. I leave it playing for a few songs, but I quickly tire of the radio and all its incessant carpet, insurance and furniture adverts and go back to road noise to keep my brain occupied.

The radio was strange anyway, they played a song that was quite familiar to me, I was humming away to the tune and belting out the chorus, but the DJ said it was a new release after it played. I put this down to DJs being idiots, but I stopped for a piss in the hedge and popped out a tweet.

Ever heard a brand-new song on the radio and known for sure you have heard it before? Sure you know it very well even?
  #WhatsThatAbout ?

I have a vague inkling that something like that had happened before to me, maybe when I was a kid. I couldn't explain it then and forgot all about it.

Back on the road the rest of the journey is uneventful, aside from one cow I had to swerve to avoid. These things happen.

Oh, and I stopped at the graveyard too, desolate and lonely here on the side of a hill near the coast, the Atlantic spray only a handy distance away. The remains of the small church are now just a few stone walls and nothing more; the roof is the wide blue sky. Thick and hardy green moss softening the edges of the rocks, sprayed with tiny pink flowers no bigger than a grain of rice. But after deliberating for a while, I didn't go into the graveyard in the end. What would be the point? Just bones in the ground. I don't believe in any kind of afterlife.

I arrive at the familiar, but now very overgrown, driveway. I think if humankind left Ireland for a generation or so and then came back, they would find that the brambles would have entirely taken over, started some kind of government and order and built cities and efficient train networks.

I turn the van off, but I can't bring myself to get out just yet. I sit for a few minutes looking at the building. Perhaps a part of me is hoping Dad will wave from the window and open the door with a mug of coffee in hand and his pipe in his mouth.

The last time we made something in this workshop together must be six years ago. I brought measurements and wood, Dad helped me make a window frame, showed me how to set up the router, use the guides, join the corners so they would be immensely strong. He always knew how to do everything, no matter how complicated or obscure it was. I'm suddenly jolted to reality by a thought, did I bring the keys? Adrenaline and confusion and some digging in my bag, and I find that yes, I did bring the keys. A huge bunch. I also brought a lantern, spare batteries, a towel - because you should always know where your towel is, and a bottle of water. I also note that the cellular networks still don't consider this area worth covering, and my phone is disconnected from everything: 'NO SERVICE', much like myself.

. . .

After trying six keys in the door, I finally find the one that fits; I don't think anybody alive knows what all the other ones fit. The door is stiff, a swift kick to the base only budges it a bit, two more kicks plus pressure at the top, and it finally opens, swollen by the weather, no idea how I'll get it shut again without ripping the door handle off.

Of course, there is no power on here; the window is mostly covered by junk on the inside and brambles on the outside, so I flick open the lantern and step into the past.

There's a particular type of silence here; there's rarely any traffic, the thick walls mostly insulate the wind. Peace and quiet, I can see why Dad spent so much time here. I brush the sawdust off a work stand and sit for a moment, soaking in the familiar smells. Coffee, pipe smoke, sawdust and tools, just general tools, there's a certain tinge to the air that nothing else can muster.

Looking around at the ridiculous array of every tool anyone can possibly imagine, I'm reminded, and quite daunted of the task ahead, how the feckin' hell am I going to move all this stuff on my own in one day?

Lost in my thoughts, pondering the sanity of my situation, I'm just thinking of grabbing the big stuff I can carry and calling it a day, maybe that will have to do? But in the still silence, barely audible above the sound of the blood in my ears, there's a faint sound. I don't think I noticed it at first, but now I realise something is there that is maybe out of place. What could be making a clicking and droning noise, coming from somewhere under a bench?

Using bat-like sonic echolocation, cupping my ears and turning around, I think I've pinned down the direction, so I start shuffling equipment, a cement mixer, a generator, not functional - I tried, a welder, three power drills, a seriously heavy box full of files and hammers - what the fuck? And about three-hundred miles of wound three core mains cables, and there's a big wooden box deep under the wide bench.

Pulling it out required some serious effort and leverage from a broken broom handle, but this is definitely where the sound is coming from now. Still not very loud. On the top of the box is written:

"No rest for the conflicted !!"

In my dad's unforgettable handwriting, in black permanent marker. Messages like this are all over the place, not least the ever loved -

"If all else fails, read the fucking manual !!"

The box is sturdy, something like the size of a big suitcase, but a bit deeper. Finger holes on the short edges for handles, made of an unfinished board, the edges solid with

Dad's typical exact carpentry. It has a lid, hinged at the back, clasp at the front. Inevitably, I open it up.

There's a contraption inside, that's it, undoubtedly a contraption! It spins gently, causing the sound, I think it is catching on something underneath, causing the regular clicks.

The spinning part is made of brass, I think. A kind of low cone shape studded with a spiral of small black discs, like magnets. It's in the middle of the box, I can't see what it's resting on, but there's a small gap between it and the bottom of the box. At the sides there are flat areas that have hand shapes, left and right, drawn on in the same black marker pen. Seems to be on copper circuit board, thick red wires connect them to somewhere under the cone.

I've never seen this thing before, even though I've spent many an hour in here with Dad, making stuff, breaking stuff, talking about the nature of the universe, the things he was working on. I've messed with most things in here before, so what is this thing? There's no chance it was made by anyone else; I can tell the trademark style, the routed edges of the internal wooden structure are clearly built on his router table. I recognise the bevelled edge, I broke that router bit something like eight years ago when I tried to rout through a screw, oops, so this thing had to have been made at least eight years ago I reckon, but how have I never seen it?

Touching the spinning cone feels like it buzzes with electricity, like when you touch a poorly earthed metal device, but there's no power connection. Oddly, touching it doesn't seem to slow it down at all, even pressing quite hard doesn't disturb the angle or slow the spin.

There's a smell too, a bit like an impending storm.

So I'm guessing there must be a battery or something in the box, how else is this thing propelled? But I haven't been here in years; no one has, what kind of battery could last this long? I think I'll take this back home and investigate further in my shed, under good lights and with a cup of coffee.

There's a lot of equipment to sort through still, to decide what is coming and what is staying, so back to the task at hand.

Using an ancient wheel cart thing, formally employed moving beer kegs around in the 1700s by the looks of it, I drag and heft the box and its mysteries out to the van and load it in. Followed by a vast array of power tools, sheets of plywood, planks of floorboard, eighty-four router bits in a beautiful wooden chest, three large boxes of assorted and sorted resisters, cable ties, an AntiStatic Mat - always thought that was a cool DJ name! LEDs, switches, buttons, knobs, capacitors and other 'odds and sods' according to the labels, piled on with every other thing I could grab and looked like it was worth the effort.

After some time, some sweat, some swearing and some rips in my T-shirt the van is pretty much full, so I guess that's it.

That's it for the workshop anyway, I took all the computer equipment from the office in my car years ago, boxes of disks and old computers. One day I will get round to collating all the data from the multitude of disks into one storage array.

. . .

I get back home and it's late. A heavily loaded van is a beast of a thing to drive on the bumpy rural roads. I was starving on the way back so stopped for chips, it delayed me a bit but needs must. I'm cream-crackered after the long day; I'll unload the van tomorrow. I go straight to bed and collapse.

Chapter Three

SUNDAY 26TH AUGUST

I'm not a morning person, but there's still a lot of work to do to unload the van, so my alarm sounds at an evil hour. Only the thought of a nice big breakfast rallies me from the bed. I get up, stick the kettle on for tea. I also start the coffee machine because I'll need two types of caffeine for this job! As I wait for the water to boil, I have a niggling memory of the dream I just woke from, and pop off a tweet.

Last nights dream: Excellent production value, good casting, almost realistic plot. Can't remember a damn thing now. 7/10

There's a group text message on my phone too, from my family, asking how it's going. Presumably, they mean the moving?

They decided to up and leave a few years ago. Mum inherited some money and a house in Italy, up a mountain or something. I haven't been there, it's much too hot for me. But they prefer the weather there, and we can easily keep in touch. I send a photo of the full van back to the group chat.

. . .

Looking in the fridge, I see that not only do I have no milk, but I don't have any eggs, any sausages, any bacon, any beans, anything decent at all. Damn! A significant gap in project planning here. Toast and black tea will have to suffice.

My house, if you can call it that, once described by an estate agent as 'pile of stones, vaguely house shaped' is quite a distance from the nearest shop, and I don't fancy driving a van loaded to the max down to the grocery store and back. The joys of living the rural life, I have space to waste outside as I please, but it comes at the cost of distance to amenities.

After my 'big breakfast' I head out to the shed, which is more of a stone out-building than your average wooden slatted garden variety. Rusty tin roof, rough stonework, one door, one window. It does have electricity though, and plenty of space, which is what I'll need today. A quick shuffle of boxes of old junk, sweep up and I'm ready to start unloading.

I'm thankful to the weather deities that this weekend is absent of rain and horrific wind, in fact, it's quite nice, light breeze, blue sky. Some music courtesy of my phone and a set of speakers and the whole task doesn't seem so bad.

Unloading is at least a bit easier than it was loading up. I've rigged up a few planks which I brought with me, so I can just roll things down almost straight into the shed door. From there I'm dumping things inside, making sure they are safe and moving on to the next.

Breaking for lunch involves a frozen meal and the microwave. It tastes like cardboard and wallpaper paste, but at least it is more than toast. I check my emails, Twitter, news, text messages. Nothing of interest; no one else has contacted me, seems like a typical weekend. Quite often I find that from the time I leave work on Friday evening, to the time I go back on Monday morning, I have absolutely no human contact. Suits me.

Maybe I should sell some of this stuff? I mean, what am I ever going to do with five routers? A bench mounted metal hole punch? A set of vintage antique planers and profilers? A band saw? None of this stuff is much use to me, but it is valuable equipment. For now, it can stay in the shed I guess, selling gear like this is not fun, people ask too many questions and want to chat about it, and what it was used for. Even if I wanted to, I couldn't tell them.

Occasionally I find something that triggers a distant memory. The hammer I smacked my thumb with, when helping Dad nail down floorboards in an extension he was building. The set of chisels I bought him for a birthday one year, still in perfect condition. These things slow me down as I bathe in the nostalgia. But, I guess that's the whole point.

Slowly the van empties as the shed fills. I'm getting towards the back now and I notice the mysterious box again, sitting there placid, at the bottom of the pile, filled with all of Pandora's secrets. I will be able to drag it out once I get the last row of boxes out. But these final boxes are filled with pure lead by the feel of the weight, either that or I'm getting tired.

"Fuck!"

. . .

Blood and pain, and I drop the box on my foot after scraping my forearm up on a nail sticking out of the door frame. I rush into the house and grab a towel, wrap it around my arm and hold it above my head while I look for bandages.

It turns out it wasn't too bad, big scrape down my arm. Not deep, but I've ruined a good towel with blood, and it is quite sore. Luckily I'm finished unloading the van now, I think that's enough for today, I'm calling it a job done. But I might need a tetanus booster though. Wonderful!

After a cling film wrapped shower experience, so I didn't get the bandage wet, I brave the freezer and find yet another microwave dinner. Unsatisfying, but I am exhausted, and I fade away to bed. I have another early start tomorrow to take the van back before work.

Chapter Four

MONDAY 27TH AUGUST

I'm not used to all these very early starts, my body revolts. To get out of bed is a brutal battle between my muscles and my brain, but in the end, the pressure in my bladder wins and I get up. Everything aches, things I didn't know I had ache, even the aches ache. Nevertheless, I dress, gulp down toast and tea and head away in the van to the rental centre which is in the middle of the town. From there I can walk to work and back to reality.

I often wonder if being sick of work is enough to take a sick day? I would probably never go in if that were the case. As I trudge through the halls to my desk I pass familiar faces, barely a nod in their direction as I keep my eyes down, pretending I have something interesting to look at on my phone, headphones in, volume up.

"Good weekend?" my colleague Jeff barks at me over the cubicle wall as I plonk down my bag and begin unpacking my laptop. He's ever jovial and about twenty cups of coffee ahead of me in the 'being awake' race.

"Same old shit," I mutter, reluctant to start a conversation at this early hour on a Monday morning.

He doesn't get the message though.

"Thought you were going down to your dad's old workshop or something?"

"Oh, yeah, I did, I ache all over to prove it. Cut my arm up too." I hold up my bandaged arm as proof.

"Well that's not the same then, is it? You don't do that every weekend!"

"Fuck off, Jeff. I need coffee."

I walk away to the canteen and press buttons on the coffee machine, curse a few times, press more buttons, eventually ending up with a cup of something barely resembling coffee. I pour three sugar packets into it; carpe diem!

I check my phone and note I have a meeting in twelve minutes. Oh, joy.

The meeting room is darkened for the projector, cramped and hot; it feels like all the oxygen has been sucked out. I'm suffocated in these windowless meeting rooms. I always sit near the door in case I need to exit rapidly. The fools up near the projection screen have no chance of getting out of here quickly. This is a regular progress meeting for one of my numerous customers. No progress is ever made, yet we have the weekly meetings anyway. The first eight minutes are wasted as people figure out, yet again, how to use the conference call speaker, and while various people dial in. Some from an underground satanic nightclub by the sound of the background noise, some apologies for being late, some having several other conversations at once, some heavy breathing Darth Vaders. Around the table in the room we make the same exasperated sighs and eye rolls at each other as we do at every meeting. The other people in the room with me are sales or something, I'm not sure what they actually do, but they seem to show up for meetings and write things down, so I assume they have some purpose? Everyone on the dial-in is muted eventually, and they start the action tracker list of things no one will ever do. I tune out, my mind is drawn back to the mysterious box I found in the workshop, I forgot about it because of all the rushing around, but the boredom of the meeting allows me to drift off into my thoughts. What does it do? Where did it come from? When did he make it?

"... Terry?"

Oh, shit, someone was asking me something, I have no idea what they said!

"Sorry, I was distracted, can you please repeat the question?"

This type of thing is usual; no one ever listens to anything anyone else says, only waiting for a pause so they can butt in and show how great they are.

"Did you hear back from the vendors on the price of those cards?" The voice of Judith Greene on the conference speaker repeats, mildly annoyed. She's the project lead for this customer.

"Oh, no not yet, I will send a chaser mail."

"Only it's getting quite urgent now that we get this locked down."

"Yeah, as I said, I will send a chaser, and I'll make sure they know it is urgent."

"Thanks, Terry, let me know if you need anything."

Yes, I do. I need a new job, I need a holiday, I need a

million Euro to fall from the sky into my lap, I need a lot of things, but none of them will come from this meeting...

After the meeting, I slope off back to my desk, thankful to the office gods that no one is around. Must be break time already? I can look through my hundred-and-eighty-seven unread emails in peace.

Delete, delete, delete, ignore, one line answer, saving the interesting ones for later, moving the annoying ones down the pile of shit I will never do.

My calendar tells me there are still three more meetings to get through today, most of these daily meetings are carbon copies of each other, some with customers, some internal only, some that I can just dial in and tune out. Others require me to say something. I don't enjoy presenting, but by now it is second nature, and I churn out the same old crap to an uninterested audience.

Lunch in the canteen is always the same. Every single dish, no matter what it is meant to be, is laced with celery. I have a theory that the chef has a brother who owns a celery farm. I fucking hate celery. I sit down at an empty table, hoping that no one will see me and sit next to me, but they inevitably do. They talk about sport, cars and their kids. Patios, barbecues, dinner parties and holiday plans, none of which interest me, so again I tune out. In any case, I find it hard to hear and focus on individual voices amongst the crowd, so even if I wanted to listen, I couldn't. I'd prefer to eat out of the office, on my own, but the industrial estate restaurant is equally awful and to go into town is too far just for lunch. Sometimes I bring sandwiches and sit in my car, but today, I must suffer the celery and chit-chat.

Time, For a Change

"Did you find anything interesting, down in the workshop?" Jeff slams down his tray opposite to me.

"Just a load of tools, what else would you expect to find?"

I'm not going to mention the mysterious box; don't need the Inquisition right now. I'm still aching and tired from the weekend; I just want to run a hot bath and soak away the pain.

"You never know, wasn't your dad a mad scientist or something?"

"Not mad, just a scientist."

Jeff is distracted by someone hurling office banter abuse about the woeful sports team performance over the weekend, I am offered a chance to vanish, so I do.

"Need to catch up on emails," I mutter to no one in particular as I get up, no one listens or cares anyway. I grab some salt packets as I leave the canteen. Need to stock up on slug-person repellant.

I spend the afternoon between meetings researching a cheap but good external disk drive; I'm planning to take the sixteen or so drives I have of my dad's and copy all the data onto one, much more straightforward to keep it all safe and search through things. All sixteen disks are ancient and small capacity, so the data from them should all fit on one new big disk. Dad was always amazed by the progress made in computers; he'd often tell stories of the stone age machines he worked with in the sixties and how he thought new equipment seemed to defy the laws of physics. It's going to take some effort and time to transcribe all those disks down to one, but it will be worth it, assuming they all still spin up after years in a cardboard box in my cupboard. There must be some notes about the mysterious box somewhere in all his documents, just need to search through it all.

. . .

Five o'clock eventually ticks around, and I pack up my bag and head to the car and impending traffic.

You'd be forgiven for thinking there can't possibly be any traffic in Ireland? Aren't there only like eight people in the whole country?

C.S.Tech HQ is in the USA, I have heard all the ridiculous assumptions many times.

"Do you guys eat Haggis for breakfast?"

"No, that would be in Scotland."

"Oh, I thought Scotland and Ireland were the same things?"

"No…"

Well, the cities outside of Dublin and Cork are quite small, but the roads are still packed, and sometimes, like five pm on a Monday, I still have to sit in traffic for a while, despite there being only seven other people in the entire country.

As I sit in my stationary vehicle and stare at the back of a dirty truck, I ponder on what Jeff was asking. Now that I think of it, he was probably expecting me to be clearing out a science lab type of room, rather than the DIY tools I was actually clearing. The science equipment went long ago when my dad's company decided they no longer had any use for him or the gear. Sold to the lowest bidder. None of that stuff is left now, only the plumbing, woodworking, power tools, masonry equipment, none of the weird and wonderful stuff a layman might expect to find in a lab. Just that odd box, of course, spinning into infinity with no explanation. I need to take a look in the shed.

I connect my phone to the car and search for some Chopin to relax my brain. But as I near the grocery store, I remember that I have no food at home, so I reluctantly have to stop for a shop.

I have an ability, or maybe a curse, of being able to instantly extrapolate the entire life story of a stranger after a microsecond glance. At least that's what I tell myself, I could be totally wrong, probably am, but it doesn't matter. I usually just look down at my own shopping and avoid eye contact, or any kind of contact with the normal humans, but occasionally one slips through.

There's Phil, diminutive, small headed, slightly balding side parting, unusually long eyebrows, face creased with the pressures of life.

He's parked his trolley in such a way that my path and shelf destination are blocked. I will only allow twelve seconds before I tut and move on. Phil lives a blissful life, in that bliss is only in abundance where ignorance is present.

Never married - no ring. His late middle aged life is mainly meals for one, confirmed by his shopping on display; one carrot, two onions, half a litre of skimmed milk.

He has a profound and disturbing obsession with train crashes throughout history; an expert on the subject. He can give you intricate details of railway disasters since the dawn of the age at a moments notice, his pub mates can attest to this fact, as they too become familiar with the highlights of the genre, through his uncanny ability to steer any conversation toward his favoured topic.

His jacket makes shushing noises as he moves, his spotless brown shoes squeak on the polished floor.

On his nightstand by his bed is a pocket watch that his

Grandfather left him, it hasn't worked for decades, but he keeps it dusted and clean. He doesn't have a dishwasher, preferring to wash up by hand - size small, yellow rubber gloves and green dish-soap, he's partial to dark chocolate and cheap red wine.

He uses a sniff as punctuation to indicate he's just announced something profound or poignant.

He's got a day off work tomorrow to go to the dentist; floss, mouthwash and new toothbrush. He works in a factory as a quality inspector, walking around with his clipboard, hard-hat and 'hi-viz' vest, checking the widgets are neatly aligned and accurately fabricated, ticking things off on the dockets.

He still uses VHS tapes to record off the telly, cassette tapes to record off the radio. He's thinking of getting a laptop for 'research purposes'.

His favourite armchair faces a fireplace, not the TV. He has €80,000 saved up in a shoe-box, and intends to retire early, so he can travel the world, making pilgrimages to his favourite train crash sites of history, and bathe in the macabre atmosphere. One hundred and one people died that night in 1918, Nashville, Tennessee.

Phil continues to deliberate over the choice of Manuka honey.

I tut and move on.

Once I get home, I make beans and eggs on toast; the staple dinner of the lonely nerd. Then head over to the shed for some investigation.

Time, For a Change

I heft the wooden box up onto the bench and open the lid. There it is, spinning gently, the twist of the black studs mesmerising as I stare. That smell - like new rain, storm brewing, lightning struck air, electrical. I pull up a stool, sit down and look inside.

Weird thing, when I looked into the box before, I didn't notice that there's a set of controls at the front. There are four black knob dials of the kind you might see on an old amplifier, with labels under them, at the front of the spinning cone. I found a small drawer full of these exact knobs amongst the equipment I pulled out of the workshop in a cabinet marked: 'Odds and Sods' - otherwise known as variable potentiometers.

Y, M, D, H. They are all turned as far right, clockwise, as they will go. There's no scale on the dials though, it looks unfinished as if there would eventually be something to align the knob to, but instead, there's blank wood behind them.

Turning them has no visible effect, the cone spins as it always does, no lights come on, there's no sound. I set all of them as far left, anticlockwise, as they will go. It seems like that would be the zero baseline setting.

Left and right of the spinning wheel are flat copper pads with hand shapes drawn on in marker. Not hard to work out what they are for, but what happens when you touch the pads? Maybe they work like a heart rate detector on an exercise bike? There's nothing that would indicate a measurement though. Only one way to find out I suppose!

I reach down and put my hand on the left pad, fitting my fingers into the outline, there's a tingle, and the brass cone seems to wobble for a moment but it quickly stabilises and continues its perpetual spin. I reach down and hover over the right-hand pad, pausing, but decide 'fuck it' and put my second hand down…

A sudden change, a drop in temperature, the feeling of falling fast. Darkness, no weight. Silence, a rapid fade of all external senses.

… [please hold while we try to connect you] …

A pulse, a pattern, a universal dial tone… Now everything starts to come back into phase. I feel cold; there's a smell like snow in moonlight, a taste of sugar on my tongue. There's an overwhelming sense of euphoria, I'm thrilled and awoken, the joy is saturating and stimulating like five cups of espresso. Adrenaline floods my veins, a tingle in my nose. There's warmth now, even though there's still cold. I can't move anything, I try and open my eyes, and they don't work, I feel disconnected from my body.

… [Your call is important to us, so please stay on the line, and we'll be with you shortly] …

Gradually, then suddenly, some senses return. There's a regular, repeating sound I vaguely recognise, can't put my finger on what it is though, figuratively I mean, I still can't physically move any digits at all right now. It's still dark, I can hear a muffled voice but can't make out who or where. The regular repeating sound gains clarity.

. . .

I... I think it's a printing press, a hand operated model. Made by Adana, my dad had one when I was a kid; he would do invitations, business cards, letterheads, whatever people needed. He did it at night usually in a tiny cupboard room that was cut out of my bedroom. That's precisely what I can hear now. As the lever is pushed down, the rollers slide up over the ink as the inking disc twists around, evenly spreading it out. There's a sticky slurp of the thick ink, squelching over the rollers, which then roll down over the metal type, making it ready to impact the ink on the paper. The type is reversed, upside down, tightly bound in strips of thin wood, padded and clamped perfectly into place, then the ink covered metal impacts on the paper, leaving the mark. That's the sound I can hear now, over and over in a production line way, each cycle ends in a bell-like tinkle. These are sounds I haven't heard in thirty-something years.

After some cycles, the hand press stops. Some muffled shuffling and typing on a loud keyboard, now another sound starts, loud, percussive, very fast. Machine gun fire. No. An old computer printer, a daisywheel, the type that takes paper with regular holes down each side that you can tear off, tractor feed fan-fold I think it was called.

I try again, and my eyes open this time, blurry, dark. A slit of light under a door. I'm in a small room, standing next to a small bed.

There's a smell now, familiar and acrid, pipe smoke. Are you fucking serious?

I hear a cough, the printer sound stops, then...

In the shed, my phone is ringing, I try to stand up to reach it, but my legs have gone numb. I pull myself up on a shelf: 'UNKNOWN NUMBER' I sigh and sit back down without answering.

What was that? Was I asleep? Dreaming? Seemed like a very vivid memory, I haven't thought about that printing press for decades. No idea where it went, Dad must have sold it long ago. Why would that come up now? Did I black out?

It's getting dark outside, how long was I in here? I didn't note what time it was when I sat down, but it seems like the sky is darker than it should be. My hands smell like copper, I'm disturbed and discombobulated somehow. I stand up, and out of the corner of my eye I notice something different. I look at the controls, and there's tiny writing next to the Y knob at the leftmost setting. '78'. The cone still spins, unaware of the confusion it is causing.

I find myself walking along the lane that leads from my house to the main road, twisting and narrow, a grass strip down the middle, just wide enough for one vehicle. The evening scent of summer is calming, a gentle cooling breeze blows away the strange feelings, and I can focus.

I'm a logical and rational person, I trust in science, I'm sceptical of fanciful claims, but something odd just happened to me, and I can't help but think I was really in that small room for a moment, my old bedroom? I try to figure out when that would have been, I know we moved from that house before I was five years old, so something like 1977, maybe 1978? '78'… That's the number that was written on the dial for Y.

For a long while, Google Maps didn't even know my lane existed. Now they do, but it seems like they gave up halfway down. No one else calls this plot of boggy turf-land home, not unless you count the cattle that roam around from a nearby farm almost unfettered. At night it is completely dark, no streetlights pollute the black, so when it is clear, all the stars of the universe are mine. In the winter it is even more crystalline and pure, but this will do. The air chilled, silence enveloping the world. Occasional rips of sod torn from the ground as a cow chews. These are beef cows so I don't have the daily churn of mud and shit on the road, as some would have, when they lead them to milk.

There are no natural predators here. I feel utterly safe in the dark. I know most people would find that odd or unrealistic; but to me, it is natural and incredibly calming. I sometimes sit out on the bonnet of my car, contemplating nothing in particular for hours until I decide it is time to stop.

There is peace and sanctuary in being alone. But there is also terrible loneliness. I sometimes act out in my head how I would show a mythical son or daughter how to change a wheel by the road. How to program a computer and how to cook. How they would be well versed in science and electronic engineering, be eloquent beyond their years and maybe invent something world changing. How I'd learn from them and all their mistakes, as they utterly deny to learn from mine as all children do. Everyone must learn for themselves.

How my wife would lie sleeping peacefully as I get up and pick flowers for our breakfast table, or some other clichéd romantic tripe. The trouble is that society and humanity are poisoned, and they cannot trust in sincerity, and instead of friendship, there is only anger and violence on the tips of their tongues.

That is why I remain alone, it is safer and easier and exposes less risk. I do sometimes wonder though if the risk is worth it? How soon is now?

I turn around and head for home, intending to pull open the files and disks I took from Dad's office many years ago now, and maybe find some answers to the myriad questions I have.

Chapter Five

TUESDAY 28TH AUGUST

I'm irritable and tired today, well, more irritable than usual perhaps. Couldn't sleep much last night, too much on my mind. When I did finally drift off, I frequently woke, disturbed. 'Busy head' is what I call it, a repeating cycle of thoughts I just can't get rid of. At the time they are intense, the only thing that matters, violently raging in my brain, but once I get up, walk away, distract myself, they fade into nothing. I can barely remember what was so important. Sleep is a weird thing when you think about it. Lying unconscious, hallucinating wildly, acting out bizarre situations with your muscles switched off and then quickly forgetting the details of those visions when you become conscious again.

There are occasions where I admit that sleep is not going to happen, and I get up and watch something, or read. My insomnia hasn't been too severe lately, since I discovered melatonin and the need to be exposed to sunlight during the day. This typically means going for a walk around the car park at lunchtime; even just that gentle stroll outside is good enough to make a significant difference. Gets me away from the stresses of work anyway, so wins all around. My sleep patterns have been a bit disrupted lately, though. I probably should try and get some good sleep and rest.

Ever have one of those days at work, where you know you won't get anything done? Too tired to concentrate, and too bored to do anything simple. It's overwhelming and depressing honestly, I don't want to waste a day, but I'm not in a fit state to do anything useful. Even multiple cups of coffee and a walk after lunch does nothing to boost my energy. I tried to search through some of Dad's old disks late last night, but it was painfully slow to find an adaptor, and search each disk individually. Also, I don't know what I'm looking for, so opening file after file of notes and drawings and designs became very frustrating. I didn't find anything relating to the mystery box.

[14:23] O'Brien, Ted:
   Shtory?

Ted pops up a message window on my screen. I welcome the distraction, pop on a headset and set my status to 'Busy'. The headset is so passersby don't think they can bother me. Any casual attempts to make pointless conversation can be met with a thumb and small finger 'I'm on the phone' gesture and a quick eye roll, indicating my disappointment that I won't be able to shoot the shit with them for fifteen minutes, as they walk back from the jax. Only the determined lollygagger will persist after that.

[14:23] Ward, Terry B:
   Well Ted.
   Feck all.

Tired as a canteen sandwich.

[14:24] O'Brien, Ted:
Yah. One of those days.

[14:24] Ward, Terry B:
They should pump the office full of oxygen like a Vegas casino.
Instead, I think they suck it all out.

[14:24] O'Brien, Ted:
Tis a bit suffocating alright.

I want to discuss the weird experience I had with the mystery box with someone, but I fear it would lead to too many questions that I have no answers for, too many sideways glances at my sanity. Even someone as understanding as Ted may fear that I need to rest up and stop being a weirdo. Best to keep it quiet until I understand what is going on I guess. I mean, for all I know it was just a weird dream, maybe I nodded off for a minute. I'm severely out of shape, the early starts and physical work probably just took their toll. I'm too old to burn the candle at both ends these days.

[14:25] Ward, Terry B:
Any craic?

[14:26] O'Brien, Ted:
My kettle broke!
Couldn't have tea this morning.

[14:27] Ward, Terry B:

Disaster!

[14:27] O'Brien, Ted:

I know.

I'll get a cheap one on the way home.

[14:28] Ward, Terry B:

My Father always said 'I am not a rich man, so I can only afford the best.'

Did you know most American households don't even have a kettle?

Don't even know what it is.

[14:29] O'Brien, Ted:

How do they heat water?

[14:30] Ward, Terry B:

Pot on the stove.

Or microwave.

[14:30] O'Brien, Ted:

That's mad.

[14:31] Ward, Terry B:

Yeah. It led to that 80s ballad 'How can you live without a kettle?'

A Duet.

Barry Manilow and Barbara Streisand.

[14:31] O'Brien, Ted:

Really?

[14:32] Ward, Terry B:

Oh yeah. Was massive in Europe.
Especially Bulgaria for some reason.
Number one for weeks.

[14:33] O'Brien, Ted:
Google doesn't know about it…

Ted knows I'm talking shite. This is how we communicate; it makes perfect sense because it is total bullshit. In other words - it is better than the dull reality of the office and all the dull people who inhabit it. The bit about the Americans not having kettles though, that's 100% true.

[14:35] Ward, Terry B:
Yeah, well, it wasn't well documented.
Due to the power shortage in postwar Bulgaria.

[14:37] O'Brien, Ted:
Which war was that?

[14:37] Ward, Terry B:
Falklands.

[14:38] O'Brien, Ted:
Was Bulgaria involved in that?

[14:40] Ward, Terry B:
Well no, probably not, but there was still a power shortage at that time.
And consequently, the details of that song were lost to the mists of time.

The mists of time are what bother me right now; I feel

like I passed through them by about forty years back to my childhood, and a bedroom I have long since forgotten, to the sounds and smells of my dad printing business cards into the night. Back then he was also working on a sophisticated computer program to predict the future of the Football Pools, based on historical results and some algorithmic system; I was much too young to understand it. Never won of course, but Dad was always chasing a big dream, never content to sit and wait for it to come to him. Green screens, huge beige keyboards, reams of folded printout of code, ever-present pipe smoke and coffee.

[14:42] O'Brien, Ted:
It seems there are some details available online of other popular songs of the 80s in Bulgaria.

[14:43] Ward, Terry B:
Oh sure, you will find some details.
Not everything is lost.

[14:43] O'Brien, Ted:
How did you find out about it?

[14:44] Ward, Terry B:
Good question…

How can you know all the things that have been forgotten? How do you know that every day isn't another expiration of millions of memories worldwide? What if we forget the same things over and over? Who will ever know or care?

. . .

Time, For a Change

I look up and see Eoghan Williams walk by. Pace quick, head down, trying to avoid being noticed, which is almost impossible for a lad of his stature. I need him to work on my projects, so I take off the headset and plan an intercept course. He's heading for the canteen no doubt. Looks like he's going via the throne room, so I have time to get to the coffee machine before him.

I time it so that coffee is pouring into my cup just as he approaches.

"DeltaWave Eoghan."

"Ugh!" He genuinely looks upset by the mention of the customer name. I'm not surprised, they have ridiculously complicated requirements, and getting the information from them is harder than asking the dead for lottery numbers with a Ouija board. I hate them too, but such is life.

"Yeah."

"What now?" He looms over me at an awkward stoop of six-four. You might be intimidated if you didn't know he was as soft as the melting marshmallows on my coffee.

"They want to refresh all their projects, update everything. New configs, extra hardware, the whole eight point two meters."

"Did I mention I'm taking three months vacation, starting now?"

"Ah, you love it. Keeps you occupied. I'll set up a meeting, and we can go through all the stuff."

"Can't wait."

"Where would you go anyway?"

"True."

. . .

Eoghan can be obstinate, slow, overly worried about things no one needs to worry about, and he brings a new meaning to the 'glass is half empty'. He would explain in laborious detail how the glass is safer being half empty; if it was full, it could spill and cause liquid damage to your computer. That could cause a fire, which would burn your house down, causing you to become homeless. You'd end up in jail for stealing apples, turn to drugs for some small solace, and end up dead in a bin behind SuperMacs. He's still the only techie I trust to work on my projects. All the other lads in that team are about as useful as a basket of farts on a windy day, to them, this is 'just a job' and not a passion like it is for some of us, technology in our bloodstream.

When I get back to my desk Ted, has gone offline. I have a conference call coming up, but I only need to listen vaguely, so I think I'll dial in as I drive home. No one will notice I snuck off a bit early. I sometimes work from home so it doesn't make any difference. It's not like I'm getting any useful work done sitting here anyway.

I find an Amazon package on my doorstep when I get home. That will be the disk I ordered, so I shall start off the tedious copy process later. It may take several days to get everything copied. I should have done this years ago, but I just couldn't bring myself to even think about it. Emptying the workshop, gathering up all the data from the disks, all the paperwork I found, all this seems like an ending, a closure that I haven't been ready to face.

. . .

After several hours, I've got three disks copied over, slow going, but so far so good. While the copy process does its thing, I'm leafing through paperwork, three large boxes full. Bills mostly, threatening letters about bills, final demands. Nothing of interest. I dump most of it in the bin. Don't need reminders about ancient debts. It makes sense that anything relating to the mystery box would be a file on a disk rather than a printed document anyway, but can't hurt to check.

I need a break, so I wander over to the shed. The box is there on the bench where I left it; I was planning to have a look again at the controls, but I can't face it now. All the other tools and equipment are there too, a heap of memory triggers again. This is all a bit too much.

    Instead, I go back inside; check my work email, nothing worth bothering with. I put on some random YouTube and fade away, exhausted and empty.

Chapter Six

WEDNESDAY 29TH AUGUST

I don't know how I forgot, but I'm due to be going on a work trip to visit a new customer next week; I am duly reminded by the account manager this morning on the conference call. I guess I didn't really forget, I just forgot it was next week, or I forgot that next week was next week. I'm a bit messed up with days and times right now. The account manager, Sean Woods, is based in our Glasgow office. We will meet at Heathrow and then travel together to Chicago, then rent a car and drive to Ohio where the customer is based.

It sounds glamorous, other people at work might be envious, but honestly, there is no fun in it at all. I would rather stay at home. Long hours, barely any sleep, time zone changes, jet lag, always hunting for good WiFi. You don't get to see anything interesting anyway, and once you have experienced an industrial estate a hundred times you have seen enough. Hotels are always the same, and everyone always wants to go drinking and socialising once the meetings are done with. I don't drink anymore because it irritates my gout, and I find drunk people quite offensive to be around.

First world problems, I know, but I just can't get excited by it anymore. My jaw tends to ache after hours of fake smiling, and the constant chit-chat that is inevitable when around people. I don't find silence awkward, I prefer it to pointless talking.

I did try to argue that this trip wasn't really needed, couldn't we achieve the same thing over the phone? But humans do like their face to face meetings, so I was unable to get out of this one. Apparently, it shows our commitment to the customer and makes them happier about working with us, or some bollocks like that. I'm the technical representative, presenting all the different ways we can configure their equipment, blatantly lying about how long it will take to set up, and how much it will cost them.

I haven't been out of Ireland for a while now; I'll need to check all my travel documents, passport, and all the bookings; that's the rest of my week totally messed up! I'll get nothing useful done now.

When I go on trips like this, I like to have every tiny detail planned and accounted for. Everything is printed out and placed in the correct order that it will be needed in a ring binder, and also in electronic format on my phone. By being as organised as I can possibly be, I find it takes away some of the stress of travel. I even 'drive' the route from the hotel to the customer office on Google Street view, so I know what it will look like when we get there. Nothing fancy about it, just a dull grey office building like all the rest.

I also forgot that I had scheduled a meeting with Eoghan today, so I need to prepare for that now.

. . .

I set up camp in the meeting room early so I can make sure the air conditioning is set as low as possible and the lights are all switched on. People seem to want to roast to a dark death in these rooms, but I prefer it cool and light. I rarely bother with projecting slides up on the screen; people aren't capable of reading and listening at the same time, so I find slides utterly pointless. When Eoghan shows up, I've already set my bait of a pack of biscuits on the table.

"I forgot I have to go to the States next week, so I need to leave this DeltaWave crap with you."

Eoghan slumps down in a chair as far away as possible from my seat.

"Oh, that's nice. You swan off on a free holiday while I sweat my hole off?"

"Yeah, that's about the size of it. I'd rather not be going, honestly." I can see doubt in his eyes, but he lets it go.

"Bring me back a present."

"Here's your present lad!" I gesture to the biscuits I just went out and bought to sweeten the deal. That was my meeting preparation; I tend to wing the technical part. He looks annoyed, but shuffles over and grabs a biccie.

"You can keep the whole packet; I hate these."

"Thanks. So what exactly do they want now?"

"Well, you'll be delighted to know everything is super urgent of course, and they want it all done yesterday."

I explain as best I can about the technical requirements of the projects we're setting up, going into intricate details and promising to have all of them recorded on the tech-sheet before I go. Not that anyone will read it of course, and when I get back I expect it to be in a worse mess than how I left it, but you have to try at least.

Time, For a Change

After the meeting, Eoghan asked me to come for lunch with him and the lads in the canteen, but I don't fancy celery pie again, so I politely decline.

I head back to my desk and type up some notes, but while I'm doing that, I remember I haven't seen Jeff in his cubicle for a couple of days. No idea where he's gone. I don't really care, but it seems odd, as he's usually sat there opposite me and being annoying, he chews gum incessantly. He's part of a different team; I don't directly work with him, so perhaps he's gone out on a trip too? Whatever.

With all the meetings for the day done, I head out for lunch. By head out, I mean I drive home, by lunch, I mean I stop at a petrol station and get a nasty sandwich, and eat it at the 'dashboard diner' in my car. I'm not skiving off; I just find it easier to do my organisation work in the comfort of my own home. Plus my head is killing me. Not the typical almost daily low-key headache I've been having for months now; this is like I got mugged with the lead pipe in the conservatory. No idea why, but it sucks. I have loads to do for my trip, so I can just tip away at my leisure and get everything sorted. Then I have packing to do, and I want to copy a few more of Dad's old disks over.

Chapter Seven

THURSDAY 30TH AUGUST

I actually got a load of work done this morning. Surprising what you can achieve if you ignore all the phone calls and people harassing you. I had to get all the tech-sheets done for the DeltaWave projects before I fly off, or Eoghan will never let me hear the end of it. I was feeling quite good about things by lunchtime, maybe the trip won't be as bad as I think? I even went with the lads to the canteen, but I just bought a sandwich as they can't sneak celery into them, pre-made and sealed up as they are.

My phone buzzes on the table, I see the name Judith pop up. I ignore it, but it buzzes again, the same name. So I reluctantly pick it up and read the messages.

> *Terry - big problem on last DeltaWave order*
>   *Call me ASAP*

I feel the familiar thud of adrenaline, a punch in my guts and instant headache that bad news always brings. Fantastic, just what I wanted. Something is wrong so they start the witch hunt with me; after all, who else could have fucked up?

I amble back to my desk, wondering what now? And make a phone call to Judith.

"Hi, Judith how are you?" My real geniality has worn off on the walk from the canteen; this is now my work persona bullshit. I don't give a slippery shit how she is really.

"Just got your text there."

"I've been trying to get hold of you all day Terry." Her accent all matter-of-fact and business-like, so fake and insincere. She's from somewhere around the home counties of England, which is essentially where I am from, but I've lived in Ireland so long now that an English accent seems weird to me, apart from mine of course which has no doubt picked up a tinge of rural Ireland here and there.

"Yeah, been busy offsite with a customer." I lie comfortably because I don't give a crap what she thinks anyway. I was working on her fecking projects!

"Whats up?" Let's cut to the fucking chase here.

"DeltaWave ordered five-hundred systems a few weeks ago; they shipped out a few days back."

"Okay." I know that. I had to nurse them through every step of the configuration process in painstaking detail.

"They have the wrong software on them."

There's a pause of silence for effect on her side. My mind is racing, did I fuck something up or is this someone else's fuckup? Not that it matters because it will be me who has to figure out how to fix it anyway, and get the blame.

"What do you mean, wrong software?"

"They updated the version and sent a new one about a month ago. They sent an email."

I open up my email, search for DeltaWave. I have hundreds of emails on the subject; all look the same, it will take hours to dig through all this to see if there is one about a new software version.

"I don't recall that, can you clarify when exactly and who sent it?" I need to divert the attention away from me, so I have some time to see what is going on.

"Yes, I will copy the mail to you now." I hear her clicking and scrolling her mouse-wheel, looking for the email.

"They are screaming and threatening to go elsewhere. The new projects we are doing now are in jeopardy, they want to cancel the big order for the end of the year."

She pauses again for dramatic effect.

"That's a two million pound order, Terry."

Yeah, yeah. I've heard all these threats before, over and over. They wash over me. I know it's a massive fuck up, I don't need it emphasised, so best just to ignore this hyperbole. She wants me to be shocked, jump to attention, somehow change the situation immediately, but none of that will happen. I get the email and open it up; I was copied on it, but the subject is the regular meeting notes subject, it doesn't stand out as significant. But down at the bottom of the email, under the link to download the new version, the customer notes that this is to fix a critical bug they found and it must replace all other versions we have stored. Awesome. I missed it, no one mentioned it since then, no one checked it during tests, and now it is all my fault that five-hundred computers are incorrectly set up. Fucks sake.

"Where are the systems now?"

"Well that's at least some good news, most of them are still in a warehouse in the Netherlands, but some have already shipped out to end users."

"Okay, can we get a list of where they are now?"

"You know DeltaWave supply oil rigs in the North Sea?"

Oh, this gets better and better! There's no way I'm going round oil rigs with a memory stick updating software!

"Do they have internet on oil rigs?"

"Apparently, but not fast enough to download this update, it would take weeks."

This is a mess; I don't have time to fix it before my trip to the States.

I don't even know how we can fix it yet; my throat tightens, my head aches, I hang up the call promising to send an update once I have looked through all the information and figured out a plan. There will be daily status calls, correction plans, root-cause analysis, quality metric impacts and 'lessons learned' meetings after. All utterly pointless, no lesson will be learned, no one will change anything, next time a critical piece of information is sent in a generic email and lost in the mire of hundreds of unread messages, the same set of processes will kick off again.

I download their software update; it's a series of massive files that take hours even on the super-fast connection here. I start preparing a memory stick that will flash the update onto an affected system. It is quite simple, just overlay the new version onto whatever is already there, but it will take a couple of hours per system, and a human has to plug everything in, and kick off the update. I have to presume we will be able to send the software in the post somehow, surely they get the post on oil rigs? How are the computers going to be delivered? I start working on a step by step guide on how to do the update, down to the level of 'plug a power cable into the rear of the computer.' With photos and arrows and smiley or sad faces indicating the correct way around to plug things. Never underestimate the ingenuity of fools. Eighty-five units in total shipped out but the remaining four-hundred-and-fifteen also need to be updated in the warehouse. Luckily, I already have a step-by-step guide on how to replicate the memory keys from last time this type of balls-up happened. I also had to go back and update all the work I did this morning as it all references the same old files.

When I look up finally, it's nine pm, how did it get this late? No one else is in the office; I'm starving, exhausted and pissed off, so I get Chinese food on the way home.

Chapter Eight

FRIDAY 31ST AUGUST

Couldn't face the office today so I'm working from home. I sent all the instructions for the DeltaWave fix to Judith; now it is up to her to coordinate the technicians to go out and do the update. I was expecting a follow-up phone call, but she hasn't sent anything or even replied back to my emails. Suits me, I have other things to sort anyway. I may have missed this update, but someone should have called it out and not trusted one email to issue a critical fix like that. I'm trying not to feel bad about it, but these things get to me. It took hours to get to sleep, and when I finally did, I had horrible dreams. Not really nightmares, just disturbing, repeating thoughts that simply won't fuck off.

Thankfully it's payday, and I get a text message from my bank.

A large deposit has been made to your a/c. Pls do not reply to this txt.

A large deposit? Some hope of that!
Translation: You've been paid. Congratulations fucker.

You can now just about cover all your bills until next payday. You won't have a penny left again at the end of it, but at least you can keep afloat to continue to serve the man. Could be worse I guess.

I was curious about Jeff too, because it's been all week since I heard from him. I checked on instant message, and he wasn't showing up, so I tried to look him up in the company directory: not listed. I sent an email, but it bounced back. Weird.

I look him up on LinkedIn. After a bit of scrolling, I find him and his profile picture that looks like a mugshot, but this must be wrong, it says he works at another company, miles away in Dublin. For the last six years?

> **[11:23] Ward, Terry B:**
> Don't ask.
>
> **[11:23] O'Brien, Ted:**
> Well, Terry. Ask what?
>
> **[11:24] Ward, Terry B:**
> Total and utter balls-up on my project. ***sigh***
> Spent all day yesterday trying to sort it.
> End of the world and all that.
>
> **[11:25] O'Brien, Ted:**
> Yay. You love balls-ups!
>
> **[11:27] Ward, Terry B:**
> Yeah.
> Hey, do you know Jeff Maloney?

[11:28] O'Brien, Ted:
Nope.

[11:28] Ward, Terry B:
Hmm.
He sits opposite me in the office.
Or he did.
Just wondered if you knew him?

[11:32] O'Brien, Ted:
Never heard of him.

[11:32] Ward, Terry B:
Hmm.
Strange.

I guess Ted may never have met him as he doesn't officially work in this office anymore. I don't even know why I care as he was annoying, but something odd is going on, and I'd like to know what. I send Jeff a message on LinkedIn, and he replies within a few minutes, sad fecker.

"Hi Terry, wow, long time no speak. Must be ten or eleven years since we were at XpressPrint? I heard they shut down a few years back? Guess they couldn't survive without you as the IT manager! How are you keeping? I see you are at C.S. Tech now? Meant to be good money and healthcare there?"

What the fuck?

No, not good money as Jeff should very well know. Average money, average healthcare, that only works if you go to a specific optician halfway across the country, and never seems to cover any medical things anyone might actually need. I did work at XPressPrint before this job, that was a long time ago, a different life I can barely remember now. I haven't thought about that horrible place for a long time. Glad to hear they shut down! I'm sure it wasn't my fault though. I left the IT systems running smoothly.

I step away from the computer and heat a can of soup for lunch, and then head off down the lane for a walk to clear my head.

Along the road, I meet John, the farmer from nearby, poking around in his field with the cows. We talk for twenty minutes about the weather and the feckers from the forestry department, ruining the road and causing potholes with their huge trucks, and the water tax rebates and nothing in particular, and I'm harshly reminded about the massive divide between the two worlds I inhabit. The high-tech environment I work in, surrounded by computers and allegedly intelligent people solving complex technical problems, and the low tech world where I live, where cow shit and silage and welding an iron gate are important things in your day, instead of software version updates on oil rigs in the distant ocean.

Back at my desk for the afternoon and things are quiet, only a few junky emails I can ignore. No one tries to message me, Sean confirms travel plans a final time and I log off early, and zone out in front of some mindless YouTube junk.

Friday evening and I have nothing to do and nowhere to go, and I'm okay with that. Other lads at work would think it is odd to stay at home alone when there are pubs to go to, especially after the shit week I've had, but I don't find the pub a source of entertainment, quite the opposite. I can't handle the noise, the people, the smells and the drunk people in my face. I'm boring I guess. Sosumi.

There are four disks left to copy from my dad's old collection. I kick another one off and make some dinner and play some music, filling my house with pleasant smells and pleasant music, very loud, because only the cows will hear it.

Chapter Nine

SATURDAY 1ST SEPTEMBER

I was hoping to lay in this morning and catch up with sleep; I really need it. But I woke early anyway, had to piss like a Russian racehorse. Trying to go back to sleep was a waste of time, so instead I got up and scrolled through Twitter, numbing my mind with endless nonsense, I guess that is almost as good as sleep?

I ran a hot bath, lay soaking in the bubbles and almost drifted off to sleep again, but my phone pinging with messages woke me. My family in Italy, wishing me a safe flight, instructing me to let them know when I arrived in Heathrow and Chicago, asking for presents to be sent from America. They are a day early; I leave tomorrow.

After lunch, which turned out to be eggs on toast, I finished copying the last of the old disks onto my new one. That's a lot of data in one place, probably numerous duplicates of photos and files, but now I feel like the data is safe, at least for a while.

. . .

I head out to the shed. I need some answers before I go off on my trip. As I sit down at the bench, I see those words again written on the box

"No rest for the conflicted !!"

What does it mean? I tried searching through Dad's files for words like 'rest' and 'conflict', but I didn't find anything interesting.

The storm smell washes over me as I open the lid; the device inside happily twisting into infinity. I still don't know what makes it spin. I don't want to take it apart though, I may utterly balls it up in the process.

Last time I set the knobs all to the minimum, so this time let's try maximum. I turn everything as far clockwise as it will go, Y, M, D, H and reach down onto the hand pads. Dropping my left hand onto the copper, nothing changes. So I lay my right hand down, flinching slightly. Nothing happens. Well, nothing apart from a guy in a shed reaching into a box anyway. This is not the same as last time. I take my hands off, rub them together, maybe it needs moisture or something? Nothing happens again. Okay, well, perhaps the maximum setting isn't hooked up correctly? Maybe there's a cable come loose inside the box?

I fiddle around with the knobs, turning back and forth a couple of times randomly, and try again.

My stomach wrenches and I drop through infinity, darkness; I laugh for no reason, just felt the need, tingling in my fingers and slowly some senses fade in, sudden intense pain in my

head now. I hear a background drone, muffled voices, the scent of air-freshener... Am I at work? I try to look up but my vision is fuzzy, slowly blinking into clarity, and I am looking at my desk and the screen of my computer. These are the notes from the meeting I had with Eoghan the other day, I look around me, gently because my head throbs with pain when I move, I stand up, turn around, this is the office alright! People walking by, laptops open in their arms, headsets in their ears, a guy I recognise nods to me as he passes by, I realise I am staring so look away. I turn around and look at Jeff's desk, just opposite mine, empty, the cubicle is vacant. I thought he had a sports scarf pinned up on the cubicle wall and a photo of his favourite football player over it? But it has all gone, the desk is completely clear, not even a monitor or a keyboard. I was in the office just two days ago, I try and remember if the desk was clear or populated? It is hard to think; this isn't making any sense.

I sit down again; my head feels like I was run over by a tractor, I close my eyes.

As I open my eyes again, I'm in my shed, I reach up, and it feels like there's a lump on my forehead, sore to touch, must have banged my head on the box or something? I stand up and feel dizzy, sit down again. Need to chill for a moment I think. The Y control knob is set to maximum, the M, D and H are all somewhere roughly around the middle. Interesting.

An idea pops into my head. I turn the M dial a tiny bit more anticlockwise and try again, reaching into the box and gently placing my hands on the pads.

. . .

It feels like dropping in a lift from fifty stories, too quickly. A wave of pain rushes over my head, darkness around me, but I'm getting used to this now, and I let the senses return and blink my eyes open. I'm at my work desk again, I have headphones in, music playing, my phone in my hand. Usual work clutter is open on my screen; emails, browser windows, spreadsheets, a database, a notes app and my calendar. The calendar is open on July 27th, 2018, the day of the email from DeltaWave that I missed before. I switch to my emails and look through the massive list of unread emails that day. There it is, from DeltaWave, I open it up and see the little note about the critical software version update that we need to use.

What if I leave this email open on my screen now so I'll definitely see it?

I take out the headphones and look around. People are going about their day, nothing weird, no one is watching me, I close my eyes, job done?

I slowly walk over to the house and get a cold bottle of water from the fridge, and pop two soluble painkillers into it. Sipping on the medicinal liquid, I wander back over to the shed; I want to try something and prove a theory I'm developing.

I set all the knobs in the middle, pointing straight up, halfway around their travel.

Nausea returns as I drop into the blackness, probably should have let my headache subside a bit before trying this again, but I'm impatient, I need to act on my impulses immediately, or I can't concentrate on anything until I do. There's a smell, salty ocean air, clean and fresh, moist on a brisk wind. A gentle sway under me, a distant throbbing engine. As I open my eyes, blinking to clear the blurriness, I'm standing on a huge boat, looking out at the open sea; sweat suddenly pours from my brow, motion sickness hits me like a train. I stumble and walk back towards a doorway into a room off the deck. Steadying myself on the wall, I look around. There's an escape map of the boat deck on the wall, showing the name: 'Irish Ferries, Isle of Inishmore' This is the car ferry from Holyhead to Dublin, I recognise the little shop. I was on this boat maybe twenty years ago when I came to Ireland for the first time. There are people dotted around, standing at the railing, sitting on benches. I go through into the lounge, carpeted and furnished like a cheap hotel bar from the 70s, colourful and fake.

I walk around the bar area, incredulous, still dizzy, but this is so unreal that I push the nausea aside. Everyone is reading magazines, paper books, drinking pints of Guinness, smoking! Kids are playing card games; not one single person is using a smartphone or tablet. Not even any laptops visible.

Then I see him. Dad. My heart stops, I almost collapse but steady myself on a chair. He's asleep on a lounger, his jacket rolled up as a pillow, his bag under his legs, he's young, alive, embarking on a new chapter of his life, this is our first trip to the Emerald Isle, just me and Dad, everyone else came later. We scoped it out, reported back, then decided to emigrate. I'm frozen; I can't move my legs. I feel like I will burst into tears, but the lounge bar is busy, people are already avoiding me, I push forward, sit in the seat next to Dad, don't want to wake him up as there's a long drive ahead from Dublin. I allow the tears to flow finally, picking up a magazine to hide behind and close my eyes.

. . .

In the shed, I find my face wet with tears and my head woolly with pain and emotion. I sit motionless and silent for what must be five full minutes; my brain just cannot comprehend.

Eventually, I stand up; I'm shaky, disconnected. But I look around at my reality here, and the rough stone walls of the shed ground me somehow, the tension subsides, and I can focus again. I glance at the control knobs on the box, just above the Y knob a tiny '98' label joins the '78' on the far left.

Back in the house, I finish packing my suitcase, unpacking it, repacking it, taking things out because they are heavy, putting them back in because I might need them. Finally, I slam it shut and watch old Star Trek DVDs until midnight, which was stupid because I have to leave the house at five am to get the first flight.

Chapter Ten

SUNDAY 2ND SEPTEMBER

The flight to London only takes ninety minutes, but all the bullshit surrounding it takes forever. I get to the airport later than I wanted, after hardly any sleep, but hopefully I can nap on the plane. I check in my bags and head up to the security desk and straight through with no issues. Barely anyone around at this time on a Sunday morning so I needn't have rushed. There's a bar just after the security check, and I still have some time to kill, so I grab a coffee. It's 6:45 am and someone at the bar is drinking a pint of Guinness. Unreal!

Sean sends a text that his flight has been delayed but he thinks he should still make the connection. Hope so as I don't fancy doing all this customer stuff on my own if he misses the flight to Chicago.

It seems utterly ridiculous to be flying east to go west, but I guess this is just how the schedule works out sometimes. Coming back is the killer, after seven or eight hours on the plane, flying right over Ireland to have to keep going, wait in London and then come back again is just torture. Give me a parachute over Shannon; I'll take my chances!

Time, For a Change

. . .

The flight is smooth, comfortable, no screaming babies, no drunken louts, I spend ninety minutes trying to nap but failing, my thoughts bounce between the mysterious box, that trip on the boat to Ireland, the cock up with DeltaWave at work and the weird situation with Jeff. I can't really explain any of it, so my brain flits between everything, maybe trying to correlate it all subconsciously. I've done zero prep for this customer in Ohio; I can't even remember the name now or what they want. Sean can explain it on the flight to Chicago. Actually, I remember I screen-grabbed their street view photo of the building on my phone, so I pull it up and look at their logo. FutureCloud. Some kind of Cyber-Security-Cloud buzzword-bullshit company. Probably half their own staff don't know what they make and sell.

We land and exit smoothly, I have woken up a bit more now, becoming efficient, powering past all the laggards dawdling their way along the thousands of miles of corridors and on through to the terminal. I need food as I couldn't face eating when I woke up at arse-o'clock this morning. My body needs time to adjust from sleep mode to be able to process solids. Luckily I don't have to change terminals so I can linger here in T2 for about three hours until the onward flight. I wonder where Sean is at now, I haven't got any messages from him, so hopefully, he's on his way from Glasgow right now.

I message my family, let them know I have arrived at Heathrow, send a photo of myself in front of the arrivals board so they know I'm really here and then go hunting for food. I find myself in a place called 'EAT.' I wonder what they do? I guess it pays to be obvious in this confused society. I get a breakfast roll that is surprisingly good, and a bucket of coffee and sit down by the window. Airports are great places for people-watching.

A woman sits at a table next to mine, wrapped in muted colour scarves, greens and dull blues, lace trim. A hat of such girth that it must slow her down considerably through air resistance. Let's assume she's a Gerty, all smiles and 'darlings', sensible flat shoes, but red shoes, a flash of passion amid the caution. A handbag so vast that undiscovered tribes may inhabit its lower realms. Her coffee has spilt on the trip to the table; she slurps it from the saucer. I shudder. Her perfume is so strong that any nearby dogs would be stunned into spasming fits on the ground, flowers wilt, milk sours as she passes. An almost visible aura cloud of scent like bug killer spray mixed with mustard gas. She was an actress, am-dram, trod the boards in many a town hall. Now she lives vicariously through her book club and the younger members, always listening for scandal and gossip. Her phone rings from somewhere deep in the abyssal handbag, she pulls out three sets of spectacles and fumbles between them to find the correct phone answering pair. By the time her vision is adequately corrected, the phone stops ringing. She sighs and mutters a curse and hurls the device back into the bag. Many seconds pass before a splash can be heard, echoing through the thick, brown, Stegosaurian leather.

Gertrude has £750,000 in various bank accounts, inherited from her late Father many decades past, but she refuses to heat her house for fear of the bills. She's travelling now because someone has died. Not someone she cared too much about, but someone who gave her a 'look' in 1982 that she's never forgiven. Glad to see the old cow buried even if it means spending money on a trip.

Gertrude slurps at her curdling latte and glares at a magazine article about cake frosting. I look away.

I get a text message from Sean; he has landed at Heathrow. Good, because if he hadn't then I'd be arranging a flight home as soon as possible. I can't deal with a customer visit on my own right now. I have made these trips on my own several times, but that was years ago, before my confidence and enthusiasm were ground away. Especially as I haven't done any preparation at all, and honestly, it seems pretty pointless to me anyway. I reply I'll meet him at the bar, which is undoubtedly where he wants to be, even at this relatively early hour. I meander over via the various shops, stocked with absolutely nothing I would ever need or want.

"Hey, Buddy!" I turn around on my stool and find Sean's hand extended.

"Hey man, you are looking well." I give him a hearty firm shake.

"Drink?"

"Ah you read my mind, pint please!" I motion to the barman, slipping into my work persona.

"A bit early, no?" I smile.

"Been up since the crack, so this is lunch time for me!" he dumps his bags down and sits on a stool next to me.

"Fair enough." I make sure to get the bar receipt for expense claims later.

We shoot the shit and catch up while Sean downs this, and another pint, before we decide to head over to the gate for the flight to Chicago. I've been sipping on sparkling water.

At the gate, Sean pulls out his laptop and takes me through the basics of the customer deal we're trying to sell on this trip, and the detailed agenda. The initial presentation of customisations available, how we can make their life easier, blah blah, same old. Nothing out of the ordinary. They are trying to get a presence in Europe and so need the help of a company like us to build that up. Sean will handle all the sales talk; I will get into the nitty-gritty of their technical requirements. We've got Monday at the hotel to get our presentation together, and come to terms with the time zone, then Tuesday is all day meetings led by Sean, and Wednesday is my turn to 'deep dive' into the technical stuff. Thursday is also my day for looking at their existing set up with their engineer, and gathering all the data I might need for the project setups to follow. Friday morning we pop in and say goodbye, and then drive back to Chicago, staying in some dive airport hotel. Saturday evening we fly back on the 'red eye', so it will be Sunday afternoon before I am back at home. A full week wasted. I set a mental note that I am owed three days in lieu for travelling all over my weekends.

By the time we board the plane, I am already bored of scrolling Twitter, bored of what I was reading on my kindle, bored of whatever is happening in the news, bored of sitting and waiting. But this is just the start, there are nine hours of absolutely nothing to do now, and I wish I could sleep and wake up in Chicago, but I know that won't happen. I hadn't thought about it before, but I ask Sean if we are sitting together, and turns out we aren't anywhere close. I'm in a middle seat, and he's four rows back on an aisle. I fucking hate the middle seat.

After the shoving and jousting of the boarding, overhead baggage locker stowing, drudgery of the emergency procedure, and the tiny thrill of the take-off, I take out my laptop and wait for it to boot up. Sean emailed me all the presentation stuff and all the details of the customer. I may as well read up about them now as I've shite all else to do for hours. I haven't even glanced at my fellow seat neighbours. I try not to make eye contact because I don't want to spend nine hours learning about someone's ailments, life history, sisters in Illinois, new carpet in their back bedroom or any other small talk shite that inevitably gets churned up when someone thinks you are interested.

I stare only forward, tunnel vision, but I think there's a woman on my left next to the window and an older man on my right at the aisle. Thankfully neither of them have attempted any contact so far.

My laptop finally boots and I open up the files. There's a list of contact names, all the various models of computer they use, the rough outline of what they want to do, all the standard stuff. I read through everything, and I'm horrified to discover that only fifteen minutes have passed, and there's still a million hours of flying left with nothing to do. They should have an option to be anaesthetised for the trip. I'd willingly pay for that. Perhaps that's what the in-flight magazine is designed to do?

The attendants start bringing round what is probably lunch, but who knows in which time zone this plane is operating? At least that will ease the monotony for a while, as I try to figure out how I am meant to fit all the packages they give me onto the tiny pull-down tray, and not spill hot coffee into the guy next to me's lap.

After the food is eaten and cleaned up, I slump down into my chair as much as possible without reclining the seat, because, why would you do that? I try to take a nap, but my head quickly fills with confusing thoughts again, the mystery box specifically. The minimum setting was back to 1978; I was standing in my small childhood bedroom, my dad working in his even smaller print room. The maximum setting didn't work, but a little less than maximum was a few days ago and then right in the middle was 1998 on a boat to Ireland for the first time. It seems to span a forty year period of my life. A time travel device for just most of my lifespan to date?

I meant to do some more searching through all Dad's old files, but this trip has interrupted my research. I was thinking of bringing the disk with me, but I didn't want to risk losing, or damaging it, so left it on my desk at home. Not much I can do about it now anyway until I get back to Ireland.

Something jolts me, and I wake with a start, must have dozed off I guess, still on the plane, my wrist sore from being bent back, holding my head up as I slept. I feel like all my blood has been replaced with mercury, heavy and slow. A flight attendant is looking at me, waiting for something expectantly.

"Sorry, can you repeat that?" I notice the lady next to me has her tray down with a cup of something steaming.

"Would you like a coffee, Sir?" Her accent American, can't tell what State. She seems irritated, but so am I now.

"Oh, yes, black, lots of sugar." If I'm going to be awake I may as well be awake!

They woke me up to ask if I wanted coffee? Is this prison or something?

She hands me a small cup of a brown liquid resembling coffee, and two sugar packets, and moves on.

I load up the navigation page on the tiny screen on the seat-back in front of me, it shows land beneath us instead of the ocean, two hours to landing. I must have slept quite a while. My bladder confirms this theory and I need to empty it quickly. Not going to be easy with this tray in front of me and the gent next to me also has his tray down, sipping red wine like this is a fancy bar in New York or something! My only hope is that he'll need to drain the lizard soon, too.

Twenty increasingly painful minutes pass and eventually the aeroplane sommelier folds his tray up and gets up and goes for a walk. I follow quickly, heading down towards the can. I pass Sean on the way, he's asleep, snoring like a hibernating bear, a beer can empty in his hand. Classy.

I have to wait outside the toilet area; there's a queue, three awkward people waiting for the chance to piss into a hole fifty-thousand feet above North America, all pretending that this is perfectly normal and not making any eye contact. There should be something to read up on the wall by the toilets. We're all standing here like we forgot to bring a book to shit with, in the pre-smartphone era, desperately reading the back of shampoo bottles in four languages.

When I finally get my turn, I can barely get my lad out before I piss myself. But we're safe and dry, and I feel so much better now. I know this feeling will be short lived though. This is why I need an aisle seat. I make a mental note to try and change my seat allocation on the way back. As I go back I try and stretch my legs out a bit, and then I drop a wadded up bundle of toilet paper on Sean's lap, as I pass him. A spur of the moment childish prank, but it might cause some confusion and fun when he wakes up. In this environment of boredom, you have to do something for amusement. It's a squirt of liquid soap inside the condom that is wrapped up in the tissue, and it was a fresh one from my wallet, unused, but he won't know that! It was probably long past the use-by-date anyway, been in there since before the internet was invented!

I sit down again with a smirk, not even caring that I had to ask the aisle seat fella to get up so I could sit down, the window seat lady is not here, so we'll all have to play musical chairs again shortly anyway.

Only about ninety minutes now to landing, I can handle that. I pull out my phone instinctively and then immediately put it away again, remembering I don't have a connection here so I can't scroll an endless page of snarky comments on Twitter.

Instead, I try and pick up the book I was reading, but the words won't sink in; I go over the same paragraph seventeen times before giving up and stare at the rotating satellite navigation screens. Bit chilly outside apparently and winds of over five-hundred miles per hour. Brrr.

. . .

"WHAT THE FFFFF!!" I hear Sean's unmistakable accent yell out from behind me. I guess he woke up and found the wee gift I left him. I try very hard not to laugh or smile; he sounds very annoyed. An attendant quickly walks by towards his seat. I pick up my book again and try hard to read and not look up.

"This is absolutely disgraceful!" I hear the Glaswegian cry, I can't make out what the attendant is saying to him, but she soon walks by again, shaking her head, but I am pretty sure I saw a smirk on her face too.

The seatbelt sign pings on, the landing announcement comes on the P.A. The ordeal is almost over.

We land eventually and exit ungracefully with shoves and head bangs on lockers and backpacks in faces. Chicago is warm and dry at least. Standing at the baggage claim, I see Sean and wander over to him.

"Good flight, Sean? I slept half of it, thank fuck."

He turns around, sees me and shakes his head in a disbelief way.

"You won't fucking believe what happened to me!" I raise my eyebrows inquisitively. His voice has turned from a softly spoken Scott to an angry Glaswegian.

"Some cunt left a fucking used Frenchie on my lap!"

"A what?"

"A condom! Some fuckers joined the mile-high-club and left the wee wrapper on my lap while I was asleep! Unreal! Wait till I write to the airline, that's disgusting like!"

"Oh man! That's revolting! Mile-high-club eh?"

"I could fucking catch some disease!"

"Did you touch it?"

"Naw, it was wrapped in tissue, but the tip of it was

sticking out, touching my trousers! I'll have to fucking burn these pants now!" He points to a wet circle on his leg, I nearly die trying to stifle the laugh, and I have to look away.

"There's my bag!" I run off around the belt and grab my suitcase, and wait for Sean to catch up, trying all the way to hide my grin, but when I'm far enough away, I explode with laughs. That's cheered me up no end! I'm sure he'll expense a pair of new trousers on the company credit card anyway, so not a bother.

While I remember it, I send a photo of the baggage claim area to my family so they know I have landed safely. Sean rolls up soon, and we walk over to the car rental depot and then pick up a fancy Chevrolet. The steering wheel is on the wrong side, there's a pedal missing, but otherwise, it is in excellent condition, and it has lovely cold air conditioning and cup holders everywhere! I fire up the SatNav app on my phone, and we head away to the unknown wonders of Columbus, Ohio. Or at least, an industrial estate and a hotel somewhere close to Columbus, Ohio. I'm driving, Sean 'forgot' his license.

America is too damn big. On the map, it looks like a quick jaunt from Chicago to Columbus, but it is an epic trail worthy of the pioneers! The satNav app says it will take five and a half hours, and that is with a good wind and no stops. I'm glad I got some sleep on the plane, or this would be almost impossible, and we'd be finding a hotel somewhere along the way. This is going to be an extraordinarily long day.

At least the car more or less drives itself. Once we got on the freeway out of the city, all I have to do is point it in the right direction; the cruise control keeps us in the legal speed

Time, For a Change

limit, the map shows me where I need to turn. Not too bad, but still not what I would have chosen to do after an already epic journey.

Our first stop is just outside Chicago, urine and caffeine, a bag of pretzels and several weird energy delivery devices including tablets, concentrated drinks and regular cans. Your average rest stop here is set up for the long-distance truck driver, complete with sketchy looking prostitutes loitering in the parking-lot.

We pass by a wind farm of proportion I have never seen before, miles and miles of amazing large wind generators, stretching back as far as I can see on both sides, a fantastic engineering achievement. It reminds me of just over a week ago back home in Ireland near Dad's workshop, passing by the epic towers collecting all that Irish wind. The scale here is significantly bigger, but I guess that is to be expected.

The wind farm continues for what seems like miles, the spinning veins gently turning, hypnotic.

I exit off the freeway and into a car-park, sorry, parking-lot, of a Taco Bell for some grub.

"I have absolutely no idea what to eat here, but I hope you like Mexican?" I prefer not to talk much as we drive along, Sean seems to agree, so we enjoy the miles mostly in peace. But now we're out in the world, its okay to talk again.

"Me either! But Mexican is good; we'll figure it out as we go along!"

We both stretch our legs, exiting the vehicle and wander slowly over to the door. I hadn't thought much about it, but we are two novelty acts here in 'middle of nowhere, Indiana' the second we utter a word. I hate having any attention directed at me, so I try to say as little as possible, but there's no escaping it, they will know immediately we aren't from around here. After a pit stop, we go and browse the menu, but to me, it is horribly confusing. I'm not privy to their offers and deals; I just want something to eat that doesn't taste like cardboard. I end up with some kind of burrito and nachos and a bucket of ice slush, Sean gets something similar. The girl at the counter was so disinterested in her role, that she didn't even notice our accents. A lucky escape this time.

We get back on the road, and the satNav indicates still another three hours; will this journey never end? I can't remember any other life than travelling from Ireland to America.

It starts to get dark, yet we still carry on, crossing over to Ohio now out of Indiana, stopped for another piss by a shop that looked like a giant candle. Also noticed a huge Jesus cross by the side of the highway, must be a hundred feet high. I wonder what that's about? What was the intent of the people who put it up? Do they expect me to see that huge cross and suddenly believe in their mythical saviour? Or is it just brand reassurance, like cola adverts, just keeping all the believers happy. Yep, good ol' Jesus is still here saving your asses!

Eventually, we roll up into the hotel parking lot. I am so tired I can barely speak, but we manage to check in, and I go directly to my room and collapse on the bed. I barely even looked around the room. Sean said he was going to see if the bar was open! I guess he forgot about the trouser spunk situation for now. We are to meet for breakfast around nine am. I set alarms on my phone, turn off the TV that came on as I entered the room, with a message for a Mr P. Word, welcoming him to the Inn. If I see Mr Word, I'll pass on the greeting.

I lie in the darkness, so tired but unable to fall asleep, probably due to the many energy drink things I have consumed; my brain is buzzing. The image of the road flashing by my mind's eye, rolling on and on, the sound of the car droning. This is why I hate work travel; there has been no glamour coming here!

Chapter Eleven

MONDAY 3RD SEPTEMBER

I set six alarms for this morning and I slept through all of them. But I eventually managed to get out of bed at nine am. My body rebelled. No wonder. I was Futterly Ucked. Sent a text message to Sean that I would be late for breakfast. I scramble around unpacking, and finding suitable clothes and plugging in things to charge, that I forgot to do last night, I get down to the dining room by 9:30. Not bad considering. There's no sign of Sean though. Maybe he already ate and went back to his room? Fecker didn't reply to my text message anyway.

The bacon is weird, the eggs are complicated, the juice is strange, and their idea of tea is not the same as in my universe. Coffee is okay though.

I try calling Sean's mobile, and it says not in service. I have no idea which room he's in to knock on his door. We are meant to be doing the prep work for the meetings today. I wander back to my room anyway. I'll see if he emailed me or something on my laptop.

. . .

Time, For a Change

There are no emails or messages from Sean once I managed to get on the terrible hotel WiFi, and then onto the work network. I forgot all about the time difference. Back in Ireland it is already three pm so I've got dozens of emails to wade through. Oddly there is nothing from Judith about DeltaWave.

|10:23| Ward, Terry B:
Hey. Can I ask a favour?

|10:25| Williams, Eoghan:
Whats up?
Aren't you in the States somewhere on your free holiday?

|10:25| Ward, Terry B:
Remember the DeltaWave update we did about a month ago?
Some fecking crap holiday by the way...

|10:26| Williams, Eoghan:
How could I forget?
What happened?

|10:26| Ward, Terry B:
Can you check the software version we deployed at the time?
That would have gone out on the recent order of five-hundred systems?

|10:26| Williams, Eoghan:
This sounds bad. What have you done?

[10:26] Ward, Terry B:
Just fecking check it and let me know the version?

[10:26] Williams, Eoghan:
Okay, okay, Sheesh. Give me ten minutes.

Eoghan goes off, presumably to pull the log files of the orders.

I'm getting concerned I still haven't heard from Sean yet, so I try calling again, but his phone is still dead. I hate calling reception on the phone, so I wander down to the front desk.

"Hi, I'm trying to find my colleague Sean Woods. We checked in last night around eleven. I don't know what room he's in and his phone isn't working." The receptionist's face feigns concern almost well enough to convince me she cares, but not quite.

"Well I'd love to help you Sir, but I can't give out any personal details." She smiles her plastic smile.

"I don't want any personal details; I only want to know which room he's in."

"I'm afraid we can't give out that information, Sir." Her smile is now so fake that she could be an exhibit in Madame Tussauds. I can see there's no point in arguing with her.

"Can you please call his room for me?"

"Oh sure." She looks relieved and fiddles with her computer for a moment, and then picks up a desk phone, and puts it on the counter in front of me, and types in 439. She hands me the phone. I sigh inwardly but flash her a fake smile of appreciation. Fuckwit.

The phone rings out; no one answers after way too long, so I hang up.

I head back to my room but stop at 439 on the way. Just down the hall from me. I knock on the door, no answer. I try and peep through the peephole, but I can't see anything. Well, this is great. Where the fuck is he?

I go back to my room and check my laptop.

[10:41] Williams, Eoghan:
There was a software update about five weeks ago.
The version was 4.2, and that is what was deployed on the five-hundred units.

[10:48] Ward, Terry B:
Thanks, dude.

I check my notes. 4.2 is correct. I recheck the email from DeltaWave. Sure enough, 4.2 is what they asked us to update to and the same version that I downloaded and made a fixing USB stick.

Well, I'll be…

I need some thinking time to parse what just happened, plus I feel sticky and gross from the travel. A bath should fix both of those problems.

The bath is quite shallow, but it's hot, and the water flows fast. There was a tiny bottle of bubble liquid, that smells like pine toilet cleaner, but I threw it in regardless. Feels good to soak away the aeroplane and travel dirt and pain.

My phone is ringing; I wake up with a jump, my body suddenly realises I'm freezing, in the bath. I fell asleep. I feel like a bucket of prunes all wrinkled up and slimy. I get up, grab a towel and run to my phone on the desk, but it isn't the mobile ringing, it is the hotel phone on the nightstand. I pick it up just as it stops ringing.

For fuck's sake.

The phone rings again, this time my mobile.

"Hey, buddy!" Sean's voice on the phone.

"Where the fuck have you been? Where are you now?"

"I'm at reception downstairs."

"What? Where have you been?"

"I'll tell you over a pint mate! Come down to the bar? My phone died, just plugged it in here at the front desk."

"I'm just having a wash. Be down soon."

I hang up. What has the fool been up to?

I check my watch on the nightstand. Two-seventeen pm. I must have slept for ages again. I'm too old for this travel lark. My body is utterly broken.

Down in the bar, I see Sean sat on a stool, looking quite rough.

"Heyyyy, buddy." He's got a big shit-eating grin on his face, like he just got told a Great Aunt who he never knew died, and left him a million quid in her will.

"You won't believe the night I've had!" Oh, wonderful. Here we go. Those words never precede a sensible and restrained evening, followed by a restful sleep in a comfortable hotel bed.

Time, For a Change

"Go on…" I give him a frown and then order a coffee from the barman.

We move over to a table with sofa seats next to it, and Sean tells his story of binge drinking, and how he slept on some dude's floor in the city. Apparently, he met a woman in the bar here last night, this very seat he tells me, she is on a business trip in Columbus like we are, but she's from Georgia, her name is Candy Cain. I asked three times and got it spelt out, Candy fucking Cain, he showed me her business card. She sells security systems. She was enthralled with Sean's delicious Scottish accent apparently. They got bored and went into the city in an Uber and hit up some nightclub, from there they met a group of hipsters who invited them back to their place, where they had a load of weed. Next thing he remembers was about an hour and a half ago, waking up in the apartment on the floor behind a couch, no sign of Candy Cain and the hipsters were too sober to understand his accent, so he just made his way back here.

"Fuck's sake Sean. All I did was sleep!" He chuckles, I think he's still drunk and high.

"You better go off and get cleaned up, mate."

"Aye."

We agree to meet back down in the bar at around six pm after he's got his excrement all centrally located, and he's stopped stinking like six bags of arseholes mixed with vodka.

I go back to my room and check my work emails, nothing exciting, so I google for some decent restaurants around here, and make a list of places we could go out to eat. I'll drive, because I want easy access to get the fuck outta there quickly if Sean starts acting like a twat again. We are meant to be at the customer site tomorrow morning at ten am, so he better not mess around tonight. I guess I'm the sensible, boring one on this trip?

"There's a Japanese place?" I know Sean will turn his nose up at this, but I put it out there first as I would love some sushi. Sean makes a face. He's had his nose in his phone messaging someone.

"I can't face that right now." At least he's showered and changed and cleaned up a bit, and smells less like a gents and more like a duty-free aftershave shop.

"Steakhouse?" I see his eyes light up.

"That's the ticket!" Fair enough. It's a short walk from the hotel. Easy, and I don't even have to drive to ensure safety.

"Are we going to do any prep for tomorrow?" I feel like a sad, boring fecker even saying it, but maybe he's forgotten why we came here?

"Naw mate, it's all in me head! I'll just spoof it." He probably will, too.

We wander over to the steakhouse, I'm starving, Sean is ravenous, but I bet he hits the bar first.

As we go Sean is giggling at his phone like a teenager. Quite annoying but I don't indulge him by asking who he's texting. The restaurant isn't too bad, booth seats, a bar, low music, TVs everywhere showing sport. A waitress approaches us and asks if we want a table, but as predicted, Sean heads straight for the bar. I haven't got much choice but to follow. But I make sure and ask the girl for two menus.

Sean gets a glass of local ale, I get sparkling water, ice and lemon. I used to enjoy the odd interesting beer, now and then, but I absolutely don't appreciate the horrific pain that gout brings me, so I gave it up completely. No point in beating around the bush, because one leads to more, and more can lead to trouble. I'm not fussed; booze is overrated and expensive.

A blonde lady approaches us, must be in her fifties, pink dress suit, hair in a mullet like she's from the '80s. Shoulder pads, matching pink heels.

"Hi Scotty." She reaches over and rests her hand on Sean's shoulder, he turns around, and the childish grin returns to his mug. This must be Candy Cain.

"Scotty?" I look at him sideways, raising an eyebrow in a mock Spock.

"Ah, this is my good buddy, Terry from Ireland!" He introduces me to Candy who reaches out a manicured hand for me to shake. Her nail polish matches the rest of her outfit, naturally.

"Charmed." I flash a fake smile and turn back to the menu in front of me.

"Can I get you a drink, Candy?" Sean asks. The likelihood of her turning that down is equal to the likelihood of spontaneous formation of sub-zero centigrade water molecules into a unique fractal pattern in the realms of Hell that only politicians inhabit.

"Vodka and tonic, lots of ice." Bingo.

"I'm starving lads, so I'm going to order food, you can stay at the bar if you want?"

"Ah no, we'll all go get a table, eh?" Sean winks at Candy who nods in acceptance.

We move to a booth. I make sure I sit on the outside so I can get out quickly.

"You don't sound Irish?" Candy looks at me over her Vodka glass. Pink lipstick is already staining on the rim. I was hoping to avoid this interrogation, but I suppose it's inevitable.

"I'm not." She looks disappointed.

"But Scotty told me you were from Ireland?"

"Originally from England, lived in Ireland for twenty years." Knocked that one on the head pretty quick. Scotty indeed!

Her phone chirps from her matching pink bag, it sounds like a Star Trek communicator. Now things start to fall into place! She glances at the phone and dumps it back in the purse with a scowl, and then instantly flashes the grin again as she looks over at Sean.

"So, what are you two fine fellas doing in a place like this?" She sounds the part too with her southern drawl.

"We're on an away mission." We all laugh. Smooth, Sean, smooth.

Sean is doing his best impression of a kid in a candy store. Ha. No pun intended. I keep quiet because I don't know what story Sean may have spun her; for all I know he could have said we were Russian spies! It turns out he didn't tell her much at all, and he explains that we work for a big prestigious software company, and we're here to enable the overseas sales presence of cloud cybersecurity, for all of Europe. A somewhat embellished and glossy version of the truth I guess, but not technically a lie. Candy seems impressed anyway.

We order food, finally. Candy gets swordfish and more vodka, Sean a huge steak. I order steak too, I mean, when in Rome… But I'm keeping my corporate credit card safely in my wallet for this bill - if Sean wants to figure out how to expense a swordfish dinner, and gallons of booze for Candy, that is his problem with the auditors and not mine. While we wait, I find the restaurant WiFi and scroll through Twitter while Candy and 'Scotty' exchange anecdotes about life in Glasgow and Atlanta. I'm not listening, but I throw in the occasional nod and chuckle, so that I can continue to be ignored. Feeling like a third wheel here but they don't seem to care, and I have already offered to piss off and leave them. Food arrives, and it's pretty good actually, and there's plenty of it. Just what I needed.

As the evening rolls on and everyone else gets more drunk and annoying, I get tired, fed up and then bored. They are still yakking away, drinking and enjoying themselves. I guess I don't resent them that, but there's no fun in being the spare prick. I get up to leave.

"Sean, I'm off. Remember we are at FutureCloud by ten am, I'm leaving at nine-fifteen with or without you."

"Aye mate, no bother at all."

"So I'll see you at breakfast then at eight-thirty?"

"Aye Aye, Cap'n!" He does his Scotty impression, Candy bursts out laughing.

I walk away, but I turn around by the door.

"Live long and prosper." I make the Vulcan V sign. They both laugh and make the V sign back. Thankfully the restaurant isn't busy.

I decide to pay for my food, so I go back to the counter and settle up for my meal, and leave a generous tip on the company card, and then stroll back over to the hotel and my room and bed.

Chapter Twelve

TUESDAY 4TH SEPTEMBER

I think this is the first decent night's sleep I've had in months. I get down to breakfast at precisely eight-thirty, showered and ready for meeting the customers today. Feeling good and awake, adjusted to local time.

To my surprise, Sean is already at the breakfast table.

"Bloody hell, you're early!"

"Been here ages mate." Sean is reading a newspaper, he doesn't look up.

"Oh?"

"Candy got up at six."

"Oh!" He sniggers and looks up from his paper at me with a cheeky wink. I guess they had a fun night together then. But he seems subdued.

"Aye, I don't know how she does it, we got to her room at about two." That explains it I guess. He's on no sleep.

"You all set for the customer meeting?"

"Aye, it'll be fine." I go load up a plate with breakfast stuff from the buffet. Sean has paid for two nights in a hotel room, and not slept in his bed yet. Seems wasteful. I eat in silence and Sean reads his paper until it is time to leave.

Time, For a Change

. . .

We get to the customer office a little bit early, the drive was easy, and just as I had already rehearsed in google street view; I love technology. Sean hasn't said a word the whole trip, but the second we walk through the customer door, he switches to work mode, enthusiastic go-getter. Pointless though because we are met with a receptionist barrier, who quizzes us on who we are, why we are here, who we are meeting and the license plate number of the car, which I didn't know, and had to go outside and check. We sign a book and fill in forms and have to wait while she prints us temporary guest access badges, which we must 'wear at all times above waist height and visible'. Then she takes the serial numbers of our phones and laptops. She then makes us watch a five-minute 'emergency procedure video'. We have to sign another sheet of paper, to say we are now versed in the fire and emergency procedure. Insurance companies and lawyers run the world. I can see these guys are going to be fun.

We are now ten minutes late. All my planning ruined. I hate that. Now we have to wait for our contact to come down and let us into the actual building. There is a bowl of mints on the reception desk, so I grab a handful to compensate. The receptionist flashes a toothy smile.

A hefty man comes through a door, balding, tall, stuffed into a suit. He walks with a proud authoritative gait, hand outstretched well in advance, left hand ready to grab onto an arm. He rolls up to Sean with vigour.

. . .

"Pete Schenk. You must be Sean?" Sean shakes his hand firmly and long.

"That's me, pleased to meet you, Pete."

"And you are?" he steps over to me, the same handshake, enthusiasm shining in his eyes.

"Terry Ward, I'm the techie on this mission!" I do my best to match his candour, but I'm light years behind.

"Ah excellent, the man who does the real work!" I laugh, knowing he's joking, but also knowing he's right.

"C'mon, let's get you guys some coffee. Did you have breakfast?" Before we can answer he's away, holding the security door for us. We walk up two flights of stairs and enter into a big open office area. Vastly more upmarket than my office back in Ireland. Beanbags dotted around, big desks, nice computers on them, pleasantly air-conditioned, green plants everywhere. A big wide open office space, with plenty of natural light. The people wandering around look happy and smart. We are led to a break room with a coffee machine.

"Help yourself; my desk is just around the corner. Hop on over when you have some caffeine, and we'll get going!"

I feel like Pete has already had about twenty cups this morning.

The coffee machine is free apparently, and it pours out lovely coffee. There's also a range of syrups to squirt into it. I grab two shots of Hazelnut. I'm jealous of the employees here already. Our machine back home pours out brown shite, and we have to pay for it. Sean gets his cappuccino, and we head around to Pete's desk.

Pete is on a phone call, so we have to stand around awkwardly chatting for a few minutes, nodding and smiling as other people pass by.

"There's some decent skirt in here, eh?" Sean accurately observes in a whisper to me.

"Yeah, bit different from back home."

Pete gets off the phone and walks over.

"Sorry about that guys, had to deal with a salesman out in the field. We have an introduction meeting scheduled so you can get to know everyone."

We are led through a maze of corridors to a big meeting room, windows overlooking the car park area. We take seats and set up our laptops while Pete plugs in to a projector.

Today is going to be boring as hell for me; I have heard all these sales pitches before. They tell us about their company, we vaguely listen, then we tell them about our company and they ask questions that make them seem smart and unique. We tell them 'Good question!' and they feel happy. The business dance that must be done before real work can be started.

A lady comes in, tiny, but feisty looking. She drops down a laptop and leaves again. A dude comes in, sees us and heads over with outstretched arm.

"Hi, I'm Russ, sales lead, you must be the guys from C.S. Tech?"

"That's us. Sean Woods, project lead, and this is Terry, he's the technical man." Sean handles the intro. I'm okay with that; my jaw already aches from fake smiling. I am forced to shake hands though. Another bone crusher.

Russ sits down and stares intently at his laptop screen.

Sean is also looking at his screen; I can see that he tried to get on the WiFi but failed, so he's just clicking around and doing nothing, making it look like he's busy. I leave my laptop shut. Sean didn't bring a U.S. power adaptor for his charger, so he's borrowing mine. If I don't get that back, I'll be very annoyed.

The small lady comes back in, sits down and says nothing to anyone. She's latino; hair pulled back tightly, smart casual dress, covered in 'bling' I think it is called? Bracelets, necklaces, rings, all of them too big, too gold, too jingly for my taste.

Pete coughs to get attention and begins his business talk. I am getting ready to phase out, listen-only mode, but still be prepared to pipe in occasionally when I hear something on which I should comment.

"I thought we'd start off with a quick round-table introduction." Painful, but inevitable. I have my spiel off by heart more or less. Pete starts off and talks about how he's project lead on this European move, and he's been with FutureCloud three years, which is almost as long as they have existed. A newish venture then.

Russ next, and he talks about his sales stuff. I have no idea what he said. He immediately goes back to his screen once he's done his intro speech.

The small lady, Yolanda. She's the marketing lead, and I can only make out one word in seven of what she's saying, so heavy is her accent.

Now Sean gives his pitch; he's the project lead for Europe at C.S.Tech, based in Glasgow, but covering all of Europe, the Middle East and Africa. He's been with the company for eight years and worked with high profile customers on many complex projects. The FutureCloud people nod, impressed.

My turn comes round, and I blurt out my spiel. Ten years in the company, often working with Sean on many of his complex accounts, I'm the project manager focusing on the customisation and the technical side. Based in Ireland, where we have our engineering office and factory lines.

Back to Pete, and he tells us that one person can't be with us this week, Toby, who is the engineering lead for

Time, For a Change

FutureCloud. Excellent, so who am I going to pitch my stuff to? None of these people will have a clue what I am talking about! Apparently, Toby injured himself on vacation and will be out for a while.

"But don't worry Terry, we have a very capable stand-in, who Toby was training up just before his vacation." Pete looks directly at me, assuringly.

This sounds bad. They have handed over the crucial technical stuff to an intern, who won't have a single clue. Well, this is rapidly going downhill. My entire point for coming along was to get into the nitty-gritty of the technical details, and now I'm wasting my time. I tune out and open up my laptop, pretending to make notes.

The warm sun and the air conditioner battle it out all morning, but the room stays nice and cool. I wish my office was like this. We break for lunch after an arduous two-hour discussion between Sean and Pete, Russ occasionally throws in some sales numbers, Yolanda has said nothing since her introduction. I piped up here and there with some technical jargon that no one understood, but it probably sounded good. At least they sent in a tray of drinks and cookies to keep us going.

They don't have a canteen aside from the small break room, so Pete takes us out to a restaurant which is just a two minute walk away, but for some reason, we drive in his 'truck'. I shudder at how much fuel this tank uses, and also wonder why we don't walk? Russ and Yolanda went their own way elsewhere. Pete starts talking about sport with Sean, and again I'm lost and uninterested. This feels like it has been a massive waste of time for me so far. All that travel and hassle and now I don't even get to talk to a techie? I should have stayed in bed. No, I should have stayed at home, and in bed, where I could do something useful, like scratch my arse, for instance. Pete mentioned several times how much they appreciate us coming all the way from Europe to set this project up. He seemed sincere, so I guess Sean had a point about the customer feeling better about working with us, but my part in this is minimal and maybe non-existent.

We arrive very quickly at the restaurant. I can still see the FutureCloud logo on their office building. Fuck's sake, how lazy are they here?

It's more like a small café than a restaurant, but the food is good enough and quite cheap.

Sean got something called 'biscuits and gravy' which turned out to be neither biscuits nor gravy, but in fact a savoury scone covered with a white sauce, that had lumps of sausage meat in it. Apparently a favourite with the locals here.

I got a salad, trying to be healthy I guess.

Pete loaded up on a huge burger and seasoned fries. I would much rather be having that, but after the steak last night I think I've put on five stone in weight, and I've only been in America a couple of days. Anyway, the salad was pretty good.

Sean and Pete continue talking business stuff. I feel almost as useless as last night with Candy. Sean is doing all the talking; I'm just sat around wasting my time.

I would like to walk back and get my daily few steps done, but we get in the truck again and make the twelve-second journey back to their office.

When we get back to the meeting room, Russ is already there, but Yolanda is nowhere around. Pete doesn't seem to care and carries on with the meeting regardless. Russ gets more involved this time, he and Sean talk sales figures in great detail; charts are thrown up on the projector, big tables of numbers, details of shipping countries and spare parts locations, support agreements, projected volume forecasts for each fiscal quarter into the next year. I'm well out of my depth and once again, sitting here like a brussels sprout, that no one wants to touch at Christmas dinner.

Pete tells us around 2:30 that he has other meetings to attend at three, so we begin to finish up. I'm getting a bit concerned; I am meant to be presenting technical details tomorrow, and spending time with the engineer on Thursday.

"Pete, I'm planning to deep-dive into the technical details tomorrow."

"Right, you'll be working with our very talented new engineer, Rachel."

"Okay, great." Interesting. I wasn't expecting a woman to be the stand-in engineering person, but fair enough.

Pete takes us down to the reception exit, and we say our goodbyes. On our own we are at the whim of the receptionist again, and we have to pull out our phones and laptops, and she has to check off the serial numbers from the forms we filled in earlier. We head back to the hotel.

"I thought that went very well!" Sean chirps.

I look over to see if he's kidding, he isn't.

"Seriously? Their technical guy is out, and I've got an intern to work with."

"Ah, it will be fine, he said she's very talented."

"Right." This is going to be a disaster. I wish I had been stronger and pushed to stay at home for this gig. No one is doing my normal day to day work while I'm away, so I'll have to catch up on churn back in the hotel this evening, on the terrible slow WiFi, with a five hour time difference; everyone back home has already finished.

Back at the hotel, Sean convinces me to join him at the bar for 'one'. I agree, but I make it clear I have to do some work before we get dinner. Apparently, he doesn't have any work to do. Lucky him.

"So will Candy Cain be joining us for dinner again?" I grin and roll my eyes at him.

"Naw. She had to leave today, gone off to the next sales deal."

"Oh, sorry mate." He seems sad about it. Who'd have thought a pink Candy Cain could stir emotions in this Glasgow lad! I will save up the chance to call him 'Scotty' on a conference call once we're back home, and all this is forgotten.

"Ah, no worries, ships that pass in the night." He takes out his phone, checks the messages, puts it away again.

"So, what's the plan, man?"

"I'm no eating any raw fish, so you can forget that."

"They have other food apart from sushi, you know!"

"Aye, but I don't want to watch you eating Cthulhu's children all night."

"Whatever! What do you want to eat?"

"What's around?"

"Anything really. Throw a stone, and you could hit five restaurants here." There's a vast difference between my usual choice at home. I have to drive twenty miles to get a takeaway pizza that doesn't taste like a vacuum bag was emptied onto it.

"Glasgow is pretty well served these days too; I want something you can only get here in Ohio."

"Hairy muff."

"Heh?"

"Fair enough."

I pull out my phone and search close by for restaurants. I find a place called 'BJ's Brewhouse', and clearly that has to be the winner for Sean. The reviews look good, the food photos look decent, and once I show Sean the huge line of beer taps he's sold entirely. We arrange to meet back at seven, and go for dinner. I go up to my room, and while my laptop boots, I wash and change.

Work is the usual wave of semi-spam emails, newsletters no one reads, big-win memos, all the general clutter of shit that muddies the water every day. But I see one from Judith, so I open it up.

Terry,

Thanks for the work you did on DeltaWave. I've been out of office unexpectedly the last few days, but I got a note from the customer to say they made a mistake, and the five-hundred units do actually have the correct software on them. The person who checked was looking at the wrong reference. So all is well!

No, all is not fucking well! No apology, no sorry for stressing you out unnecessarily! I lost sleep over that balls-up, questioned my sanity, wasted time working on a fix for them, and planning how to send software to oil rigs. This is a typical customer response. They fucked up and caused a load of work and panic, and they think nothing of it. When they thought it was us that screwed up it was the end of the world. I reply back that I would like to see more careful checks in place in future, to avoid this sort of problem, but I know I'll be totally ignored. We just have to suck it up.

I go down to the bar at seven and find Sean already there, sipping on a glass of something. He's in the same seat he was when I left earlier, and I wonder if he's actually left at all. He sees me, gets up and claps his hands together.

"I'm famished! Let's go eat!"

The restaurant is close, but it is on the other side of the highway, which means we have to drive. Apparently, walking across a road is illegal here.

I had scrolled through dozens of photos of the restaurant on my phone, so even though I have never been here before, it looks familiar. We inevitably sit at the bar and Sean's eyes light up as he studies the thirty or so beer taps.

"It's a shame you don't drink, buddy." He looks over at me, "We could do some real damage here like!"

"Yeah, no doubt Sean, but even when I did drink I was never much for getting shit-faced."

"Ah well, more for me!"

Sean orders a taster tray of the brew-pubs own beers, they do look and smell good, but I'm not touching any. On top of the usual reason, I have to drive to get back to the hotel now, and I wouldn't ever consider driving even after a sip. The last thing I need is local cops finding a weirdo foreigner driving under the influence, and then spending a night in jail before being deported back to Ireland. The cops have guns here and aren't too worried about using them.

Time, For a Change

. . .

We move over to the tables and get some food. Burgers, onion rings, all on big ostentatious plates, with seasoning dusted over the whole thing. Little towers of chips and vegetables. They make an effort, but it's a bit over the top for pub grub out of town. Still, there's nothing wrong with the taste, and it goes down nicely.

Sean was asking me about the early days at C.S.Tech before he joined. I'm only a couple of years longer than him, but his office in Glasgow is primarily sales oriented, and no technical stuff at all. I tell him about the software testing I started on; we'd download every known operating system in various languages onto loads of different test systems, and made sure everything worked well. If it didn't, we'd report it to the development teams, and they'd patch something and send it back for more tests. I was the team lead, which meant nothing really, but my team would have to come in once a month at three am and do a night shift, because we weren't allowed to make changes to servers during regular business hours. I remember one Monday coming back in after a night shift on Friday, my manager asked me if I had a good weekend, I said sure, I installed a new version of some software on my home machines. Updated everything. He looked at me like I was from Mars. I spent all night installing software at work, and then went home and did the same thing on my own computers. I had to laugh; I hadn't considered it weird until he pointed it out. Well, whatever makes you happy, right?

After we eat we move back over to the bar, and Sean decides on the next beer he'll try. I get a mug of coffee.

. . .

"Ay up!" Sean nudges me and gestures with his thumb towards two women who have come in and sat down at the other end of the bar. Here we go again!

"Ah, I don't like the look of yours, Sean. Come to think of it; I don't like the look of either. I've seen more attractive things hanging in a butcher's shop window."

"Ah, c'mon, where's your sense of adventure?"

"I left it in Ireland, years ago."

Sean gets up and heads over to annoy the ladies. I stay firmly put. I can see his animated gestures across the bar, the tell-tale signs of the women preening, they adjust hair, change pose, even blush. He's only been there a minute. How does he do it? No force in the universe would make me go over to strangers and start up a conversation like that. Drinks appear, and he hands over dollars to the barman. He points over at me. Fuck no.

I have zero desire of interacting with these people, not just because they aren't my type, but because I don't want to meet people and 'have fun' the way normal people do. I'm fine here alone, thanks.

One of the women waves me over. I pretend I didn't see. Fuck's sake. What has he got me into here? Sean approaches. He better fuck off, or I'm outta here, and he can find his own way back.

"Terry, these ladies find my accent very appealing shall we say! I told them you are from Ireland and they want to hear an Irish accent."

"I don't even have one!"

"They won't know that!"

"Dude."

"Aw, come on over. There's two of them, so there has to be two of us."

There's a certain point at which it becomes hard to

extricate oneself from a situation, without appearing to be a total prick. So, under duress, I follow Sean over. I don't know what he expects to happen here, maybe he doesn't either, and doesn't care?

"This is my good buddy Terry from Ireland."

"Err, hello."

"Dinnae mind him the-now, he's just a wee bit shy." He's putting on the Scottish thick here. He never talks like this usually.

"Sean, I think I'm going to head back."

"Oh, no! Stay," One of the ladies protests.

"I love to hear an Irish accent." Ah, for feck's sake, like.

I have no desire to be complicit in this subterfuge but what do I do now? If I walk away Sean will be pissed off. if I tell them I'm not even slightly Irish and I just happen to live there, they will know Sean is bullshitting. So I say nothing.

The conversation goes much like last night with Candy, same topics, same anecdotes, different restaurant and different beverage choice. I'm bored of it. I'm saying as little as possible and avoiding answering questions. I'm uncomfortable, nervous, annoyed, and desperately trying to think of a reason to leave without seeming rude. I don't know why I care, I should just go. But social norms pervade, and I don't want to cause hassle. I don't think Sean has decided which one of these ladies he wants to pursue. I haven't even bothered asking their names because I simply don't care. I feel like I'm in one of the many work meetings where I'm just phasing out reality, and drifting into my own universe.

I come up with a plan and rehearse the lines in my head, several times, and try to guess all the likely responses and then my responses to those. I think this will work.

"Hey, sorry to be a party pooper, but my head is killing me. I think the jet lag caught me or something."

It didn't come out like it should have, in my head I was smooth and natural sounding. But that sounded cliched and fake. Seems to work okay anyway, I don't think Sean cares anymore, and the ladies are eating out of his hand. He's telling stories of the whiskey distilleries he's visited and the differences between blends and single malts.

"You'll find your way back, Sean?"

"Aye, mate, no bother. See you in the A.M."

Chapter Thirteen

WEDNESDAY 5TH SEPTEMBER

"You are the worst wingman ever," Sean announces as I find him at the breakfast table.

"Ha. I know." I pour myself a coffee, and I get an orange juice and a bottle of spring water. My mouth is as dry as a nun after lent this morning.

"Didn't go well then?"

"Ah, it's okay. Still made it!" I shake my head in disbelief.

"You're going to catch something nasty. Which one?" He grins and sniggers childishly.

"No!"

"Aye." The dirty little bastard.

"How do you do it?"

"Alcohol mate, you should try it."

"Ah, it never did anything good for me anyway. Here? In the hotel?"

"Yeah, well their apartment was further away." I guess he finally slept in his hotel bed. Or at least used it!

"They're gone?"

"Aye, left about half an hour ago. Stacy had her car."

"But… Oh well, whatever, nevermind."

When we get to FutureCloud, we are met with the same barrier of bullshit by the receptionist. We have to sign forms, fill in who we are meeting, and the license plate of the car, which I again can't remember and have to go and check. Then we have to wait while the receptionist prints us new badges that we must wear 'above waist height and visible at all times'. Thank fuck we don't have to watch the stupid emergency procedure video again; Sean managed to get us out of that.

Pete comes through the door after a minute and ushers us up the stairs to the meeting room. We are precisely on time today, because I allowed extra just in case. No coffee stop this morning, straight down to business. We sit down, and I get my laptop out, I'll need to connect up to the projector, as I'm going to be showing my slides and doing my configuration spiel.

Russ is in the room already; he nods a hello. Pete is busy on his laptop. I'm not really sure what we are waiting for, but nothing is happening just yet. Sean is looking antsy but saying nothing.

A girl walks into the room and drops down a laptop opposite me at the table.

"Ah, Rachel, nice of you to join us." Pete looks up from his laptop, then gets up and takes his stance in front of the projection screen.

The girl makes a face at Pete as he turns around to look

for whiteboard pens, and then flips him off with her middle finger. I don't think anyone else noticed. I stifle a laugh. She's gorgeous, long dark hair, piercings, a bit goth-metal, and clearly super-cool. She must be half my age, and I wonder what she's doing in this boring meeting. Suddenly I realise. This is Rachel, the intern who I'm going to be working with on the technical aspects of the project. Fuck.

"So I'm going to kick off the meeting, but then I guess it is over to you Terry to impress Rachel here on all the configuration stuff."

"Uh, sure, okay," I mumble. This has knocked me a bit sideways. I thought I was prepared to roll out my tired, dull presentation, but I wasn't expecting to have to deliver it to this audience.

I look over at Sean, and he gives me a wink and a grin. He's noticed my predicament I take it. He's going to be feck all use!

Rachel looks over at me and flashes a grin. She sits back and folds her arms.

Pete starts off with a high-level description of how they run their operation here in Ohio. Apparently, the ground floor here is a mini factory. They take in brand new computers in one end, install hardware and software, configure them automatically, and then re-box them and ship them out the other side direct to end users, who will then use them in their businesses to run their 'Cloud security' or whatever shite it is they do. Seems a bit like a mini version of what we can do back home. I'm sure we can make it work, but there are dozens of technical details I need to know. I guess Rachel will be able to explain all that stuff. Maybe over dinner? No, shut the fuck up, Terry.

"So, over to you, Terry. I've got a meeting to jump to, so I trust you are in good hands." He leaves the room. Russ has already gone; I didn't even notice. Sean goes off to use the bathroom. I'm alone with Rachel.

"So, I don't know how much you know about C.S. Tech?" I fumble around with the projector connector and try to get my laptop to show its screen, but it doesn't work of course.

"Jack shit, dude." She's watching me and trying not to laugh.

"Okay. Yeah, well, we can take care of more or less all the configuration in Europe the same as you do here." I finally get my screen showing on the projector.

"Yeah, yeah, I get it. Hey do you want to go see the factory?"

"Oh, yeah, sure. That would be great. Should I leave my stuff here?" She's already gone. I follow, but not before I password lock my laptop and close it.

"You came all the way from Ireland to Ohio for this?" I catch up with her on the stairs; she's bounding down two at a time.

"Well, yes, Sean sort of insisted."

We get to the ground floor, and instead of going out to the reception and exit, we go back into a security protected door, Rachel swipes her card and motions to me to go through first. The noise level suddenly jumps up, and the plush office environment is replaced with a factory type view. Racks and racks of computers, conveyor belts, stacks of boxes, people pushing little carts around, general bustle and commotion, but organised. We walk all the way through down to the back, and there are a couple of cubicles set up just aside from the factory area. Rachel dumps down her laptop in one of them; the other is empty. I guess this is her desk.

"So let me take you through this from start to finish, and you just butt right in if you have any questions. Okay?" She flashes a grin.

"Cool." I try and act cool, but I'm probably not. I tried and failed to avert my eyes from Rachel's butt the whole time she led me through the factory floor. I wonder if she knew somehow, and that's why she mentioned butts?

"Well, forget all that crap that Pete showed you upstairs. That's all bullshit. He thinks it runs smooth like that, but it don't."

"Oh." I wonder what she means. It looks like things are running quite smoothly, albeit busy.

"For one, none of it is automated. We have fellas running around, manually doing everything." I guess she read my mind.

"Ah, okay. Maybe we can help you with that? Almost everything we do is automated as much as possible." I'm feeling a bit more in my element now, this type of thing is a frequent customer situation.

"Sweet, maybe we can chat about that later." It sounded like a statement rather than a question, but I nod anyway.

We go back through the whole factory, and Rachel shows me every step in detail, she really knows her stuff. I ask her how long she has been here; three months. She's learned quick I guess. Straight from a university on some kind of internship placement.

By the time we get back to the other end, almost two hours have passed.

"Well I guess that's most of it, I hope you remember all that?"

"Uh. I mean, sure."

"Just kidding. It's cool. I will email you all the details." She smiles in a very pleasing way.

"Well, I got shit to do, so you should go get your buddy, and go eat or something." She holds the door open for me to get back to the corridor and stairs.

"Okay, thanks, I really appreciate the tour. Um, we are scheduled to meet again tomorrow and go through… Oh, I guess we just did all that?"

"Are you saying you want to see me again?" She laughs and tosses her hair back.

"Yes! I mean, we're here for another couple days."

"Cool. Text me when you get here." She hands me a card, and I pull out my wallet and give her mine in return. The first time I have handed one out in years.

Rachel Brooks
Junior Engineer

I climb the stairs two at a time, navigate the halls and find Sean on his own in the meeting room, a coffee in his hand.

"Where the fuck have you been?"

This time it is me who has the shit-eating grin, "Rachel gave me the tour."

"Oh, aye?" He gets a sparkle in his eye.

"She really knows her stuff. Pete was right, she is very talented."

We head off, Sean pops by Pete's desk and tells him we are done for the day, so we head back to the hotel, deciding to eat there.

"What's the story then, buddy?" Sean is fishing for gossip.

"Their factory here is very manual, for all the talk Pete gave us, it isn't true. We can definitely sell them on some automation processes."

"No that, you daft ape! What about Rachel?"

"What about her?"

"I think you like her - you're grinning like a baboon!"

"Yeah, she's a solid engineer, she'll rock the industry in a few years."

"Are you fuckin' blind, mate?"

"Yeah, I did notice she's quite attractive."

"Quite attractive? I'd crawl twenty miles, over broken glass, with my cock out, just to see her in a bra."

"That sounds painful."

We get to the hotel and Sean makes for the bar, as usual. I go up to my room. I want to wash and change, check email and make sure all is well, before we go for lunch. I fire up my laptop and check my phone, and I have a single message from a US number.

What's your sign?

I don't know what that means, or who it is from, until I pull out the card Rachel gave me. It's from her number. My sign? I'm lost. Something to do with the software we use? I reply with a question mark, and leave the phone on the desk, and go wash and change. I hate wearing smart clothes. Generally, in the office in Ireland, I wear jeans and T-shirts every day. No one cares. Only when I go to meet customers do I get done up like a dog's dinner. My phone buzzes on the desk.

Star sign dummy. My cards said I would meet someone interesting today.

Am I interesting? First I heard of it! I don't even know what my star sign is, so I google it and reply: Taurus. I wonder why that is important?

I head down to the bar to meet Sean for lunch. I'm starving now. My phone buzzes in my pocket along the way.

Oh boy.

Is that a good or bad thing? I have no idea how astrology works. Never put much thought into that kind of thing, or the occult. I know a lot of people believe in it, but it has never made any sense to me, so I mostly just ignore it. I reply asking if that is good or bad.

The universe doesn't work like that!

I'm perplexed now. But I get to the bar and find Sean, who has already made enquiries and found the hotel has no food at lunchtime.

"Now what?"

"Go out somewhere?"

"Pain in the hole."

"Pizza?"

"Sorted."

I google for local pizza, and find dozens of options. Some of the same restaurant chains even have duplicates within a mile radius of the hotel. I'm always amazed at the density of restaurants in America. I can't understand how they all make money? We choose one at random, place an order online, and wait for it to come. I go up to my room and get my laptop, and bring it back to the bar. I've got some emails to respond to for my real work, the usual stupid questions, the answers I've already given three times, but someone has lost the info yet again, that sort of worthwhile admin task. As it turns out, the WiFi is much better in the bar, and I can get online quickly. That must be a sign! Speaking of signs, I recheck my phone, but Rachel hasn't messaged me again. I haven't replied to her last message because I didn't know what to say honestly. Interesting girl.

The pizza arrives, and we find a quiet corner of the bar area to munch. Sean is already on the beers.

Massive competition for pizza has led to excellent quality. I could eat this all day. My phone buzzes in my pocket.

So, you gonna talk to me?

I don't know what to think. Why is this girl interested in me? I reply with - I don't know anything about astrology.

I figured.

Sean is scarfing down pizza, but he's noticed I'm messaging someone and grinning.

"You sly bugger!"

"What?"

"I bet you are texting that Rachel?"

"Well, yeah, but she started it!"

My phone buzzes again.

Do you like sushi?

My mind races. Yes, I love sushi, but why is she asking me? Do I ask her for dinner? I only just met her, she's half my age, lives thousands of miles from me, what is the point in going further with this? I reply that yes, I do.

Cool, pick me up at 7:30

She sends an address. What just happened? I reply: Okay, is this a date?

The universe knows what it's doing.

I can't help but feel a nervous fuzzy feeling in my stomach. I'm entirely lost here, and I'm being led into the unknown.

"You okay finding dinner yourself tonight, Sean?" He laughs.

"You little fucker! Yeah of course buddy, enjoy yourself!"

I'm not going to be able to concentrate on work now, so after we finish eating, I head up to my room and run a hot bath. I need to think and relax. I have my deepest thoughts among the bubbles.

I find the address she sent. It's about twenty-five minutes' drive away.

As I drive the route my phone is sending me on, I can't help but wonder what I'm doing? I feel somehow disconnected from reality like I'm just watching someone else perform the actions. A bit like when I use the mystery box back at home, I can see things happening, but I'm not sure if they are happening as they did, or if I'm influencing them in the past. There's a disconnect but also a strong feeling of being there. My throat is tensed up, my stomach churning, I don't even know why, and I don't know how to stop it. I keep distracting myself from what is happening, but with only a few minutes drive left to Rachel's address I can't think of anything else. The last few hours have been torture.

My phone buzzes and I glance at the lit up screen.

Hurry the fuck up would ya?

I check the time: 7:20 pm. She's impatient! There's no point in stopping to reply now. I'll be there in a minute. Sheesh!

I arrive at the house, an old looking wooden structure, I've seen many like it around. She's on the porch at the side of the house, and when I pull into the driveway, she jumps down quickly and gets in the car.

"Well, what are you waiting for?" I can't see what she is wearing but she's looking fabulous, I don't have time to take in the view though, she seems to want to get out of here. The car fills with her perfume. It's like a drug that melts me away.

"Let's go!"

"Er, hi. Where are we going?"

"Sushi, dude!"

"There's a Japanese place right behind my hotel?"

"There you go."

I pull back out onto the road and turn around, and head the way I came.

"Fancy car."

"Thanks. All on the work credit card."

"Can I put the radio on?" She doesn't wait for an answer and starts pressing buttons. She finds a classic rock station and turns it up loud. I'm okay with that.

A song plays that she knows well, but I have never heard before. She sings along to it, her voice is fantastic. I'm in an utterly alien situation with a stranger, but it feels natural somehow. There's no guard up in front of her. Nothing false or pretentious. She is raw and visceral, and she says exactly what she means without a filter. There's no bullshit here. She must feel safe with me; a total stranger in his car; does she trust me already? I never trust anyone; I need an escape plan, a plan B, or I feel vulnerable. I couldn't do something like Sean did the other day and sleep on a stranger's floor, in a city I have never been to before. I need comfort and safety and walls between me and the rest of the world. But somehow this girl is perfectly comfortable, and her ease is making me feel better. I have no idea where this is going, but it doesn't matter right now. All I know is I have a beautiful girl next to me singing her heart out, and we're going to get sushi. What more do you need?

We arrive back at the hotel, and I park in the same spot as I had earlier, near a side entrance.

Rachel turns off the radio as we stop. "Where is the restaurant?"

"Right over there." I point behind us, about two-hundred meters over the road.

"I have heels on, dude!"

I don't even complain, I start the car back up and drive out of the hotel parking lot, down the road and into the restaurant parking lot. We drove further than it would have been to walk. Rachel seems satisfied.

I get out and walk around the car, and dramatically open her door for her.

"Oh my god, don't you dare say something like 'M'lady'!" She laughs and steps out, and I make an overly theatrical bow, and offer my arm for her to walk with me.

She takes it, and I feel her close to me, and chemicals start to rage in my brain. I sense a grin explode on my face unwillingly.

"You okay there, mister?"

"Fine."

We go into the restaurant and stop to take in the environment. It seems decent. There are tables as in any dining room, but there are also chairs around little grill areas where you can interact and watch the Chef cooking or preparing the food. A small Asian man approaches us.

"Two? You want table or counter?"

Rachel and I look at each other and say together: "Table!"

No way would I want to be at the centre of attention at a counter.

She takes her coat off as we are seated, and she's wearing a tight black dress, fishnet shirt under it. Every nerve in my body pulses gently. I sit down opposite and pick up a menu.

"Soooo, do they have beer here?"

"I would think so, yes."

"You getting one?"

"I don't drink."

"Oh boy. Well, I do!"

I wave at the waiter, and he comes back over. I order Rachel a Japanese beer and a coke for me. I bet he assumes the other way around.

I'm looking at the menu, but I can't focus on anything,

can't concentrate, keep wondering if this is a real thing that is happening now or if I'm dreaming?

"I don't get this menu." Rachel looks up at me with a frown.

"Have you ever had sushi before?"

"Nope."

"But, you suggested it."

"You like it."

"That's true but…" I trail off and look back at the menu for something simple we can order.

"I always wanted to try it."

I look up at her, but she's looking at the menu again. This restaurant is pretty close to where she lives, and there are probably dozens of other places to get sushi around here.

"My Mom never took us out to anywhere fancy." She's doing that thing again where it seems she's reading my thoughts.

"I worked in a Japanese hotel for a little while, when I was about your age I guess." I hadn't thought about her being so young. She looks up at me, pauses, but doesn't say what it felt like she was going to say.

"You know what to get then?"

"Yup." I plan to ask the waiter just to give us a selection of sushi and some tempura, that should be plenty to start her with.

The waiter brings our drinks and puts the beer in front of me, and the coke in front of Rachel. I snigger and wait for him to go and then swap the glasses over.

"So, what's wrong with you then?" She sits back, folds her arms like she did earlier in the meeting room, and looks straight at me.

"How do you mean?"

"The universe brought us together for a reason. Just have

to figure out what it is." She keeps talking about the universe like this, like it's a sentient thing imposing will on us.

"I don't know what you mean?"

"Okay, well, I guess it will take some time to find out."

I shoot her a raised eyebrow look.

"My cards told me I'd meet you today, and you would need some help."

"What cards?"

"Tarot."

She's a hippy. A techie hippy! A Teppy? That explains the astrology and the intuition. I guess it doesn't matter too much. I'm not averse to it, I just never got interested in that kind of thing.

"Oh. I don't know anything about that."

"Go figure."

The waiter comes back to the table, and I order a selection of food for both of us. Rachel seems happy that I know what I'm doing and sips her beer.

"We are heading back on Friday." I feel I need to be clear about the situation, I don't know where this is going, but there's no point in denying the fact that I will be thousands of miles away soon.

"What's your point?" She holds her glass up, empty.

"Well, you said it might take some time."

"You got internet in Ireland?"

"Of course."

"Okay then!"

I wave the waiter over for more beer.

"Anyway, there's nothing wrong with me."

"Sure. Everything is peachy, right?" I suppose everything is not entirely peachy. But how could this girl possibly fix my life? Also, why would she do that? What does she get out of it?

"I'm quite complicated really."

"Yeah, I see that." She smiles her heavenly smile and gets up to go to the restroom.

While she is gone, I take the opportunity to look around the restaurant. It isn't very busy, but there are people dotted around. Some sit at the counters and watch the chefs flamboyantly make their dinner with fire and knives, and lots of things thrown up in the air. Others sit quietly at tables as we do.

Rachel returns, her replacement beer has arrived.

"See that couple over there?" I nod towards a table close-by.

"Don't look!" She looks back at me and laughs.

"They are about to break up."

"Really?"

The couple are in their fifties, salt of the earth types.

"That's Ron and Martha. They are on a road trip vacation of the mid west states."

"Oh yeah?"

"Yup. Ron owns a corn husking business, Martha is prominent in the church community. She bakes a lot. They have been married thirty-seven years now. Two kids all grown up.

Their son, Jack, well he moved to Alabama a couple of years back. Married a sweet girl who makes little characters out of sponges, she sells them online. She made $378.76 last quarter.

Their daughter, Emmylou, she's in love with a Texan. Ron hates him, Martha thinks he's just fine thank-you-very-much.

They have a dog called Reagan. Ron laughs inside every time he yells out for Reagan. Martha is fed up with finding poops on the lawn."

Rachel is giggling and looking over at the couple who innocently slurp at their noodles.

"Don't look! I haven't got to the interesting bit yet." She looks back at me.

"What is the interesting bit?" She bites her lip and fiddles with her piercings.

"I'm getting to it. Ron has saved up $93,000 in a bank account that Martha has no idea about."

"The sneaky asshole."

"Yeah, but what he doesn't know is that Martha has saved up $126,000."

"How?"

"Bake sales."

"That's a lot of baking!"

"Yeah, I said she bakes a lot. They both have a plan to leave each other and go off and travel the world for their retirement, and they both planned to do it tonight at this very restaurant.

Ron wants to go to Iceland and wander the landscape, to fulfil his passion for geothermal energy and volcanoes.

Martha wants to go to Spain and learn about bullfighting and Flamenco, because she finds it fascinating and immensely passionate.

They have sat on these dreams for almost four decades, and now they can finally live their lives." I pause for effect.

"But now I think they won't do it."

"How come?"

"The noodles."

Rachel looks at me sideways, quizzically.

"They are both slurping the noodles."

"So?"

I let her sit for a minute, while I sip my drink. Taking my time. She raises her eyebrows and leans forward.

"They are so dependant on each other, so ingrained in each other's habits and lives, they can't be apart now.

They are about to realise that they both didn't even notice each others' slurping, and they didn't mind it one bit, in fact, it reassured them, made them feel safe and happy.

Instead they will pool their resources, and with their $219,000, they can go to Iceland and Spain together, and while they might complain at the cold or the heat, they'll be okay. They'll put up with it and stick together because, deep down, they are connected, and they love each other more than silly problems could ever overturn."

"Wow… What makes them realise?"

"This."

I take out a napkin from my lap. I've written on it with a pen I picked up in the hotel.

STOP
FUCKING
SLURPING

I ball it up and throw it onto their table while their heads are down in the noodles.

Rachel laughs out loud, stifles it with a hand over her mouth.

"Shhh!" I cross my lips with a finger.

"Oh my god, you nut job!"

The waiter brings our food on a trolley, and sets about putting a multitude of plates and dishes on our table.

Rachel discovers that she's a huge fan of sushi and tempura, we both go crazy and try some of everything.

She tells me about her home life, which isn't great. She has no father; he did a disappearing act when she was a baby. Her mother never had a good job, surviving how she could, getting random guys to pay bills and buy groceries. But somehow through all the poverty and unstable home life, she managed to study and win a scholarship to Ohio State University to take computer science. From there she got the job at FutureCloud.

"You want to know why Toby is really gone?"

For a second I have to think who Toby is. But it comes to me. He's the senior engineer I was meant to be working with, instead of Rachel. Pete said he was out.

"How do you mean?"

"Pete told you Toby injured himself on vacation, right?"

"Yeah, I think, something like that."

"Yeah, he's injured alright, but it wasn't on vacation."

I look up at her, "Huh?"

"He's out because I broke the motherfucker's arm when he tried to hit on me."

"Oh! Shit."

"Yeah."

"I'm sorry that had to happen to you. Men can be total wankers." She looks blankly at me.

"Jerks."

"What did you call it? Wankers?"

"Yeah, that's what we say!" She laughs.

"They gave me more money and put me in charge of the engineering department. He won't be back anytime soon. His wife kicked him out. He's back with his mama."

"Well, his loss is my gain! I get to work with you instead, right?"

"Right." She smiles her most heart melting smile and knocks back the rest of her beer.

"They got anything else to drink here?"
"Uh, they might have some sake."
"Sucky?"
"Sake!"
"Sucky Sucky, love you long time! Ten dollar!"
"Stop!"
"What is it?"
"Rice wine. You can get it hot if you want."
"Get it!"
"It can be very strong."
"Dude. I'm a pro."

I wave the waiter over and ask for a hot sake, turns out it does cost $10, and we laugh when he's gone. I get sparkling water, lots of ice.

"How come you don't drink?"
"Ahh. Well, two reasons really. I get gout." I wait for her to recoil in horror but she looks blank.

"It's a kind of arthritis and it's incredibly painful, alcohol aggravates it."

"Okay, that makes sense. What is the other reason?"
"I don't like how it makes me feel, I prefer to be in control of my body and mind."

She pauses for thought for a moment.

"I have a big book of herbs and shit. I'm gonna look up that gout thing. I guarantee there's a simple fix."

"Yeah, I can go to a doctor and get medicine for it, but it's preventative, which means I have to take it every day of my life. I don't want to have to rely on a prescription medication for the rest of my life."

"Right, dude, so herbs will fix you right up."
"I'm sceptical."
"I know, but do what I tell you, and you'll be fine."
"Okay, Mum!"

"Fuck you!" she laughs.

The waiter brings a small pottery jug filled with hot, sweet sake, he pours some into a little cup, and offers it to Rachel, she takes it and sniffs.

"Goddamn!"

The waiter offers me a cup, but I wave it away. He sets down my water, and I sip it, watching Rachel as she wonders what to do with the cup of hot wine.

"Well, only one way to find out!" She chugs it down in one shot.

"Take it easy!"

"Damn, that's good!"

"Seriously, take it easy, I don't want you to pass out."

"Ha, why not?" She gets a mischievous look in her eyes.

"Could end up in trouble."

She picks up the other cup and chugs it down.

"Let's see what the universe has planned for us." She leans back in her seat, her cheeks flush red.

I wave over the waiter and get a coffee for myself and jug of water for Rachel, even though she protests she's okay. I think the food will soak up most of the drink, but no one wants a hangover, and water never hurts. She asks me about my life, my family, I tell her they all left me one way or another, and I'm alone in Ireland in a house that needs work that I will never do, and a job that I barely care about anymore. I want to tell her about the box of mysteries, I feel that out of everyone in the world I could talk to, she is more likely to understand, and not just assume I'm a fruit-loop, but I keep that in my own thoughts for now. I never usually tell anyone the details of my life, but with Rachel, I feel open and safe. She doesn't judge, doesn't mock. She comes from an entirely different world to me, where drunk boyfriends smash TVs in fits of rage, and get arrested for drugs. Where no one has ever had a stable job, and sleeping on a friend's couch is a reasonable and acceptable way to live. It's all quite weird to me. Scary, even. I wonder what the universe thinks I can offer this strong-willed young girl?

I pay the bill as the evening goes on, and it feels like we have stayed here long enough. Once the waiters start hovering around, it's time to leave. I paid on my personal credit card instead of the work one.

Rachel seems happy, a bit hazy perhaps, but generally very merry. Once we get outside though and the cool breeze hits her, she flops against the pillar of the porch and looks a bit woozy.

"Are you ok?"

"Ugh. Take me home!"

"Okay." I smile at her. "Told you to take it easy!"

We get in the car, and I program in her address into my phone again and set off driving. She slumps into her seat, doesn't touch the radio this time. As we get onto the highway, she looks up and around outside.

"Where are you going?"

"Taking you home."

"No, douche! YOUR home!"

"Oh! My hotel?"

"Well, Doh! Where else?"

I get off the highway at the next exit, and turn around and go back.

. . .

We arrive back at the hotel, and I park in the same spot again, Rachel exits on her own, and she seems to feel better than a few minutes ago, on the other side of the street outside the restaurant.

I want to ask her if she really wants to do this, we are mostly strangers after all, and she just told me how she broke some dude's arm for trying it on. I know this isn't the same situation, but I can easily misinterpret these things. Someone once told me a girl could come up to me wearing a T-shirt that said 'I WANT TO FUCK TERRY' and I'd be thinking 'Oh, lucky guy.' I want to know for sure I have a green light before I step on the accelerator.

"It's okay." She reaches over and grabs my hand as we walk to the side entrance of the hotel. Is she reading my mind again?

"Just remember, the universe brought us together for a reason."

I want to believe her, but what is that reason?

We get up to my room, and I am thankful I left it reasonably tidy.

"Fancy hotel." She takes off her coat, throws it on the floor and slumps down on the bed.

"Ahhhh, comfy bed too."

"All on the company credit card." I set my phone to play some music through a tiny set of speakers. Rachel sits up and finds the light switches, and fiddles with them until the main light is off, and only the dim bed-side light is on.

"That's better. You gonna come here or stand there all night like a vegan at a barbecue?"

I move to the bed next to her, sit on the edge and turn to face her.

"Jeez, dude! See, this is why you need a drink!"

She grabs me and pulls me down on top of her. I guess this is the green light?

We kiss and caress and fumble, her perfume is intoxicating, I feel the heat from her breath on my neck and her hands down my back.

"Lie down and turn over," she orders me, and I obey.

I feel her straddle me and then her hands on my back and shoulders.

"You are so tense, dude, lighten up."

"I don't know how." I really don't want to be tense in this delicate situation, but my body does what it does, and I apparently don't have any control over it.

Rachel gets up and goes into the bathroom.

"Get naked!" She yells from the bathroom.

"Umm!"

"I can't massage you through clothes, asshole!"

I stand up and do as she says. She seems to know what she wants and who am I to object? But I get inside the bed covers once I'm undressed, I'm out of shape and mid-forties, and she is gorgeous, and in her twenties, there's no doubt who would win the naked competition here.

She comes out of the bathroom, stripped to just her bra and panties.

"All I could find is this lotion, so I guess that will have to do. You can take off the rest later." She notices me staring at her body. I look back at her face quickly, embarrassed.

"My tits are down here." She points at her ample bosom and laughs.

"Okay, turn over and please try to relax."

I turn over, and she whips off the bed sheets, I feel a slap on my arse, and she laughs and straddles me again, and squirts body lotion from a tiny hotel tube over my back. It's cold, but I try not to tense up. I feel her hands on my back, gently rubbing in the lotion, then up on my shoulders, I sense her bra fabric brush against my back as she leans over. I slowly melt into the bed, almost drifting to sleep as she presses and squeezes and rubs her way up and down my back. I've never felt so relaxed and aroused at the same time. After what seems like years she lifts off her hands, and I sense her get back up and roll over onto the other side of the bed. I could have stayed like that forever, but that was just a starter, now I'm ready for the main course.

"You gonna help me with my underwear?"

I turn over and face her.

"Oh, hello Mister!" Her eyes pop as she notices my dick standing to attention.

"I guess you liked that?"

"I fucking loved it." I reach over and pull her toward me, finding the hook of her bra quickly, and undoing it in a fluid motion. I have no idea how I did that. But it was damn smooth.

"Oh my god, how did you do that?"

"I practice every night on a shop dummy." She laughs and pulls her arms out of the straps.

"Just kidding, pure fluke!"

I pull off the bra and bury my face in her chest, smothering her with kisses and caresses and slowly move down her stomach and to her panties, red lace. I pull them down her legs and off her feet and look back up at her naked body.

"Oh, fuck!" I suddenly back off her.

"What's up?" She looks shocked.

"Uh, I don't have a rubber." I used the last one on the plane to prank Sean with, but it was a hundred years out of date anyway. I haven't needed one for a long time.

"Oh, dude. You scared me there for a second. Don't do that!"

"Sorry, I just realised."

"Its okay, just pull out."

"Really?"

"Yeah…" She pulls me down, and I once again do as I'm told. I thank the universe for this intervention, and whatever the reason was for bringing us together, I'm fucking grateful!

Chapter Fourteen

THURSDAY 6TH SEPTEMBER

I think I got twenty-five minutes of sleep before my alarm went off at five am. Rachel has to go home and change before she goes to work, so we need to leave the hotel before six am so she has time. We fucked all night, over and over. I discovered just how incredibly out of shape I am and how sweaty I get when exerting that much energy. I thought hauling all those tools from Dad's workshop was hard work, but making wild and passionate love with a beautiful young girl is like running a marathon. We showered together after the third time, but I got sweaty when we did it again. After that, I collapsed, and Rachel lay down and snuggled up next to me. I feel like I now know what being 'royally fucked' means.

She's in the bathroom, getting ready. I'm already ready, having brushed my teeth, pissed and got dressed, all in five minutes. She's been in there twenty-five so far. I check my phone while I wait, but I don't have any messages. I realise I haven't even looked at Twitter for a while, so I scroll through. Nothing new, same old snarky comments and the occasional funny picture. I post a random thought:

What happens if you put anti-caking-agent into cake mix?

Rachel finally emerges from the bathroom, she's wearing the same clothes as last night of course, but she's wiped what remained of her makeup off, and put her hair up. She still looks amazing.

"You look better with no makeup," I blurt out.

"Shut the fuck up!" She laughs and seems a bit shy about it, so I shut up.

"We better go. It's almost six am." I'm exhausted, but I have to take her home.

Outside, the light is a dim shade of sunrise that I have rarely witnessed. I'm not a morning person, but in my youth, I would occasionally stay up all night in chat rooms and see the sunrise as it happened through my window. Or a family holiday as a child, when we'd have to leave the house at crazy o'clock, and Dad would drive for hours across the country. This light reminds me of those days.

The drive to Rachel's house is quiet, we don't say anything, there's not much traffic. She scrolls through her phone on and off as we drive, I leave her to her thoughts.

I pull into her driveway, and she opens the door and jumps out, but then gets back in and leans over to me and we kiss again, long and soft and so good.

She reaches into her bag and pulls out a small black velvet drawstring bag and hands it to me; it has several lumpy things in it.

"What's this?"

"Keep it with you all the time."

"Okay, but what is it?"

"Stones. You need them more than I do."

"Oh. Thanks." I wonder why I need a bag of stones?

"Text me when you get to work, okay?"

"Yeah, we are meant to get there at ten again."

She's gone, into the house by the side door. I back out onto the road and head for the hotel.

Driving back I feel an emptiness, a gap, I look over at the passenger seat and touch the cloth, there's no body heat left, there's no evidence she was even here. In my exhausted state, I can't help but wonder if I dreamed all of what just happened. But if I did, why am I out driving at arse o'clock in the morning. Pull yourself together, Terry. Then I remember the little bag of stones she gave me and it makes me feel better.

By the time I get back to the hotel, it's seven am, I head straight to the dining room and get coffee, water and orange juice again. I'm feeling a massive headache coming, probably from dehydration. I must have sweated a gallon last night.

Too early for my body to eat just yet, but the coffee goes down well, and after a while, I start to feel a bit more human. I'm still exhausted, but I at least have enough energy to go up to my room and wash, grab my bag and get ready to go to FutureCloud again. Our schedule was that I would be working with Rachel today while Sean and Pete and Russ thrash out the commercial side, whatever that entails. I'm in no fit state to be much use today, so I guess it is good that we had already been through the details of their setup and customisation requirements yesterday. If only all meetings were as smooth and efficient as that.

I go back down to the dining room and get some eggs and bacon and more coffee.

"You're up early!" Sean arrives at the table.

"Couldn't sleep." Technically that is true. I couldn't sleep because I was busy doing other things.

"No luck last night then?"

"Depends what you class as luck I guess?" I smile.

"You sly bugger!"

"What did you get up to on your own?"

"Ah, quiet one mate. Went back to the steakhouse place, lovely meal. Had an early night for a change. Feel better for it."

"Nice one. Does you good now and then!"

"Aye."

I can tell Sean is itching for details, but I don't want to go bragging about my fantastic evening. I don't know how Rachel would feel about it and I don't want to discuss the gory details.

We finish up an extended breakfast and head off to FutureCloud, nice and early this time for the inevitable security procedure. I have the license number of the car in my phone now.

There's a different receptionist this morning as we enter, she makes us do the entire process all over again, including the safety video, because there was 'no record' of us having done it before. If a tornado hits, I know who I'll be snuggling up with in the basement! This doesn't help my headache at all. We have some ridiculous procedures at C.S.Tech, but at least we don't make people go through this torture over and over when they visit.

I text Rachel we are in the building and head upstairs with Sean. Pete looks panicked this morning, no banter, a bit curt and annoyed. I feel a buzz in my pocket, Rachel sent a message:

Hey, shit is going down here. Get you in a bit.

I wonder if that is the same shit as is causing Pete frustrations? I text back and offer to help if I can.

Actually, you might be useful. I'll get you now.

Pete dumps us in the break room to get coffee, he's got some important calls to make apparently. Sean is meeting with Russ first, so he heads off to a smaller meeting room in the central office area. I linger at the top of the stairs waiting for Rachel.

She waves from the landing; I walk down to meet her. It has only been a few hours since I saw her, but it feels like ages ago. She's changed into jeans and a baggy shirt, and she's still delicious looking. She's stressed, though. Clearly, some nasty shit has happened here today.

"What's going on?"

"We got this massive order come in, for like five million bucks. Biggest order we ever had. It's for medical systems or something."

"Okay." I know how fussy the healthcare industry can be from tragic experience.

"We can't get the firmware versions to work. It errors every time, we've tried on like a dozen computers."

"Right." I think I know what the problem might be, but without seeing the error messages and log files I can't be sure, so no point in getting her hopes up yet.

"Can I see the systems?"

"Yeah, I'll show you the one in my cube."

We walk through the factory floor together again, and I can't believe it is only twenty-four hours since I met this incredible girl, let alone made love with her.

We get to her desk, and she shows me the computer, connected up to a keyboard and screen on a little trolley. It shows a red FAIL on the screen and a familiar blinking cursor underneath.

"Can I get online here? On my laptop?"

"Um, yeah, let me get the WiFi password for you."

While she looks for the password, I try some commands on the failing computer. It's a server, I'm not familiar with the particular model, but I've seen hundreds like it. It has the FutureCloud logo on the front.

"Do you know where the error logs are? I can't find them."

"Yup." She nudges me out of the way, navigates the network and pulls up the log files. To most ordinary humans these are text files filled with utter gibberish, but to nerds like us, they contain valuable information. I scan through for a few minutes looking for the fail info.

"Okay, I think I see it. You want version 2.4.8 of the firmware on here, right?"

"Yeah, I know that." She looks annoyed.

"Well, you already have 2.5.1 on here."

"Yeah, I know that too."

"Well, sometimes a firmware update is one way only, you can't downgrade it."

"Shit! They like, MUST have that version, something to do with the medical license."

"Did you get that WiFi password?" She hands me a sticky note with it written down.

"Did you set this?"

"How can you tell?" The password is 'T0by=A$$H0L3!'

My laptop gets connected, and I can access the C.S.Tech systems back home. I get the make and model of the failing computer and search our archive.

"I'll need a blank USB key."

"Okay." She goes round to the other cubicle and comes back with a selection.

"Pete is shitting his pants; the CEO is up his ass about this order. There's like two-hundred-and-fifty servers to do, and they have to get done this week. He thinks everything fucking magically works down here, but he hasn't got a clue."

This sounds horribly familiar. She could be talking about my job. Managers never understand or even pretend to understand the details. They only care about when it will be fixed. Rachel seems upset about this. Maybe because she's also tired from last night. I have woken up a bit. Nothing like a technical problem to stimulate the grey matter. I'm skimming through technical manuals and downloading a file that should do the trick. Just need the correct commands.

"Okay, you have to put it into manufacturing mode to do the downgrade."

"How do you do that?"

"You put this USB key in when I've made it, and you hit F12. Give me an hour to build and test it here then you can replicate the USB and do the rest."

"Seriously?"

"Yeah, should work. Maybe this is what the universe had in mind?" She looks at me to see if I am mocking her, but I'm not. She smiles.

I get the file and then write a little script that resets the server into a mode only used in a factory usually, but it allows things that normal operation would block. Then I program the firmware downgrade to happen, which is pretty quick. It then resets back to the normal operation mode and shows the green screen if it all went well. It only takes me about thirty minutes to get the key done. Pretty simple stuff. Rachel has gone off to the factory floor to do her regular duties while I'm working.

. . .

"Hey."

I feel a shake. I must have dozed off in her chair.

"Is this done?" She points to the server.

I look up at the screen, it shows a big green PASS.

"Oh, let me check it." I open up the log files again on the system, and scroll through to the firmware section. 2.4.8 as it should be.

"Yup."

"Oh my god! Dude, I love you!" She throws her arms around me and plants a kiss on my lips.

"You're welcome!" I don't usually get that response when I fix a technical problem back home.

"One thing. I probably shouldn't have handed out that software. Do your fix, then delete all the keys, okay?"

"Okay."

"If anyone asks, I only told you how to do it and you got everything from the internet yourself."

"Got it."

We set about making ten duplicates of the USB key, and a very brief instruction sheet on what to do, and Rachel takes them over to the factory operators. They have a lot of machines to fix, but if they can do ten at a time, it won't be too much of a disaster. She's going to explain the fix to the factory supervisors and demonstrate it on a couple of failing systems. She also sent an email update to Pete saying we had found a fix for the problem and it should get done today if they run a second shift.

"You want to get lunch?" Rachel comes back to her cubicle, all smiles.

We get outside, and I make a point of checking Rachel's shoes. Flat. No heels. I insist we walk over to the café. I feel like I haven't walked more than a hundred feet since we got to America.

"I need sunlight and exercise," I complain, but I don't think I'll have any trouble falling asleep tonight. Tonight... I wonder if she'll come to my hotel again? I wonder if she wants to? I wonder if she meant what she said when I fixed her technical problem, or if it was just an expression? 'I love you.' People do tend to use those words frivolously and out of context.

"You got plenty of exercise last night." She grins.

"True."

We head towards the café, and she reaches over and grabs my hand. I look over at her. I feel the thrill of passion, but also sadness. Will I ever see her again? Sure we will keep in touch with phone calls and messages and emails, photos, even video chat, but will that be enough? I'm reminded of how I haven't seen Ted at work for years, but yet we still talk every day, and I can tell his mood just from a few words of text. Not the same with Rachel. I have no desire to smell or touch Ted!

As we get to the café, just outside, I stop her and turn her to face me, my hands on her shoulders. I want to bring her with me to Ireland, to wake up every day and see her pretty face next to me. But there are a million reasons why that isn't going to happen. I was planning to say something profound, emotional, unrealistic and ridiculous. But words don't come out of my mouth.

She looks at me, puts her finger to my lips, and then kisses me.

"Everything will work out how it should be." She looks like she believes it, but I just can't see how.

We go in and sit at the back. I get an All-Day Breakfast and a bucket of coffee, she gets soup and salad and some lemon and lime drink. She doesn't seem to want to talk about the future, so we talk about her hobbies, or more specifically, her interest in all things occult. She tells me how many tarot decks she has, and all the ones she wants but hasn't managed to get yet. How her Mother threw out her books and cards and little bundles of sage when she was younger, because they were 'the devil's work'. I'm reminded that this part of America is subtly more religious at its heart than catholic Ireland. Maybe not more, just manifesting differently. I think most people in Ireland only go to church for the craic.

I believe in science and technology. To me, that is a real religion, and I marvel at the miraculous creations like the internet that will enable me to talk to this girl even when I am thousands of miles away. When you think about it, the elements needed to make a smartphone and a worldwide fibre optic network have existed for millions of years. But only now have we learned how to wield those tools in a new craft, formed over many decades by dedicated people, working hard to build something incredible that the world has never known before. The trillions of dollars invested in hardware, the software that has thinned the hair of many programmers, devices so complicated and secretive to make, that the factory workers are sometimes stressed to the point of ending their own lives. We all walk around absent-minded of the powerful computer in our pockets, holding the combined knowledge of humanity in the palms of our hands. What do we use it for? Watching funny cat videos and arguing with strangers.

Time, For a Change

. . .

I pay, and we amble back to the FutureCloud office, in no rush to go back to what is currently work. But I can't get the thought out of my mind, looping over and over, my brain extrapolating all the possible outcomes of the question I want to ask. In the end, I blurt it out.

"You want to stay with me again tonight?" She looks at me and smiles.

"Well duh! You are so funny!"

She giggles at my expense. Well, I guess that went better than I expected! I do realise that I waste billions of brain cycles worrying about stupid pointless things, but it seems to be out of my control. Even as I am thinking the thoughts I know it's ridiculous, but there's nothing I can do. I sometimes yell at myself out loud "SHUT UP", but until the cycle is broken with a resolution or a massive distraction, it doesn't help.

"After I'm done at work I'll drive to your hotel. That way I can drive myself to work in the morning."

She's answered my next set of questions already. I feel better. I open my mouth to voice my final concern, and she pre-empts it again.

"I'm crazy tired, so we can't stay up all night again."

"That's what I was going to say too. I have to drive to Chicago tomorrow."

"I know, dude. It's cool."

I find Sean in the big meeting room we first congregated in, he's sitting on his own, looking at something on his laptop.

"Hey, buddy!" He looks up as I enter.

"How's it going?"

"I hear you saved the world!"

"Oh, well. Not really saved the world."

"That's what Pete thinks!"

I guess I may have saved them an embarrassing business fail, but I'm sure Rachel would have figured out the problem if she had more time. I only know about issues like that because they have happened to me many times. I guess decades of fuck-ups teaches you something! In any case, I don't want a load of attention now, especially as the method I used may not strictly have adhered to company software distribution policies. Whatever works.

"I just showed Rachel what to do." Sean winks at me, conspiratorially.

"With the firmware downgrade!"

Pete comes into the room, his gait has returned to the proud bounding, rather than the troubled stoop it was earlier.

"Hey, hey! The man of the moment!" He comes over to me and offers a handshake, I stand up and accept. I don't like when people stand next to me while I'm sitting. I feel vulnerable like a deer in a forest.

"It was nothing really." I don't know exactly what Rachel said in her email, but people don't need to get all excited. There's still a load of work to do to fix all the systems.

"Well, you got us out of a big hole! Dinner is on us tonight!"

Oh shit. I did not want to spend my last evening in Ohio with Pete at dinner! I was looking forward to a quiet evening with Rachel.

Sean and Pete are talking about where to eat, and more importantly, where to drink. I leave them to organise the piss-up-in-a-brewery and sit down and send Rachel a message about Pete's dinner plans. She replies within seconds.

I know, he emailed already :(

I guess at least she will be at the dinner then. Maybe we can sneak off early somehow?

Pete and Sean have agreed on a plan. We all meet in downtown Columbus around seven at a bar, and then go to a restaurant called the Ocean Club, I googled it and looked at the menu. It seems very nice, but that hardly makes up for the stress of having to eat dinner with a bunch of business folks I couldn't care less about. I'd rather eat pizza out of a box in my hotel room with Rachel.

Rachel is on my mind a lot. I have to remind myself that I only met this girl yesterday and that I'm leaving tomorrow. But that's just it. I want to spend the short time I have with her efficiently. There's no way I can get out of this now without breaking all of society's unwritten rules.

With the plan made, and Sean's meetings all complete, we head back to the hotel. I messaged Rachel a goodbye, and she replied that she'll come over around six, after work, and she's stopped to pick up some stuff from home. That only gives us a few minutes before we have to make our way downtown.

"I think you've done it, Terry." Sean is looking at his phone as we drive back.

"How do you mean?"

"That fix you did, I think that was the push they needed to sign this deal with us. I just got a mail from Russ, he's doubled his sales forecast for Europe."

"Oh, wasn't it already a done deal?"

"Nothing is ever a done deal until the papers are signed."

Maybe I'm a bit naive of business operations, but I was working this whole time on the assumption this was all real work and not speculative. If I had known that this could go nowhere, I would never have got on the plane in the first place. But if I had done that I would never have met Rachel.

The universe does work in mysterious ways.

When we get back to the hotel, I head up to my room. Sean bypasses the bar for the first time too, and he goes to his room to make some calls.

I collapse down on the bed.

I'm woken by thumps on the door and my phone ringing. I jump up, startled, look at my phone and see Rachel is calling. I open the door and find her standing there glaring.

"Sorry, I must have fallen asleep."

"No shit." She stomps into my room.

I check my watch. 5:53. She's early.

"Were you waiting long?"

"Hours, dude! Just kidding. I just got here. Do I get a hug?"

I smile, and we embrace. I feel like crap now, having slept in my clothes and for just that wrong length of time, not long enough for proper sleep and not short enough for a nap.

"I have to wash up. Be right back. Make yourself at home."

I come out of the bathroom and find her at the desk with a mirror on it, doing her makeup. She is using the lid of my laptop as a tray for her various little pots and brushes. I'm glad it's just my work machine and not my own personal one.

"How did the fixing go?"

"They had like half of it done when I left."

"Great news! Do you know the place we are going for dinner?"

"That fancy place downtown? No, I've never been anywhere like that."

I planned to meet Sean in the bar at six-thirty and I'll drive us downtown. I'm pretty sure he'll be making his own way back, much later, fuelled by alcohol and whatever debauchery he can find this evening. We head down once Rachel is changed and made up. I changed my shirt too, I feel like that is more than enough effort.

Sean waves us over at the bar. He's got an almost full beer glass in front of him, which I mistakenly think will mean we'll be stuck here waiting for him for a while. But he's gulped it down in two chugs, and we're ready to go. He tried a friendly 'Hello' with Rachel, but she just nodded and smiled.

"Do you know the way?" Sean asks. He must be forgetting who I am.

"No, but my phone does. Who is coming?"

"Pete, Russ and us, I think that's it"

I hate city driving. It makes me nervous. Sometimes the GPS signal get's a bit confused because of the tall buildings, and I lose where I'm going and have to guess. We went several streets too far, and I had to navigate back again. But after a lot of cursing, we find the parking lot I had planned as the destination. The bar is just around the block, and the restaurant is right next door.

We get into the bar just after seven and find Pete and Russ already at a small circular table, with interesting looking beers in front of them. As we approach there's a wave of handshaking and small talk bullshit, but I noticed no one tried to shake Rachel's hand, or comment on the coincidental arrival of her with Sean and I. Forgot to plan for that, and have her arrive a few minutes later or something. Oh well.

Everyone gets a beer of some kind, and I get sparkling water again. I don't want to be the weirdo who shocks everyone when he says he doesn't drink alcohol. I'd rather that drinking alcohol in public wasn't part of the social norm at all, and people who have reasons for not doing it weren't shunned, as if crazy hermits or outcasts, and probably dress up in their dead Mothers clothes and prance about, after killing women in the shower. None of that has ever been proven!

An unhealthy amount of clichéd chat is thrown around the table between Sean, Pete and Russ. Rachel and I are more or less left out of the banter. She's very quiet, just sipping her beer and trying to shrink away invisibly into the stool. She's a young woman out with four boring old farts. Not surprising really. I imagine she is dreading bumping into someone she knows in here.

Under the table, I compose a text message to her. I don't send it, I just show her my screen as she's sitting right next to me.

'Are you okay?'

She takes the phone and types back.

'Yeah, just hate all the people and shit. Pretty tired too.'

She gives me the phone back, I reach over and hold her hand under the table. She squeezes as thanks.

Time, For a Change

. . .

Pete announces they do wonderful Martinis here and he goes to the bar to order them for everyone. Well everyone except Rachel and I, who declined.

I can see him at the bar, 'educating' the bartender on how to make the ultimate Martini. He's a booze snob. I'm sure the bartenders have people like him high up on a list of annoying customers. I imagine attending a barbecue at his house would be intolerable too. 'Now, you gotta flip the burgers just right, or they don't get the good grill pattern...' His wife must either be equally annoying, or some kind of saint.

As the level of inebriation goes up, so does the noise level. It gets quite busy in the bar, and the sound forms a barrier around me. I can no longer pick out an individual voice; it's just a constant drone. The occasional screeching laugh, or booming yell and clink of glass, I feel disconnected from everyone, the more I see other people drinking, talking, flirting, gesticulating and acting out stories to their friends, the more I feel like I want to get out of here and hide in my hotel room. I've long since lost track of the conversation, but the others don't seem to notice my lack of participation. I look over at Rachel, she looks tired.

Eventually, the group decides to move to the restaurant. I'm glad to get out of the bar, and I exit first, followed by Rachel, we stand outside in a little plaza area and wait for the lollygaggers to catch up. The street feels like a massive relief and my head slowly lets down the barriers, a few seconds pass before I feel like I can hear and speak again.

"I don't like noisy, busy places."
"Yeah, me either."
"I want to get this dinner over with as soon as possible."
"For real."

The others eventually roll out, midst some anecdote about the time Pete visited Scotland in the 90s, and thought he was in the movie Trainspotting. Sean does a 'choose life' impression and they all roar with laughter. Rachel rolls her eyes at me. I'm sure she has no idea what they are talking about.

I guess this is how business is done, this friendly banter is mortar between the companies, wet and sticky right now, but once it hardens, we'll be glued together. That sounds disgusting now I think about it!

We get to the restaurant and climb the stairs. Greeted as we enter by a sickly smiling sycophant, head tilted in self-deference. Once Pete confirms his reservation we are led to a table, overlooking the street below. A chair is pulled out for Rachel, and I take a seat next to her. Sean sits opposite, and Russ and Pete take the ends. I don't like this dynamic, but the choice is made now. Pete gets a wine list. Here we go, he 'knows about wine' too, I bet. Sean and Russ jump in with wine suggestions, and they settle on some 'informed' choice. I guarantee they could be drinking grape juice mixed with vodka and they wouldn't know the difference. I noticed they have a cocktail menu too, and I'm quite sure that will be brought out before the night is over. I plan to have 'exited stage left' well before then, taking the young lady with me.

The menu does looks delicious. Too good. Everything is over the top with flourishes and sprigs of garnish, but I'm not

Time, For a Change

going to complain, because no one will understand my point. Rachel looks at the menu like it's written in an alien language, so I help her make a choice.

"Why is there juice with the meat?" Rachel whispers to me.

I look at the menu again, trying to see what she means.

"Oh, jus? That means sauce, like gravy." I laugh, but I hope she doesn't think I'm mocking her. She rolls her eyes. I agree. The menu is pretentious beyond any reasonable level. It feels like it was designed to trip up the novice. Only fancy people can dine here. The Emperor's new clothes bullshit.

I suddenly realise what the numbers are next to each dish. They aren't prefixed with a dollar sign, presumably because that would be uncouth and brash, so I didn't notice before, but each number is substantial. Glad I'm not paying. This dinner for five is likely to hit five or six hundred dollars once they factor in a few cocktails. No wonder Rachel has never been in here. I wouldn't be here either if I were paying. I could grocery shop for a month and not spend that much on food. I settle on a steak with some side dishes, Rachel goes for salmon. We skip the starters.

When the waitress comes around to take the order, she makes all the appropriate facial expressions to indicate what a fantastic choice we have all made. That's what the extra money pays for. 'Ego boost with your steak, Sir?'

I get another fucking sparkling water, because what else am I going to do? Even that probably costs more than a whole meal anywhere else. Rachel got one too, I think she's exhausted now, I just want to take her back to the hotel, but we are stuck here for a while longer.

When the wine arrives, there's an inevitable cork removal and tasting ceremony, and Pete just laps it up. He sent back the first bottle. I'm sure he doesn't know that means his jus will be spat in and they'll stick on some extras onto the bill. Never piss off the people who bring you food! Once he is happy with the booze, he toasts to the future of our business partnership, and throws in a little nugget for us nerds by thanking us techie guys for making it all happen. We clink glasses, and I sigh inwardly. It would be nice if I were going to make any cash from this deal, but I'm salaried. Not linked to any sales commission, so it won't make any difference. Sean is looking at a nice cut of the action. I'm guessing the double forecast he got earlier means he can add all leather interior to his next Merc.

The food arrives, and it looks picture perfect, smells delicious. There's nothing wrong with it all, but it feels off somehow. Everything is too perfect, like an early 3D animated movie, the uncanny valley of fine dining. Give me something to legitimately complain about for fuck's sake, even a chip in the plate or a fingerprint on the glass would be something.

It is good. I dive in like a flock of pigeons on a bag of mouldy bread.

Rachel seems to enjoy her food, but she is picking at it. The others could be on another table now, I feel like Rachel and I are just a hindrance to their enjoyment. I thus form a plan for our escape.

I write a message on my phone again and show it to Rachel.

'You want to get out of here?'

She takes the phone and writes back.

'Hell yeah.'

'Okay, say you don't feel good, and I'll offer to take you home.'

'Plan.'

We execute, it works, everyone feigns concern for

Rachel's well being and thanks me for gallantly taking her home. Pete even tells her to take the morning off if she needs it. I think they are secretly relieved, so are we; everyone happy.

"Smooth, bro."

"I thought so." I smile.

We walk back to the car, and then head back to the hotel.

It hasn't escaped my thoughts that this will be my last night with Rachel for - I don't know, forever? For a while? I've been pondering how I can come back here independent of work. I have enough holiday saved up to take a week or two off, and I could squirrel away enough money to get here in a few months. The costs add up quickly though. Right now work is paying for hotel, food, car, flight. If I have to fund all that on my own it will be pretty tough. But then what? I only get so many days of holiday per year, I can't afford to travel to America multiple times a year, plus the authorities don't like that kind of travel, it makes airport staff suspicious.

Am I in a relationship? I don't even know for sure what to think. My instinct tells me just to let it go and see what happens, but my brain insists on some kind of answer. Sean can love them and leave them, and seemingly not be too troubled about it the next day, but I don't function like that. I like this girl, a lot, we connect and fit, and everything feels natural with her. I don't need to pretend to be someone I'm not. I get the feeling she understands, and I'm pretty sure she likes me back. I mean, she's in my car now going back to my hotel. Willingly! I have to reassure myself things like this. Just in case there is some way I could have misunderstood.

But I didn't come here looking for a relationship, and I

don't know how to manage a long distance thing. I'm not a fuckwit though. I'm not going to let this go.

We get back to the hotel, and I have to piss, as usual, I wash up while I'm in the bathroom. When I come out Rachel is in bed, her clothes in a heap on the floor, she's wearing one of my T-shirts by the looks of things. There are moist tissues with multi-coloured stains on them in a pile on the desk. I can't tell if she's asleep or just lying down, but either way, I undress and join her in the bed as quietly as I can.

"We didn't find out what is wrong with you yet." I guess she wasn't asleep yet, just resting.

"No, well, if I don't even know myself…" I'm not sure what she wants to hear, but I want to tell her about the mysterious box back home. I'm suddenly reminded of it. I can't tell her I have a time-machine though, because as understanding as she is I don't think she'd be able to believe me. I don't even know what to believe myself, so I find a more natural way to explain it.

"I have these dreams." She looks up, props herself on one arm. I feel her leg wrap around mine and her hand on my back.

"Since I went down to Dad's old workshop a couple of weeks ago. They feel so real. I'm right there in the dream. Like a vivid memory, almost a lucid dream I guess."

I tell her about clearing out the workshop, how I should have done it years ago but couldn't bring myself to. How my shed is now full of tools and equipment. I tell her about the first dream, the printing press sound and my childhood bedroom, and how I knew my dad was just a few feet away in his little print room, that I could smell his pipe smoke, hear him cough. Then I tell her about the boat trip to Ireland. How the motion of the boat made me feel sick and how I saw my dad asleep, how it brought tears to my eyes to see him again, so vivid and alive.

Then I tell her about the DeltaWave fuck-up at work, and how I dreamed about the email I got from the customer, how the problem seemed to disappear after that. I tell her I don't know what to make of these dreams, that they make me feel dizzy sometimes, very emotional others. Then I remember the weird situation with Jeff. How I worked with him, sat opposite him, and then he vanished and turned out to work at a different company in a different city.

"Have you had any more dreams?"

"Not since I came to America. I guess I haven't slept enough to dream." She smiles and gently strokes my back. She ponders for a while.

"Just see how it works out. Your brain is trying to tell you something. You have to let it happen."

"What do you mean?"

"Let them come. Don't try and stop it, or overthink it. If you have another dream, write it down as much as you can remember right after you wake up."

"You want me to email them to you?"

"Sure if you want to." She scrunches her nose up in thought again

"You still got that bag of stones?"

"Yeah, it's in my work bag."

"Keep it with you."

"Okay, but why?"

"Vibrations and energies, they will help you."

"I told you I was complicated." She smiles.

"Everyone is, dude. You miss your dad?"

"Every single fucking day."

"I never had one to miss."

"I'm sorry."

We kiss, long and soft, and then make slow, gentle love, I want to stay in the moment forever, but we fade away to sleep, entwined and exhausted.

Chapter Fifteen

FRIDAY 7TH SEPTEMBER

I snoozed my alarms over and over, but eventually I had to give in. As I sit up, I notice Rachel isn't in the bed, I panic for a second. Has she run away, was it all a dream? I tell my brain to fuck off and give me a break for once and ignore it. Rachel comes out of the bathroom wearing a towel, dripping wet from a shower.

"Hey, sleepy-head." She comes over to me and drops her towel, but then runs away giggling.

"Ah, you little tease!" I get up and go to the bathroom.

I check the time, ten-fifteen. Oh shit. Sean will be wondering where I am. I check my phone. No messages. I wonder if this is a repeat of Monday when I couldn't find him and then he turned up later still half drunk. Whatever. We don't have a set time to leave today since the flight is tomorrow. We can take our time getting back to Chicago. Rachel got the morning off, so no harm done. I needed a good sleep anyway, so I'm fit enough to drive.

We take a good long while to get dressed after some pleasurable messing around, and then I realise that the hotel breakfast is probably long gone.

I send Sean a message asking where he is. Hoping I don't have to call the cops or scour every bar in Columbus looking for him. He replies after a minute that he's still in his room, just woke up. Fair enough.

Rachel has her coat on, and her bag over her shoulder, I realise she's ready to go, and this is goodbye, and a thump of adrenaline pumps through my veins.

"Oh."

"Yeah. I want to stop at home before I go to work."

I go over to her and squeeze her as tight as I can, taking in her scent, and her warmth, and I can't stop the tears from coming despite trying. I hold her until I gain control of myself and wipe my face dry. She's smiling through wet eyes, and she promises me this is a beginning, not an end and that the universe will bring us together again. She makes me vow to keep her bag of stones with me, all the time and not lose them, she wishes me safe travels, and to text her when we stop and, when we get to Chicago. She tells me not to get into any crazy shit with Sean. I assure her that I have no intention of doing anything crazy with Sean or anyone else. I never do. Except for these last few days with her, I guess.

She leaves, waving as she closes the door. I sit on the bed, devastated and shocked at how I can be so affected by someone after so little time together. She smashed a massive hole in my protective shields, and now I'm incredibly vulnerable. My phone buzzes on the desk.

I love you, please don't be upset.

I reply 'I love you, too' and it's the first time I have used that phrase in a long, long time. I will see her again somehow, that's for fucking sure.

. . .

My phone buzzes again, this time it's Sean, he's heading down to check out of the hotel. I haven't packed anything up yet, so I dash around and scrape up all my stuff into the big bag. I can pack appropriately for the flight tonight. I check and double check and triple check that I have the little bag of stones though. I do a final visual in the room and bathroom, the desk and the plug sockets and I'm gone. Some fun times in this hotel room!

"How was your stay?" The receptionist asks me as I pay. Her fake smile plastered on thick.
 "Emotional."

I find Sean lingering outside, and we head to the car, load up with our suitcases and bags, and I enter the hotel at the airport as our new destination into the satNav app. The original plan was to go back into FutureCloud this morning, but that was hours ago, so I'm assuming that ship has long since sailed.

"Mah fuckin' heed!" Sean complains. I haven't looked at him yet this morning, but I turn now and wish I hadn't. He's got a black eye and a thick lip, and he's apparently got the hangover from hell. Here we fucking go!

"It's no as bad as it looks," Sean grimaces.
 "If I hear the word boyfriend or pimp, I'm stopping the car, and you can fucking walk to Chicago."
 "No, no, nothing like that."

"Come on then. Out with it."

"You should see the other guy!" He tries to laugh but coughs instead.

"Yeah, I'm sure he's right now cursing the day he ever met Sean Woods from Glasgow, nursing a slight bruise on his little finger."

"Fuck off!"

Sean explains the whole sordid deal from when Rachel and I left. Of course, it begins with cocktails at the restaurant, a wide selection of them, until Pete had the fantastic idea of going to one of the many strip clubs out of town. They paid the hideously expensive restaurant bill and grabbed a taxi to Pete's favourite skin joint, where he is fond of one of the girls.

We approach a big pharmacy store, so I stop the car and go in, leaving Sean in the car to fester. I grab an instant ice pack, some painkillers, a pair of big cheap sunglasses and a bottle of water. That should sort the fecker out. I make sure to keep the receipt for my expenses.

"Ah, you fuckin' star. Cheers." Sean sticks the ice-pack on his mug, and I get back on the road. He fumbles with the water and the painkillers but finally manages to swallow a couple. He carries on with his story.

The stripper that Pete wanted to see wasn't on duty, at least he couldn't find her. They stayed for a few beers and some lap-dances, then Pete realised this was the wrong strip club, the girl he was after worked at another place he frequents. Dirty Bastard. They grabbed another taxi and headed out to the other venue, all the way across the city. Pete found the girl he wanted; 'tits you could bounce a fuckin' peanut off' apparently. He settled in for a lap dance. Sean and Russ hit the bar and paid fifty bucks to watch two girls drink shots off each other's crotches. Usual classy stuff.

"What happened to your mug?"

"I'm getting to that." He's put the sunglasses on now, and he looks like he's from a B-rated road-trip movie that ends in the trunk of a car in the desert.

"I had to pish like a fuckin' fountain, so I flew into the bogs. Didn't see there was a willy-wonka on the floor."

"A what?"

"A love glove! A fucking raincoat! Fairly full of baby juice by the sound it made when I stepped on it! I went sliding like an olympic skater and slipped over. Tried to get my balance by grabbing onto the sink. Smashed my face into the door handle of a cubicle as someone came out."

I look over at him, my mouth agape.

"You did it to yourself?"

"Aye."

"You daft fucker! Not having much luck with the old used johnnys eh!" I remind him of the flight over. He scowls and complains about a perfectly good pair of pants he threw into the hotel room trash the next day.

"You want breakfast?"

"Aye."

I pull over at the next food venue, which isn't far, and we load up on pancakes, American style. I message Rachel that all is well and we stopped for food. She replies promptly.

All the servers are fixed, we got the order done in time. xxx Thanks so much!!

I reply with a load of heart emoji and smiley faces,

realising I'm now acting like a teenager, but not giving a single shit.

Sean flicks through his phone and email, his face lights up after a minute, and he chokes on a gulp of coffee he just drank. When he stops coughing and spluttering, he shows me his screen.

"We fucking did it buddy!"

"Huh?"

"This is the signed statement of work from Pete!" I look at him quizzically, I've no idea what that means.

"We won the deal with FutureCloud! Three thousand servers per year!"

"Oh! Nice one. Congratulations."

"It was you who made it happen, that techie fix you did swung the deal."

"Ah, that was nothing. I shit better solutions than that!" But a thought occurs to me, and I begin to form a plan so cunning, it could be appointed Professor of Cunning at Oxford university.

We get back on the road. Sean seems to be feeling a bit better now. Still four hours of driving to go before we get to Chicago according to the satNav.

Sean fell asleep just before we exited Ohio into Indiana state. The epic towering 'Jesus cross' brings back the memory of the trip here at the start of this week. Not long ago, but it feels like so much has changed since then. I put music on from my phone and relax into the drive. My plan is pretty simple. I'll be working with Rachel for the European replication of the FutureCloud configuration work. Once all the set-up is done, which can take about a month or six weeks, we'll need someone to validate everything is correct, and just how it would be if it came out of their little factory in Ohio. That validation could all be done remotely via the internet and photos, but to do it properly they would need to send someone over to Ireland to check it in person. It is pretty complex after all, and might need some tweaking on the fly, which would need an engineering resource familiar with all the work they do. That resource can be Rachel! I'll start sowing the seeds of this plan into the weekly meetings that will begin once we get back. I can be fucking subtle and smooth when I need to be.

The sky seems dark. I think it's going to rain. Within ten minutes my prediction comes true, this isn't Irish 'soft' rain though, this is something entirely different. It started slow, but quickly has become level three wipers, and even that isn't helping much, each raindrop; a bucket-full, splashing with force. I slow the car down and huge trucks pass by me like trains, they can't afford to slow down just because of a splash of water. This is a storm now, at least by my classification. I can barely see the road ahead, so I plan to pull off at the next exit. We think we have mastered the planet and live in civilisation, we think we can travel the world and fly to space. We can do all those things, but only at the sufferance of nature. The planet is still in charge. A downpour can slow us down, a blizzard can ground us, a gust of wind can blow our houses down. We should listen to what the planet is telling us. I pull off at the next rest stop and watch the rain for a while.

It can't last long at this rate? I can't even see if there is anything here, the visibility is so bad you can't see your own arse in front of your face. So we have no choice but to sit here and wait it out. Sean woke up and is flipping through his phone.

"Hmm," he mumbles something and then looks up.

"Just heard a few people in our office got laid off."

I look over, and he seems quite troubled.

"Fired?"

"Tapped. Redundant."

"Shit." These waves of redundancies tend to happen every few years as policies shift, and people change their minds about where in the world they think the cheapest people are currently located, or where tax breaks exist. I've survived several of these culls already. I'm not too worried.

"Yeah, all in IT."

"Doubt it will come to us though?"

"No, probably not, we're showing a good profit these days. Don't want to seem quiet though."

"Good job we just won this deal!"

"Yeah, for sure."

The rain dies down a bit, but it's still heavy, we decide to drive on anyway. Sean is quiet, he took some more painkillers for his headache and washed them down with an energy drink. I'm planning every detail of how I'll get Rachel to come to Ireland, already embarrassed at the state of my house. I wonder if I can significantly fix it up in a month or so? Probably not. The work involved to make it 'woman-friendly' is probably beyond my budget now. Almost easier to knock it down and start from scratch. FutureCloud will be paying for a hotel, anyway.

The flight isn't until nine pm tomorrow. Should have planned this a bit better, I could have stayed another night in Ohio with Rachel. There was no need to come to Chicago so early. Why didn't I think of this earlier? When all this was booked, of course, I had no idea Rachel even existed and couldn't have possibly conceived of any reason I'd need to stay in Ohio another night. Too late now! I wish I had thought of this yesterday. I could have easily changed bookings and moved plans around. Sean wouldn't have minded. I feel terrible now, I've wasted a day and a night. Now I'm in a dirty looking airport hotel, and I'd be willing to bet that the staff are on first name terms with the pest control guy. My room is down a level from the ground floor. Not quite a basement, but somehow half underground. The bathroom stinks of drains, and the shower dribbles out a piss poor stream of tepid drool. The carpet feels sticky, and I don't want to touch the blanket on top of the bed. We really should have stayed in Ohio.

I sent Rachel a message to say we arrived, but I didn't mention the total logistical fuck up.

I'm freshening up before going up to reception to meet Sean again, and see what we're doing for dinner. If he's planning any kind of piss-up, he's on his own. Social rules or not, I've had enough, and all I want to do is tidy up my suitcase for the flight, and make sure all my travel documents are correctly ordered and ready. To me, this is just part of the journey now, not a stop on the way. I have no business in Chicago.

. . .

I think we are both exhausted and burned out from the week. We settled on delivery pizza again, because it was the easiest thing to do.

Chapter Sixteen

SATURDAY 8TH SEPTEMBER

I stayed up late last night messaging Rachel, but it doesn't matter since we have a day to waste here. I got up just as housekeeping were banging on my door, despite the 'do not disturb' sign I hung on the handle. We messaged for hours, and she sent me funny 'memes' and videos, I asked about her family and her childhood, told her about my own experiences that were so different, twenty years previous, and in a different country. We are as wildly different as gas and liquid, but I think, made of the same basic molecules. Rachel thinks we may have known each other in a previous life, which is why we are drawn together, and why things feel so familiar. I don't believe in reincarnation or souls or spirits, but I can't deny the obvious. There is something I can't adequately explain about the whole situation. I barely talk to anyone, have no interest in socialising or 'having fun', but I want to spend time with this girl, and I feel sate with her, like I can be myself. This hasn't happened in my life up to this point. I didn't tell her about the plan I have to get her to come to Ireland. I'm not sure if it will work out yet, and maybe she doesn't want to travel that far. I'll see how it goes for a while before mentioning that to her.

She messaged me this morning asking if I had any more weird dreams. Not yet. I don't remember any actual dreams now, but there was something about endlessly driving and dying for a piss but never being able to find a toilet. I have that one often.

This zone around the airport is grey and depressing. Everything seems dirty. I don't want to stand still too long because I think I'll either catch something or stick to something. After we checked out of the hotel, we went to find some breakfast elsewhere, since we didn't fancy eating anything from that place. I had to fill up the car anyway to take back to the rental depot, so we ended up eating 'gas station burritos' and drinking large cups of coffee in the car.

"You gonna see that wee Rachel again?" Sean's mood has vastly improved since yesterday, and he got a good sleep. His face still looks like he argued with a toilet door, which he did, but it's less swollen, his lip is almost normal again.

"I hope so."

"You should get her to come over and do the validation, once the projects are set up."

"Yeah, I was thinking that."

"Aye, I bet ye were! Dirty bastard!" He chuckles and gives a knowing wink.

"It's not like that. Well, I mean, it is. But it isn't." Sean chuckles again and gets back to his burrito. I've already scoffed mine, but I'm sipping the bucket of coffee.

"Ya soppy wee fucker!" he announces.

"Let me know if I can help you out!"

"How do you mean?"

"I think I can influence Pete, so he will believe it essential that she goes to Ireland for the validation. There won't be any question about it."

"Thanks, mate. Don't say a word yet. I want to talk to her first."

"Aye, okay. You done?"

"Yup. Now what?" We've got about six hours to kill here. I don't want to sit in the airport all day.

"We should have stayed in Columbus another night!"

"I know! Why the fuck didn't we?"

"I thought you booked it all?"

"I thought you did?"

"Oh."

"Well too late now. May as well make the most of the day."

I don't want to stray too far away from the airport. I also don't want to sit in a bar watching Sean get wasted again. There has to be something to do around here?

I pull out my trusty phone again, the answer to all life's questions, almost. I search for things 'to do' and a list presents itself immediately.

"There's a Legoland!" I exclaim, probably a bit too enthusiastically. I realised as I said it that Legoland isn't a place for two adult work colleagues to go together.

"No."

"Yeah. Okay. There's a park and a pier and all kinds of

touristy things not far from here. The magnificent mile, fancy shops and skyscrapers and all that shite."

"That's the ticket!"

We head off to see what we can see.

Finding somewhere to park is no fun at all, but eventually, we get sorted and meander down the 'magnificent mile'. It feels like wandering through any big city to me, there are some lovely old buildings, well maintained. But aside from those, I see the same shops as I see everywhere, more or less. A monument to obsessive retail commercialism.

Sean was more excited, and he bought some trinkets and clothes and stuff. There's nothing I need or want here so I tag along making snarky comments at the prices, the other customers, the staff, anyone I can think of really. We walk all the way down the road and then onto the pier, a bit more established than anything I have seen before, but a pier nonetheless. We stop at a crab restaurant for lunch, which was very pleasant, then we wander down the end where there's an outside bar. Sean gets a beer. This is all very nice and interesting, but there's something off about the day. I realise, I should be doing tourist stuff like this with Rachel, not with Sean.

Heathrow is as surly as I left it, grey and miserable and all matter-of-fact and by-the-book. Sean is off to fly back to Glasgow, and I'm on a connecting flight back to Shannon. I only have about thirty minutes to wait.

"Well, good trip buddy, safe journey home." Sean sticks out his hand.

"Yeah, same. Very interesting all told!" I've no idea when I'll see Sean again, but we'll be in touch almost every day for months now while we set this FutureCloud stuff up. Daily emails, twice weekly calls. Maybe he'll pop over to Ireland to watch over the validation too.

I figure out my connecting flight gate, and wander over. It's already boarding, so I'm glad I didn't linger. As we hop over to Shannon, I read my book again, but I'm distracted thinking about the life I'm returning to. The box in my shed, the house falling apart, the monotonous churn of work. None of it has changed just because I've been away for a week. I may have, but nothing else has.

Chapter Seventeen

SUNDAY 9TH SEPTEMBER

I get home around one pm local time. I forgot to stop at the shop of course. I have no food, so I'll have to go out again later. I message everyone I'm home, put on a big pot of coffee, dump my bags and change out of my smelly travel clothes. I put the water heater on for a bath later too. Though it might be classed as 'not fit for human habitation' by some, barely above the level of cow-shed to others, I still feel a massive relief to be home. Once my coffee is made I take a flask out to the shed. I want to see if the box is still there, still functioning, still weird as fuck.

I'm standing in a queue, there's a smell of chip oil, the dim light of one bare bulb. An old lady stands behind a table; white hair, wearing an apron. A single chip fryer behind her on another table, a box of coins, a shaker of salt and a bowl of ketchup in front of her.

I turn and look around, I'm in someones living-room, a small dark house, the room is emptied of furniture, but you can tell what it once was. There are outlines of removed picture frames on the walls, papered in a dull pattern, a fireplace unlit, carpet that doesn't quite reach the walls, frayed. On the wall by the door a handwritten menu on an oddly shaped piece of cardboard.

I know this place. We called it the 'Grim Chippy', a house at the bottom of a hill, near a pub that we aren't allowed in anymore. The only item on that menu is chips, either wrapped or unwrapped, same price of fifty-pence. The cardboard menu is written on the back of a tights packet, forty denier, tan colour.

If you ask for wrapped you get more chips, so that's what we all do, those of us who are only alive because of this grim chippy, surviving on pennies we can scrape together or drag out from the ten quid a week we live on. I found a pound coin in a phone box last night, so this is a luxury lunch I can afford. This is college life, must be 1991 because by the first term of '92 this chippy had closed. We never found out why or what happened to the old lady.

I reach the end of the queue and ask her for chips, wrapped. She replies with a simple 'Yes' and busies herself, nervously bundling up a portion of deliciously hot golden chips into paper. The burned crispy chips serve as a stabbing device, to use to impale the others. I hand over the pound coin, and get back a fifty-pence-piece. I turn around and give it to Wayne for his chips, or we'd only be sharing mine otherwise; he spent his last quid on fags earlier. I then unwrap the chip paper and add a sprinkle of salt and some ketchup from the bowl with a silver plated spoon, the plating long since eroded away.

I wait outside. Wayne comes out presently, already munching his chips, he motions down the road to the bench we always sit on. We amble down, passing the real chip shop, where the prices are double, you get less chips, ketchup is five-pence extra for a tiny packet, and the chips somehow don't taste as good. Then the pub that we are barred from, the Steamhouse, where Wayne would sip dregs from left over pints, and where we all bought our first pack-of-three from the johnny machine in the bogs. The landlord a cocky prick, he knew we were underage and then kicked us out for not buying any drinks, twat. Wayne and I sit down on the bench, distant and quiet, tired, contemplative. One of our mates died last night in a car crash. The words from the song we played over and over into the early hours from Danny's 'sad tape' on repeat in my ears, I'll protect you from the hooded claw, keep the vampires from your door… I close my eyes and return to my shed.

I can't even remember who died now, I don't think we were close, but the fact that someone in our group could be killed was a shock, we thought we were invincible, protected somehow, owning the college halls like no one else before. What a load of shit that was. The reality was that we passed through the classes like thousands of others, and no one else will remember that we even attended now. I barely remember it myself. We grew up a little bit that day.

We loved that chippy, and the next two years of college were simply not the same without it. There was an evident sadness in the white-haired old lady, a nervousness at us rowdy students. I have no idea why she ever decided to open up her living room as a chip shop, but many poor students are indeed glad she did.

Travelling with the box is emotionally exhausting. I guess it still works. I had set the dials to somewhere left of centre. A little '91' has appeared above the Y knob.

. . .

I go back to the house and open up my laptop and write down the details of the box-journey and send it to Rachel as promised. Maybe she can make some sense of this?

I wonder about taking a nap for a while, because I'm tired as a hooker after five-dollar-blow-job-day, but then I remember the anti jetlag mantra, and Beastie Boys song: 'No sleep till bed-time' so instead, I get back in my car and drive to the shop. It took a few minutes to get used to driving on the left when I came home from the airport earlier. That's fine now, but I just tried to get in the passenger side door…

I walk around the store in a daze. I have to go back around several times because I can't remember what food is, or what I like to eat, or barely even my own name. I suffer from paralysis of choice. I sometimes wish there was just a big box called 'Human food'. I recognise the staff as I come here at least three times a week, and have done for years, but I've never once said a word to any of them. I don't feel any need to. Dad would know everyone's name, everyone's life story, what they are looking forward to, what problems they have. He was friends with everyone. I'm friends with no one. I eventually get the basics and check out.

I go home and make eggs on toast and a mug of strong tea. My staple food. Now I'm finally home.

Rachel has woken up. She's read my email and wants to ponder on the meaning of my 'dream'. She asks me about the details; I tell her I went to college in Cornwall in the south west of England, I studied hotel and catering management. I have no idea why now, as that is not what I ended up doing. I tell her that a sixteen-year-old kid shouldn't be asked to make a career decision that will affect him for the rest of his life, since he hasn't got a fucking clue what life is all about. I tell her about my mate Wayne who I haven't seen for a long time. He joined the forces, travelled the world, we lost touch over and over, but he's the sort of solid lad who I know I could find twenty years later, and he'd still be the same. I tell her I haven't thought about that day for many years, but it was so vivid and real, I could taste the chips, smell the air, feel the emotions like I was there. Like I travelled back in time and spent a few minutes in 1991. I run a deep hot bath and wash away the travel pains and smells.

If it wasn't for the 80s music playlist I had on and Rachel messaging me, I probably would have fallen asleep in the bath again. That happens a lot. She said she couldn't unravel the specifics of my recent dream, but that the sum of what I've told her already hints to a more profound problem, something in my past that I can't let go of. All the dreams are from emotional or stressful times, or things I vividly recall. She has a point. Sweet dreams are made of these, indeed…

I get out of the bath and start the suitcase unpacking procedure, putting all my chargers and cables back where they belong. Being in the office at my desk reminds me of work tomorrow. I'd like to take a day off, but there's likely a massive backlog of crap to deal with anyway. Another day away will only prolong the inevitable. I'll work from home though, because I've travelled enough.

I'm exhausted now, but I need to stay awake, so I wander over to the shed again.

Headlights shine up the narrow road, and I fling the car around the corners. I know I can blast through the lanes at night because I'd see the lights of an oncoming vehicle on the hedges, and it would give me time to stop. The car is an old Ford Fiesta, my first car as it happens. A pile of rust really, but it got me around. I pull up to the house, no lights on, everyone else probably already asleep. I go in and creep up the stairs to my room and switch on the telly and computer. While it boots up, I go down to the kitchen and stick on the kettle for a tea. My habit is to watch terrible late-night TV while I read usenet and catch up on my daily email discussions with Mary from Houston, about cats and the differences between English and American ways of life. Then I usually mess around in chat-rooms with anyone who might still be around. Costs a fortune on the phone-bill, but I don't care. I fund it with my meagre wages somehow. I wait for the kettle to boil and tap my fingers on the cup.

"Hi, Terry."

I turn around, a thump in my chest, Dad walks into the kitchen from the back door, he's got a little workshop out there, he must have been working on something after everyone else went to sleep.

"Hey." The word comes out, but I'm not in control, I want to rush over and hug him, to tell him how much I've missed him, but none of that happens. In this time period, I just saw him a few hours ago before I went out. He's young, short hair with barely any grey, covered in oil and dirt, he must have been working on the Land Rover engine again.

I'm tapping on my cup, the kettle boils, and I pour the tea.

I'm itching to go upstairs and go fiddle around on the internet, but Dad seems to want to talk. My stupid young self doesn't realise the value of being able to sit and talk to Dad and that one day it won't be possible anymore. He lights up his pipe.

"I got that fuel pump working!" He's rebuilding an engine from scratch. That way he knows how to fix every single part of it when it fails.

"Cool." I am dismissive and bored.

Dad opens up his flask and pours the dregs of his coffee into a cup.

"You finished with the kettle?" He comes over and starts making another pot of coffee. It's already after one am, but he's not tired, and he could be planning to work on the engine some more.

"Yeah."

We get talking about fuel, and the inevitable price increase, as humanity uses up the stores of dinosaur oil. We talk about hydrogen as a clean fuel, then electrolysis, solar and wind energy, and the natural vibration frequencies of elements. We talk about perpetual motion, over-unity, magnets and free energy, and the universal laws of conservation, hidden energy, sub-states of atoms, black holes, aliens and time-travel. We talk about these things without any presumption that they may be impossible or ridiculous; we discuss everything with excitement about potential future inventions and discoveries.

It is five am when I finally go up to my room. I turn the computer and TV off and climb into bed. I hear Dad come upstairs eventually too.

The Y knob on the box gained a little '94'.

Time, For a Change

We talked about time travel that day! The theory of time being a series of snapshots that we pass through, stretching from infinity past to infinity future, and we are perpetually somewhere in the middle. We talked about the possibility of being able to change our point on that line, and jump around to anywhere we wanted, if we just knew how to alter our perception.

I find myself wandering down the lane from my house with tears in my eyes, a headache forming in my skull, confusion and sadness in abundance. I feel a buzz in my pocket.

You okay?

Rachel messages me from thousands of miles away. Dad just talked to me from decades ago. I barely know if I am okay, but I tell her 'yes' anyway. I wander back to the house and make some dinner.

After I eat, I write down the details of the experience I had, and send it to Rachel. I told her it was a dream I had while taking a quick nap earlier. We talk about it for a while, she orders me to get some sleep, and maybe tomorrow I'll feel better. I bought a bottle of her perfume in the airport, planning to give it to her when I see her, but I pass a spray of it over my bed and pillows before I get in and pass out.

Chapter Eighteen

MONDAY 10TH SEPTEMBER

[10:36] O'Brien, Ted:
Hey, good trip? How did you find America?

[10:36] Ward, Terry B:
Well Ted.
I didn't find it, I assumed the pilot knew where it was.

[10:37] O'Brien, Ted:
Haha.

[10:37] Ward, Terry B:
Not too bad in the end!
Fecking tiring though.

[10:38] O'Brien, Ted:
Any auld craic?

[10:38] Ward, Terry B:
Well, now you mention it, there was a small bit!
I met a girl…

|10:39| O'Brien, Ted:
> A girl you say?
> I've heard tell of them folks.
> Strange mystical creatures, by all accounts.

|10:39| Ward, Terry B:
> That's for sure Ted.
> That's for fucking sure.

I tell Ted about Rachel, how she's the lead engineer for the project we're just starting now, how we connected instantly, and things sort of happened without me even knowing what was going on. He wants to see a picture, and I realise that I'm a fucking idiot, because I didn't take a single one of her while I was there. How could I not do that? I haven't even bothered connecting to her social media; it didn't occur to me. We have been messaging without the need for it. So I don't have a photo. I don't want to go sneaking around now trying to find her Facebook account, so I will have to ask her later to send me some selfies. She won't be awake yet.

This morning has been a mess at work. I had millions of unread emails to skim through and mostly delete, two regular phone conference call meetings about old projects that I don't even touch anymore, and a bundle of expenses to file and submit from my trip. I welcome the break to chat with Ted for a while. When I asked him if anything unusual happened while I was away, he said 'feck all.'

. . .

I wander over to the kitchen and make my usual breakfast of eggs on toast and a strong tea, and scroll through Twitter on my phone. I've been ignoring the world lately, so I fire off some words of wisdom.

Hind-sight: that feeling of looking at your life up to this point and realising just how much of an arse you made of everything.

I suddenly remember the disk archive I have of all Dad's old files. I plug it into my laptop and try a search through everything for the word 'time'. The index builds slowly, adding dozens of files. Clicking on a few of them finds nothing of interest, I guess my search term is too broad. I try variations on 'time-travel' and get nothing.

There has to be something on that disk that explains the box in my shed?

My work laptop bleeps at me, telling me I have another conference call coming up with DeltaWave. Lovely. I ping Eoghan on IM and see if he's done any work at all while I've been in America.

   [11:46] Ward, Terry B:
     Morning.

   [11:47] Williams, Eoghan:
     Hey. Welcome back from your holiday.

I see Eoghan is his same old cheery self. It doesn't take long for me to become disillusioned by the drudgery of work after a trip away.

[11:47] Ward, Terry B:
How are the new DeltaWave projects going?

[11:49] Williams, Eoghan:
Almost done. Just need a few more days.

[11:50] Ward, Terry B:
What have you been doing all last week?

[11:52] Williams, Eoghan:
You know these are complex, don't you?

[11:52] Ward, Terry B:
Wait 'till you see the new one I have for you…

I give Eoghan a rapid summary of the FutureCloud work before dialling into my DeltaWave meeting. I don't mention Rachel or any of the shenanigans that Sean and I got up to in America. Too much information would impede his workflow.

Judith opens up the meeting in her usual monotonous way, the same tired jokes and comments that we open every call with, waiting for people to join, muting people with loud background noise. We go through a list of items for discussion, even if there is nothing to discuss. Boring and irritating to listen to. Previous orders shipped is a topic. They briefly mention five-hundred units that dispatched and then move on to the next item, which is future projects. I notice that no one apologised for the software mix-up thing. Feck them! I give an update on status, which is mostly fabricated, I tell them our top engineer is working on the details right now. He's got the bulk of it done already and needs to tie up loose ends and then we can test the first units. They seem satisfied, and Judith types up her notes and moves along. I mute myself for the rest of the call and pick up my phone for some distraction. Rachel just woke up and sent me a selfie. Fucking gorgeous.

I spend most of the day doing some notes and preparation for the FutureCloud project. I have a lot of technical details to note down. Rachel has emailed me a process map, now I need to extrapolate all the small details and make sure every step is possible within our internal process. Should be okay. I didn't see anything over in Ohio that I thought we couldn't do. Our first regular meeting is tomorrow, late-afternoon.

Sean sent a trip report summary to everyone he could think of, by the looks of things. It's all high level; how much of a big win the deal is for us, and the incredible possibilities going forward. I can't read most of it, too much work bullshit-speak for me. Dozens of people are copied, and they all hit 'reply-all' and spam everyone with: 'Good job!', 'Great win!', 'Can't wait to see what's next!' emails. All the usual crap, so the world can see how much they all care. I selected all of them and hit delete, because I don't care.

I check my diary for tomorrow and see a one-to-one with my manager. I more or less forgot she existed, because I barely ever need to get in touch. We have a regular meeting once a month, and that is plenty for me. I run my own day. A lot has happened since last time, but I'll use the edited highlights version. She's based in Tennessee, and thankfully she leaves me alone most of the time. I guess I can get my expenses signed off quickly anyway.

I shut down my laptop on the dot of five and turn around to my personal laptop. I try some more searches on the disk archive, and I turn up a load of nothing. Maybe there are no files to find? Maybe the data is corrupt? Maybe I missed a disk when I cleared out his office? Maybe the data is encrypted, and I can't see it? There are loads of reasons why I might not ever find anything, but there's still a lot of data to look at.

I have a moment of doubt, could Dad really have invented a time-machine? Wouldn't he have told me about it? Did he use it? Did he travel through his life, revisiting memories, as I have been? Was it an experiment? Why was it buried under a bench? I have so many questions and no answers. He worked on some odd projects, I know, but perhaps nothing so bizarre as this?

Rachel said to see what happens, go with the flow. So, I head back over to the shed, and maybe I'll find some answers?

I open the lid of the box and randomly fiddle with the dials, let's see where this goes. I'm getting used to the smell and weird feelings that come with using it now.

"Two cheeseburgers and two large chips," Dad calls out to me from the hatch.

"Right." I grab two burgers from the freezer and slap them on the griddle, meanwhile dunking a batch of chips in the fryer and toasting the buns, preparing the dressing and spinning the burger flipper up in the air.

This is the burger and ice-cream bar we opened in the summer of 1992, Megabites. I was the cook, Dad was on the window talking to the punters. I finish the order and put it up on the counter. The food is for Pickles and his girlfriend. Never found out what her name was. Pickles is a fisherman out of Newlyn. A regular customer when he's on land. He once asked us for a hot dog bun and slapped his dick in it, squirted mustard and ketchup on it and offered it to his lady. I don't think she found it funny, she switched to burgers after that. They drive off in the back of Mike's Mustang and Dad pours himself a coffee, then goes out for a smoke.

I look around the little kitchen, a griddle that I meticulously cleaned every night, a deep fat fryer, fridges and freezers all crammed into a tiny room, with a hatch window out to the promenade of Penzance. Not much more than the 'Grim Chippy' really, but it provided us with food for a year. We never made any real money, but it paid back the investment, and it was fun for a while.

I go over to the hatch and look outside. Dad is talking to a weirdo who often comes around here. He told us once he was a radio DJ, but we never found out from which station. Never seems to have any money, but he would trade weird things for burgers. I got a T-shirt, frisbee and a pack of cards; he got fed.

A car pulls up, music blaring out of it, the windows vibrating. Wayne and Danny get out, leaving the music on. I wave to turn it down a bit because we have residential neighbours, and the last thing we need is cops hassling us. I don't think we have a license to be selling food here.

Time, For a Change

Our menu was quite vague. You could get what you wanted if we had it. This is the night Danny invents the 'Piccalilli burger' which is essentially a cheeseburger with mustard piccalilli relish all over it. We put it on the menu after that, but perhaps, unsurprisingly, no one else ever ordered it.

I make us all some chips, and we sit on the wall outside. There are no customers around, and if some come along, I'll go back in. The 'DJ' bums a fag from Wayne and Danny plays his latest mix-tape. The evening is warm. Wayne and Danny stayed on my bed-sit floor that night after we'd messed around on the prom till two am. Trying to run from one set of steps down to the beach to another and back up, in-between the waves of the tide coming in, without getting wet, screaming 'ROOOXANNE - You don't have to put on the red light' as loud as we could.

Those were good times from what I can remember. We all took turns to work at the burger bar. Life seemed more straightforward back then. People asked for food, we gave it to them, and we got money. We were pretty broke, but it didn't matter, at least that's how I remember it. Things are very different now.

I go back to the house and put on 'Smells Like Teen Spirit' and turn it up full. My windows rattle in their loose wooden frames. Outside in the field around my house, cows are rocking out to Kurt Cobain with me. I haven't had any teen spirit for a long time. Feels good to go crazy for a while.

I tell Rachel about the burger-bar and my nasty bedsit. The bitch who lived in the flat underneath mine, who would freak out if I so much as fucking farted after nine pm, and my bike that was stolen from outside my window, and how I laughed because it was shite, and the wheels fell off if you rode it over a bump. I tell her about the shower in the shared bathroom, that cost ten pence for thirty seconds of cold water, and was so small that the disgusting slimy curtain would cling to you. It was like showering in a sleeping bag, but colder, and probably had more pubes stuck to it. I tell her about the ice cream freezer, that I had to keep in my tiny single room for months, after the burger-bar had to shut down, and that we'd eat ice-cream in the car on the way to college for breakfast, because we had nothing else. I tell her all these things, and it makes me feel better, brings back memories of my youth that I haven't thought about for years, maybe decades.

Chapter Nineteen

TUESDAY 11TH SEPTEMBER

I have a meeting in the office today so had to come in. My desk is mostly as I left it, but I notice that someone has removed the salt packets I had around. Must get some more from the canteen later. I don't want slug-people all over my stuff.

Some executive is over from the US, so we all have to make an appearance and pretend like we're neat and tidy and working hard. They do the rounds of the worker's desks after the big meeting, and ask empty, pre-prepared questions, and we're all meant to have fascinating answers ready just in case we are picked. I usually make sure I head to the jax when I see the suits coming. Because, fuck that.

[09:35] Ward, Terry B:

You are missing out not being in the office for this crucial all-hands meeting at 10.

[09:36] O'Brien, Ted:
Yeah, I know. Shame.

[09:37] Ward, Terry B:
   I could make a video of it if you want?
   Live stream it even.

[09:38] O'Brien, Ted:
   You're grand.
   I've seen enough of them myself.

They are always the same: Slides up on a projector showing charts with happy or sad faces against them, an inspiring talk from the visiting executive, and then the Irish site leader. Suits flapping in the breeze from all the hot air. Microphones poorly set up, so there's always feedback and distortion, the person showing the slides forgets to turn off their IM, so we all see their messages pop up. I wasted good diesel driving in to see this shit.

I go for coffee before the 'show' and arrive early to get the good seats. Those are the ones right at the back; only the extreme dweebs with the twelve-year-old-boy haircuts sit at the front and ask questions.

Eoghan sits next to me. He's also got a coffee, and he fumbles around with a lid, sugar packets and a wooden stick. He's so inept that I take it from him while he gets his shit together, for fear of there being a splash of hot coffee in my lap if someone doesn't take charge of the situation.

"Thanks."

"Welcome."

"Did you bring me any presents from America?"

"Guess."

"Fecker."

"I'll take you through the FutureCloud stuff later if you want? It's pretty intense, but should be okay."

"Sounds wonderful."

Time, For a Change

The meeting starts, and we're greeted by a lanky tall American who was obviously the sports star in his high-school. He's all smoothed down and greased up. The spotlights shine off his face as he bounces around the little stage they have put up for the occasion. The seats are uncomfortable and too close to each other. I have way too many people much too close to me for my liking. I'm at the edge, of course, in case I have to evacuate suddenly, but I still feel closed in and breathless. I have no intention of listening to a single word this fool says, nor his stooges or sycophants that are talking later. The agenda up on screen shows many topics no-one cares about followed by a 'fireside chat' with the grease-ball. Apparently, it will make us feel better about his salary, that's likely to be six times what I get paid. I slide my phone onto silent in my pocket and sneak it out under my leg so I can scroll Twitter during this torture show.

I wonder if there are people in this room who do care about this crap? Are they so naive and disconnected from reality, that they think this shiny man cares deeply about the 'unique talent' that the Irish team has? That he wouldn't fire all of us in a heartbeat if a tax incentive came up in a cheaper country? I'm reminded of the redundancies that Sean mentioned last week in the Glasgow office. I wonder if we're next? The projector shows a slide about all the amazing charity work that our office does. They love to make a big deal about that, cram it into everyone's face as much as possible about how caring and generous the company is.

I tune out and sip my coffee. I wonder if anyone would notice if I put on my headphones? Better not, I guess.

I think about what seventeen year old me from 1992 would do in this situation. He wouldn't fucking be in this situation! He'd have ignored it, stayed in bed, made fun of the fools who did go to the meeting, argued that it was all utter bollocks. Maybe I should listen to the inner me more often.

The torture ends, and there is the usual deathly silence, after the man on the stage asks if there are any questions. They love questions because it lets them put people down. Someone will eventually stand up and blurt out some contrived shit about sales revenue, and the stooges on stage will either fire back with numbers that only they are privy to, or in the case when they don't have a come-back, they will say 'good question, let's talk about that offline'. I'm ready to duck out of here fast, I need to piss again, and I have another meeting coming up.

Thankfully the only question was a joke one. Probably a plant. What is his favourite Irish sport? I don't give a fuck. I'm out. I'm unquestionably inspired to 'do my best work' now. Cheers for that, fella!

Back at my desk and I'm five minutes late for my next meeting, because the bogs near my desk were closed for cleaning. I had to walk all the way across the office to the other toilet block and then wait for a cubicle. I hate urinals.

This is an internal, Europe only, call about FutureCloud. Sean set this up to bring the rest of the team up to speed on our trip over to Ohio. The call later is with the customer. Rachel will be on it. I haven't heard her voice since we left Columbus so I'm looking forward to it, even though it is a work call.

Sean goes through his topics to cover, and the other sales folk around Europe chirp in with their comments and suggestions, all trying to seem smart and worthwhile. They'll all get their cuts of this deal, for doing bugger all while

Time, For a Change

Eoghan and I slave away doing all the real technical work, and get nothing extra out of it. Oh well.

I chime in when I think they are misunderstanding the technical points, but mainly I remain muted and let Sean sort all this out. That's his job after all.

They want to know when it will all be finished and ready to sell. I give my standard estimate of about four weeks from now, but it depends on many factors that I have no control over. We'll need to get stock of some parts in and set up the customisation scripts. We'll need all the right hardware and software in place, and then we'll need to test it all. Salespeople can't hear those words. They just heard four weeks, and then I can picture them all getting out the calendars and calculators, and loading up the BMW configuration website in the background.

After the meeting ends I decide to get lunch early. I've got the one-to-one later and then the FutureCloud customer call and the usual bloat of emails to delete that come in every day, no matter what. Also, now is probably when the vapid suit will come around the desks, and awe people with his dedication and knowledge of the industry while remaining true to the common man. Prick.

As I stand up to go to the canteen, I notice the empty desk that is opposite mine. That's where Jeff should be sitting. I never found out what happened to him. My mind is muddled and confused about that. He's apparently worked somewhere else for years, and in a different city. But I swear he had lunch with me here two weeks ago?

I got something that was advertised as chicken curry, but

it had very little chicken and no curry flavour. It did, of course, have the obligatory sheaf of celery. I fucking hate celery. Eoghan sits down opposite me, he's got the same curry. The popular choice today I guess.

"Hey, do you know Jeff Moloney?"

"Nope, doesn't ring a bell."

"Really? He sat opposite me. Always happy. Really annoying."

"Don't know him, lad, sorry."

"He wasn't in our department, but you must have seen him around?"

"What does he look like?"

"Grey hair, always wore a blue shirt."

"Can you be more specific?"

I pull out my phone and load up LinkedIn, and find Jeff and his photo and show it to Eoghan.

"Don't know him, sorry."

For fuck's sake. What is going on? I decide to change the subject because I'm freaked out here now. We talk about the FutureCloud factory and how they do everything more or less manually. Eoghan agrees it can be vastly improved and he's got some ideas of what we can do for them already. I knew he'd like this one because it has some complication, and needs some coding that isn't just a copy and paste from another simple project. This one will require some real thinking, and that's what us nerds do best!

I go back to my desk, making sure to pick up some salt packets on the way, and start to prepare for the afternoon meetings. A one-to-one with Joanne the boss first, so I make notes about all the projects I have worked on since the last time we spoke. I go into great detail about the FutureCloud deal, leaving out anything to do with Rachel, Sean and his booze habit, and especially the software that I used to fix the issue they had. No need to bring that up!

|13:23| Ward, Terry B:
> ugh and stuff.
> ***headache***

|13:25| O'Brien, Ted:
> Yup. I know what you mean.

|13:25| Ward, Terry B:
> Fecking manager meeting is coming up now.
> She wants to do video chat.

|13:27| O'Brien, Ted:
> Better make sure you wear pants so!

|13:28| Ward, Terry B:
> Good point.
> I usually do in the office.
> But you never know I guess…

|13:29| O'Brien, Ted:
> I always work naked.
> Feels more real somehow.

|13:30| Ward, Terry B:
> Are you naked now?

|13:32| O'Brien, Ted:
> Yah, of course.

[13:32] Ward, Terry B:
Well, there goes my lunch!

[13:33] O'Brien, Ted:
Under my clothes anyway.

I haven't been for my walk around the car park yet. I head out now before the meeting. I need to find an empty meeting room too, just a quick lap around the building to try and get some air into my lungs. I usually need an energy drink to get enthusiastic enough for a manager meeting; I find she prefers if I'm super positive about everything, even if it is a problem. She wants to know everything is fine and then I'm left alone, so worth the bit of bullshitting to get her off my back.

There's a spot of rain outside, but it's only soft rain. Nothing to worry about. Feels good to get out of the building. I send a photo of the office to Rachel. Showing her where I work. It's nothing special, but maybe she'll be interested. Perhaps she'll be able to visit soon?

I wander back to my desk, grab my laptop and find an empty room and set up. I have black tape over my camera by default, just in case IT are bored and think they should snoop around and see what I'm doing. I peel it off and clean the lens and get ready for the one-to-one call.

I'm sitting here like a bacon sandwich at a bar mitzvah for ten minutes waiting, and about to pull the plug when she finally shows up.

"Hiiiii, I'm so sorry I'm late!"

Joanne appears on my screen, heavily tanned, and with more gold on her than a Tutankhamun statue, her voice is squeaky and sounds fake; everything is emphasised too much.

She lives in Tennessee, but I don't think she's from there originally. I've only met her twice in person over the last couple of years. She's just the latest in a succession of managers I've had in the same role.

"No problem, how are you?" I like to get my 'how are you' out before she can ask me, because I know she doesn't want to hear the truth about how I am. I'm awkward like a fart in a crowded lift, I have to try and ignore the fact that I'm projecting my image halfway across the world or I freeze up. I'm not comfortable with being on any camera, let alone a live video.

"Oh, good! So busy though!" Yeah, I bet, busy planning her next junket to Asia no doubt. Seems like she's always travelling somewhere on the company card. I know I've just done that myself, but I went to see a legitimate customer. I think she flies around the world for the hell of it.

I tell her about the FutureCloud trip and emphasise all the good points, and how we can help them improve their processes and automation, and how we won the deal we set out to get, doubled it in fact. She's ecstatically happy about it. A bit too much if you ask me, but that's managers for you. Better happy than pissed off, I guess.

She tells me my annual review is coming up soon. Oh, joy. I'm obliged to write a self-assessment and list all my achievements for the year. I bring up the ever popular subject of a pay rise, since I'm now in the company ten years, she replies with the standard crap about a freeze on pay rises right now, but she'll certainly try to consider me for the next available review. Funny how that sounds good and means precisely the opposite. I haven't had any pay rise in five years now, which effectively means I've had a pay cut if you take into account average inflation. We finish up with her profusely thanking me for 'all the incredibly hard work' I do, and she hopes to come over to

Ireland sometime before the end of the year. Great. It went okay I guess, and she signed off my expenses. Over for another month anyway. I scoop up my laptop and go back to my desk.

I've got a choice now. Either stay here and get some work done before the FutureCloud call and then drive home after; or go back now, do the call at home and miss the traffic. A no-brainer, so I pack up and feck off.

I stopped on the way for pizza, so I don't have to cook later, and got home just in time for the meeting. I log-in and see Sean, Pete, Rachel, Russ already on. The gang from last week all together again. I say 'Hi' and we exchange pleasantries about the flight back, and great dinner, and how they look forward to the next time we come over, all that meaningless crap people say. Rachel didn't say anything yet. I guess she is just listening. I send her an IM outside of the meeting.

[16:02] Ward, Terry B:
Hey!

[16:02] Brooks, Rachel:
'Sup!

[16:02] Ward, Terry B:
How are you today work colleague? :)

[16:03] Brooks, Rachel:
Stressed, dude. You'll see why in a minute.

Time, For a Change

[16:03] Ward, Terry B:
Oh. Shit. :(

I feel a wave of nausea come over me. Has something happened? Another factory issue?

[16:03] Ward, Terry B:
Is there something I can do?

[16:03] Brooks, Rachel:
Hmm. I don't know.

Everyone has joined the call now, and Sean starts off his spiel with his agenda for the meeting. He's going to talk through the plan to set everything up, then go to the timeline of when everything will happen.

"Hi, this is Pete Schenk." Pete interrupts.

"Hi, Pete."

"Yeah, we need to cut straight to the chase on this."

"Okay…" Sean sounds a bit perturbed.

"We just won a huge deal for our server product for pretty much every airport in mainland Europe. This is that extra sauce Russ was talking about."

"Oh, that's great news!" Sean perks up, but Pete butts in again.

"Here's the catch, we need to deliver before the end of September, the first week of October is the absolute latest. They have to spend the money before the budget is cut."

"How many units are we talking?"

"About five hundred."

"Okay, and that gives us about three weeks?" Sean is shitting it now. I can feel it.

I see what Rachel was talking about now. There's no fucking way we can pull this together that quickly.

[16:07] Woods, Sean:
Can you do it?

[16:07] Ward, Terry B:

That's going to be dangerously tight.
I'd typically say four weeks was the absolute minimum and THEN we'd do the validation.
This means we cut about two or three weeks off the timeline.

[16:08] Woods, Sean:
Aye, but can you do it?

[16:08] Ward, Terry B:
No pressure?!
Uhhhhh… I need to think.

If I put everything else on hold and work on this directly with Eoghan every day, maybe pull some weekends, and late evenings then I guess it is possible. But an idea hits me like a train in a dark tunnel.

I switch to the IM window with Rachel.

[16:09] Ward, Terry B:
Hey.
Can you come here?

[16:09] Brooks, Rachel:
What? To Ireland?

[16:09] Ward, Terry B:
Yeah.
I'll need your help to pull this off.

[16:10] Brooks, Rachel:
OMG.
Ugh! I guess!
But I've never been on a plane!

[16:10] Ward, Terry B:
You sure?
I can make it happen…

[16:10] Brooks, Rachel:
I mean, yeah okay!
Holy shit.

I flip back to Sean's window:

[16:11] Ward, Terry B:
I need help.
Send Rachel here.
She knows their stuff inside out.

[16:11] Woods, Sean:
Plan.

Back on the call, everyone is talking about numbers and delivery schedules and how great the opportunity is. Sean cuts in and sells Pete the idea.

. . .

"Hey, Pete — I've just had a quick discussion with Terry over IM. We realise the importance of this deal, and we're committed to making it happen even though this is a very tight schedule."

"That's great Sean. I knew you guys would pull this off."

"We think it would help if you guys could send your engineering resource over to help Terry get this set up."

"Rachel?"

"Yup. If we rely on doing this over the phone, we'll never hit the deadline."

"I guess that makes sense. Hey Rachel, what do you think?"

"Er. Hi. Um, sure…"

Those are the first words I've heard her say since she left me last week, she said the universe would bring us together again. Well, that was pretty quick! Nice job universe!

The deal is done. Pete agrees to fund the whole thing. Her travel is a drop in the ocean compared to the value of this deal. Rachel will be on a plane in about a week, and she'll stay until the order is set up and complete. It still means a lot of work under a lot of pressure, but I think we'll get it done with her help.

After the call, I'm emotionally exhausted. I've just committed to a shit-load of work, but I'll also get to see Rachel again, so soon. My brain is fried so I go for a walk down the lane to clear my head.

My phone buzzes in my pocket, it's an audio call from Rachel.

"Hey."
"Oh my god, dude."
"Yeah, I know."
"No, like, I'm shit scared of flying."
"Oh."
"Yeah."
"But you said you never flew before?"
"Exactly!"
"Well, I mean, how do you know you are scared if you never did it?"
"Dude!"
"It's just like getting on a big bus that happens to fly."
"I never went on a bus either!"
"Ah."

I manage to calm her down after a while. I tell her it will be fine, it's more tedious than anything else. All you have to do is show up and sit still. Luckily she has a passport already because she was planning to visit Italy a few years back with a friend, but it never happened in the end. I tell her I have family in Italy so maybe one day she'll get that trip after all.

I reach the end of my lane and turn around, we switch to a video call, and I show her the road and the fields around my house as I walk home, she says the countryside looks nice and all, but not the same as home. Then she sees my house and laughs.

. . .

"You live there?"

"Yup."

"No offence, but it looks like a shit hole!"

"Yup! I know. But it's all I got."

"Is that your car?"

"Yup again!"

"Well, that looks fancy."

"I gotta have something nice!"

I take her inside the house and show her around. She's not impressed. I knew she wouldn't be but what more can I do?

She hangs up because she has to go upstairs to a meeting Pete has called. I remember my pizza, which is probably cold, but I take it to my office anyway and start researching posh hotels near work.

Chapter Twenty

WEDNESDAY 12TH SEPTEMBER

When I got to work this morning, I went straight over to Eoghan, then his boss, and gave them the fantastic news about the FutureCloud deal, and how I'd be focusing on that, and nothing else, for the next few weeks. Luckily Eoghan has 'almost finished' the DeltaWave stuff he's doing. He's agreed to work with Rachel and I when she arrives. I didn't tell them the engineer they were sending was a pretty young girl. Don't need to freak the lad out just yet.

I'm almost excited; work has turned from monotonous drudgery and churn, to an exciting project, with side benefits, and a complex technical challenge, under a load of pressure. Still work though, and I'd rather be doing something else, but I have to admit, this is more fun that it has been for a long time.

I head down to our lab with Eoghan to start putting together a list of things we'll need - hardware and software. It turns into a pretty big shopping list, and we may need some more items later, for now, I send the details to Sean to approve, and we head to the canteen for breakfast.

. . .

"You're enjoying this!" Eoghan smirks at me, incredulous.

"Huh?"

"I haven't seen you interested in a project for a long time. What's different about this one?"

"I like a challenge. Wakes up the old grey matter."

"No, that's not it. The DeltaWave projects are challenging. This is something else."

I shrug and tuck into my eggs and toast. They aren't fried to my adequate specification, and they have been lingering under a heat-lamp for millennia, but they'll do. We only recently got the toaster in the canteen, after many years of toast famine. When I asked the chef why they didn't have a toaster once before, he told me it was a 'fire risk'. I just shook my head and walked away. I guess now they are at the stage of not caring if we burn and die, at least we can have toast before we go to hell.

When I get back to my desk, Sean has already approved our shopping list. He didn't blink, even though we spent about €30,000. This deal must be a deeper vein of gold than I imagined. He could be finally getting the Porsche he always wanted! I send the list to our procurement mailbox and set it all to expedited delivery. Should have it in a couple of days.

Until we get the hardware we've asked for, we can't do too much more of the engineering work, but I can spend time on the tech-sheet. Luckily this is only one product we are doing, so there isn't a multitude of things to work on all at once. I plug in headphones and select a suitably rocking playlist, and start working through the technical details. It will probably take me the rest of the week to get it all filled in anyway. There are hundreds of things to fill in and verify and then triple check against the FutureCloud specification.

I found a great hotel in the middle of town. Modern and very posh and probably insanely expensive, but we aren't paying, so I don't care. I send the details to Rachel and offer to book it for her. I suggest their 'Superb Suite' since she'll be there for a while, and it may as well be as nice as possible. I was going to say she could stay at my house, but that plan went out the window when it seemed like she didn't think it was habitable for human life. But I will be her chauffeur while she's here. She told me she 'can't drive a stick' and didn't like the idea of driving on the other side of the road anyway. I'll pick her up at the airport, and I can even claim mileage expenses for doing it. I don't know if I can assume that she'll want me to stay with her at the hotel, so I'll play that by ear.

I cancelled all my other meetings and commitments for the next three weeks, and explained the urgency and situation in an email to Joanne; just in case anyone moans that I'm not doing their other projects for them. They can wait.

I decide to go home and work on this tech-sheet. There are too many distractions in the office. I'm getting interrupted every few minutes by something or someone. Also, I am not paying for more celery in the canteen for lunch.

When I get home, I heat a bowl of soup and take it to my desk, I open up the tech-sheet and carry on where I left off. But after ten minutes of staring at the same data, and not being able to concentrate, I get up. I know that if my brain is refusing to co-operate, then I can't influence the situation. I need a break, so I go out for a walk. But the shed door catches my eye, and instead, I wander over there. I might not get much time to go fiddle with the mystery box when Rachel is over here, so I want to make the most of it now. Am I going to show this to Rachel? Maybe she could try it out too? Will she think I'm a fruit-loop if I tell her I have something like a weird time-machine? Undoubtedly. Maybe she already thinks I'm a fruit-loop? Perhaps that's why she likes me? But she's in touch with the occult and the mystical and unknown, possibly she can explain it somehow?

I'll play that by ear too I guess. I don't want her to freak out.

Why does she like me anyway? I'm double her age, boring, set in my ways. I'm not hideously unattractive physically, but I could do with losing some weight and getting more exercise. I know she thinks the universe brought us together for some reason, but is that enough for the basis of a long-term relationship? Is that even what she wants or expects? Does she see this as temporary fun? Fuck this train of thought. My brain is being a twat again. I jump into some random past.

I pull into the familiar driveway at my parent's house and get out of the car. Dad asked me to come over. Probably wants me to help him carry a lathe or something. I go in and find Mum making lunch.

"Hi, Terry." She comes over and hugs me, her eyes are red like she's been crying.

"Hey, are you okay?"

"Fine. Are you staying for lunch?"

"Yeah, what are you making?"

"Roast Chicken."

"Grand job!"

She tells me Dad is in the workshop as usual, so I walk over. It's the same workshop I cleared out the tools from, the same workshop in which I found the mysterious box. I open the door and see Dad pottering away with his tools. The scent of pipe smoke fills my nose.

"Hey, Terry."

"Hey. So what are we moving? Saw bench? Lathe? Huge wooden benches?"

He laughs, "Nothing today." He opens up his flask and pours a coffee and takes a sip. He's looking frail, getting older. We smashed down a concrete block wall in here about a year ago, with sledge-hammers, and then tossed all the debris out the window. Now it doesn't look like he could even lift up a sledgehammer.

Something is off with this situation. Something doesn't feel normal.

He leans back on the bench and looks over at me.

"The stent they put in isn't working properly. I had a test done, and it's apparently a tumour on my pancreas."

"What?" All the blood vanishes from my body, I am limp, and I can't move anything.

"Cancer."

"But…"

"I'm starting chemo next week. They reckon it will take care of it."

"But… Pancreatic cancer? That's what Steve Jobs had?"

"Yeah."

There's nothing to sit down on in the fucking workshop,

but I need to sit before I fall. I wipe the dust off the generator and flop down.

"But…"

"It'll be okay. Be right as rain before you know it."

The intercom rings, the signal that Mum has lunch ready, so we go back over to the house for chicken.

FUCK YOU, BOX. Why did I need to see that again? I leave the shed and get in my car and drive nowhere very fast, steering through tear filled eyes. Of course it wasn't fucking okay, of course he wasn't right as rain. The chemo did nothing except make him weaker.

I find myself at the beach. I must have been driving for a while. This is my secret empty beach that no one seems to know about. I've been here before when times were rough. I walk to the shoreline and stand and watch the water go in and out. Listening to the waves wash up and down calms my brain, and after a while, I go back to the car and go home.

When I get home, I realise I have a load of work still to do, but I feel like talking to Rachel for a while if she's around, and not busy. I send her a message, but she hasn't answered by the time I've made a pot of coffee, so instead, I write down the details of the 'dream' I just had. It is painful, tough to write the words, but I want to do this. If the universe is trying to tell me something, then I need to listen and understand.

I can't believe I am thinking like this. A week ago I would have laughed at the concept of mystical shit like this.

A week since I met the girl who has rapidly changed

everything, it feels much more than a week. It feels like I've always known her, but yet I know so little.

I go back to my desk and wade through the lake of emails flooding in my inbox, delete, delete, delete, ignore, one line answer, saving the interesting ones for later, moving the annoying ones down the pile of shit I will never do.

I switch back to the tech-sheet and fill in some more details, cross-referencing with five or six documents on every single tiny aspect and point.

Rachel replies to my message, says the hotel looks lovely, please book it, make sure we get a big bed. I guess that's an invitation to stay with her? A while later she messages again, she's sorry I had that dream, she wishes she could cuddle me right now, make it all better. I wish the same thing.

She tells me her plan for next week. She'll drive up to Chicago with her mom, and then her mom will take her car back home. That makes sense. Then she will get the same flight I got to London, then over to Shannon. I'll get her from the airport. We'll go to the fancy hotel and fuck like wild animals, and then start work that afternoon, once she has had a rest from the travel. The animal thing was her idea. I'm not going to argue.

I book the hotel and make sure we get early check-in, because I am boring and I think ahead about that kind of detail.

She's worried about the flying part again. I tell her it's like a job interview or a medical exam, the anticipation is always much worse than the actual event. Don't think about it, don't even acknowledge it, and just show up at the airport and before you know it, you'll be in the air and bored shitless and wondering why you were so scared. As we say here: it'll be grand.

The universe knows what it's doing, I tell her. She tells me to suck a monkey's dick, and then she says she loves me.

Women!

I finish up work, there is still a load of detail to fill in on the tech-sheet, but I can't look at it anymore. Rachel is busy now with work and preparing for her trip, so I leave her alone for a while and make dinner.

I think I need to start cleaning up a bit. My house is a mess, and even if Rachel isn't staying here, she might visit. I'm not in the slightest bit 'house proud', quite the opposite, but there are probably too many empty pizza and Amazon boxes around for general health and safety reasons. I probably should vacuum everywhere and bleach the entire bathroom too. I don't like to disturb the dust bunnies, because they make me sneeze and, really, who are they hurting just sitting there in the corners of the room? I flood the house with heavy metal, loud, visceral, rhythmic and raw, and plug in the vacuum cleaner.

I clean the house like it was a murder crime scene and I'm hiding evidence. I throw out more rubbish than a hoarder reality TV show. I vacuumed up more spider webs than a haunted house after Halloween, I even pulled out the fridge and vacuumed behind there. I cleaned the kitchen stove so you could see your face in it, I cleaned the dining table so well, you could eat your dinner off it.

My house is clean! But I'm sweating like a drug smuggler at the airport. I need to shower now, but I cleaned the bathroom too, and I don't want to mess it up again. I feel like I've painted myself into a corner. Now I can't live in my house until Rachel visits, or I'll fuck it all up again.

It takes a minute, but I realise this is ridiculous. I have to live in my house! Rachel isn't the health inspector, or an overbearing Great Aunt, deciding which of her relatives will inherit her vast fortune, based on cleanliness alone. As long as there aren't vermin running around like the pied fucking piper is passing by, then it will be fine. I shower and feel better, but I rinse out the shower after I use it.

It's getting late, I message Rachel I'm going to bed, and she sends me a page full of Xs and hearts and a photo of her lips up close to the camera lens.

Chapter Twenty-One

THURSDAY 13TH SEPTEMBER

I'm staying home today. No point in going to the office just to be distracted all day. I can get this tech-sheet finished today, if I am left alone. I started early, woke up at stupid o'clock and decided to make a start on things. I got a load of work done before most other people logged on and the deluge of email started again.

This work is tedious and laborious. I find I can only concentrate on things like this with some background music playing, to drown out the constant brain chatter.

[08:17] O'Brien, Ted:
Starting early?

[08:17] Ward, Terry B:
Been working for ages already, Ted.
Big important stuff happening next week.

[08:18] O'Brien, Ted:
Oh yeah?

[08:18] Ward, Terry B:
>You betcha!
>Rachel is popping over.

I tell Ted the story of the sudden FutureCloud order, and how the only way I could make it happen quickly, is by working directly with the customer engineer here, which happens to be the girl I wanted to see. Nice handy one there!

[08:25] O'Brien, Ted:
>Yeah, I might have to get one of those girlfriend things.
>I hear they are quite expensive though.

[08:25] Ward, Terry B:
>They can be for sure.
>Expense one on the company card!

[08:26] O'Brien, Ted:
>Haha.
>Let me know if you need any help on the coding.

[08:26] Ward, Terry B:
>Thanks, dude.

I make a second pot of coffee and go back to my desk, but I'm distracted, disturbed, the memories that came from the box yesterday are pervasive and destructive. I'm angry and sad at the same time. None of what happened is news, but to have it all replayed in such vivid ultra high definition 3D was shocking.

It's like when a song gets stuck in my head, I can't get it out until I play the song again, sometimes over and over. Inevitably I wander over to the shed.

There it is, sitting on the bench as always, the gentle whir of the innocently spinning cone inside, defying logic and physics somehow. I need to apply some rules to this. So far I have more or less randomly skipped around the decades, but I think I need some order to this chaos. I set everything to maximum and try the hand pads. Nothing happens, as expected. My guess is that maximum setting is NOW, whenever NOW may be. So, there's nowhere to jump? It doesn't go into the future apparently. Only the past. I already know what minimum setting is, so instead I go back about a quarter on the Y dial and give it a blast.

I'm at a desk, but this isn't my usual work desk, the seat feels different. The smells are more industrial. It's roasting hot, a fan rotates around and blasts warm air over me, loose pages flap around in the breeze and blow onto the floor. There's a big screen in front of me showing a business card for a local company, they do industrial refrigeration units and air-conditioning, I wish they'd come and install something here! I'm uncomfortably hot in my jeans and T-Shirt, but I'm fecked if I'll wear shorts. I spin around in my seat and see I'm in the print company I used to work at, XpressPrint. I was the IT manager, and I hated every single day of it. Maybe even more than my current situation. The only reason I didn't walk out every day was the mortgage. The office is on the top floor of a cheap warehouse. The roof is just corrugated iron with no insulation, so in the winter it's bollock freezing, and the summer is an oven. When it rains, it bangs on the roof like being inside a snare drum at a marching band parade. There are maybe three days a year where it is comfortable inside.

The computer connected to this screen is suffering from narcolepsy. It falls asleep randomly in the middle of work.

Especially now in the summer heat. I'm here to fix it. But I know what the problem is now, I didn't back then though. Eventually, I found a cooling fan was disconnected inside the case, but I tried loads of software fixes first. Now I know what to do straight away. I shut it down and get down on my knees on the floor, and pull out the tower from under a mess of cables and dust bunnies. It's a simple fix, literally just plug the fan back into the little connector.

I get back up and brush off all the shit that's now on my jeans and power the computer back on.

"That should sort you out. It helps if the fan is connected up inside."

"Thanks, Terry!" Jeff beams his annoying smile and sits back down at his desk.

"How did you know the fan was unplugged?"

"Didn't get to be IT manager without knowing a thing or two!" I tap the side of my nose and wink.

I go back to my desk on the other side of the office and see how my movie downloads are progressing. I have bogger-net back at home, so I have to get all my downloads done at work.

'07' is the code now above the Y knob on the box. I dial them all forward a little and dive back in.

I pull into the car park at work, it's pitch dark, the clock on my dashboard says 2:30 am. I go in through the security door, and walk through the empty factory, all the way down to my lab at the back. The factory closed about three hours ago. We have to give all the systems time to finish their installs, before we shut everything down and do the updates to the code. The radio blares extremely loud, I can't tell if it is louder than usual, or just that there's no background noise now, with all the machines turned off. Either way, it's annoying. Terrible pop music surrounded by carpet and insurance adverts all fucking night. I forgot my headphones.

I get to my lab and unlock the door with my badge, I'm the first one here. The other lads probably won't get here for another half hour. I set about organising all the test machines, and getting the monitors and keyboards on trolleys that we need ready. Some fucker has stolen one of my screens. It's on another bench belonging to a different team. I take it back, and also steal their power cables and pens they left out. Arseholes.

Everything is ready now for my 'team' to come in and start the testing. We'll be here all night, and the canteen isn't open. I've got my flask of coffee, dunno what everyone else is doing. I make the long, arduous trek to the toilet block before everyone else arrives. You can smell it a mile away, the stench of factory worker shit in a hot environment that never gets any fresh air. Fucking delightful. As I kick open the door with my foot, daring not to touch anything at all, I am greeted by the naked hairy arse of a fine gentleman as he bangs a squealing woman on the sink. I promptly turn around and exit. Now I'll have to hike another six miles to the next toilet block. How romantic, a swift shag in the stinking jax at three am at work. Love knows no bounds, huh?

A minute later, the aforementioned woman passes me as she fast walks through the factory to the exit, cursing in Polish. The young man follows shortly after, he turns to me briefly and raises his hands in a 'what can you do?' gesture and then runs after the girl. I'm thankful he pulled his pants up first. I guess that means I can go back to the original toilet block, but note to myself not to attempt using the sink.

Time, For a Change

. . .

'08' appears on the box above the knob. That's when I first started at C.S.Tech after leaving the print shop. That was before I was broken and disillusioned by the constant stress and jobsworths doing anything they could to avoid actual work. Battling against people who think 'it's just a job' for ten years will do that to a man. My hands smell of copper now, but time for one more run I think. I turn the Y knob a tiny bit further and lean into the box again.

The view from the window is fantastic from this height, forty-eight floors above Shanghai, looking out over the night-time cityscape. The explosions below are fireworks. I've never seen them from above before.

It's the week after Chinese new year, these are the final celebrations ringing in the year of the Ox. I'm in a plush bar, vast soft couches everywhere, small tables dotted around. Everyone else is out on a balcony watching the celebrations, but even with the high railing, there's no fucking way I'm going outside at this height. I can see fine through the window, thanks. We're here to negotiate with a computer manufacturer about automating our services onto the machines as they are built. But that doesn't start until next Monday. I go back to the free food bar and get a plate of melon balls and sushi and a tiny bottle of ginger ale.

The lads want to find the Irish bar in the city later. I rolled my eyes at them, seriously? You want to travel all the way to China and visit an Irish bar? Not even ironically? I don't approve, but my choice is either stay in the hotel on my own or go with them. I'm not entirely comfortable navigating around without some company just yet. The taxi drivers don't speak English, all I can do is show them my hotel card, and they bring me back. We went to the counterfeit market earlier, I bought something that unquestionably isn't an iPhone, but it looks vaguely like one. It was about twenty dollars, but I had to haggle even though I didn't want to. Probably won't last very long. I bought it only as a keepsake from China, not actually to use as a phone.

'09' is now above the knob on the box. The automation process we went to set up never worked properly, despite all the effort and expense. But I got a free trip to China that undoubtedly would never have happened without work sponsorship.

I should get back to work on the tech-sheets, so I wander back to the house and check email to see what is going on. Eoghan got word that the first parts from our shopping list will arrive into the office tomorrow, so I better go in. We can start to put things together in preparation. I put the music back on and get back to work.

I manage about three hours by logging out of the instant message service and email and switching off my phone. The music blocked out my brain, and I was able to churn through. I think the tech-sheet is done. I've gone over it so many times now, that I'm blind to it, so I log back into email and send it to Eoghan to check. I also copy it to Rachel in another mail. I want her to give it a look and make sure I have every detail covered. The consequences of fucking something up, even a tiny detail, are too stressful to think about. We're already on a tight deadline, there's no room for any mistakes. The customers demand perfection, so that's what we try and deliver. Rarely works out that way though.

I'm starving now, so I have breakfast for lunch and then wander down the road for a breath of air.

The walk acts as processing time for all the muddled thoughts in my head. I'm thinking specifically about the XpressPrint box-journey. I was fixing Jeff's computer from narcolepsy, triggered by overheating. Jeff worked at XpressPrint with me, not at C.S.Tech? He said he hadn't heard from me since those days when I contacted him on LinkedIn, he doesn't even live here anymore. But he sat opposite me, he made stupid comments every day, he chewed gum incessantly to the point where I had to put headphones in and stack boxes high on my desk, so that I couldn't see him, or I would've ended up battering his brains out with an ergonomic keyboard.

I try to think when he started working at C.S.Tech, when I first remember him joining? He wasn't there when I worked in the factory lab and came in for three am shifts. He wasn't around when I travelled to China either, I worked in a different area of the building then. I can't put my finger on a time, it just seemed like he was always there. I can't even think what job he did or who he worked with now. 'Some other department' is all that I ever knew. I wonder if the box has done this? Have I changed something in history?

The DeltaWave email that caused five-hundred systems to have the wrong software installed, but then it turned out to be a mistake by the customer. Did I change something there too?

Most of the box-journeys I've gone on so far were passive, I didn't seem to control what happened or even what I said. It felt like a dream where I was observing, but sometimes I felt like I had a bit of control and I could make things happen. But did I? Or was I just acting out those thoughts as I would have anyway? What if things have changed? What decision was it that altered them? Did anything else change? Has anyone else's life been modified because of something I have done? Has my own life changed because of it? What if a version of me from the future returned to a time when I was in Ohio and did something to set me up with Rachel? What if Dad used the box before me and changed things even before I knew about it. If he could do things like that, why didn't he change his own fate? Perhaps some things are destined to happen regardless of how we try and influence them. I'm more confused than ever now, the mysteries of the box remain an enigma.

By the time I get home there are another thirty-seven emails in my inbox, but only one of them I want to read, from Rachel. She says she'll look at my tech-sheet later, right now she has loads of stuff to organise for the Ohio factory while she's away. She said Pete was going to ask Toby to come back and cover, but they couldn't get hold of him. She said she hopes he went to hell. I send her back a load of Xs and tell her I'll leave her to work and she can call me later if she feels like it. I put the water on for a bath and start to make some dinner.

Chapter Twenty-Two

FRIDAY 14TH SEPTEMBER

I got to the office just after the delivery courier came with a load of our new toys. It's amazing how fast you can get stuff when you are willing to pay extra. We got a server configured more or less the same as FutureCloud need, but we have to change out some disks and memory and add some extra cards to match it identically. I'll leave Eoghan to do that dirty work. He loves the smell of new computers. Anyway, I didn't do my static electricity training course this year, so I'm not allowed to touch the equipment officially.

Rachel called me last night, and we talked for hours, she was nervous about the flight again, so I told her in detail every step of how to traverse the airport at Chicago. How to get through security quickly, and then get to the gate, what to expect when she gets on the plane and off again at the other side. Then how to go from the exit in Heathrow to the Shannon flight gate. I told her to put the address of the hotel in Ireland on her phone and print it out too. I told her how to organise all her paperwork, so she has everything in the correct order, and all of it backed up on her phone, ideally on a cloud server too so, even if she lost her phone she could log in and find the details somehow. I also have a copy of everything and all her flight details. I'm a fucking project manager!

I churn through my work emails and check my calendar, it's almost empty of meetings for the next three weeks, and it feels like I'm unburdened and free. Of course, I'm not free, there's a massive amount of work to do yet, but it's just one project and one customer, so it feels much more straightforward. I still have to keep Sean up to date and join the afternoon calls with FutureCloud, but that isn't anything to worry about.

I realise Rachel will need a desk and chair while she's here. She'll be in and out of the lab of course, but for general catching up on emails and taking phone calls she'll need somewhere quiet to sit. There's an empty cubicle opposite mine, so I commandeer it and put a note on the felt covered wall. 'Reserved for visiting customer.' I should get some salt packets for her too. Don't want slug-people leaving slime all over her area.

Eoghan appears in my periphery, majestic as a lion as he stealthily pads around, blending into the savannah of the office. He's looking worried, but I can't tell if that is the usual level of worry or if something new has happened. I flag him down with a wave.

"What have you broken?" He looks at me startled, in disbelief.

"It's okay. There's a spare connector on my desk."

"Ah, for fuck's sake, lad!"

"It's not my fault the pins are so easily bent!" his voice notches up a few semitones.

"I thought you knew how to build a computer?"

"I do!" His voice has reached new octaves previously unknown to man.

"You want breakfast?"

"You buying?"

"I am in me hole!"

We get overcooked eggs on barely warmed bread and big mugs of tea. The stingy feckers charge extra for butter packets, so I hide three of them under my plate as we go to the checkout. It's the principal! It's not even good butter.

Over breakfast, Eoghan tells me he'll have the base system built by the end of Monday, but it will be bare metal, no software, no firmware updated, no additional stuff at all. That's fine, that's how the machines will come to us. After that, we can start all the automated configuration on top of it. We add the whip of cream and cherry to the top of the cake, and then parcel it up in fancy wrapping, ready to ship around the world and 'delight and excite' the end users. Apparently.

So far things are going pretty well. It can't last though. Something will inevitably go wrong. No matter how much I prepare, and how many things I take into account, there is always some minor detail that gets missed. That's why we need Rachel, because it is entirely possible that I have misinterpreted something from her documents, or they didn't contain one small, but vital piece of information. Or maybe I wasn't listening when she was explaining something in the

Ohio factory, because I was too busy staring at her tits. That's very probable.

We go back to the lab, and Eoghan shows me what he broke. Fecking heavy handed lad! It isn't too bad, and he has a replacement, but we only had the server five minutes! I watch him replace it but now he seems nervous, so I go for a wander around the lab and leave him to it. Reminds me of when I started here. Different location, but same benches and shelves and screens on wheels. Racks and racks of computers, all wired into network and power, flashing and humming away.

I notice some DeltaWave logos on a few of the systems on one rack.

"Thought you finished these?" I have to roar over the fan noise.

"Almost."

"What?"

"They are literally doing the final download test now."

I wander back over to Eoghan, "You know there's a very tight deadline on these FutureCloud ones?" I tap on the server but realise I'm not wearing an anti-static strap so I back away.

"I am aware."

"Massive deal, huge pressure, engineer coming over from Ohio. If this goes wrong we'll all be fucked up the arse, with a frozen kipper, repeatedly, and without lube."

"Yes, it will get done."

. . .

I've heard that before, but I let it go. This time I'll be here every day going through everything in detail with Eoghan and Rachel to keep it all on track. What could possibly go wrong?

Until the server is entirely built, I'm as much use here as a spare wheel on a pogo-stick, so I may as well go home and finish up there.

Had to stop at the supermarket on the way home. Once I had loaded up on food for the weekend, I stood in front of the flowers they had out for five whole minutes. Deliberating if I should get a bunch to have in my house just in case Rachel comes to visit, but I don't know when that might happen, if at all, and I don't know how long flowers last until they dry up and start to stink. Also, would she care if I put flowers out for her benefit? Would she think it was weird, is it too much? What kind of flowers does she like? In the end, I walk away. I have insufficient data required to process this situation. I can't extrapolate all the potential outcomes adequately, so my brain sends back an error message. My house is still pretty neat and tidy anyway so that will have to suffice.

It starts to piss with rain on my way home, heavy, but nothing like the deluge we had going back to Chicago last week. Ahead of me on the road, I see dark grey skies, but in my mirrors I see blue. A metaphor for life…

When I get home, I put a pot of coffee on, open up Twitter and fire out a notion that occurred to me in the car.

#RandomThoughts: Do things ever really get wet, or do they just have water on them?

Before I fire up the laptop and see if anything happened at work, I wander over to the shed, it's becoming a habit, but I want to get as much 'boxing' done as I can before Rachel comes over.

I try the box again without adjusting any of the dials from how I left it last. Nothing happens. No visions, no flickers of the past. A big load of sod-all occurs in fact. Is it broken? Can I not travel to the same time more than once? Does it need a reboot? I fiddle with the dials and try again.

It's dark and hot, and there's yellow glass fibre insulation under me, a single bare bulb strung from a rafter above. There isn't enough room to stand up. A hole in the floor streams light up from the space below. I'm in the loft of my house. I have a roll of cable, a hammer and a pocket full of clips. From below I can hear Dad singing some inane ditty he's making up on the spur of the moment. It involves a lady with magnificent talents and many profanities. I push a cable through a hole in the ceiling.

"See that?"

"Yep."

"Can you tie a knot in it?"

"Said the actress to the bishop!"

I crawl over to the loft hatch and climb down the ladder into my bedroom, but right now it isn't a bedroom, it's a building site. The walls are lined with a wooden frame and some insulation on one wall, but there's no plasterboard on anything yet. We are dry-lining inside the ancient stone walls because it is the only way to make this room even vaguely warm in the winter.

"Not much fun up there."

"If it were fun we'd all be doing it!"

Dad pours a coffee from his flask and then knocks out his pipe through the open window. He fills it up from a pouch of sweet-smelling tobacco.

"Making some good progress now."

I swig from a bottle of water. The loft insulation has caught in my throat.

"Yeah." I manage to cough out a word in response and gulp down the rest of the water.

I never feel bad asking Dad to help with my house projects because he loves doing things like this. Any opportunity to use all the tools he's collected for decades, and kept clean and sharp in his workshop. In fact, if I didn't ask him to come over, he'd probably be offended. I feel sorry for people who didn't have someone around like Dad, who could do anything he set his mind to. I don't ever remember him saying he didn't know how to do something. Anything was possible, no matter how obscure. Even better if it required some exotic and expensive tools to be acquired.

We talk about computers as we often end up doing. I recently got a new laptop, so I show him the thin slab of metal that is capable of so much. While most people take for granted that a new computer will be much faster than the previous version, and not give any thought to how or why, Dad marvels in the engineering required to achieve these feats of technological ingenuity. Where the laws of physics seem to preclude silicon chips from running as fast as they do.

We work late into the evening on my bedroom walls, almost finish the cabling and insulation. I help him load his tools back into his van, and he goes off home. A long drive now but he doesn't seem to mind. I gave him some money for diesel and offered to make dinner, but he said Mum had something in the oven for him.

A little '12' appears above the Y knob on the box. I wander back to the house and go into the bedroom, the walls are flat and exact, smooth with plaster. Dad made all this possible. I wouldn't have done it without his help and motivation. If you look at the whole house casually, you'll see it is falling apart and shite, but the little details like this were all handmade with love and care and attention. Good intentions too. I planned to finish all the work, but… Situations change. The idea of hiring someone else to do work like this never even occurred to me until recently. It just wasn't something we did in our family. Dad would make fun of other people who needed to call a 'man' to come and do maintenance or work on the house. If there was already a man there, he said, then they wouldn't need to call one in…

I go back to my desk and google for things to do in the west of Ireland, in case I have an opportunity to take Rachel around to see the sights. I've lived here for twenty years, but I haven't really done any tourist stuff. Sure, there's time yet!

It turns out there are lots of touristy things to do, I guess because a significant part of the revenue in Ireland comes from tourists and travellers. Everyone loves to claim a single digit percentage of Irish heritage, so there is a considerable business in it. No matter how far back it came from, the claim is always proudly made. Personally, I don't think I have any

Irish blood, but I've spilt enough of my own here that I reckon that counts towards something now?

I head back to the shed for another box-journey. Feels like I'm binging on a Netflix series, but this is my own personal epic forty season soap-opera, in 3D smell-o-vision, with full body sensation.

That gives me an idea. What if I can go back to the first fun evening I had with Rachel in Ohio last week? Maybe I only get one go at it? I should probably save that trip for a special occasion. Anyway, she'll be here soon.

I try something else instead.

I'm in a parked car outside a building, not familiar with this place, but it looks like a large house. I'm in the passenger seat. There's a laptop on my lap, and I'm uploading some files to a machine over WiFi. Presumably the WiFi from the building I'm outside. This is Dad's old car. Ashtrays are full of pipe tobacco, there's a shaker of salt and a bottle of vinegar in the door pocket, and various charge cables rigged up to the cigarette lighter socket. My laptop is plugged into one of them. Dad isn't here.

I look closer at the laptop, perhaps it can give me some indication of what is going on here as I don't remember this at all. The filenames all begin with MediDB_ and then various identifiers. Now I understand. We built a software package for general practitioner surgeries, a database customised to doctors needs. Only one doctor ever bought it, this is his practice. I'm doing a remote software update to his build from the car. Dad is inside. I chose to stay in the car rather than sit in the waiting room with all the sick patients.

Plus I wanted to try out the wireless networking. This is quite a new thing in 2001.

Once the files are finished transferring, I close my laptop and go into the building.

"All done, need to reboot now."

We start with the receptionist's machine. She's talking away in Gaeilige to an old man. This is Connemara, in the Gaeltacht area of Ireland. I haven't a single clue what they are saying, but the whole conversation is very animated, and seems to focus on the prescription paper he's holding.

We finish off the software update, and test everything is still working, with no data loss, and then head back.

Over the course of the long drive, we discuss quantum mechanics, and the fate of Schrödinger's poor cat, at least, Dad does, and I listen, trying to keep up. We stop for dinner at a very down-to-earth place outside Galway city. The tablecloths are a thick, shiny vinyl for a quick wipe-down. You get your food at the counter, and you make your mug of tea or coffee afterwards. It's good sturdy breakfast-for-dinner food.

Eventually, we get back home, Dad drops me at my place, and then he drives on. He has an unlimited capacity for driving and not getting tired or needing to piss.

I'm exhausted after the long day, even if I sat on my arse for most of it.

There's a little '01' on the Y knob now. I hadn't thought about the medical software we did for a long time. Of course it didn't sell, and eventually, we had to shut down the one practice we set up. Connemara is beautiful untouched landscape, a different world to where I live.

. . .

I go back to the house and look in the fridge at what I bought earlier in the supermarket, but I feel drained after the box-journey. Instead, I decide to drive a forty mile round-trip and get a Chinese takeaway. There is a closer place, but it isn't great, and I felt like driving for a while. I send Rachel some Xs before I go, and tell her I can't wait to see her, counting down the hours now using an app on my phone. It's about ninety.

Chapter Twenty-Three

SATURDAY 15TH SEPTEMBER

I intended to do some work today, maybe even go into the office. I feel like I should be doing something more, there's a nagging doubt in me like when I was at school and didn't do my homework. I'm conditioned to believe that I can't take a break without feeling guilty. But good intentions wash away with the morning shower. The bed was too cosy to exit and the Saturday morning Star Trek binge too distracting. By the time I get dressed it is already midday.

I make a second pot of coffee and scramble up some eggs for a change, and after breakfast, I wander over to the shed. It's raining, the tin roof amplifies the sound to a wash of metallic white noise. It isn't cold, and the rain smells fresh, so I leave the door open and stand inside watching the falling drops for a minute. All the other tools and boxes of odds and sods, and bits and bobs, are all still lingering in the back of the shed. I still don't know what to do with it all. Maybe I should start cleaning things up and selling them online?

That is definitely a job for another day though. There's no harm in the stuff sitting there procrastinating a while longer.

I sit down at the bench and open the box. I realise I

haven't been telling Rachel the 'dreams' I've had. Maybe I'll write them down this afternoon. She's been busy anyway.

I'm stuck behind a group of slow people walking through an airport, I can see planes lined up outside. The miles of featureless corridors, clean, shiny floors, dull colours that enforce the desire to exit quickly and get back to something the mind can recognise. Finally, I edge past the group, talking in Dutch I think. I'm pulling a suitcase along, and in my other hand, I have my passport. Signs on the walls indicate this is Schiphol airport in Amsterdam. I exit eventually and hail a taxi. Luckily the younger me knows where he's going. A hotel in the city. The cab cost fifty euro for a twenty-five-minute ride. I feel bad now I didn't try and get the train or bus, but I had no idea it would cost this much. I carefully file away the receipt. Fucked if I am paying that myself. As I get out of the taxi, a stench of rotten food hits me, a pile of rubbish bags down the road is probably the cause. I climb the steps and push open the door. Inside is like a church, dark and cavernous, but modern and lined with plush couches and rugs. I check in. I have to fill in too many forms for my liking, so by the bottom of the sheet they stand little chance of ever reading my writing.

My room is revolting and expensive, the colours are vulgar, the angles all wrong somehow, there are three steps inside the room up to the bed area, which is cramped and dark. I'm on the ground floor, just off the reception but in an oddly shaped corridor. Behind layers of curtains, I finally find a window and wish I hadn't. The view is a brick wall only feet away. I'm beginning to think this whole trip was a huge mistake. It has already cost way too much, and I haven't had dinner yet. The customer meeting isn't for another two days.

How was I to know there was a public holiday in the Netherlands when I booked all this months ago? It'll be okay, they said. Have a day in Amsterdam.

I tried to shower, but the bathroom was so small I kept knocking my elbows off the walls of the shower cubicle. I'm increasingly pissed off, but I need food, so I go out. Surely there's somewhere to eat that doesn't cost a fortune?

After staring at menus in windows for far too long, I settle on a steakhouse. I don't even want steak, but everywhere else was too busy, too noisy, too jovial. I wish I had stayed at home now. Calculating the possibilities of just going back to the airport and getting on the next flight. I persevere through and get food that is unsatisfying. I pay and leave and wander around trying to find a shop that will sell me just a simple bottle of water, but everywhere is uninviting, dangerous, repelling. I am shrinking more and more into myself with every step. I'm too nervous to take out my phone and try and find where I am, so I keep walking straight. After maybe twenty minutes I see a shop open, and I buy my water, three bottles because I don't want to pay hotel prices. I make the trek back and go directly to my room and my bed. Instead of a day in Amsterdam, I've had a nightmare in my agoraphobia. I'm never going on a work trip alone again. Fuck this. If I were with someone everything would be different, I'd be joking and drinking with the boys, maybe head down the red light district to point and laugh. But on my own, I'm lost in a head-scape of fear and anxiety. The price of everything made it worse. I can't afford any of this myself, but I know my boss will question every expense I put through. Even worse, I must have left my kindle on the plane, because I've emptied all my bags three times and I can't find it. Fuck.

. . .

I spent the next day hiding behind the 'do not disturb' sign in the hotel room, flicking through dreadful TV channels and only sneaking out for food when I had to. I didn't travel for work again until Ohio. The customer part was okay in the end, they were a little startup trying to sell their server-based appliance product into the bigger market.

The deal never happened though, and the trip cost the company almost a thousand euro in the end. I got it all signed off eventually, but I felt terrible about it. Best to sweep those memories under the rug and ignore them forever.

'13' now joins the cluster of numbers on the Y dial.

Everything is different now, and I couldn't give a shit if a trip costs ten thousand, if that's the price of business then so be it. I know we make it back many times over. I dial the Y knob back a couple of ticks and dive into the past again.

"All the coins have fish on them!" I turn to Ted showing him a handful of silver coins. He laughs and turns them over in awe. I don't think he has ever been this far from home. We're on a small bus. The landscape outside is barren and windswept. It could almost be the west of Ireland, but there's a charred black feel to the rock under the green and orange lichen. It's volcanic rock, this is Iceland. We're on the little shuttle bus from the airport into Reykjavik.

The sky is dull, but it isn't dark as I had expected. It's October, the dark days are not yet upon us!

We arrive at the Hilton, up on a hill above the city. It looks modern, plush, and the reception staff are friendly and efficient. My room is incredible, looking out over colourful roofs and mountains in the distance. We will meet in half an hour down in the bar and then go into town for the first gig. This is Airwaves, the annual music festival.

We try a local beer, decent and refreshing, but I'm keen to head into the city, soak in the atmosphere and see some bands play. We grab a taxi into town. It isn't far, but it's more than a quick walk. I almost dozed off in the back, it's pitch dark now outside. We are starving, so we find a restaurant first. Ted is a vegetarian though so he misses out big time on the utterly wondrous smoked salmon I had. I got a second plate of the salmon and egg salad because I've never tasted fish like it.

We find the Airwaves information centre to get our wristbands, and pick up a booklet with all the music and venues listed. It's complicated though, so in the end, we just walk around and head towards some music. There's a bitter wind blowing, which I guess is actually Arctic, and not just metaphorically Arctic. The band is playing in the back of what looks like would normally be a gym — everything becomes a venue in Reykjavik for this festival. It isn't very busy, but we stand towards the back, out of the crowd. The lighting is mainly blue through the smoke with columns of red and purple, and flashes of white. The band are intense, powerful, well suited to the explosive geography. No singing, just acoustic metal telling a story in the melody and rhythm. This is why I came.

"Terry?" Ted is tapping me on the arm.
   "Huh."
   "You okay?"
   "Yeah, why?"
   "I think you were asleep there for a minute!"
   "No. What? Was I?" I am exhausted. It has been a long

day of travel. But I'm still standing up and still in a gig. How could I have been asleep?

"*I think we'd better head back to the hotel!*"

"*Ugh. Yeah, fair enough. Takk fyrir.*"

My only regret about that trip was how short it was. Only two nights. I could have stayed a month in Iceland and explored the wild landscape and geothermal springs. There wasn't much time for anything, but we did see some great bands. I head back to the house and eat left-over Chinese from last night for lunch.

I send Rachel a good morning message. She must be awake by now? She responds with a photo of a squirrel standing up, holding a beer bottle and flipping me off. She sends a page full of Xs after. She's going to the store today to buy a suitcase, as she doesn't have one. She asked me if I slept well, I said I didn't know because I was asleep. She tells me to shut the fuck up. I write down the recent 'dreams' and send them through to her.

I still have the nagging feeling I should be doing something productive. I'm reminded of that ancient Chinese proverb: *Man who goes to bed with itchy bum-hole, wakes up with stinky finger.* I switch on my work laptop and let it boot up.

There is the typical avalanche of bullshit email. Newsletters no-one reads, planned downtime for a system I haven't used in seven years, but can't get off the mailing list for, sales wins-of-the-week intended to boost moral I imagine, but it has the opposite effect on my state of mind. I select all and delete. There is nothing that looks interesting or important. I check my procurement requests, and they seem okay, I check my tech-sheet once again, and can't see anything wrong with it. I can't think of anything I am missing, so I shut down the laptop and go for a quick walk down my lane in the rain.

I'm restless in anticipation of meeting Rachel again soon, I hate waiting for things, and on top of that, I am not used to having a spare day to do nothing. I'm antsy, nervous and bored. I need to find something to distract myself or I will go crazy sitting here. I know normal people do things like watch TV shows or sport, or go to the pub and 'socialise' but none of those things make me happy. I don't socialise. In the many years I have lived in this small village, I have never once been to the local pub, and barely ever go into the local shop. Only when I need to get fuel in an emergency situation, do I go to the local petrol station.

I wander back to the shed again. Fuck it. I can make my own entertainment with a box-binge.

I'm in a big kitchen, stainless steel countertops and huge cookers, sinks as deep as loch-fucking-ness and with all manner of monsters in them too, this is a hotel kitchen, we're making breakfast, but this is not a typical hotel. Hidden away in the Wiltshire countryside, there is a hotel that almost only caters for Japanese visitors to the nearby Honda factory. The building is old, probably some kind of converted mansion.

Time, For a Change

I'm a contract chef, earning twice what the real employees make, but I'm temporary, and I could be dumped any minute.

Rice for breakfast, lunch and dinner, the guests at the hotel are quite simple to look after. Dinner is more fun, but I'm not allowed to make sushi, just prepare for it. I often spend an entire evening shelling king prawns in those deep sinks, they are still semi-frozen, my hands bitter cold. This morning I'm working the kitchen on my own because Kamikaze, sorry, Yamazaki-san hasn't shown up yet. I'm guessing he was up till all hours playing Mah-Jong with the other lads as usual. They play for big money when they aren't at the massage parlour in town. Fucker didn't even prep the rice machine for me.

I grab a bowl of noodles and go back to the staff room, breakfast is nearly over, and the dishwasher fella is working away. He's a local, so I made him hash browns and fried eggs.

My apron is already filthy, I throw it in the laundry pile and grab a clean one. The boss moaned at me for getting too dirty before, I told him I'm the only fucker who cleans the grill properly, so kiss my shiny arse. I could walk out of here any time, and my agency will find me another chef placement. Not everyone wants to cook here, the food is weird, the knives are funny, the sushi chefs are miserable cunts, and they barely speak English.

Kamikaze finally shows up in the staff room.

"Nice of you to join me, Yamazaki-san," I stand up and mock bow. He's looking whiter than my clean apron though, he pours a coffee and sits down, he's shaking, looks like he's seen a ghost.

"So sorry, Terry-san. Did not sleep well."

"You okay?"

"Something attack me in room. I will never sleep here again!"

"What?"

Between his shaking and his pigeon English, I finally get information from him. Well, the waitress did when she came in, she calmed him down, I only wind him up.

He slept in the staff quarters, which are in the old building above the central hotel. He said he was woken in the night by a sound, something rattling in the wardrobe. He tried to get out of bed, but he was paralysed, he felt something pushing on his chest, he thinks he saw something, a light, a figure, he can't explain, he's genuinely shit scared. He did see a ghost, at least that's what he thinks. He's almost in tears, he wants to go back to Tokyo. Caroline, the waitress, brings him a whiskey from the bar.

"Which room was it?"

"Six. Close door, lock up! Not safe!"

"I'm staying here tonight. Put me down for room six."

I did stay in room six that night, I went home after breakfast and napped the rest of the morning, then I packed my overnight bag and went back for the evening stint. After work at about midnight, I finally took off another filthy apron and went up to room six. I couldn't sleep because after a busy shift I'm buzzing, I put the TV on and watched 'Poltergeist', because it happened to be on. I slept like a log, didn't see any ghosts, didn't feel anything, didn't hear anything. I asked for that room every time I stayed afterwards too, and nothing ever happened. Kamikaze thought I was insane, he never forgot that night. I tried to explain to him it was sleep paralysis. A normal process when your body is still half asleep. It's to stop you acting out your dreams. He didn't understand, or didn't believe me, probably went back to Japan with tales of haunted English mansions.

I chuckle to myself, it was hard work peeling prawns for hours on end, but I had some laughs there, and earned decent money for the first time in my life. I spent it all on computers and CDs. A little '96' appears on the Y dial.

Chapter Twenty-Four

SUNDAY 16TH SEPTEMBER

Apparently, I fell asleep while chatting with Rachel last night, I woke up around midday with my phone in my hand, battery dead. When I plugged it in, I saw several messages from her.

Am I that boring?
LOL
Well, goodnight, I guess!

And then a bucket load of Xs. The timestamp on the messages was around four am, so that must be when we were talking until.

We talked about life, the universe and everything. Her family are being 'annoying assholes', and she is looking forward to getting away for a while now, even with the stress of the airport and flight. She showed me all the stuff she was packing in her new suitcase. I told her the power is different here, that her weird hair straightening device may not work in Ireland, even with an adaptor for the socket. I ended up ordering her a new one from Amazon. I let her pick it out because I have no idea what the pros and cons of these devices are. Evidently, it is vitally important that she has it immediately, so I got fast shipping.

I also described to her the last 'dream' I had about the Japanese hotel, she laughed, but then she told me about some apparitions she has seen at her house. A civil war soldier, a dark beast with smouldering red eyes at the edge of the woods, a little boy and girl who died a long time ago, buried somewhere nearby in unmarked graves. She was utterly sincere when she described them all, in great detail. Personally, I don't necessarily disbelieve in spirits and ghosts and strange creatures, but I have never witnessed these things with my own eyes, so I have no basis for reference. When I stayed in room six, part of me was trying to prove to Yamazaki that there was nothing to worry about, but part of me was hoping I would see something eerie. It would have made for a better story to tell.

I make some breakfast and get dressed. My plan for the day is to do as little as possible, but I need to think about what stuff I'll take with me to the hotel as well. I can easily drive home if required, but I may as well bring any stuff I might need.

My suitcase still sits on the bedroom floor, some clothes and bathroom stuff still in it from when I got back from America recently. I intend to unpack, wash and repack some things, but thinking about laundry returns an error message. 'Unable to process at this time. Please try again later.'

Fair enough. Instead, I wander over to the shed for a quick blast around the past.

I'm sitting at an old desk, littered with knick-knacks and junk, otherwise known as antiques to some people, I believe. A large diary planner book dominates. The only nod towards modern technology is a telephone, but even that is relatively ancient. The pages of the diary are divided into seven with scrawled lines, barely even meeting the edges of the sheet and far from ruler-straight. In-between the lines are names, credit card numbers, addresses and phone numbers. Various distinctive ink colours and handwriting styles. I recognise my writing on some of the entries. I look around me, the little office is stuffed full of more junk and opens out to a dark hallway.

The telephone rings, obnoxiously loud, breaking the silence.

"Good evening, Abbey Hotel, Penzance, how may I help you?" I take a booking for a room next week, as I turn the pages of the book, some of them are thick and crusty with dry correction fluid, where someone has changed a booking. The guy on the phone said his name was David Bowie, and he wanted 'something grand' so I booked him into the suite for two nights.

I check things in the kitchen, everything is clean and tidy, ready and waiting. I go up to the lounge, a big room with rugs piling up on top of each other, faded and threadbare. The fire is still lit, I poke it a bit and throw another coal on, then check the dining room. The fire here is almost dead, well, it never really lit, because the wood is damp, and there was only one fire-lighter left. I gather up old candles and some sugar and throw them in. It flares up for a minute but will probably go out again soon. I go down to the cellar, finding the key up on the top of the door frame, and grab a bottle of orange juice, then go back up the stairs, up to the attic floor. The stairs are narrow, steep and dark as the lights are off, but I leave them off. Valerie, the housekeeper, won't come up here in the dark alone, she says there are evil spirits.

The hotel is hundreds of years old, but anytime I am here in the evenings on my own, I wander up to the top floor, and I've never seen or felt anything strange.

I hear a faint ring of the doorbell, so I rush back down again, shit, a customer?

I pull open the enormous heavy wooden door, must be eight foot tall, and find a woman, small, frail, and shivering in the cold.

"Are you open?"

"Oh, yes of course." *I wave her in and close the door against the winter wind. I shuffle around into the office and stand behind the hatch window.*

"Do you have a room for two nights?"

Shit. I was hoping we'd have no guests and I could sneak off early.

"Yes, we have seven. A single?"

"Yes, please."

She's old, maybe in her eighties, she's got one small battered looking suitcase with her. I take her name, and tell her the price of the room. She doesn't bat an eyelid at the ridiculous amount.

"Did you park in the car park?"

"Ah well, I tried to, but I couldn't get it in. My car is outside, would you be so kind as to park it for me?"

She hands me her car keys. I look through the window, and see she's just abandoned her car on the road, there isn't room to pass by it on this narrow lane, so it can't stay there for long. The car-park is a cobbled stone courtyard behind the hotel, it can be tricky to squeeze into sometimes, but right now only my car is there. There's plenty of room for a bus. Her car is tiny.

"And could you please bring in my large suitcase?"

"Yes, of course."

I don't know if I should leave her waiting here while I move her car, or show her up to the room first and then go back and get the car. In the end, I grab her small suitcase and take her up to the room first, but as we move to the second flight of stairs, she stops.

"Oh, I'd rather not go any higher."

"Oh."

"Do you have any rooms on this floor?"

"Yes, but they are double rooms, more expensive."

"That will be fine, young man!" She waves me down the stairs and points to the door of room one. None of the doors are locked, so I show her in. It's a vast room, in mostly blue, the bath is freestanding in the middle of the en-suite bathroom. The windows are firmly shut with decades of coats of paint.

"This is lovely." She smiles and flops down on the bed.

I go and move her car and bring her bag up, it weighs a ton. I'm dreading asking, but I have no choice…

"Er, would you like to stay for dinner?"

"Oh yes, that would be lovely."

Shit. I'm the only person working, that means I'm chef, receptionist, waiter and housekeeper.

She complained because I left her handbrake on too tight and she couldn't get it off the next morning. Didn't leave a tip either when she went.

I worked in that hotel for four and a half years and probably made less money, even including the odd tip, in that whole time, than I do now in six months. Times are very different now, but I'm so glad I got out of catering!

. . .

Time, For a Change

I go over to the house and put the water on for a bath later. I like a good soak. Stimulates the old brain cells and eases the pain in my feet. While the water heats I make some lunch and scroll the inane tweets of the day. I fire out one of my own:

It seems ridiculous to me that the mid-90s were seriously 20+ years ago.
  #FeelsLikeYesterday

The world has changed so much in the last twenty-five years, me included. I was online then, barely, but not many others were. Back then to send a photo to someone required an actual photo and a scanner and a lot of time and effort and money. Now we flood the internet with billions of photos every day and don't think twice.

I do my laundry finally, and empty out the suitcase, the bathroom stuff can go straight back in, and I don't need to worry about the weight of bags now, as I'm not flying, so all my chargers and cables can go in my laptop bag. It feels weird to be even packing a suitcase just to stay in town half an hour away, but what else would I do? Throw stuff in shopping bags? I may as well use the correct tools for the job.

I run the bath and put my phone in a waterproof pouch so I can message Rachel if she is awake yet. I send a photo of the bubbles. She replies promptly.

Cherries

Cherries? I ask her what she means. She tells me she's been researching herbal remedies for gout. I thought she had forgotten all about that. She says black cherries have something in them that helps maintain healthy levels of uric acid. She tells me to get a cherry supplement and take it every day. I say I will, because why not? Seems better than the drug company chemicals I'd have to take if I went to the doctor. I googled and found a site that has various herbal remedies and seems safe and genuine, and has free fast shipping. So I buy some while I'm still in the bath.

I'll have to work from home the next couple of days now as the delivery couriers will be coming to the house. I have anxiety about couriers, I can't take a shit on days when I'm expecting a delivery because the second I sit down on the toilet is when they drive up my lane. Guaranteed every time. Delivery shit syndrome. Well known phenomena.

It's windier than the staff room at the Heinz factory outside today. It howls through the gaps in the walls, the cool air brings a shiver even while I'm in the water. The choice now is top up with more hot water, or get out and do something productive. I don't fancy going for a walk in the wind. Messes up my hair. I don't want to touch the work laptop. I suppose I'll go back to the shed once more, because I might not get another chance to play with the mystery box again for a while.

I'm in a bed, curtains pulled all the way around, hospital curtains. I'm desperate to take a shit but they told me I couldn't move my leg, so I can't get up. I'm a patient, dozy, faded, tired and high on whatever drugs they have pumped into me. I fell off my motorbike, my knee fought with the road and lost.

There's a lot of whaling and moaning coming from someone on the other side of the curtains, I don't know what is going on, but it doesn't sound good. I haven't been able to shit for the whole week I've been in here, but now I have no choice.

"Nurse!"

I yell uncomfortably, no one comes. I try to read the Viz Magazine Dad brought me, but I can't concentrate because of the bowel pressure.

I was going home from work, a late shift in the restaurant. Finished up around eleven pm, collected my share of the tip pot and got on the bike to go home. Wasn't gone very far and then I don't know what happened, I think I blacked out, hit the kerb and tipped over on the bike. Next thing I can remember is trying to stand up and pick the bike up. I spent a long time fixing it up with Dad, one of the indicator stems we fitted is snapped off and lying on the road, lifeless. Someone stopped and called an ambulance. I said I was fine, just needed to get back on the bike. They told me to look at my knee, I did, then I fell back down. A black hole half way down my trousers and a sudden shock of pain. After that, an oxygen mask in an ambulance. I asked the medic to call my parents, tried to give him the phone number, but I couldn't speak properly, and it took a few tries to get the numbers out. I think people came to visit me, here in the hospital, but I don't know if I could converse with them, I don't remember who they were, maybe someone from work? Everything is a bit of a hazy blur. Only yesterday did I learn I've been here a week. Now I want to get the hell out and go home.

"Nurse!"

I don't want to shit the bed. I understand they are busy

with someone who is obviously in a lot of pain, but my fucking arse is going to explode.

A male nurse sticks his head through my curtain.

"Sorry, we are a bit busy right now."

"I need a bedpan!" I guess the urgency must have reflected on my face because he looked annoyed at first but then sniggered and went away again. He returns after a minute with a shit bowl and a piss jug that I awkwardly use. The relief! It was no fun trying to balance and also aim and then wipe. Not doing that again! I need to be able to walk to the bogs.

Eventually, the noise from outside subsides, and they open the curtains up, and the nurse takes away the effluent of a weeks' backup.

When I said I wanted a bike for my sixteenth birthday, Dad got me something that was two wheels with a lump of metal between them and a seat on top. It was a hundred quid, and I paid for fifty of it. The engine didn't run, it didn't have any electrical circuits working, the brakes were worn out. It wasn't just a bike, it was a project. We took it apart, bit by bit, over weeks, he showed me everything from the piston to the spark plug, the suspension and the brakes. We took the cylinder block to get over-bored and skimmed, and then got a piston to fit. He explained how to gently tighten the spark plug so as not to strip the thread of the aluminium block. We bought a Haynes manual, and went through every step. We rewired the entire lighting system, bought a new battery. We fitted a new exhaust too, so it didn't sound like a machine gun firing as I rode around. In the end, I painted over the light blue with red spray and then black hammer finish over the top. It looked cool. It ran smoothly, all the lights and brakes worked flawlessly. The gearbox was always a little crunchy, but I got used to it. I knew everything that there was to know about that bike, because Dad taught me. Then I went and wrecked it by falling asleep on the way home.

What I wanted when I was sixteen was a bike, so I could go anywhere I wanted, when I wanted, and not have to ask for a lift. I didn't want to spend weeks covered in oil. But now I realise why it was so important. Dad passed on his knowledge to me, made me understand what I was using, so when it stopped working, I would be able to fix it. I've taken the same deep interest in everything I touch since then. From computers to cooking. I'm not content to know enough to get by, I need to understand everything about it and know how it works.

Chapter Twenty-Five

MONDAY 17TH SEPTEMBER

I couldn't sleep for hours last night, I forced myself to go to bed at a reasonable hour, but I just lay there tossing and turning, well, not actually tossing… But turning for sure. I tried to read, but the words wouldn't soak in. I tried playing ambient music, it only woke me more. My head filled with thoughts, randomly firing on an infinite loop, things I have to do for work, all the memories the box has brought me, how I'll see Rachel very soon and all the things we can do together. What will happen when she has to go back again? After that, will I ever see her again? I still don't have any idea where this is going. I feel like she is just letting things happen naturally and not worrying about it, but my brain needs a closing bracket on that sub-routine or every time it runs that code it returns an error.

In the end, I got up and scrolled Twitter, messaged Rachel for a bit, watched DVDs, made a sandwich, pissed five times, and oiled the squeaky lock on my bathroom door that had been bugging me for months. By four am I was so scared I would oversleep through my alarms that I thought I'd try and stay awake. Then I woke up at eight am, my throat sore, my bladder full. I'd give away next week's lottery numbers if I could have a week of proper restful sleep, and not have constant ridiculous thoughts spiralling around in my head.

I put the coffee machine on and fired up the work laptop. Now I'm churning through all the shit-mails that came in since I last checked.

Eoghan should be working on finishing the FutureCloud build today, but he's showing offline. I'll try him again in a while.

I got dressed in a hurry this morning in case a delivery came to the door, and then sat on the toilet nervously listening for a van driving up the road. Nothing happened except my stress level went up a notch.

I pop out a tweet to mark the occasion.

Amazon deliveries… the only reason to get dressed in the morning.

Sean has put a meeting on my calendar for ten am, a general catch-up on FutureCloud status. If I don't hear from Eoghan before then, I'll have to bluff it with what I already know. The test hardware has mostly arrived, the base system is work-in-progress of being built. The tech-sheet is done, and I'm focused entirely on this for the next couple of weeks at least. Rachel is due to land in the country in about fifty hours, and she knows exactly how it is all meant to go together. I've done all my due diligence, let's see if the salespeople have done anything at all since we last spoke.

I put on a second pot of coffee before the meeting starts. I'm going to need all the caffeine in the world to stay awake, with barely any sleep and a boring phone conference.

. . .

Sean opens up the call on time, but then we wait the customary seven minutes for everyone else to join and get settled and mute. I don't know a lot of people on these calls, they are from other departments who seem to show up when there's a sniff of money. You never hear from these type of people again after the deal is done.

I haven't been able to contact Eoghan, I have to assume the fecker is on a Monday sick-day. He better be actually dying, or in the hospital with no limbs, or have been abducted by aliens. I made the importance of getting this stuff done on time super clear.

"Hey Terry, can you give the team an update on progress from your side?"

"Yeah, sure." I elaborate the details, explain the next steps, run through all the things that could go wrong, and how I've pre-empted them. Sean seems happy, some other people on the call asked some stupid questions. Of course, they weren't listening before so I have to repeat myself. I ask them how they are doing with the product purchases, the actual five hundred units that we'll be configuring. Apparently they haven't started that yet. How surprising! Sean got quite annoyed when he heard that, he asked for a reason, but nothing tangible came in the reply. Basically, they didn't pull their fingers out of their arses for long enough to actually place the orders. If they don't get that done today, then I don't see how we'll have all the units available in time. All the work we've done to get ready will be a massive waste of time in that case. Sean can chase that up. I have enough to do already.

I'm not saying I never fuck anything up, but I do at least try and get things done on time when there is a good reason.

Sean announces he'll be coming over to Ireland for the final build. Don't know what he hopes to achieve by coming over, aside from a free holiday in Ireland, with all expenses paid, but whatever. He asks me which hotel Rachel is staying at, I tell him on the call I don't know, up to her. I don't need random people knowing all my personal information. I'll email him later. He doesn't need to stay in the same place anyway. What would the point of that be? I think he's just trying to wind me up. My delivery comes during the call. I muted my headset and rushed to the door. It's the Amazon parcel with Rachel's hair straightener thingy. I bring the box back to my desk and put my headset back on, they are all still yakking away, and nobody seems to have noticed I wasn't around for a couple of minutes.

Sean finishes up the call and asks everyone to join a followup call this afternoon and another tomorrow morning, probably the only way to get people to do their jobs.

I try and contact Eoghan again, but no response. I can't do much more work now without that test unit fully functional. I don't even know how far he got with it, or what is left to do. Do I go into the office and see if there's anything obvious I can do to progress it? Or do I forget it for now? I think I'll ignore it because I'm not officially meant to be messing with the hardware. What if I break something? It would be a can of worms to sort out. I'll go in tomorrow, if there's still no progress and I can't find Eoghan, I'll go to his manager and get someone else assigned to help. #executiveDecision.

Must be breakfast time, I make my customary eggs on toast and throw in a slice of bacon for the craic. If you can't live a little on a Monday what's the point in it all?

After breakfast, I go back to my desk, but, since I have no

way to progress the situation, despite the urgency, I may as well sneak off for a quick romp around in history.

There's a gap on the left side of the dial. The 80s are unexplored so far. I'm not too keen on visiting my childhood though, it feels too far away, too disconnected and distant from my life now. I'll give it a go though. I turn the dial back almost all the way, and dive in.

Darkness, warmth, safety. I'm sad, hiding, no one can see me be upset. Dad is calling me, but I'm not going to come out. I peek out under the tablecloth, the track is still there, Scalextric, all around the room and out into the hall, we spent all day making it, now Dad said we have to pack it up because it's in the way. I wanted to race again.

"Terry. One more go then."

I look out from under the table. Dad has the WD-40 can and the Scalextrix controllers and a jar of gherkins. I love gherkins.

I crawl out, and we have another race.

A tiny '80' appears on the left of the dial. The smell of WD-40 always reminds me of Scalextrix even now. I could murder a gherkin, but I don't think I have any. I turn the Y dial a notch forward and go again.

Space Invaders fill the TV screen. I'm clutching a joystick and blasting them out of the sky. No one will beat my high score!

Time, For a Change

Mum is making dinner, so I have to go soon, but I need to clear this screen first.

A helium balloon floats around the room. I've stuck a lump of plasticine on the string, so it doesn't go too high. Dad measures some wood. He's making an arch instead of a door. I had to hold the end of the tape for him earlier, and he'll probably do the saw again soon. I don't like the sound it makes, but I hold the end of the wood sometimes. It makes my hands feel tingly.

"Terry, food's ready."

"In a minute, Mum!"

I blast the motherships and the last aliens, and check my score. Yes! Beat my record!

We had many different computers when I was a kid, but I loved the Vic20 the most. It had big cartridges that plugged in the back, and games would load immediately. I was killer at Space Invaders. Dad had a computer shop back then, he'd bring home whatever was new and fun, and I'd always have a play with them hooked up to the tiny living room TV. They sold telephones too, and Dad would tell stories of 'phreaking' and round-the-world phone calls using secret exchange codes, so it didn't cost anything. That was 1981. I wind forward a few notches on the Y dial again.

"Forty-Two!"

"What?"

"Forty-Two! That's the ultimate answer!"

"Oh, yes it is!"

I was reading until midnight last night, and then I woke up early and picked up the book again. It's so funny! I want to write a book like this when I grow up! Dad said he'd get me a typewriter so I can start writing now. He said my story about the strange hotel was funny, but I knew the jokes were a bit naff. I think I'll get a job with computers and then I'll write stories about them. It'll be super-cool.

I want to get all the other books in the trilogy. There are four books now, so it isn't a trilogy anymore, but that's why it's funny. Dad said there's a new video game of the book too, so I want to get that, but we don't have the right computer yet. He said 'don't panic' though, we'll probably get it soon!

I still love those stories today. Some people have based their entire business and culture around them. It was truly a sad day when I heard that Douglas Adams had passed away. I never did get around to writing the books though. I guess there is still time…

I should go and see if anything is going on at work and maybe Eoghan has woken from his weekend hibernation? But there are just a few more junk-mails that I immediately delete and a short email from Rachel. She's at work early because she's finishing up all the prep before she comes over here. She'll be leaving tomorrow morning from her house and here in Ireland the next day! I'm excited, nervous and overall, horny. While I remember it, I should put the bottle of perfume I got for her in my suitcase, but I take a sniff of it first, it makes me shiver, that's how you know it's the good stuff.

I make a bowl of soup and some cheese on toast for lunch and then take a wander down my lane. The weather isn't too bad, just a bit of drizzle which spots up the glasses. I should get some contact lenses. It seems like it is much easier to blink than it is to wipe the rain from spectacles.

Sean's afternoon status call was only five minutes long, the salespeople finally ordered everything they needed to, and we should get delivery of all five hundred units to be processed about two weeks from now. Then we have about one week to get everything done before they have to go back out all complete and configured. The schedule is very tight, we would ordinarily allocate much longer for this type of work, but what can you do? That's all we needed to hear for today. I logged off after that since there's still no sign of Eoghan.

I'd love to take a nap now, but if I do that I'll probably just mess up my sleep schedule once again. Best to stay awake and go to bed at a reasonable hour. May as well go back for another spin through the 80s while I wait for Rachel to finish up at her work.

I'm walking along a tree-lined avenue, big houses, set back from the road. My digital watch says 13:05, 16/09/88. I just started a new school, I don't know anyone and don't want to. The teachers are smarmy bastards, the other kids are vicious and aggressive. Intelligence seems to be a punishable offence here.

I'm walking down to the town for lunch. There's a baker that has the softest iced-buns in the universe. I can afford three of them and a can of drink. The kids in my old school would tell me how unhealthy that is, and I should be eating dark brown bread that tastes like wood or something, but no, thanks. They are probably doing Eurythmy right now, prancing around with copper rods, pink smocks and ballet shoes. I don't know which fate is worse.

I've already been down to the town once this morning. Home Economics apparently means going to Co-Op and doing the teachers shopping for her, at least if you are a boy. I like cooking, but she doesn't think boys should be in the kitchen. I told her Marco Pierre White has two Michelin stars, she sent me to buy washing powder. In my old school, boys and girls did the same things, because, why wouldn't they?

This uniform is uncomfortable and ugly too, we didn't have uniforms in my old school. What makes it worse is that they let the kids vote on the colours the shirt and trousers should be this year and they chose blue and cream. I voted black and black, but here I am wearing these vile coloured clothes.

Yesterday was a gym day, so I stayed at home, I'm not interested in cavorting around naked with these imbeciles in the showers after. I don't see the point in going to this school anyway. They are teaching subjects I covered last year, and the other kids call me a smart-arse if I tell them the answers. I said it wasn't my fault they were all fuckwits and got detention. Dad said I 'don't suffer fools' and to ignore them. He said I could get out in two years and then I could do whatever I like.

'Whatever I like' turned out to be a bit of a challenge. I failed almost every exam because I had terrible hay-fever that summer. I could barely read the paper let alone concentrate on answering the questions. All I learned from that experience was holding in a sneeze for too long makes me sweat and burn up and almost pass out. So getting into a college wasn't easy. Then they asked me at the college why I didn't study computer science instead of catering, I told them I already knew more about computers than the teachers did. Maybe an exaggeration but that's how I felt.

I think I've had enough of the 80s, so I dial the Y to the other side. There's a gap between '13 and the maximum, let's see what happens.

I've had junk cars my whole life, but this one takes the star prize. It's spent more time in the garage than on the road, and I'm sure it costs me more than a new car would in maintenance alone. This is the last straw, stranded in the middle of nowhere, pissing rain, the engine just stopped and won't start back up. I don't know why and honestly, I don't care. The battery is getting low now too, so I called the AA. I'm waiting about an hour so far, and I've worked out how I can scrape together a deposit, and I'm fucking buying a new car. New-new. Not another junk heap from some fella who swears it's grand. I want a five-year warranty, I want new car smell, I want clean seats that don't have odd and questionable stains on them. And I want to get in it every morning and know it will get me where I'm going, safely and efficiently. I can't keep dumping money into shit-mobiles.

This is the first time I've used the AA, because Dad would always come and tow me home before. No matter how far away I was, he never complained, I think he enjoyed being the hero. Not this time though. I can't rely on Dad anymore… If this were another decade we'd have stripped down the engine and figured out what went wrong, and then fixed it, it would have been a fun weekend in the garage. But times have changed. I don't have time to do that anymore, and I can't live or work without a functioning vehicle. No public transport meets my needs here.

So, I sit here in the dim evening light, watching the rain streak down the windows, listening to the tick of the hazard lights and the occasional whoosh of a car passing by. I think about all the times Dad had car troubles, money troubles, house troubles, health troubles. All the constant stream of problems that he just batted out of the way and carried on through. He always had a solution and a plan, he always knew what to do and how to make everyone around him feel okay about the situation, even when he was in the hospital, he had a plan, and everything would be fine.

It wasn't fine though. It wasn't fucking fine at all.

Dad was invincible, a super-hero, a genius and the planet-sized rock that everything balanced on. But he died and left us, and I don't think I will ever get over it. I don't know how to function now. I am not like he was, and I don't have a plan for this.

Through blurry eyes and blurry windows, I see the flashing orange of a tow truck pull up behind me, and I'm saved. Dump the car in a fucking ditch for all I care. Take me home.

That's how I come to have a 'fancy car' as Rachel put it. She probably thinks I always had a nice car, but this is the first time. I am not a rich man, so I can only afford the best. Actually, I can barely afford it, but it hasn't let me down once so far, and I think it costs less per month than the previous heap of shit. She'll get to see it in person very soon. I haven't 'christened' it yet… Maybe we can have some fun?

Chapter Twenty-Six

TUESDAY 18TH SEPTEMBER

More out of panic, than logic, I headed into the office early today. I needed to make sure that Eoghan was around and he gets the FutureCloud system finally built and working. He showed up at nine am, all jolly and bright as a button, well, as much as he ever is jolly and bright. No hint of remorse for his lack of appearance yesterday. I didn't ask where he was, and he didn't tell. I sat with him in the lab all morning and told him he 'ain't going nowhere till this lump of metal is singing the FutureCloud song.'

It got done, finally. He didn't understand why I was worried. I thought it was clear and evident that this was a big deal with a very tight timeline, but apparently not. He can start on the configuration scripting now, taking my tech-sheet, so lovingly and elegantly crafted, and turning it into all the various scripts and code to automate the set-up. With a good wind behind us, that should take a week and a half, but that almost never happens, unless the task is straightforward and been done before many times.

. . .

It was celery surprise for lunch today in the canteen. A surprise because there wasn't any celery at all in the risotto. I was going to say something sarcastic to the chef, but then I remembered, never piss off the people who make your food. I'm sure the celery will be back soon in a series of sequels — The Celery Strikes Back, Return of the Celery, The last Celery, etc.

Rachel sends me a message, she's on her way to the airport. She's nervous and panicked. Last night I had to go through the same conversation again about how to get through the airport, what to do at each stage, what to expect when the plane takes off. She heard it all before, but I think she just needed another round of reassurance.

Hopefully she'll be fine once she's bored to sleep on the plane. I told her it would be grand, and to message me when she gets to Chicago.

I left Eoghan to do his thing after lunch and went back to deleting emails. I also sent Sean an update on the test system. I forgot to join his status call this morning.

I also forgot to ask Eoghan if he completed all the DeltaWave stuff, I check in the database and it's all showing complete. I don't want to start another load of work on that now, but ideally, they would test and validate all the new work we did. I let Judith know it's good to go and she can organise a test if she wants.

[14:17] O'Brien, Ted:
Well Terry, what's the story?

[14:17] Ward, Terry B:
Hey Ted.
I'm importing a young woman from America.

[14:18] O'Brien, Ted:
Sounds fun.

[14:18] Ward, Terry B:
Making her do my job for me.
Probably taking her out for dinner.
You know, the usual.

[14:20] O'Brien, Ted:
Mmm, food.

[14:21] Ward, Terry B:
That reminds me, I should look up some fancy places to eat.
Maybe not though, she might prefer something simple.

[14:21] O'Brien, Ted:
Eggs on toast?

[14:22] Ward, Terry B:
Definitely that, yeah.

I don't know any restaurants in the city. I get takeaway usually and go home. There'd be no point in going to a posh restaurant on my own here. So I do what I always do and look it up on my phone. There's an abundance of places to eat, some within walking distance and some that we'd need to drive to. The hotel has a fancy restaurant as well, and a load of places that will deliver to our room. We won't starve, but I don't know who is going to pay for it all.

There's a FutureCloud customer call later this afternoon, Rachel won't be on it of course as she's travelling to Chicago, but I should put in an appearance since we are going to be the spotlight focus of events for the next while. I decide to go home first, and I want to get the car washed and cleaned out on the way home. I know I'm going over the top here, trying to make a good impression, but the car needs a clean anyway.

I got home just in time for the call, but my car is nice and shiny now. I even got an air freshener scent for inside the car that smells like cherries. Which reminds me to check where my delivery of cherry herbal supplements is. I hope they didn't try and deliver it earlier today. I forgot all about it when I left this morning.

I boot up the laptop and join the call, and hear Sean's familiar voice talking with Pete. They are laughing about something I missed. We wait for everyone to join and then Sean starts his list of topics. I'm number one.

"Hi, Terry, can you give an update on progress please?"

"Sure."

I don't often get to be the bearer of good news, but today I have that privilege. The test system is built, the tech-sheet is done and ready, Eoghan has started work on the scripting, we are looking good all around. More importantly, their very talented engineer is heading towards a mattress not far from my current location. I kept that part to myself. Pete seems happy, Sean is delighted. So far so good. But I don't want them all to 'come in their pants' just yet, so I add some salt to the sugar and tell them this is just the beginning and we still have a tremendous amount of work to do. But I don't think they heard those words.

The call drifts off into territory unknown to me. Finance, credit limits, tax and regulatory details for various European countries. Boring sales stuff. I pull out my phone and track my order of cherry supplements, and note that it landed at Shannon today and should be here tomorrow. Hopefully, before I have to go to Shannon myself and pick up Rachel. After the call, I log off and raid the fridge for dinner.

I spent a lot of time packing things in bags, unpacking them again and finally giving up and bringing just about everything I could ever possibly need. Tea and coffee included. My technology bag was even more complicated. I deliberated for a long time over how many laptops to bring. I need the work one, obviously, but I don't do any personal things on that, so I need my personal laptop too. I know Rachel is going to mock me for the amount of stuff I'm taking to a hotel, that isn't very far from my house. But I like to be prepared. What if I need something? It would be a ninety minute round trip to come back to my house and get it. I'm overthinking this. It will be fine.

Rachel sends me a message from half way to Chicago. They stopped for refreshments. All is well, but she's going to call when she gets to the airport, and I have to talk her through it all again. I think I will lie down for a while before she calls. I need to catch up on some sleep, and I bet I won't get much tomorrow night.

I set four alarms on my phone and set the volume to maximum. I was going to set an old alarm clock too, but the time on it is wrong, and the interface to change the time is so complicated and unintuitive, it's easier to wait until midnight and then switch it on, than try and mess with the tiny buttons. It was okay anyway, the alarm woke me up, but I felt like a herd of Camels had stampeded all over me, and then taken a shit in my mouth. I made a mug of strong tea, to try and feel like a human again. Rachel called a little while after. They arrived at the airport, she said goodbye to her Mom, and then I navigated her to the check-in desk from memory, then to security, then she had to hang up. She called back a few minutes later. All fine. I talked her through to the gate with no problem, but she was very nervous the whole time. Too many people, too many stimuli, too convoluted and confusing. Airports have made themselves into a realm of unnecessary complication of their own volition. I'm sure it doesn't need to be that way? It's just a bus station with buses that happen to fly in the sky.

She's waiting at her gate, and I'm wide awake. Now I think about it, this plan to take a nap hasn't worked out. How the bollocks am I going to get back to sleep later? I'm waiting for her to board and take-off first. I'm tracking her flight with an app on my phone.

Outside is dark, no stars, no moon, perfect darkness. I light the way to the shed with my flashlight, but I stand still for a minute and turn the light off. Just bathing in the blackness and silence. There's an occasional distant shimmer of a car going along a road, a breath of wind shivering a tree. I start to hear my own breathing, heart thumping, the creak of my shoes. I flick the light back on and go over to the shed. It's getting chilly now, I should have brought a coat, but it won't matter once I travel to the past. This may be the last chance I get to journey with the box for a while, I still don't know if I should show it to Rachel, I don't know how she'll react. Perhaps I'm paranoid, but the old saying rings in my ears: it isn't paranoia if everyone really is out to get you…

I open up the lid of the box, the heady tang of ozone courses over me, invigorating, inexplicable. The brass cone still spins with a quiet whir, and a gentle tick. The Y knob is still on 2015, I turn it back about ten years, the only other gap in the years I've explored these last few weeks.

I'm holding the end of a sheet of wood, Dad feeds it through the saw-bench, the noise is unbearable, sawdust sprays in my face, I can't let go though, the cut would get messed up. I try to blow dust out of my nose and squint my eyes. The wood glides along, smooth and slow, the spinning blade barely noticing the wood fed into its brutal teeth. The shudder of the end of the cut means I can open my eyes again. Dad turns off the saw and the pressure of sound releases against my ears.

"Nice cut." Dad runs his finger down the edge we just made. I take the spare and put it on the pile of 'odds and sods' then brush away the saw-dust that is all over my face and hair.

"Now to test the new jig!" We take the cut wood and move to the router table, Dad has already rigged it up, with a

cutter barely protruding from underneath, he puts the wood into a perspex jig which slides along grooves in the table. It clamps in, and when slid, will run the edge gently past the spinning bit. It's the bit that I broke, it's the bit that was used to make the mysterious box.

I don't have to hold the wood now, so I stand back while Dad switches on the router and quickly glides the wood along, another spray of dust spills out onto the floor behind the table, nowhere near me this time. Dad turns off the machine and takes out the sheet, inspecting the edge.

"Lovely grub!"

I go over and look, and the edge is smooth, clean cut, still hot from the cutter.

"Nice! I might make some shelves with that one."

Dad pours a coffee from his flask, and knocks out his pipe on the edge of the saw-bench. The black ash falls onto the clean sawdust on the floor. Then he fills the pipe from a packet of sweet smelling tobacco and lights it up, I sip from a bottle of water.

"Thought you gave up the pipe?"

"I did. Then I changed my mind."

There are many more cuts and bevels to make yet, so we go back to the saw bench and Dad's cutting plan and slice up the rest of the sheet. My ears are ringing, I'm covered in dust, but it doesn't matter. It's fun to make things in the workshop. Mum is making dinner later. Roast chicken with all the trimmings.

I stand up and look at the mysterious box in front of me, the bevelled edges, the smooth, clean finish, the wood is dirty now, but there's no doubt, this box is what we made that day.

Chapter Twenty-Seven

WEDNESDAY 19TH SEPTEMBER

The last thing I remember from last night is watching Rachel's flight depart on my app, she sent a message that she had boarded, and was in a window seat over the wing and was 'freaking out'. I told her again it will be okay, this happens a million times a day, it's just the same as getting on a train or something. She didn't seem to be convinced, but what else can I do? I slept through my alarms this morning, woke up an hour late, I panicked for a moment and ran around the house, getting dressed, putting on a coffee pot, switching on the laptop, then I realised it doesn't matter too much today. Rachel's flight to Shannon lands around one pm, I have plenty of time to meet that. She messaged me that she landed at Heathrow already, she said the flight was okay, she slept most of it. I'm glad it went well and she calmed down. One more step and she'll be here.

As I sit down on the porcelain throne and make a morning download, I remember the box journey from last night. I helped Dad make that wooden box? Why didn't I remember that? There's a manufacturer stamp in red ink on one of the sides, we cut that same exact piece in 2005. There's no doubt that the box on my bench is the product of those woodcuts we made.

But the contraption inside? I don't know how it even works! So I doubt I had anything to do with making that, Dad must have worked on it afterwards.

I finish my ablutions and pour my coffee, and check work stuff. There are no calls today thankfully, and Eoghan is showing online. Hopefully, he's busy with the FutureCloud coding and setup. I still didn't mention to him that the engineer who is arriving today from Ohio is a pretty young girl. It shouldn't matter, but I know it will. He'll be nervous, twitchy, he won't voice his opinions if he thinks something is being done wrong. He'll have to get over it. I'll be there too, so he can talk to me. He usually has no problem with telling me I'm wrong!

There's nothing else immediately important going on, so I delete all the spam that's accrued in my mailbox and think about some breakfast. As today is a special occasion, I mark the event with a special meal, eggs, bacon, beans and sausages, all on toast, and a big mug of strong tea. The breakfast of superstars!

My delivery of cherry supplements arrives, and I sniff at the little tablets cautiously. They smell like grass or something, very earthy, not as I expected. I shrug and take two of them and pop the bottle in my tech bag.

I notice my suitcase, ready to load into the car. It weighs a ton. I'm embarrassed by it now; there's way too much in it, not even counting my laptop bag which is stuffed to bulging, even before the two laptops are in it, I open the big suitcase up and take everything out again. Only putting back absolute essentials and dumping the rest in a pile on the windowsill. If I need it, I'll have to come back and get it. Stupid shit like this shouldn't matter, but my brain just can't leave it alone. Minor details are what make up a big picture. Like the FutureCloud tech-sheet, pages and pages of tiny details, that form a whole working system at the end. I almost forgot the hair straightener I got for Rachel, I get it from the office and pop that in the case too, and then take it out to the car, ready to go, now it is done and out of reach. I can't add to it. I leave the bag of tech as it is; I need all that stuff.

I tidy around the house, clean the kitchen, load the dishwasher, throw out all the things that are past the use-by-date from the fridge and pour bleach down the toilet.I even vacuum around the living room again. I get in the car and head to Shannon airport. Nervous and excited with anticipation.

There isn't much to do at Shannon, I pace up and down the length of the arrivals hall, at least I'll clock up some steps on my exercise tracker app. My phone buzzes in my pocket, she's landed. She's here, just a short distance away, but still customs and baggage claim to go before she walks through the door into my life again. I feel a pulse of adrenaline course through my veins, a gurgle in my stomach. Perhaps I shouldn't have had that big breakfast? I pace up and down some more, stopping in the little shop, and get a pack of indigestion antacids.

People start to emerge from the arrivals door, so I walk over. There's a couple of other people waiting, but it isn't busy. I try and stand in a manner that looks cool, but I'm writhing and tortured, I want this moment over with so I can relax. The faces coming through the door look tired, happy, bewildered, some business people come through amidst an animated and loud conversation, direct and to the point, they head straight to the car hire desk without looking around. An old couple stop right outside the door, blocking the exit while they gape around, discombobulated, as if let out of a dark dungeon after twenty years, rubbing their eyes - so this is Ireland? No, it's the fucking airport! Get out of the way!

Then she appears, slow motion, she sees me and smiles, I wave like a kid watching a Disney parade, my heart thuds in my chest and my guts decide this is the best moment to let out a gruesome fart that would stun a troop of Marines returning from war. I quickly walk away from the almost visible cloud of noxious gasses, and throw my arms around Rachel, sweeping her up off the ground and burying my face in her chest.

"Wow, someone is pleased to see me!" I put her down and stand back so I can focus.

"Hey." I try to act cool, but I guess that illusion has already been broken.

She's wearing black leggings, a green knitted sweater and

a black leather jacket on top, she's pulling her new suitcase and carrying a big purse.

From Shannon to the hotel is only about thirty minutes drive. I show Rachel the points of interest along the way, like Bunratty castle and a ruined tower by the road. I tell her that further back along this road, towards where my house is, the route had to be changed when it was being built because of a faery tree that the builders didn't want to disturb, for fear of upsetting the 'little folks' and never getting a good nights sleep again. Maybe I accidentally disturbed a faery tree somewhere, and now I'm cursed with the same affliction? I doubt it, my garden is quite wild and free to grow however it likes. There could be whole tribes of faery folk out there, and I'd never know.

The hotel is posh, acres of polished floor in the reception area and an epic stairway up to a balcony. There's art all over the walls, and things that I can't tell if they are art or furniture. We check in and Rachel seems subdued as we stand at the reception desk. It's her room really, but she seems happy that I'm doing all the talking. She's probably tired from the travel. I ask if she wants to get a drink or food or anything, before we go up to the room but she said she's fine.

The suite is impressive, huge and opulent. Almost embarrassingly too much. Rachel dumps her bag down and takes off her jacket, flops down on the bed. I'm reminded of a similar scene not so long ago in Ohio, I dump my bag and flop down on the other side, and turn over towards her.

"Hey."

"Hey." She laughs, and we kiss and start to fumble around like teenagers, finally left alone together.

"I need a shower. The flight was hot and sticky."

"Oh, yeah I know, okay."

Rachel gets up and digs around in her suitcase, finds a bag of stuff and goes to the bathroom.

"Woah, dude this is fancy."

"Yeah, it should be for the money it's costing your company!"

The shower comes on, and clothes fly out of the bathroom doorway and land in a heap outside.

"You coming or not? These titties and ass ain't gonna wash themselves you know!"

I don't need asking twice, so I jump off the bed, I pause though, do I need my shower kit? Nope, jump in and enjoy the ride!

The shower is big enough for two to stand under at the same time, without the usual situation, where one person is pressed up against a wall getting cold. There are also coloured lights that come on, shining through the water, with a variety of spray formations and patterns. They certainly had shower fun in mind when they designed this. I approve, this is well worth the money that FutureCloud are stumping up. I pay particular attention to making sure Rachel is thoroughly soaped and washed all over, and she helps me scrub my back and front. Good job we were in the shower because things got pretty dirty there for a minute! We get out and move to the bed, remembering to pull the curtains first, and I open the door a crack to slip the 'do not disturb' sign on the doorknob while holding a towel around me. I take it off and set it down on the bed, and then lie on it, so we don't have to sleep in a damp patch later. Rachel gets on top of me, leaning over to kiss me, and I reach around and grab her arse and pull her down onto me.

I'm exhausted, but relaxed after our epic frolic. We lay entangled for a long time until I got my energy back, and things started to rise again from the ashes. She laughed and said later maybe, and got up and grabbed my T-shirt from the floor and put it on. It's like a short dress on her, she looks very cute. I get up and find a pair of clean underwear and another T-shirt and sit back down on the bed.

"Are you hungry?"

"Yeah, a bit."

"Oh, shit." I suddenly remember the reason either of us is in this expensive hotel room.

"I was meant to go to work today!" I realise there's no way that will happen now, but I haven't even checked mail or phone for hours now. Fuck it. Whatever is going on can wait a day.

"Screw it, dude. It can wait."

"Yeah. What do you want to eat?"

We settle on getting a pizza delivered because neither of us can be bothered to get dressed and go out. I do put on a pair of jeans though, because I wouldn't want to get an eyeful of hairy legs when I brought pizza to someone's room. Although thinking back to my days in catering, if it were me delivering to a hotel room, I'd expect to see some 'crazy shit'. Still, no one needs to see my shit, and I prefer to be modest.

"Hey, you got that hair straightener?"

"Oh, yeah." I pull it out of the suitcase and hand it over. She looks happy and goes off to the desk with the mirror and unpacks it.

"You guys have different power here?" She looks incredulous at the plug.

"Different voltage, two-thirty instead of one-ten."

"I can't take this home and use it?"

"No, I don't think so."

"Weird."

She swipes it through her hair and looks pleased with the result. I thought she looked good all ruffled up with sex-hair, but this is good too. When she reaches up above her head with the straightener, the shirt rides up, and I get a delicious glimpse of her naked arse.

"What about my laptop?"

"Well, electronics like that are designed to have worldwide transformers in them. So phone and laptop chargers, stuff like that, will work anywhere if you can plug it in."

"Are you checking out my butt?" she looks at me in mock shock via the mirror.

"Yeah." I laugh, she turns around and hoists up the shirt and shows me the whole picture for a second.

"Good!"

There's a knock on the door, the pizza has arrived. She dives down behind the bed, hiding.

Rachel sits cross-legged on the bed munching her pizza, still only wearing my shirt, provocative in her innocence.

"Did you let your mom know you got here okay?"

"Oh shit, I guess I should call."

I've already checked the internet speed here, of course, and the WiFi is decent. She plugs in her headphones, and calls her mom back in Ohio, free. Things like this are incredible to me, because not long ago this type of long distance call would have cost a fortune, and been terrible audio quality. Now she can idly call, and not even think about it. 'HiFi on the WiFi!' It shouldn't be weird to me, I spend a tremendous amount of time on global conference calls, but that feels like work to me, with a significant corporate infrastructure behind it, and cost no object, whereas this is only Rachel and her phone.

I don't know if her mom is aware of my presence, or my age, or anything about me, so I keep quiet and move to the desk where my laptop is.

"Hey."
"I'm in Ireland."
"Yeah, it was okay, kinda boring."
"Eating pizza in the hotel."
"Yeah, Terry picked me up."
"Okay, well, I'll let you go then."
"Yeah, bye, love you too."

She turns to me and smiles.
"All good."
"Did you tell your mom about me?"
"Yeah, she wanted to know who I'd be with here."
"What did you say?"
"That I met a guy…" She grins seductively.

"Did you mention that guy's age?"

"Yeah."

"Oh, how old is she?"

"Um, I think about forty-five, maybe forty-six, I can't keep track."

"Shit, do you know how old your dad is?"

"He's like a year younger, I think."

"He's my fucking age. I'm the same age as your dad!"

"Yup!"

"Holy shit."

She laughs and comes over to where I'm sitting and puts her arms around me, pressing her bosom into my face.

"It's okay, dude. It's not weird at all. I don't even think about it."

"Well me either usually, but that kinda hit home."

"Mom dates like, eighteen-year-old assholes all the time. She can't say shit."

I look up at her, open-mouthed, she sits down astride my lap and pulls off the shirt.

"You okay now, mister?" I pick her up and carry her over to the bed, pull off my clothes and fall on top of her, feeling her soft, warm skin against mine, breathing in her perfumed scent.

"I am now."

We make slow, soft love for what seems like hours and then lie half asleep on the big comfortable bed, until my bladder forces me up. I get a bottle of water from my suitcase while I'm up, and find the perfume I got for Rachel.

"I got you this." I hand her the bottle.

"Oh, wow, thank you! This is my favourite."

"I know."

"Hey, it's open?"

"Oh, yeah, sorry." She looks at me puzzled.

"I, um, kinda sprayed some on my pillows at home. As a reminder, you know?"

"Oh my God! You are so cute!"

She embraces me again and kisses me hard.

"So, you had any more dreams lately?"

I realise I probably haven't kept her up to date on my box-journeys in the past few days, it slipped my mind. So I tell her about the 'dreams' from the 80s and my childhood, then about the car that broke down, and why I bought the 'fancy car' she rode in today, then I tell her about Dad's workshop, making a wooden box using the power tools Dad so lovingly maintained.

She says these dreams all point to a common theme, memories and experiences I've had through my life. They are trying to tell me something, subconsciously. Perhaps they are telling me to move on, past the mourning, past the loss. She thinks I'm as good at solving problems as Dad was, that he taught me everything he knew, that I'm a good man on my own, and that she loves me and everything will be okay, somehow. I tell her I love her too and we drift into a deep sleep, wrapped together in a mess of limbs, and hotel linen.

Chapter Twenty-Eight

THURSDAY 20TH SEPTEMBER

I woke up super early today. I slept soundly like a rock, but I think it was only about nine pm when we fell asleep. I don't think I've been to bed at nine since I was seven years old! Rachel is probably still a bit jet lagged, so that makes sense. I'm just old and tired. She's still asleep now, I made a pot of coffee in the room and booted up my work laptop. We have to go into the office today anyway. Work is the same as usual, hordes of junk email, a chaser from Sean to see if all is going well, a note from Judith saying she'll order the DeltaWave test units soon, but not to worry since they might have to change their software again anyway, as they found another bug. Seriously? I need to ditch that account. Nothing but trouble.

Rachel stirs in the bed, I pour a coffee for her and bring it over. She sits up, rubs her eyes and takes the cup. The room is still dark, so I switch on a desk lamp, and she blinks and shields her eyes.

"Ahh, the light!" I turn it back off again.

"Wow, I was so tired."

"Travel will do that to ya. Plus the ocean air here."

"We're near the ocean?"

"Well, the Shannon river estuary, but more or less."

"Oh wow. Can we go see it?"

"Sure! I'd love to take you. But we have to go to work today."

"Oh, yeah." She sips at the coffee and smiles.

"Good morning, honey!"

"Good morning, gorgeous!"

She goes to the bathroom, and I find some clean clothes. I'm starving. There's a couple of slices of cold pizza left from last night, but I don't fancy that. I hope the hotel breakfast is good.

Rachel must have fallen down a hole in the bathroom, it feels like she's been gone for hours.

"You alright in there?"

"Fuck off. I gotta make myself look hot for you."

"You're already hot!"

She sticks her middle finger out of the bathroom door.

She comes out, eventually, she looks as gorgeous as ever and still naked. I can't resist a squeeze as she passes by, but she slaps my hand away.

"There's no time for that now!"

"Shame. You want breakfast?"

"Can you get room service? I don't want to eat in a room full of people."

"Oh, yeah, probably." I don't think I have ever had room service before in my life, we have a little table in the suite, so I imagine it is acceptable. Fuck knows how much it will cost, but too bad. I have to keep reminding myself that this is all paid for and the deal we are enabling is worth millions. Our hotel and food is a tiny drop in the Atlantic ocean.

I can't find anything on the hotel website about room service so, in the end, I pick up the phone on the desk and call reception. I probably should have thought of that first, but who makes phone calls anymore? I was hoping I could order it online. Reception tells me food will arrive shortly, I got full Irish and Rachel just wanted oatmeal, I think that means porridge?

When the knock on the door comes, Rachel is still semi-naked, so far she's only managed to choose a bra and knickers from her suitcase. She runs and hides in the bathroom until the waiter has unloaded all the food from his little cart onto our table. It's a bit over-the-top, there's far too much equipment here for just breakfast. Plates, saucers, various spoons and knives, a toast rack, butter curls, even a vase with a flower. My full breakfast must be photoshopped because it doesn't look real, every detail is too perfect. Rachel puts a shirt on, and we sit down and eat. There's another pot of coffee and freshly squeezed orange juice. Quite a feast!

Maybe tomorrow I'll get the porridge. That looks good too with fresh strawberries and honey all over it.

After breakfast, Rachel goes back to the seemingly laborious task of finding clothes to wear. She takes out a multitude of things from the suitcase and lays them on the bed, and deliberates over the details and pairing of items. I guess this is her equivalent of me fussing over which charge cables and things I needed to bring? In the end, she settles on black jeans and a comfy looking black shirt. She plugs in the hair straightener and then goes to the bathroom again. I pour another coffee from the jug and check email. Nothing since last time, I note that Eoghan is showing online now.

[08:42] Ward, Terry B:
Morning.

[08:43] Williams, Eoghan:
Hey.

[08:43] Ward, Terry B:
I'll be in soon with the FutureCloud engineer.

[08:43] Williams, Eoghan:
I thought that was happening yesterday?

[08:43] Ward, Terry B:
She arrived yesterday, I picked her up at the airport.

[08:43] Williams, Eoghan:
She?

[08:43] Ward, Terry B:
Yup.
Did you shower and shave this month?

[08:44] Williams, Eoghan:
Feck off.

"You ready?" Rachel has been going back and forth from the bathroom to the hair straightener, she complained there's no power socket at the bathroom mirror, I said that's a good thing so people don't die of electrocution when washing their hands. She's now all made up and delicious looking and fragrant.

"Almost." She puts her leather jacket on, and grabs her handbag which looks like it has a laptop in it.

"Ready!"

The journey to the office is only about fifteen minutes even during rush hour. We aren't far away. I have to take Rachel to the main reception, and then the security booth to get her a temporary visitor pass badge, but there's no onerous earthquake procedure, or an internal cavity search or anything like the painful entry process at FutureCloud. We get through quickly, I think the ancient security guard is eager for his morning coffee break, it's nine-thirty after all. We walk over to my desk.

"Well, this is where I sit when I come in here." She looks unimpressed. Her office building is much nicer.

"Cool. Why do you have so many salt sachets?"

"Oh, err, to protect against the slug-people." She looks at me blankly.

"Never mind. I reserved a desk for you opposite." I take her around the other side and set her up with the network port and power. I knew she wouldn't have a power plug adaptor, so I left one ready for her.

"Dude, there's salt sachets on this desk too?"

"Yeah, well, you wouldn't want to be infiltrated by the slug-people either."

"What?"

"I'll explain later. You wanna get a coffee?"

We head to the canteen and pour some revolting brown

liquid into wax-paper cups. Rachel doesn't have any Euro cash, so I pay and give her the receipt for her expenses. She had no idea she could claim back money for stuff like coffee and lunch. Eoghan is lingering at the other end of the canteen, wrestling with a vending machine. We walk down and stand behind him.

"Isn't it a bit early for chocolate?" He jumps and turns around.

"I was trying to get an oat-bar, but it stole my money."

"Did you try thumping it? There's a number to call, did you try that?" There's something about Eoghan that brings out the arsehole in me.

"It's fine, I'll get some cereal instead."

"This is Rachel from FutureCloud by the way, she's their chief engineer. Rachel, this is Eoghan, he's working on the configuration stuff for you."

Eoghan's mouth gapes open, he looks at me to see if I'm joking, and then offers out a hand for Rachel to shake. It's the limpest hand-shake in the history of business, but now they are introduced.

"You busy in a minute?"

"Er, no, I guess."

"Meet us in the lab in about fifteen minutes, and we'll show Rachel our server?"

We go back to our desks and leave Eoghan to get his breakfast.

"I'm sorry."

"What for?"

"Eoghan, he's not used to seeing beautiful women in here." She laughs and blushes a little.

"It's okay, I get this a lot, dudes don't expect women to be working in tech."

"I know, I didn't expect you to be a woman either."

"Oh yeah? When did you figure it out?" She sniggers.

"Shut up! Anyway, Eoghan will be fine. I need to check email and stuff."

"Yeah, me too."

"Okay, then we'll go see the server in the lab."

"Can't wait," she rolls her eyes at the thought.

"Dude, by the way, your coffee tastes like shit."

"Yeah, I know."

I send Sean a quick update on status, delete a load of email, and check if I have any meetings or other pressing business. I don't. This is unprecedented. There's usually always something else to do, even if I don't have any meetings, there are still some stupid questions to answer, or a problem to chase up. I should enjoy the relative peace, and be happy that I can focus on this FutureCloud stuff, but I feel uneasy, like something strange is going on.

"Did you get online okay?" I stand up and peer over the wall.

"Yeah, dude. Nothing interesting, just had some stuff in the factory at home to deal with."

"Did they get someone to replace you?"

"Just one of the factory guys, I showed him what to do real quick."

"You wanna go see the server then?"

"Cool."

We walk over to the lab and find Eoghan fiddling with the latch on the lid of the server.

"What did you break now?"

"Nothing!" He looks insulted.

"Okay, you want to show Rachel all the bits and bobs?"

Eoghan opens the lid up and goes through all the things he's replaced and updated and removed from the base system, then all the add-in cards we bought and plugged in. Rachel gets out her laptop and checks her notes, and says it all looks good, except one card was in the wrong slot. I didn't notice that or see it in the build instructions. I'll have to update my tech-sheet with that detail. We're at an early enough stage that it won't be a problem. But that small thing would have been a massive pain later on, if Rachel hadn't spotted it now. Maybe even a deal breaker, because we may have had to organise a total re-engineering of the scripts and re-fit of all the cards. It sounds like such a minor thing, just plug the card in a different slot, but in the automated factory environment, there are multitudes of processes to go through, for quality and testing, especially as we're talking about rapidly processing five hundred units. We would never have got everything updated, fixed and shipped out on time.

"I knew there was a reason we brought you over." I wink at Rachel and she almost gave me 'the finger' but thought better of it and just smiled.

I send Sean a quick mail, explaining Rachel just saved the deal and justified her flight and hotel expenses, all in one five-second realisation that an essential bit of information was missing from their instructions.

"Lunch?"

"Sure. Hey, don't make a big deal about that card thing."

"How do you mean?"

"I don't want a load of attention and fuss. It was nothing really, the instructions just missed that point."

"Well, okay, but even though it was a small thing, it did save a load of pain. If anyone ever doubted the reason we flew you over, that justifies the whole deal. You are a hero now! A legend!"

"Oh geez."

I'm not going to subject Rachel to the evils of the work canteen just yet, so we go out for lunch. I stop at a sandwich place and get us a 'foot-long' each, Rachel wanted to stay in the car. We drive down to a little park by the banks of the Shannon that I have driven by many thousands of times, but never stopped at. There's a bench right by the river, and there's no rain today, just a light breeze. May as well take the opportunity to do some tourist things finally. Sure, I'm only here twenty years myself!

"This is the Shannon river. It flows out into the Atlantic further west. We can drive down the Clare peninsula one day if you like?"

"Yeah, I'd love to see the ocean."

"I know a secret beach. Well, maybe not so much of a secret anymore. But there's usually no one there."

"That would be nice."

We sit and enjoy the peace and the flow of the river while we eat, I should have done this years ago, but it never even occurred to me before to stop here.

. . .

"Do you fancy anything special for dinner?"

"I have no idea what you guys have here?"

"Well, not as much variety and restaurant density as you have in America, but there's almost everything. Indian, Chinese, Thai, Sushi…" I smile in memory of our first date.

"I never had Indian food. What's that like?"

"You never had a curry?"

"Nope."

"Oh boy are you missing out! You have to have a curry!"

I google for Indian restaurants nearby and find a selection. One is about a fifteen-minute walk from the hotel. I look down at Rachel's feet; she's wearing boots, not heels. If she doesn't feel like walking I guess we can get a taxi. I can't stand trying to park in the city, so I prefer to leave my car in the hotel car park.

"I guess we should go back to work."

"Oh, yeah, I guess. Hey, don't you work from home a lot?"

"Yeah, I try as much as possible."

"Well, home is the hotel now, right?" I look at her and smile. I see where this is going.

We came back to the hotel, but we didn't get any work done, well, not work-work anyway, I do think I got a good work-out though… Rachel is in the shower now, getting ready to go out for dinner. I guess I should check emails in case anything happened while we were 'otherwise engaged'.

Sean replied that he was delighted Rachel was useful, and he'd tell Pete that she's only been here a day and already saving the deal. I replied back that she was a bit shy about it, so don't mention it on a conference call or anything, tell Pete, sure, but there's no need to make a song and dance.

Eoghan sent an email with just a single question mark, nothing else. Does he mean where did I go? Or something about Rachel? I ignore it. I'll talk to him tomorrow and see what's going on with the scripting. I don't know if he's made any progress at all on that yet.

I shut down the laptop, pick up my clothes from the floor, and get dressed. I already showered quickly until Rachel kicked me out, because she wanted to 'actually wash properly'. I don't know what she meant, I thought I was doing a comprehensive job washing her tits and arse. She emerges from the bathroom in a cloud of steam, like a sexy elf Queen from a misty forest. Wrapped in a short white towel, streaks of black, wet hair contrasting her pale skin. Fuck me sideways, how did I manage to win this lottery?

"Don't mess with me, I have to get ready," she pre-empts my desire to unburden her of the towel.

"Fine, but I can't help having blood in my veins!" She smiles and flashes open the towel for a moment.

"Hey, you wanna see my cards?"

"Cards?"

"Tarot!"

"Oh, yeah, cool." I've never seen a deck of Tarot cards before, I don't know anything about them at all in fact, other than they are important to Rachel, and she has many packs of them.

She digs in her suitcase and pulls out a little black felt bag, tied with a drawstring. She hands it to me and sits down next to me. I can feel the heat from her body and smell her fresh, clean hair. I resist my human desires and concentrate on the little bag she gave me. Inside is a small box, thicker and bigger than a regular pack of cards.

"This is my second favourite deck. I wanted to bring more, but the suitcase was too heavy."

I open the box, carefully, and slide out the cards. They are colourful, big playing cards, but the patterns on the back are ornate, detailed, edged with silver. She takes the pack from me, flicks through and finds some interesting cards, and hands me them one by one, pointing out the details and patterns and explaining the symbolism in each one. I had no idea they were so complicated. Each drawing is laden with dozens of tiny details, making up a big picture that describes the meaning. Although wildly different, I can't help but feel this is similar to my tech-sheet, many tiny details that build up to a big picture of clarity.

"There's the cups, swords, pentacles and wands. Those are the suits, like you'd have hearts and diamonds in normal cards. Then there's the major arcana."

"The major what?"

"Just pick one out." I look at her, she nods towards the cards.

"Just at random?"

"Yeah, just shuffle them a bit and take one out."

I take the pack from her and shuffle them like I would any deck, but they are bigger, harder to manage. I spread them on the bed face down and pull out one card and turn it over. The card shows a shadowy hooded figure.

"Death! Are you fucking kidding me?"

"It's okay! It doesn't mean you are going to die."

"What does it mean then? Seems pretty clear."

"Change, the end of something. A new beginning."

"Hmm."

"Take one more."

This is quite scary now, the cards lie there, impassive, flat, but embedded with meaning. Even if I don't believe what they say, Rachel does. I move my hand back and forth along the spread and drop down, randomly. I know from programming that there are different kinds of random. This kind is my brain deciding - this is the card I should pull. The random seed in this situation is some kind of electrical impulse in my head. I turn it over. The picture is a man dressed as a court jester, with a small sack tied onto a pole over his shoulder. The text reads 'The Fool'.

"Seriously? A dead fool?" Rachel laughs.

"He's starting a new journey, he puts trust in the universe to guide him."

I look at her, disbelieving. It seems like I picked two terrible cards!

"This is good. It means you'll leave behind an old life and start on a new journey." She smiles and kisses me and then picks up her cards and packs them back in the box. "I'll do you a proper reading soon."

She spent an unfathomable amount of time 'getting ready', but eventually she emerged from the bathroom in a skimpy black dress with patches of lace, areas of fishnet and a see-through mesh over her cleavage. The air around her is heavy with the perfume I gave her, her lips a dark blood red. The whole effect is intoxicating, and I feel a burning start to kindle in my loins.

"Do I look ok?" She spins around.

"Are you kidding? You look like Aphrodite met Lilly Munster and Morticia Addams and they decided to get makeovers." She laughs and blushes a little through her powdered cheeks.

We got a taxi to the restaurant in the end, Rachel didn't like the thought of walking in the dark city. I said it was fine, this isn't a bad area, but she wasn't happy about it.

As we open the door to the restaurant, we're hit with a wall of heat and steam and feisty smells. We are greeted immediately by a small man who ushers us up the stairs to a table by a window. He pulls out a chair for Rachel and offers to take her jacket, but she shrugs him away. The restaurant is dim lit, fiery red painted walls, not too busy, which is good.

"Poppadoms." Rachel looks at the plate of flat crispy circles that the waiter just brought over, in puzzlement.

"What do you do with them?"

"You break them up and eat them with these dippy things." She takes one and does accordingly.

"Oh, I like the red onion stuff."

"Wait till you taste the curry. Do you like spicy food? I guess I should have asked that before we came here."

"I love Mexican."

"You'll be okay then."

. . .

I get a flashback of the sushi restaurant in Ohio again, because Rachel is looking at the menu utterly blank. A lot of complicated words and vague descriptions. Not very helpful to someone who has never eaten Indian. Normal people would probably ask the waiter for help without a second thought, but neither of us is ever going to do that. That would mean engaging the little fellow, and then having a conversation while he enthusiastically describes every dish on the menu. After the first few words, I won't be listening, not because he's boring or annoying, but because I will hear only the accent in his voice and the clinks of glasses at other tables. The candle flickers distracting me at every gasp of the flame, red tail-lights of a car passing by outside, anything but the words the waiter is saying. This is why I can't possibly ask for directions when I'm lost. The information is delivered too slowly, my brain loses interest between the words and moves on to something else further down the stack of processes in the queue.

Rachel chooses from the 'mild dishes' section in the end. Crises averted.

"Oh my God, this is so good!" Rachel is genuinely enjoying her korma. I'm glad and relieved because it was a bit risky to bring her for a curry without knowing if she'd like it. I'm reminded of my childhood, going to the takeaway with Dad to get dinner was a special treat. They would give me mints while we waited, and Dad would talk endlessly to the staff. I could see they were busy and wanted to move away, but they were always too polite to say anything.

"Yeah, I love curry."

"How have I never had this before?"

"Ha, if you can call that living!"

We scarf down the delicious food. Beer and sparkling-water flow like rivers to our table. Rachel said the Indian beer was weird, but she's drinking it anyway. When they bring the bill, they place it down in front of me of course, but Rachel said she'd put this on her company card. Pete told her to make sure she ate well and not to worry about the cost. Nice. Rachel gives me her card under the table because she doesn't know how to use chip and PIN. Luckily she had the PIN number in her phone, because I'm a fucking project manager! I ask the waiter to get us a taxi, and we wander down the stairs and wait outside. I'm glad to get out of the heat and let the cool breeze wash over me. Rachel is giddy, she looks tired as well, her eyes are red. She leans on me, and I put my arms around her.

"Thank you," a muffled voice comes from inside my jacket.

"For what? You paid."

"For showing me this amazing food."

"You are welcome." I kiss her head, and she squeezes me tight. We stay that way until the taxi pulls up and takes us home.

Chapter Twenty-Nine

FRIDAY 21ST SEPTEMBER

When we got to the office this morning, Eoghan was quickly over to my desk, bouncing and fidgeting around in my periphery like a kid asking to go pee-pee. I had my headset on, pretending to be on a call. Rachel was doing her morning emails on the opposite desk. I let him dance for a minute or so before taking off my headset.

"'S'up?"

"I've got the first test download ready to kick off. Oh, er, good morning by the way."

"What? Really?" Fuck that was quick. Has he been here all night working on it?

"It could fail, probably will fail for silly things, but all the software is ready to go."

"How long will the download take?"

"Probably about three hours, give or take. There's a lot of stuff in there, but it's all straight-forward once you break it down."

"That's great news. Kick it off then, lad! We'll have a squint then after lunch."

"It could fail many times before a successful download."

"That's okay, a fail is just a win waiting to happen." I can't believe I just let cheese like that out of my mouth. Rachel grins over the cubicle wall. I give her a thumbs up sign.

Eoghan scuttles off to start his download. But a dark thought buds in my head, a heart-beat skip, a thud of adrenaline courses through my veins. Once this is complete, Rachel goes away back home. They won't pay for her to stay for no reason. Eoghan is firing on all cylinders, at an unprecedented speed of work.

I stand up and lean over the wall, looking down at the goddess of love that the universe has delivered me.

"Hey."

"You okay?" She looks concerned and stands up, walks around to my side of the desk.

"When is your flight back?"

"It's flexible, anytime in the next month, I just have to book a couple of days before."

"But it depends on the sign off of the build, right?"

"Yeah, well, Pete said stay and make sure the five-hundred units get done."

"Hmm."

"What's up?"

"Nothing, it's all good. Coffee?"

"Yeah, but, can we go out somewhere for it? The coffee here is gross."

"Okay." I laugh, it isn't just me then!

There's an 'iconic Seattle based coffeehouse chain' place in the town centre. I wouldn't usually go there because it means paying for parking and walking through the city, but this isn't a normal time.

As we walk through the busy city streets Rachel seems uneasy, she holds my hand and stays very close to me. She's quiet, shy and distant, she looks down at the pavement and won't make eye contact with people. She gets this way anytime we interact with other humans. Totally different to how we are alone together. When we are in our hotel room, for instance, she is flirty, funny, loud and playful. I'm not much of a social animal either. I've been described as a hermit many times, but with Rachel, it seems different. While I am merely repulsed by most of the 'humans', she seems almost frightened and inhibited.

I never know how to order in these places. I just want black coffee with sugar in it. I don't need twenty questions about how I like it. The girl serving asks my name, I tell her 'Phteven with a P-H', Rachel giggles, the 'barista' looks unimpressed. We find a table out of the way, in a quiet corner.

"Don't worry." She reaches over and puts her hand on mine.
"Worry about what?"
"I won't vanish just yet. We aren't done."
"I…" There are many thoughts I want to voice, but I can't get the words I want to say out of my mouth. They dry up and burn away before they reach my tongue.
"What?"
I take a deep breath and try again. "I don't normally like people…" She nods in acknowledgement.
"I like you though." She squeezes my hand tight.
"I like you too." She smiles and winks.
"Can we get food in the hotel room this evening?"
"Oh, yeah, sure, whatever you like."
"It's so much effort to go out."
"Suits me."

We stare at each other for a moment, everything else in the universe melts and fades away, and my brain is at peace for a second. She breaks the spell by sipping her coffee and gazing out through the window.

"Do you want to walk around the shops while we're in the city?"

"No. Too many people."

"True."

On the way back to the office, I stop at the supermarket and get paper plates, plastic cutlery, cups, and plenty of bottles of water. That should keep us going for a while in the room. Rachel stayed in the car while I went in. I also bought a cute little stuffed animal toy for her, a furry black cat, because all witches should have a black cat.

"Ahh, he's so cute!" She visibly explodes with joy as I show her the toy.

"I'm glad you like him." She leans over and kisses me, then cuddles the little toy cat.

"What's his name?"

"Hmm. I'm not sure. Need to think about it."

I drive back to the office, but as I pull into the car park, my heart sinks at the thought. I have no desire at all to go back in. The image of the dead air, the bright fluorescent lights, the buzz of the air-conditioners. It all utterly repulses me. The server download will take a while longer to complete. I have no phone calls today, I've checked my emails already, fuck it. I turn to Rachel, and she notices my hesitation.

"I don't feel like going in just yet. Do you want to go for a ride?"

"Sure, sounds good to me. Can I put music on?"

"Yeah, go ahead." I hand her my phone, and she scrolls through my music list, occasionally laughing and groaning and asking 'what the fuck is this?' I tell her my taste in music is varied and eclectic. She settles on some old Black Sabbath and turns it up loud as I drive back away from the office.

"Ozzy!" She looks over at me.

"That's the cat's name." She smiles and nods.

"Ozzy it is!"

I drive for almost an hour, taking it easy, not in a rush. Rachel sings along to the music with her amazing voice, and I sometimes chime in at the chorus. We end up at a beach where a lot of surfers come at the right time of year. Today is quite choppy and there a few colourful boards out in the water, but mostly it's just ocean waves and yellow sand. I park up on a hill that overlooks the beach. An empty car park, that would be packed full in the summer peak tourist season. The rows and rows of caravans behind us are probably also empty now, but in August they would have been buzzing with people.

We sit for a while, watching the waves crash against a cliff face, washing up and down the beach.

"Do you want to go for a walk along the beach?"

"Oh, not now."

"But now is when we are here?"

"I have the wrong shoes on."

"Oh… Okay, you wanna sit in the back?"

"What for?" She laughs.

"Maybe it's more comfortable?"

"Okay."

We get out and then get in the back seats. Rachel leaves the Ozzy cat on the front seat, keeping it warm for her. We snuggle up close. I don't think anyone has ever sat in these seats of my car, before now!

It begins to rain a light drizzle, but develops into a downpour quickly. Inside the car we are protected, cut off. The rain smears the windows, and they begin to steam up inside. I turn and face Rachel, and move in for a long kiss, she responds, we slide down the seat, and I run my hand along her legs, stopping short before things go too far.

"Pull your pants down." She fumbles with my button and zip. I help her, and before I know what's going on, her lips are around me, her tongue caressing... She sits up, rubs a small circle in the steamed up windows and peers out, making sure no one is around. Then she pulls down her knickers and takes them off, flicks them into the front seat.

"Good job I wore a skirt today!" She giggles and tells me to sit up and move to the middle of the seat, then gets astride me. We laugh because the car is bouncing gently 'don't come-a-knockin!' She peers out of the windows again, but no one is around. I found out today why it is always useful to have a wad of fast-food napkins in the car.

At my desk, I sift through emails and find one from Eoghan. He said the download failed for 'silly things'. He's already corrected it and started it again, but as it's Friday, and everyone tends to go home a bit early, I doubt it will be finished before the end of the day. Rachel is making a call to her factory dude, he screwed something up and sent her a load of emails asking if she could call him as soon as possible. She said he was a 'douche-bag' and then went to a meeting room to make the call. I wander over to Eoghan's desk.

"Where did you go?"

"We went out for lunch. Rachel doesn't like celery either." He looks suspicious but doesn't say anything.

"The download failed, it's fine though, I forgot to take out some unnecessary tests."

"Yeah, I saw the email. No problem, I'd rather do it properly than rush it."

"You said it was super urgent? You said that all Satans demonic minions would rain down bile and retch across all four corners of the world, if it wasn't done on time. That we'd all be buggered up the arse with solid-frozen aquatic life if we didn't work on this, twenty-four-seven, until it was done!"

"I did say that, yes. But that doesn't mean we should rush it and make mistakes."

"Make up your mind!"

"Take the weekend off, come back on Monday with a fresh head."

"Fuck off!"

I take the hint and go back to my desk, Rachel has returned, she's angry looking and typing an email frantically, I leave her alone for a minute.

After a while she stands up, slams her laptop lid shut.

"Can we go now?"

"Yeah." I grab my laptop, and we're out the door faster than Eoghan can fail another download.

The drive back to the hotel is in silence, Rachel is tapping away on her phone and muttering curses, I didn't ask what happened, she'll tell me if she feels like it. Back in the hotel, she goes straight for the shower.

In my youth I would get angry at work fuck-ups too, taking every hit personally, but now, after decades of being worn down, I am no longer able to donate any excrement to the cause. I get annoyed, stressed, miserable, sure, but I try not to let it linger. There will always be another fuck-up just down the road, just like there will always be another tractor around the corner. There's no point in overtaking, and there's no point in taking things to heart. Rachel is young and passionate. She'll get over it.

When she comes out from the shower she's in a much better mood, she's just wearing a towel and sits down at the desk. She fumbles in her purse and takes out Ozzy the black cat and laughs and puts him by her hair straightener.

"Sorry."

"For what?"

"Being moody."

"It's okay." I smile. At least it wasn't me who fucked something up.

"Douche-bag loaded the wrong software onto a big order back home. Then he tried to blame me for it. He made out I told him to do it that way."

"Ah, I know that one."

"Pete was up my ass. Anyway, I think it's okay now. I'll break my foot off in his ass when I get back."

"Hugs?"

"Yeah." She comes over to me on the bed and snuggles up, her wet hair on my chest, but I don't mind.

"Fish and chips?"

"What?"

"Battered cod, deep fried, served with chunky french fries, drizzled with salt and vinegar, served wrapped in paper.

"Sounds wonderful!"

"It's about ten minutes walk from here, and they don't deliver."

"Oh, that sucks."

"But this chipper is legendary here. I'll go if you want?"

"Are you sure?"

"Yeah, you can stay here, looking pretty."

She sticks out her tongue, but she's still pretty. I get my coat and go for chips. I imagine this is something that normal people would do on a Friday evening?

Chapter Thirty

SATURDAY 22ND SEPTEMBER

I stopped at an offy after getting the chips last night. I bought a six-pack of Belgian beers for Rachel to try. They had some non-alcoholic versions too, so I got some for myself. Fuck it, push the auld boat out! She said the fish and chips were awesome and the beer washed it down very nicely. I set up my little portable speaker, and she played music from my phone, flicking through my obscure tunes, she said it was just a load of 'beep-boop' alien space noises, and that I was a weirdo for listening to that shit. I said it was beautiful and reminds me of fractal algorithms, elegant and mathematical. Then she found the classic rock again and stuck with that.

This morning passed without me knowing about it, I half woke up and went to the bathroom, but I came back to bed and fell asleep again. I don't remember the last time that happened to me. We got out of bed around noon, after some messing around.

"What do you want to do today?"

"Can we go for a ride somewhere?"

"Sure, anything particular you want to see?"

"No idea, dude, you choose something."

I pull out the phone to look at the map, and scroll around for a minute. Then I settle on a location I think she'll enjoy. We'll need some drinks and snacks, because we're going to the arse-end of nowheresville, and there's no fast food, or even slow food out there!

"Where are we going?"

"You'll see."

I drive North out of the city and keep going, past my normal home exit and on for almost an hour.

Rachel gets antsy. She keeps asking where are we going, I keep saying you'll find out soon. Then the road begins to narrow, the landscape starts to change. The green fields next to the road morph into rocky hills, flat areas like moon-scapes of grey rock. Orange-green sprouting tussocks dotted between the alien shaped outcrops.

We pass fields of grey, divided by grey stone walls. There are some small towers of flat stones piled upon each other, like primitive burial mounds, but these were probably built recently by kids, rather than the ancient druids, high off their tits on mushrooms. Then we find a clear lake stretching to distant mini-mountains.

"Oh my god! It's amazing! Can you stop?"

I pull over in a lay-by near the lake and Rachel takes her phone out and takes some photos. She tried to send one to her mom, but there's no cell signal here.

"You want a snack?"

"Mhm."

I break out our little picnic, and we walk over to the edge of the lake and find a rock to sit on.

"What is this place?"

"It's called 'the Burren', it's a vast area of rocks and fuck all else! There's caves and stuff too."

"It's so cool and weird. Mystical."

"Oh, there are some standing stones here-and-there too. Not to the scale of Stonehenge. But interesting anyway. It reminds me of Iceland a bit."

"Can we see the standing stones?"

"I think you have to walk to those, across the fields."

"Oh."

We drive North again, slowly because the roads are perilous and winding with steep drops at the edge. We hit the coast and a small town, seemingly untouched by modern civilisation in places. Colourful houses and touristy tea shops all over the place. I have to piss like a banshee, so I stop by a little pier. There's a pub nearby, but I always feel weird about pissing in a pub if I'm not drinking there. Which I never am anymore.

"Do you want a drink?"

"Like a drink-drink?"

"Yeah, you can get a Guinness or something."

"In a bar?"

"In the pub." I point across the road at the quaint building.

"I guess."

"It won't be busy."

We go in, and as predicted it isn't busy at all. There are a few people at tables and some auld fellas propping up the bar. But I imagine they would always be there, no matter what day or time it was. I find Rachel a seat at the back and head for a slash before it's too late.

I go to the bar on the way back, and get Rachel a glass of Guinness and myself my usual, sparkling water. One of the auld fellas at the bar winks at me and gives a knowing smile. I have no idea what he's winking about, so I pretend I don't see. When I take the drinks over to the table, Rachel is making gurgling noises and writhing in her seat. For a moment I wonder if she's okay, or having a seizure or something, but she blurts out what is troubling her.

"That old guy came over to me while you were gone!" It's like she's popped a cork, and all the fizz sprayed out in one short burst, now she's calm again.

She points at the winking old farmer back at the bar, his back to us now, watching sport on the TV.

I giggle at the thought of it.

"Oh yeah? You guys going on a date?"

"I had no idea what he said! It was just a load of weird noises and grunts."

"Ah, yeah, that sounds like a date alright!"

"Shut up!"

She takes her drink and tastes the smooth black stout, at first she's taken aback but then she takes another gulp.

"God damn! That's some hardcore shit!"

"An acquired taste for sure. But it's full of nutrients and minerals. Good for you, in moderation."

This is quite a voyage of discovery for young Rachel Brooks so far. I wonder what other new experiences are waiting for her?

The box… I want to show her the box, back in my shed, sitting idle, forever spinning its yarns of past times. Not today, it doesn't feel right. But soon.

Rachel takes out her phone, and she has a signal now, so she sends her mom some photos of the weird Burren landscape.

Back on the road, I take the coastal path south-west. I never drive on these roads normally, but they are a rally drivers' wet dream. I prefer a nice smooth, straight motorway these days. But back in my youth, I would have enjoyed the bends and twists.

We pass through the occasional village on the left, and the Atlantic as a constant companion off to the right, never too far from sight. I'm taking it very easy, so it takes almost two hours to get where I'm going. Rachel keeps asking where we are going and I keep saying wait and see. She's mostly content, watching the miles pass by, the fields broken by low hedges, thick with local stone, and the occasional windswept tree. Then we pass a wind-farm, casting long shadows in the dwindling light. I'm always mesmerised by these giants, no matter how many times I see them.

I slow down and pull into the driveway of a deserted property, the brambles climbing high up the stone walls. They own it now. Nature has taken it back.

"What's this place?"

"Dad's workshop."

We sit for a moment in silence, and I realise I don't have the keys with me, they are back at home in my office. It doesn't matter. There's nothing inside that would interest Rachel now. Just what remains of the tools and odds and sods, and the things I couldn't carry the last time I was here. I don't know what brought me today, it just seemed like a good idea.

After a moment of reflection, we start the long drive back to the hotel, but I stop at the graveyard, just up the road. This time we get out, and Rachel wanders into the roof-less, ruined little church. The floor lined with mossy, lichen covered gravestones. She takes some more photos on her phone. The sun now heading down rapidly. A slight mist forming on the hill below us. I walk over to Dad's grave. There's no stone, but I know where it is. I don't know what else to do, so I just stand by the mound of weeds. Rachel puts her arms around me, and we stay there, silently, until the shadows overwhelm the light, and it's time to go.

Chapter Thirty-One

SUNDAY 23RD SEPTEMBER

Rachel fell asleep in the car on the way back to the hotel last night. Understandable, with the long drive, the sea air, and the glass of Guinness, I would have slept too, but I was driving. Makes it harder to nod off. Consequently, we were up till the wee small hours, talking about life, love, the nature of the universe, ghosts and strange creatures, the source of all things, conservation of energy and the first law of thermodynamics. You know, the usual stuff.

It reminded me of the chats I would have with Dad late at night, but those were typically bent towards the sciences. Rachel brings an element that's new to me - the occult and spirituality. I've long dismissed these things as a load of hippy bollocks, but it was her talk of spiritual energy going back to a source, and then re-incarnating as something else, that reminded me of the fundamental laws of physics. That the universe is a closed system if taken as a whole. Energy flows back into the pool somehow. Then I thought about the box in my shed, the ever-spinning cone of brass, inexplicably powered by nothing. I mentioned to Rachel that I'd discussed perpetual motion and over-unity devices with Dad many times, and just because the equipment and technology we have right now can't perceive of a way to do something, that doesn't mean it's impossible. Take a smart-phone of today back in time just ten years, and you would hear gasps of awe. Take it back a couple of hundred years, and you would be tried as a witch and hung. She retorted that, just because we can't currently prove the existence of ghosts and souls, doesn't mean they are hippy bollocks. Fair enough. I had to explain to her what bollocks were.

It was late, I was tired. Plus I picked up one of Rachel's beers of the normal alcoholic kind, which led to another, which led to us giggling in bed at four am. This morning I gulped down six of the cherry tablets and a big bottle of water.

"Do you want to go out for food?"

"How do you mean out?"

"Like a café or restaurant or something."

"Not really. Can we get drive-through?"

"Oh, okay."

I don't ordinarily get fast-food, mainly because there aren't any fast-food restaurants near my house, so it typically doesn't spring to mind as an option. But this seems like a time when junk is acceptable. We get burgers and then drive to the end of the car-park, where no one else is around.

"So what do you want to do today?"

"Is there something, like, totally crazy that I couldn't see anywhere else?"

"Hmm."

I think I know where to go, but it's quite far away. After

yesterday's epic journey I'm not sure if she'd be happy sitting in the car for hours.

"Are you up for a long drive again?"

"Sure dude, I just sit here, and you do all the driving, so whatever you wanna do."

We finish eating and then head south, opposite to yesterday's adventures.

I take the old roads instead of the motorway. Rachel prefers to look at interesting things, rather than miles of plain highway. We pass through small towns and villages, and the road does become very interesting as we spin through twists and turns down steep hills, through wooded passages, dark from leaves overhead. The shape of the trees carved by the height of trucks passing through, every day for decades.

We arrive at Blarney Castle soon enough. I think this counts as totally crazy and something Rachel couldn't see anywhere else. The car park is quite full, it could be busy, but the grounds are huge. We should be safe enough.

I've been here once before, but it was a long time ago. With Dad, soon after we first came to Ireland. I had forgotten all about the experience until I saw the castle in the distance. We had climbed the steps up to the top, narrow and steep. The legend has it that, anyone who kisses the stone at the top of the tower, will gain the gift of eloquence. I don't think Dad needed to kiss a stone, he already had eloquence enough for a bus full of tourists. He did it anyway. I stayed well away from the steep drop, I won't do it today either, and I doubt if Rachel would be interested.

She saw something called the 'Poison Garden' on the map, and she got very excited, so we head in that direction first. The plants are all dangerous in some way, used in times gone by for medicinal purposes, as herbal remedies. As we walk through, she enthusiastically points out to me all the herbs that can kill you, if you don't know how to use them properly. Should I be worried? I'm sleeping next to this girl! She tells me that modern medicine is way more dangerous, and I'm inclined to agree.

We link arms and walk through the rest of the gardens, occasionally stopping for my poor old feet to rest, and for her to take photos to send back to her mom, who has never left America, and hasn't seen anything like a six-hundred-year-old castle. All the while the grey stone tower looms in the distance, jutting like a decaying tooth.

The path leads us to the foot of the stone walls of the castle. From here it looks so much taller and ominous than from the gardens. Groups of colourful tourists flow in all directions.

"Do you want to go up?"

"Are you fucking crazy? I'm not even going in there!"

"Fair enough." Instead, we follow the woodland park all the way around, past a lake and another walled garden. Everything is beautiful and immaculate, but I sense Rachel is uneasy. There aren't too many other people around us, but enough that a hushed tone is needed to talk in privacy, even while walking. When we arrive back at the car park, both exhausted. We didn't prepare for a day out, so we are also starving and thirsty.

Going to a restaurant now, tired and sweaty from the walk, is a bad idea. We stop at a petrol station for drinks and then carry on back to where I saw another fast-food place as we drove down. Stopping for pizza, which isn't bad at all, and as the sun sets once again on our day out, we head back to the hotel and a hot shower.

Time, For a Change

"We have to go to work tomorrow."

"Yeah, I know. We'll go to sleep soon, but I wanna do a reading for you."

"Tarot?"

"Yeah."

She's wrapped in a white hotel towel again. No matter how tired, the brain still has the capacity to parse the shapes of a woman, and trigger chemicals to flow. Shape recognition and chemical reactions, the true nature of love.

Rachel picks out her little black velvet bag from her suitcase, and sits down cross-legged in the middle of the bed. She beckons me over to sit opposite her, but my legs don't bend like that. Instead, I lay on my side and prop myself on my elbow.

She takes out the cards from the bag, and spreads them out on the bed in front of her, then picks them up and shuffles them as you would shuffle any cards.

"Have a question in your head, something you want answers for."

"Like what?"

"Anything really."

Of course, this is when my mind goes blank, like when I'm in the supermarket or, in the old days, a music shop. I suddenly have no idea who I am, or what music I like, or what food I eat. When presented with too many choices, the mind freezes up and is paralysed. I ponder for a moment. I suppose what I really want to know are questions I'm scared to hear the answer for. Will I ever see Rachel again after this trip ends? Where is this job going? In ten more years will I still be churning away in a job I'm utterly sick of, with people I mostly despise? How can picture cards tell me the answers to these things?

"Okay, I got some questions. Should I tell you?"

"No, just keep them in your head. Now pick out some cards, just random, whatever you feel like."

"How many?"

"Just stop when you feel like that's enough."

This all seems very vague to me, I imagined there would be a structure and protocol to follow, but Rachel insists it doesn't matter, that the universe is guiding my hand somehow.

"Should I close my eyes? Or put a paper bag over my head or something?"

"If you like."

"Would it help?"

"Not at all. But whatever you feel like doing."

The cards are shuffled, laid face down, they are already randomised. I could pick cards next to each other from left-to-right, and they would be equally as random if I just picked from across the spread. But that doesn't seem right. I close my eyes and just dive in.

'The Hanged Man'

The fella on the card is hanging upside down from a tree, and he looks a bit too happy for my liking.

"Fuck me sideways."

"You have to remember that the literal name on the card isn't the same as the interpreted meaning."

"Okay, well what does it mean?"

"The hanged man sees things in a new way, a new perspective. It's like a transition. Maybe different priorities."

"Yeah, a new way, from a rope on a tree!" She laughs.

"No, just be open to new things. Pick another one."

I look at the cards on the bed, try to see some pattern, try to choose something based on intuition, or feel guidance from some other power, but nothing happens. In the end, I think 'fuck it' and take the card from the left edge. If the universe is guiding me anyway, it really shouldn't make any difference which cards I pick. The logic is hard to find in this method of divination.

'The Moon'

"This is about intuition and fear. Self-deceit. Confusion and stress, losing touch with reality."

"Stress is a part of my normal life. For as long as I can remember."

"That's not good, dude."

"No, well, what can you do?"

"Pick another one."

'The Emperor'

That's more like it. This lad looks like he has his excrement all centrally located. He's sat on a throne holding a staff or something.

"He's a Father figure, it represents getting over something in your past."

"Oh."

"He represents power, authority, leadership. Reason and logic, taking control of a situation."

"That's a good one, right?"

"None are good or bad. They are just what they are. Take another."

This one doesn't have a name, it shows the roman numeral *VI* and a lad pushing a little ferry boat over water, but he's got six swords stuck in the vessel. That can't be good for buoyancy.

"Six of Swords. This one is about moving on to better things, moving away from difficulty and the past. This follows on from the Emperor, getting over past problems and becoming more positive."

"Another one?"

"Yeah sure, if you think."

'The Tower'

This one looks like a fucking nightmare. There's a tall tower bursting with flames, lads falling out all over the place, screaming, pain. A picnic in the park, not!

"This is about disruption, unexpected events, a breakdown of the old way, making way for new things. But you'll learn to adapt and adjust quickly."

"They are literally jumping out of a burning tower. Brutal!"

"Yeah, shit went down that day." She cackles.

"Sorry."

I reach down into the pack and gently run my fingers over the cards, come on universe, I need something substantial here.

. . .

'Death'

"Oh, lovely, so we meet again, Mr Death?"

"He's not bad, remember? Again this is about change and new beginnings, transformation. As one door closes, another opens."

Well, there's a pattern emerging here, I'm not sure what it points to, but if I'm to believe these cards, I guess something is going to happen. That could be anything though? This time I pick a card, but drop it down and take the one next to it. I don't know why, but, why not?

'The Empress'

"Oh." She pauses and looks up at me.

"She's femininity and development. Sensuality," she mouths the word and licks her lips in mock sexiness.

"She's abundance, grace and beauty."

"Hmm. Okay, last one I think."

This is another one without a title. There's the number *II* in roman numerals and a man and a woman, each holding a big cup, a house in the distance.

"Two of cups. A new relationship perhaps?" She smiles and twists her hair in her fingers. "Love, romance and harmony."

"I don't know what to make of it all." I get up off the bed and stretch my legs.

"Let it sit with you for a while. Sleep on it."

She gathers all the cards up and puts them away in the box, and then the bag.

"Be open to change, Terry. Something is going to happen."

Chapter Thirty-Two

MONDAY 24TH SEPTEMBER

The first batch of fifty of the five-hundred systems arrived this morning to our factory processing area. They are now 'on hold' waiting for Eoghan to finish his work on the coding and scripts. The rest of the units will filter in during the week.

I'm amazed at how fast we can do things if there is proper motivation. I hope everyone realises that we are now setting a precedent for all future orders to be set up, processed and completed this fast. Or will we return to normal slug-pace after this order is finished?

Sean is delighted by the progress, and he's booking a flight to Shannon for next Monday, he wants to be here when the first units get processed and signed off by Rachel. I don't know why or what use he'll be, but it's his choice, and it will be nice to see the old fucker again anyway.

Eoghan is stressed now, under pressure to get things working smoothly, his second download also failed for more 'silly things' that he wouldn't explain in any more detail. He's fixed that and kicked it off again already, he thinks it will pass this time.

Time, For a Change

. . .

Rachel wanted to stop at a bank this morning on the way into the office, but she was annoyed to find out that they don't open until ten, so instead, she gave me fifty dollars, and I gave her fifty euro back. A terrible deal for me, financially, but it doesn't matter. She wanted to go to a pharmacy and buy 'woman stuff'. I offered to get it for her as she was quite nervous about going into the store, but she said it was okay, she needed to do stuff for herself. Fair enough, I sat in the car scrolling Twitter while she went in.

A meeting pops into my calendar for Wednesday afternoon from my 'HR Representative', probably to tell me that yet again, during this round of annual pay reviews, I was not allocated an increase. Despite this deal I'm working on being worth truck-loads of cash for the company, none of that matters apparently, because I'm paid according to local averages, meaning it's cheap to hire people here on the west side of Ireland, Dublin would be much more expensive. I can't remember when I last got a pay rise, but it must be at least five years ago.

Any dealings with HR are annoying and unnecessarily fake, contrived, scripted and condescending. Their jobs are so vague and pointless that they have to come up with bullshit processes to make it seem as though they do something all day.

This particular bitch who sent the meeting to me is an evil piece of work. Maeve Tobin. She delights in telling me every year that I am not going to get more money. I can smell the pheromones of disgust off her when I walk into her cutesy little office, plastic trolls on her desk from the 90s, motivational posters on the walls, an expensive high-backed chair, because her fat arse won't fit on a standard office chair. Many years ago she called me in to 'discuss inappropriate and offensive language in the workplace' because I told someone to fuck off as she walked by in earshot. After that episode I wrote her work phone number on the back of the gents toilet door in permanent marker, 'I suck like an Electrolux - call me…' Not here in work, but in the McDonalds down in the town. HR always talk about their 'open door policy'.

She's a fine fucking one to talk about offensive language anyway. Every email she sends is littered with spelling mistakes, typos, terrible quality animated pictures she pasted from some website made in the early nineties. And she always, without fucking fail, uses the wrong tense of the word 'advice', and it drives me bananas. That's offensive language to me, but no one sees my point of view. Wednesday should be a fucking blast.

In my dreams, I imagine a day when I leave here for some greener pasture, and I can finally tell everyone what I think of them. *#LotteryDreams*

I stand up and peer down at Rachel, she's scrolling through some google results. Just looking at her eases my tension and brings a smile to my face. She looks up and smiles back.

"Lunch?"
"Yup!"

On the way out we meet Eoghan in the corridor, he says his download has passed the point of previous fails and should complete in about an hour. I tell him to cross all his digits, and we'll be back to check it out later. We have to resort to superstition to make our services work.

We get sandwiches, and go to our picnic spot down by the river. But Rachel seems quiet, even with us alone together she isn't her normal vivacious self. I asked her what was up and she just shrugged. Maybe she misses home, or perhaps this is woman stuff manifesting? We finish eating and sit for a while longer, I shuffle up close to her and put my arm around her, she holds my hand and turns to look at me.

"It will all be okay… Right?"

I don't know what she means, but to ask her for details feels inappropriate, so I look into her eyes and tell her everything will be okay, no matter what it is. She seems happier, and we slowly get up and meander back to the car, and then to the office.

I've been wondering about that Tarot reading Rachel did for me, what does it all mean? Do I dismiss it entirely? How does it help me anyway? I never envisaged myself looking to the occult for direction or guidance, but here I am pondering my future based on the turn of some cards.

I slump down in my chair and return to the grind. There's an email from Eoghan, so I click it open. I'm not surprised I suppose, but I'm disappointed. His test download failed again for some other reason that wasn't pre-empted. I should never have panicked that this would all happen too quickly. We still have some time, but I prefer to have spare time on my side rather than cut it very fine. Even if it passes, there's still work instructions to build and a run through of everything with Rachel approving it, step by step. That's a full day on its own. Realistically this part of the setup needs to be done and working by tomorrow, or we risk a disaster - having to come into work at the weekend. Balls to that.

We have a conference call meeting later with Sean and Pete, and they'll want to hear good news from us here on the front lines. I'll be able to spin some story to paint everything in a good light, but if they ask for details, I may need to fire up the bullshit-canon. The only important thing now is that when Sean arrives next week, we'll have a pretty picture to show him. A harmonious flow of approval sign-offs and factory acceptance emails, test unit inspection check-lists all ticked, five hundred units of bare stock all ready and waiting for our green light. After that, I won't care anymore. It's up to the factory people to do their part in actually processing everything in time. Sean is coordinating that part. It'll be grand.

[15:35] Ward, Terry B:
Ted.

[15:37] O'Brien, Ted:
Well, Terry.
What's the shtory?

[15:37] Ward, Terry B:
Did you get your annual review thing yet?

[15:39] O'Brien, Ted:
No, I thought that was next month?

Time, For a Change

[15:39] Ward, Terry B:

HR sent me a meeting invite for Wednesday.

[15:40] O'Brien, Ted:

Oh, maybe it's early this year or something?

[15:40] Ward, Terry B:

Hmm.

[15:43] O'Brien, Ted:

I just heard my boss is leaving anyway.

[15:44] Ward, Terry B:

Really?
Didn't you just get a new boss?

[15:45] O'Brien, Ted:

About a year ago, but yeah.

[15:45] Ward, Terry B:

You must wear them out quickly!

[15:46] O'Brien, Ted:

That's what she said!

[15:50] Ward, Terry B:

Maybe I'll apply for the position?

[15:51] O'Brien, Ted:

Go for it!
You couldn't be much worse than what we have now.

[15:55] Ward, Terry B:

Or maybe I'll start a new life as a goatherd in the mountains.

[15:56] O'Brien, Ted:
Yah, you like goats.

Rachel peeks over my cubicle wall and waves to get my attention, she looks weary and pale.

"Hey, can we go back to the hotel?"

"Oh, sure, but there's the meeting in like three minutes. Right after that, we can go."

"I don't feel too good."

"I'm sorry. We'll tie this up quick and get the fuck out."

"Okay."

"Do you need a doctor?"

"Hell no. I just need to lie down for a while."

On the call, Sean opens up with his normal jovial spiel. Pete is in good spirits too. I can see Rachel has connected to the call also, but she stays muted.

"Hi guys, this is Terry. Just want to give a quick update, because I have another meeting to attend in a few minutes."

I bullshit my way through the update with an eloquence worthy of the Blarney stone, without giving anyone time to ask questions. Sean and Pete seem happy, so I jump ship and take Rachel with me. We are out of the office in less time than it takes Sean to chat up a MILF in a sleazy bar.

Rachel flops down on the bed when we get to the room, I pull the curtains and turn off the lights and cover her with a blanket. I leave a bottle of water next to her and plug in her phone to charge on the nightstand.

"Will you be okay? I'll leave you to rest"
"Where are you going?"
"I'm going to take laundry back to my house. I'm getting low on clean underwear. Plus I thought you might sleep easier without me fiddling around."
"Oh, okay. Don't be long."
"I'll be about six foot."
"What?"
"Couple of hours. I'll bring food when I come back."
"Okay. Love you."
"Love you too."

After the poshness of the hotel, my house feels glum and dank, even when I switch all the lights on, it still seems dark. The evenings are pulling in now, and the air is cold and moist. It took a few shoulder slams to get my front door to open. There's some junk-mail in the post box that I throw directly into the recycling bin, but other than that, everything is as I left it. I pop my laundry in the machine and then find some clean clothes to take back with me.

I feel a pull over to the shed, but when I get there and see the box on the bench, it doesn't feel right to use it now. Rachel is feeling crappy in bed, I should be looking after her instead of travelling through time. But I do want her to experience the box, maybe then she can help me make sense of it all?

She's told me her beliefs in the occult, I should tell her about my time-machine. Not today maybe, I want her to feel better first, then perhaps next weekend she can come and try it herself. After that, things will be busy with the project.

I feel my phone buzz in my pocket.

Hey, are you coming back? I feel better now, but I'm starving.
   Oh, can you get Pizza?
   Do you guys have anchovies?

We do, of course, but I don't know if the pizza place has them. I'll ask. I guess if it's important I could get them separately and upgrade the pizza, postpartum, as it were. I reply that I'll be back soon with pizza, salty fish included, by hook or by crook.

Chapter Thirty-Three

TUESDAY 25TH SEPTEMBER

We got in late this morning, Rachel was in the bathroom for a long time. She said she felt better last night, but this morning she was feeling a bit groggy again. I hope she hasn't come down with something nasty? She refuses to see a doctor.

She had a tiny bottle of lavender oil in her purse, and she dabbed some on her top for the aromatherapy, and she asked me to get her ginger tea at the supermarket as we passed by.

She smells floral now. Quite a change from the usual waft of armpit that I get here.

Eoghan loafed over to my desk on his way back from the canteen. He said one more thing failed the download last night, he's already fixed it and kicked it off again, but he's now so confident that this is the final working version, that he's promised to buy the biscuits for a coffee break later, if it fails. I'm not usually a gambling man, but in this case, I take him up on the bet. I even up the stakes and make it chocolate chip cookies. He raised an eyebrow at that, but agreed to the terms.

Sean has changed the FutureCloud status call to daily now, so every afternoon all this week I have to give an update on the situation, good or bad he said, but he means only good. This means we can't sneak off early anymore. Bummer.

"Hey." Rachel peers over the cubicle wall.
"You hungry?"
"Oh, sure, actually I'm starving." We skipped breakfast at the hotel this morning because Rachel wasn't feeling good.
"Me too, I feel better now, let's go eat?"
"You don't have to ask me twice!"
"Can we get drive-through again?"
"Sure, if that's what you want."
"It sounds good."

I can feel my arteries hardening, and my stomach bloating. I'm sure they put some addictive drugs into fast food, because even as I sit here munching on a burger, I'm thinking about going and getting another one, knowing it is probably eight thousand calories. But I don't. Tomorrow I need a salad or fruit or something.

"You want to go for a walk. I feel like I ate a lump of concrete."
"Yeah, sure. I feel like shit now, too."
There's a park not far from our hotel so we motor on over. There aren't many people around in the park on a chilly

afternoon, in late September. Kids are at school, people with jobs are at work, except us. The only people around look like drug dealers and drunk winos. Everyone has to be somewhere I guess. We hold hands and walk down the wooded paths, breathing in the air, burning off the calories.

"Did you think about the reading?"

"The Tarot thing? Yeah, but I don't know what to make of it still. I mean, it said a load of change is coming?"

"Yeah, I think so."

"Well, until it happens, I can't say how I will react."

"I guess."

We sit down on a bench in a lonely spot, away from the obvious lurking dealers, trying so hard to look casual, standing around in the park during the day, but utterly failing.

"I do have something to tell you," she looks over at me, expectantly.

"What's that?"

"Those dreams I've been having. All the ones I told you."

"Yeah?"

"Perhaps I better start at the beginning?"

"Best place."

I tell her about clearing out Dad's workshop, about finding the mysterious box and taking it home. About the spinning cone of brass inside and the copper boards with the hand-shapes drawn on. That it must have been in the old workshop for many years untouched, but the cone has apparently been spinning all that time, with no visible source of power. Then I tell her that Dad often talked about ideas and concepts that were beyond my understanding.

I tell her that I have a time-machine in my shed, and all those dreams I told her about were events that I travelled back to somehow, into my younger body.

I sit back and wait for her reaction, does she call the cops and get me taken to the loony-bin? Does she run screaming in terror? Does she laugh and assume I'm pulling her leg?

"Cool!"

"Really?"

"Yeah, I mean, that's some crazy sci-fi shit. But it sounds cool."

"You don't think I'm a nut-job?"

"Well, not because of the time-machine!" She leans over and kisses me on the cheek.

"Ha."

"Can I try it out?"

"Yeah! I thought we could go over on Saturday and I would show you."

"Awesome."

That's it, she doesn't judge me, doesn't assume I'm a fruit-loop or smoking something too strong, doesn't even question my story or laugh cynically in my face. I should have told her before. No matter I suppose. A little ball of stress melts away in my neck. I feel better for telling Rachel about the box.

"We better go back to work now. See if Eoghan has fucked up again."

"It passed!"

"What did?" I know what Eoghan means of course, but I just can't help myself.

"The fucking FutureCloud download. It worked!"

"Nice one! And it only took four goes!"

"Well, five if you count the first test."

"Well done. I guess I'll have to get the cookies then!"

Time, For a Change

Cookies and coffee that I'll be buying with Rachel's company credit card.

The next step is for Rachel to check all the settings and software to make sure it is all installed correctly. There are numerous things to test and validate, so I think we'll make a start on it tomorrow morning, first thing. At least now I'll have some genuinely good news for Sean's call.

Eoghan still has to create the factory work instructions. Step-by-step details of how to set-up the hardware, remove parts not needed, add other parts in. Photos and clear instructions of every step, like a Lego set manual. The factory lads doing the actual work could be any Joe Fucker off the street, so the details we give them have to be foolproof. But, as everyone knows, fools can be pretty ingenious.

The afternoon status call went well, and we escaped immediately after. Eoghan is ready to have the test unit inspected by Rachel in the morning, and we'll be flying it if everything passes okay.

We got curry again for dinner, but this time we got delivery to the room. A mini celebration for the project success so far. Actually, for me, more of a celebration of getting the box thing off my chest to Rachel, and her not freaking out about it.

"So, if you go back in time, did you ever change anything?"

"I'm not sure if it works like that. It's more like I'm there, witnessing events. The feeling is odd. I know I'm there in the moment, but I also witness my thoughts from that time-period too, mixed up. But there was one thing I'm not sure about."

I tell her about the DeltaWave software version email, the problem that just went away when I travelled back to the day I got the email, and just left it open on my screen.

"Do you know how it works?"

"No idea. I tried searching through Dad's old files from all his computers and disks, and I found nothing. But that doesn't mean the information isn't there. It could be encrypted or something. The problem is I don't know what to look for."

"Does it come apart?"

"I haven't dared to try and mess with it. When I was a kid I would often 'fix' things like old clocks and toys, they would never work again! But I can't wait to see what happens when you try it!"

"Do you think it will work for me? You said it went back only through your lifetime."

That's a good point. It might be different for Rachel, maybe it is tuned somehow to whoever is using it at the time. I don't even know if Dad used it. He never mentioned it, neither has anyone else.

"I guess we'll have to try and see. I'm glad I told you now, I finally have someone to discuss it with."

"Why didn't you tell me before?"

"I was scared you'd think I was insane. Or on drugs or something." She laughs.

"No. Did your Dad invent any other cool things?"

"Oh, well yes, but they are quite obscure. I'm not even sure I totally understand."

"Try me."

"Well, he had an invention for a water fracturing process, using resonant frequency pulses of certain anode metals. He theorised that it caused hydrogen to mutate to deuterium, and in-so-doing, generate excess heat."

"Oh, umm. What?"

"In layman terms: it made more energy than it used. But no one could ever get it to work anywhere else. The company he worked for went bust in the end."

"That's some crazy shit."

"Yeah. You know what you were saying about the source of all things. That energy of a soul goes back to a source when you die."

"Right."

"That implies that the total quantity of energy never changes. It moves around, between say, the sun, then a tree, a lump of coal, then eventually back to some kind of source. Well, the same thing is true of the physical laws of energy."

"What are you getting at?"

"Dad's invention was theoretically impossible. But it worked! At least in his workshop."

Chapter Thirty-Four

WEDNESDAY 26TH SEPTEMBER

Rachel won't talk directly to Eoghan. Eoghan won't talk directly to Rachel. I'm sitting here like a fucking interpreter between their awkward, stilted comments, translating, adding politeness, describing what I think they mean. Project managing the shit out of this.

Rachel is checking every minor detail of the finally downloaded system that Eoghan has so lovingly prepared. He's defensive, she's thorough and questions methods that we use. Eoghan doesn't want to give away our secrets or something, but there's no magic involved, we automate things where possible. This was one of the things we sold FutureCloud on, so there's no need for the clandestine operation.

We've been here almost two hours already and I'm in desperate need of a piss and a coffee, in that order.

"Lads, are we almost done here?"

"Not really." Eoghan looks as if his life's work has been reduced to a pile of ashes. I don't know why he's so beaten up about this inspection. Everything is fine, Rachel is only asking how he did things, and why, not questioning his validity as a human being.

"Can we get a coffee break then? I'm about to burst my bladder here."

We head for the canteen and stop at the stinking pisser on the way. Rachel goes into her clean restroom with floral pastel tones and waterfalls, angels playing harps, and a full orchestra playing light classical music, and we dive into a disgusting dark pit of animal stench, faeces smeared on the walls, broken sinks, piss flooded floors. Alright, it isn't that bad, but it smells like it.

"Lad, you don't need to worry about Rachel. She's not judging you."

"I feel like I'm being evaluated."

"Why would she care? All she wants is the final system working. She's just curious about how we do stuff."

"I'm not comfortable with customers."

"No shit? But she's very nice."

We don't have time to go all the way into town for real coffee, so the brown rat-piss from the canteen will have to do. I have my pointless HR meeting later to find out how much of a pay rise I'm not getting, the miserable cow set the meeting for one pm. She probably takes an early lunch.

We sit at a table together, but we may as well be in different universes. Eoghan and Rachel are scrolling through their phones, so I follow suit and pull mine out. But I can't focus on the inane blur of Twitter. Something about Rachel's tarot reading is niggling at me. I can't put my finger on what it is though.

This morning in the hotel, she told me today was three weeks since we first met. So much has happened so quickly.

. . .

We go back to the lab and the dreary monotony of the inspection, Rachel pulls up her notes on her laptop and Eoghan goes back to his defensive stance. I sigh inwardly and try to let the stress wash away on an ocean of calm in my head.

It passed. Rachel is happy, all the software and hardware is configured precisely as FutureCloud need it. We should have some fireworks and a marching band parade or something, but instead, we have a very limp handshake and Eoghan slopes off to his desk to start work on the detailed work instructions.

I time my walk to the HR meeting so I arrive precisely at one, knock on the door and go in. Maeve is behind her desk, sat in her ergonomic chair, her laptop plugged into a screen on an elaborate stand, poised at the exact textbook angle for viewing comfort. She's got a new 'hair-do' that looks like a roadkill badger on top of her head, black and white stripes with red highlights. If I were an animal rights activist, I'd be throwing red paint at her now.

Something isn't right though. There's a fella sitting next to her, slicked back abrupt hair, bright white shirt with a tie that's short and wide in striking red, he's wiry thin, probably works out every day. They both stand up and we shake hands, her shake is dismissive and limp, her face shows the customary stapled on smile, but her eyes tell a different story. I don't like this at all. The wiry lad introduces himself as Todd Dunning from head office in the US. He insists I call him 'Todd', but I'd rather call him 'cunt'. There's an enthusiasm about him that is unnatural.

Time, For a Change

We sit down. I hope they get to the point quickly because I don't want to be in this room at all. I look around at the door to my right, noting the position of the handle and the direction it opens. A quick escape may be required.

"Thanks for coming in, Terry," Maeve opens with her nails-on-chalkboard voice. Not like I had any choice in coming, if you turn down a meeting with HR they just reschedule. I nod vaguely.

"As you may have heard, C.S.Tech is doing some global company restructuring." Nope I hadn't heard, and this is definitely going south, fast.

"That's why Todd is over now."

"I'm on my European tour!" he butts in, proud and jokingly. Does the cunt want a prize or something? I ignore him.

"I was in Glasgow last month," he adds. Something clicks in my head. A memory of something Sean was saying. I know what is coming now. A thud of adrenaline pumps through my veins, my face feels flushed, a prickle of sweat on my forehead. I'm not going to show these bastards my feelings though, that would give them what they want. I wish I had brought a bottle of water, my mouth is suddenly as dry as a camel's arsehole.

"We'll get to the point." About fucking time, lad. Todd's posture changes, he's no longer laid back and frat-boy joking, he's now serious, leaning forward, his brow creased. He's practised this in the fucking mirror, the sad twat. He's probably tapping the bottom of the desk with his boner right now.

"We're making some changes at the grassroots level." Maeve is nodding in harmony, she's the stooge here. Her smile still deeply upholstered onto her mug.

"Unfortunately, that means we have to change the way we

work too."

I thought he said he'd get to the point, this is very far from the fucking point. I think the point is in a different building and he's up a tree. We're past the point of me being polite now.

"What are you talking about?"

"We're offering a substantial redundancy package!" Maeve jumps in, spoiling Todd's thunder. He wanted to deliver the punch line and she stole it.

So this is it. Ten years of my life summed up with a 'substantial package'. Maeve and Todd are still talking but I can't hear anything else they say, I sometimes nod, look down at the sheet of paper they give me, I can't see the words, but the number at the bottom is quite a bit more than a whole years' salary. Someone said the words 'tax-free' too.

I want to protest, tell them I'm working on a massive deal right now, with a new customer, that has huge growth potential, that I've spent ten years here, slaving at this company, giving them my soul in return for barely enough money to pay my bills. But I don't say a word, there's no point in any argument, this deal was done before I came in the room. They have calculated my termination date for just over two weeks from now, my remaining vacation days have been paid into the redundancy amount.

I have to sign something and come back in two weeks for an 'exit interview'. Todd stands up and offers his hand again.

"We'd like to thank you for your service, Terry, and wish you all the best in your new life." I'd like to bury a steel toecap in his face. I ignore his outstretched hand.

Maeve turns back to her screen, her smile never faltered during the whole meeting.

I arrive back at my desk but I don't remember walking, I

shut my laptop and put it in my bag and then I see Rachel. She looks up at me, smiling, but her face drops quickly.

"We need to go, now."

In the car I tell Rachel what happened, she says she's so sorry, asks if I'm okay. I am okay. I'm devastated and shocked and confused. I feel betrayed and angry, sickened that my manager couldn't be bothered to tell me this herself. Annoyed that I have wasted such a big chunk of my life at this company just to be told to fuck off. I have roughly calculated that if I am frugal and cautious, I can stretch the money into about two years, but that is unlikely. I will need to find something else much sooner than that. It isn't exactly a job-seekers market at the moment in the west of Ireland.

The FutureCloud deal still has to be done. My instinct is just to let it rot, but I can't let Rachel down. Also, if I don't fulfil my duties until I'm officially gone, the fuckers won't pay my redundancy money. Only when that figure appears in my bank account, am I truly free.

But I am okay. Rachel reaches over and squeezes my hand as I drive to my secret secluded beach. Without her calming influence, I think I would be very much more stressed right now.

We arrive at the beach and there is never anyone around, especially today when it isn't very warm, and there's a fine mist of drizzle and a fierce wind. I don't care, and I walk down the sandy path to the water. Rachel follows, but I can see she's uncomfortable. The wind is cutting, she has her leather jacket on, but she's shivering. I don't know why I come here in times of stress, but the tidal flow seems to calm me. It's better than drinking to drown the sorrows anyway.

Rachel stands next to me, squinting against the spray and wind.

"Okay, we'll go back."

"No, it's fine. I'm okay."

"You are freezing."

"I'm fine."

"I just… I don't know what else to do."

I throw my arms around her and cough out tears, unexpected, uncontrollable, bursting and strangling at my throat, she holds me tightly and I hear her stifle back her own.

Back in the hotel and I'm reading the details of the package they are buying me off with, it works out to almost eighteen months of normal wages, in one lump sum.

There are some details about it being possible to pay no tax on this deal, if it's your first redundancy, which it is. On top of that, they will pay my health insurance for another six months. The rest is bullshit about free counselling and assistance in finding new work. Fuck them; I wouldn't give them the pleasure of going to their counselling. I'll have to go to the 'exit interview' to get the cash, but I won't say a fucking word. It makes me wonder what the point of this is? Who is going to do my job now? Who is going to baby-sit Eoghan and make sure he gets things done? Not my concern I guess, but I sure hope this decision comes back to bite them in the arse.

. . .

I turned my phone off earlier, I think we're meant to be on the FutureCloud status call about now, but fuck that. I already gave Sean an update today, everything is fine from the deal point of view. Eoghan should be okay now with only the work instruction left to do.

I think a long shower is appropriate to rinse away the stress. Rachel agrees and joins me. I told her this hairy arse won't wash itself!

Chapter Thirty-Five

THURSDAY 27TH SEPTEMBER

Among the usual junk-mail this morning I find a mail from Joanne, my 'boss' and numerous emails from Sean. I guess that was to be expected.

Joanne's mail is full of empty platitudes and apologies. It's barely even worth reading fully. 'Years of service, great job, wishing well for future.' I reply simply with 'So long, and thanks for all the fish.' I'm sure I will never hear from her again, and I'm not sad about that fact one bit.

Sean's emails were all asking me where I was, then where was Rachel, then how is the project going. I told him 'Sorry, we all got caught up with an issue in the lab with the test unit, and forgot about the call, but we fixed it, and the project is fine.'

I'm not ready to tell him about my future situation just yet. I should tell Ted though.

[10:31] Ward, Terry B:
Hey.

[10:32] O'Brien, Ted:
Morning, Terry.
How did your HR meeting go?

[10:32] Ward, Terry B:
Well…
Not great to be honest.

[10:32] O'Brien, Ted:
Oh :(

[10:32] Ward, Terry B:
I'm gone in two weeks.

[10:32] O'Brien, Ted:
What?!!

I tell Ted what happened and he's genuinely shocked. He hadn't heard of any redundancies at all. It's hard to know what to say when someone you have worked with for years is just dumped like a dead body down a mineshaft.

Eoghan is writing his work instruction today. I should tell him too, but that would probably just give him an excuse to stop work for the day. I'll leave him alone and tell him tomorrow or something maybe.

It feels strange now sitting at my desk, hard to concentrate on anything, even more than usual.

"You wanna go out for coffee?"
"Yeah." Rachel is quiet today, I think she feels bad for me

but doesn't know what else to say. We still have to work on her project, she still has a job to go back to. That fact gnaws at my guts too, now I will have all the time I need to visit her in Ohio, but if I spend all my cash on a trip like that, it won't last me long at all. I have to plan this very carefully.

"It will be okay. Remember you asked me the other day. I'll be okay."

She smiles and sips her coffee, she got some weird complicated thing today instead of her regular latte.

"I know. The universe will sort everything out."

"Are you okay?" For a moment it looks like she's going to say something, but she stops. I don't want to push her, but I'm sure there is something on her mind other than my impending unemployment.

"Yeah, dude. It's all good."

Maybe she's thinking about having to go back to Ohio, and when we'll next be together?

"I might do some travelling. I heard there are some fun things to do in Columbus?" She laughs.

"Yeah, but they are all in a hotel room."

"Sounds good to me!"

"Do you know what you'd like to do?"

"In a hotel room? Yeah, I know what I'd like to do!" She laughs and kicks me under the table.

"I mean after you are fired. What would your dream job be?"

I have to think about this for a while, but not much comes to mind. I used to dabble in coding, and I've wanted to make a mobile phone game for a long time, but there are millions of other good games in the market, how could I expect to make any money at it? It could be worth a try. I already have the equipment I need. I'd need to brush up on my programming skills a bit. Oh, and have an interesting idea for a game, too. That could be the hard part.

"I honestly don't know. Maybe something totally different? Definitely not cooking though."

"Will you cook me something?"

"If you want me to?"

"Yes, I would like that."

"Do you like lasagne? I make the best lasagne in Ireland!"

"I love lasagne!"

"Saturday then, at my house."

"It's a date!"

Back at my desk and inbox, Sean is placated, he's excited about coming over to see the final build of the five-hundred units, and probably drink as much Guinness, and drool over as many women as he can. I guess we'll have to go for dinner with him at least once. But I don't want another week of debauchery and boozing to deal with. This time he's renting his own car, so at least I don't need to worry about being his chauffeur again. He's staying in a different hotel to us, so he'll be nicely self-contained. I'll only really see him at work.

Also, the rest of the base systems have arrived now, and are all stacked up and waiting to be processed. The factory supervisors are getting whiny about the space they are taking up. I would normally reply and try to calm the situation, as this happens anytime we get in orders before we are ready to work on them. This time, I don't give a single fuck. They can whine until they call down Sasquatch from the woods for all I care.

Eoghan bounces into my periphery and waves to get my

attention. I don't even have headphones on this time. The lad is well trained at this stage.

"I could use Rachel's help on a couple of points in the instructions."

"Oh, sure, okay. We'll come down to the lab soon."

"Also, Judith contacted me again about DeltaWave."

"What?"

"Didn't you see the mail?"

"No?"

"Can you tell her to stop emailing me?"

"What do you mean? She should always come via me."

Eoghan shows me the email on his phone, she's reached out to him directly about an update to the DeltaWave software version again.

"This is what happened the last time. I had to update the software without a project revision a couple of months back."

"She asked you to do that?"

"Yeah."

"But, I thought…" I thought I had time-travelled back and fixed that problem, but she asked Eoghan to do it directly? I'm very confused now.

"Never mind. I don't care anymore."

Eoghan looks blank, and he's about to shuffle off to the lab. But I wave him down so I can lower my voice, "I got tapped."

"Tapped?"

"On the shoulder, told to fuck off, golden handshake, well, bronze handshake. I'm gone in two weeks, Eoghan."

His mouth is agape, calculating the likelihood his own income is in jeopardy. I'd be the same if I heard people in my office I worked with were being 'rubbed out'. But then, he smiles, laughing.

"You had me there for a minute!"

"No, dude, I'm not joking at all."

"Shit. Sorry, man."

"Yeah. Anyway, let's go down the lab and take a look at your hardware… That's what she said, by the way."

I have to translate again for Rachel and Eoghan while they iron out some minor details in the hardware build. This is the kind of ephemeral task that would never be mentioned in a job description, but is a vital part of my work. Relations between customers and our engineers are delicate, tense, awkward. It's the nature of the people who gravitate to these types of positions. Outside of work, I am not exactly a big socialiser, but in a professional situation, I can spoof my way through almost any problem. I should put that on my résumé, which I will need to update anyway now.

The thought of seeking a job in the real world is nightmarish. I haven't had to think about that sort of thing for a long time. Shaving for interviews, ironing shirts, polishing shoes, pretending to be interested in whatever crap they make or sell, coming up with bullshit reasons why I want to work at their fantastic company. I need money, that's why. If I didn't then I'd be happy to stay at home and piss around with whatever I felt like doing each day. It would be a very long time before I got bored and ran out of things to do. Maybe I could try and figure out how the mysterious box works for a start?

"Must be lunch time, lads?"

. . .

We go to the work canteen, partly in laziness of not wanting to go out, partly in some kind of misplaced nostalgia that maybe I'll never have to suffer the celery pie again, never have to chisel away at my fried eggs, or wring the grease from my sausages.

Eoghan sits down opposite Rachel, who is next to me. She looks uncomfortable but stays quiet. I squeeze her leg under the table.

"Have you met Sean?"

"No, I don't think so." Eoghan peers at his chicken curry suspiciously. Then tastes it and looks satisfied.

"He's been here a few times, you might have seen him around. Glasgow lad. Anyway, he'll be here next week. He'll probably want a meal out. You may as well come since you did all the work."

I hand him that bone to pick with, he'd only moan if I didn't.

"Ah, I don't know…"

"He'll pay for drinks all night."

"Oh, well, I might be able to make it."

After lunch, which wasn't too disgusting after all, we wander back to the lab and run through Eoghan's questions again until he seems happy. Tomorrow he'll finish up the work instruction and show it to Rachel for approval, and then to the factory supervisor for his input. Once those boxes are ticked, my work is more or less over. Rachel will check the first unit to be processed by the factory, and then maybe a few random samples during the week, but that's this deal done, dusted, signed off, money made. Sean and Pete will be super happy,

Rachel will get loads of praise when she goes back, Eoghan can move onto the next project. I'll still be out of a job.

The afternoon status call goes smoothly. Pete and Sean are ecstatic with the amazing progress we've made, Sean jokes he wishes all my projects go this quickly. I tell him that I can say, without doubt, this will be the quickest one I'll ever work on. I think I'll tell him the news when he gets here. It feels more appropriate. Rachel and I make like trees, and get the fuck outta here, the second the call is over.

When we get to the hotel, Rachel goes for a shower, and I pull out my personal laptop and start googling for techie jobs in the area. The results are dismal, almost nothing. The job sites let me enter in my local area for searching, but not until I include the whole of Ireland, does anything show-up at all. I'm not going to Dublin, fuck that. I couldn't afford it anyway. Instead, I download some programming refresher courses, and the latest tools for building games. May as well try that, it won't cost much. Only time, which is something I might find I have an abundance of.

Rachel comes out of the shower, moist, wrapped in a towel. I'm going to miss this view when she goes. She dries off and puts my T-shirt on again. She said she doesn't feel like getting dressed again, because it's uncomfortable. Suits me!

Chapter Thirty-Six

FRIDAY 28TH SEPTEMBER

The plan today was to get a fresh server from the factory stock, and run it through the work instruction, step by step, with Rachel and Eoghan doing the work, as if they had never seen it before, then Rachel would check it all against the final specification.

Thus far, it has taken a lot more effort and time than I imagined. Rachel isn't allowed to touch the hardware in the lab, because of insurance bullshit reasons. So Eoghan has to do the physical work. But he is easily flustered, and with us watching every step he makes, he's nervous, panicking, already bent some pins and dropped a memory stick. I would leave him alone to do it, but the whole point is that we watch it happen according to the instructions.

I think it's going to be okay in the end, but it isn't what I call efficient. I want to do as little work as possible for the next two weeks, so sitting here, actually doing tedious work is not much fun at all.

I'm also writing my shopping list for the meal I'm going to make for Rachel tomorrow. Scrolling Twitter and deleting emails. It occurs to me I don't need to worry about deleting emails anymore. Let them mount up and overflow my mailbox. The whole thing will be deleted once I'm gone anyway.

I haven't cooked for anyone other than myself in a long time, someone I cared about even longer. I'm glad I cleaned the house and scrubbed the kitchen now.

"What time did we start?"

Eoghan and Rachel look at me blankly with no answer.

"How long did it take?"

"Maybe an hour and a half, but it should go much quicker."

"We have to give the factory guys a processing time per unit. Fuck's sake. I forgot to time it. We'll have to do another one. But after lunch. It will go much quicker this time, right?"

"Yeah, just don't vanish for hours again for your lunch. I want to get out of here early."

"Me, too!"

"Does he know we are a thing?" Rachel breaks the silence as we sit watching the water flow, the wind has died down, and now it's just a grey, slightly misty day at our picnic spot.

"Eoghan? No, he wouldn't even know what a thing was if it jumped out of the toilet and bit him on the arse."

"What was that comment about? Taking hours for lunch." She sounds offended, irritated.

"He's just like that. He takes no joy in anything. Don't worry about it."

I don't know why she cares, what would it matter if Eoghan knew we were together or not? I leave it and change the subject.

"Are you excited to try out the time-machine tomorrow? It feels kinda strange the first time."

"Is that what you tell all the girls?" she laughs.

"Ha! Yeah, the queue of them at the door that I beat away with a shitty stick."

She pauses for a moment. "How come you were single?"

"Seriously? I'm a nerd who barely ever leaves his house, in the middle of nowhere."

"But it's not like you are bad looking."

"Well, thanks, but I don't go out, don't socialise, don't interact with humans."

"You weren't lonely?"

"I didn't say that. I just had no idea what to do about it."

"So you wanted to be in a relationship?" How did the topic go immediately back to relationships? I wonder what she's getting at here. This kind of discussion brings my paranoia back to the front of my mind. Are we on different pages here? Will she go home soon and I'll never see her again? What does she want from this?

"I suppose so. Am I?" She looks at me incredulously, eyes wide.

"What do you think?"

"Yes?" I venture.

"You damn right bro!"

"Okay, well, good!"

"I can't believe you would ask that!" There's a tone of pissed-off in her voice now.

"No, I mean, I wanted it to be 'yes', but I wasn't sure what you thought."

"Dude!"

"I'm not great at this."

"No shit?"

She reaches over and holds my hand and snuggles up close to me, calm again and warm.

"Yes, I'm excited to try your crazy time-machine box tomorrow! But we better go and finish that fucking server now, before Eoghan shits himself."

She learns quickly!

With only minutes to spare before the daily status call, we got the second server completed, timed, checked and passed.

I give the news to a rapturous Sean and Pete. Sean promises a slap-up meal in celebration when he comes over next week. I could do without that really, I'm not particularly in a celebrating mood.

I make sure I give due praise on the call to Rachel and Eoghan, because, without Eoghan's unbelievable never-before-seen speed, getting all the work done, this could have been a horrible disaster. My plan to bring Rachel over was worthwhile too, not just for my satisfaction, but we wouldn't have been able to sign things off, and make adjustments so quickly if she was back in Ohio, and we were guessing how things fit together.

This customer that I was reluctant even to visit just a few weeks ago, has turned out to be something I could never have imagined. I pulled off my last project for C.S.Tech with amazing speed and agility, and got myself a girlfriend in the process. If only I didn't get fired at the same time, this would have been quite a good gig.

. . .

We left immediately after the call. I didn't even bother bringing my laptop. It can stay here until Monday morning.

Chapter Thirty-Seven

SATURDAY 29TH SEPTEMBER

Rachel was shocked at how few cereal brands we have here, compared to American supermarkets. Then she marvelled at how our 'candy' was all different.

I didn't buy either of those things. We stocked up on all the ingredients I need to make my most exceptional lasagne, including some red wine for the sauce. It felt nice to walk around the store with someone, and discuss salad leaves and what real parmesan cheese looks like. This is what being a couple is all about?

As we approach my house and the road narrows, I'm nervous, Rachel will shortly see my shitty house for the first time in real life. For some reason, it's important to me that she doesn't hate it. I know it isn't much, but it is the sum of much work that I did personally, with the help of Dad. It is a part of my life and memories. Not only that, but I'm curious to see what happens when Rachel tries the box. Will she see her past? My past? Will she see something different? I guess we'll find out soon.

. . .

I pull up to the front yard and look over at Rachel, she's smiling, but I think she's a tiny bit repulsed. I haven't done any gardening or outside maintenance for a long time. When I'm at my desk, working in my office, I can't see, and don't care about those things.

I grab the shopping bags and unlock the door, leaning heavily on the wood to push it open, but it doesn't work, I have to resort to a heavy shove with my shoulder and a boot to the bottom. An epic entrance! I flip on the lights and stand aside so Rachel can see.

"It's nice!" She smiles and looks around, then sits down on the leather couch.

"Are you sure?"

"Yeah, I mean, it's not super fancy, but it's okay."

"Can I get that in writing?" She laughs, and I start putting away the shopping in the fridge. It's a relief that she's okay with it. The anticipation is always worse than the reality.

"You want a drink? Tea, coffee?"

"Your weird milky tea? No thanks! You got water?"

I bring her a bottle and slump down on the couch next to her. No one else has ever sat on this couch since I bought it.

"You want the tour? It will take about thirty seconds."

I show her the kitchen, dining room and living room all at once because they are all the same room, and we're already in it. There's a laundry room - not very exciting. Then my office which she is impressed by, I think, at least she was in awe of just how many computers and things I had managed to cram into a small room. There's a bathroom upstairs and then my bedroom, which also has a little en-suite bathroom.

"Oh, you have a big hot-tub!"

"It's not really a hot-tub, just a big tub. But it does get hot. I like a nice relaxing bath."

She smiles, flirting, touching her hair and smoothing down her shirt. This evening could be more fun than I had imagined!

Then there's the shed of course, disconnected from the house, full of tools and equipment. Oh, and a time-machine. Doesn't everyone keep a time-machine in the shed?

"It could use a woman's touch. But it isn't as bad as I thought it would be."

"You know what else could use a woman's touch?"

"Shut up!"

We go back to the living room. I flick around on my phone and music floods the house, Rachel jumps, it was set very loud since the last time I played something. I turn down the volume so it's barely there, a mix of classical with modern influences.

"You want a snack? The lasagne will be a while."

"Yeah."

I make my staple, eggs on toast, as we missed breakfast at the hotel again. Rachel insists I grind pepper onto the eggs in the pan, spoiling the pristine white, but adding spice. An interesting flare.

We eat quickly, and I tidy up and load up the dishwasher with the dirty plates, I like a clean kitchen when I start proper cooking. We're skirting around the question, but I can't wait any longer.

"You wanna see the shed?"

"I thought you'd never ask!"

We go across the yard and I take a deep breath. Once again I'm nervous beyond my control. At the door, I turn and look at Rachel, hands in her jacket pockets, expectant, smiling. It will be fine.

I open the door, flick on the light, and there it sits, on the bench, lid closed, how I left it.

"Well, there it is! It doesn't look much, but it's deceptive."

Rachel walks over to the box and runs her hand over the wood, she squints, confused, looks over at me and then back at the box lid.

"Go ahead, open it."

She lifts the lid a crack and peeks inside, pauses then opens it up fully and stands back.

"Is the machine under the tools and stuff?"

"What?"

"The cone and hand shapes. Are they hidden under all the junk?"

My heart pounds in my chest, a thud of adrenaline courses through my veins, my nerves turn to panic, and I rush over to the box. Has something happened? Has it been stolen? Broken somehow?

As I look into the box now, I see the same as Rachel sees, a box of junk, tools, plumbing equipment. There are small cut-offs of copper pipe, a rolled up sheet of thin sharp-edged brass with holes punched out here and there. Four black knobs in a small dusty plastic bag.

A sudden change, a drop in temperature, the feeling of falling fast. Darkness, no weight. Silence, a rapid fade of all external senses

... [please hold while we try to connect you] ...

Time, For a Change

Gradually, then suddenly, some senses return.

"Terry! Oh my god! TERRY!"

I look up and see Rachel panicked, leaning over me, scared, almost crying.

"It's okay." I try to sit up, but I'm dizzy, my head spins. I lie back down on the cold concrete floor of my shed.

"Um, what happened?"

"You blacked out! You scared the shit out of me!"

"When?"

"Just now! Dude, what the fuck?"

I prop myself up, slowly sitting, nausea subsides, and I stand up, Rachel offers her hand. I walk back over to the box and look inside again, just a bunch of junk and tools, pipes and odds and sods.

I lower the lid back down and read the writing on top.

"General odds and sods !!"

In my Dad's unforgettable handwriting, in black permanent marker.

"I don't understand." I feel my eyes prickle with the tears that are about to arrive on stage, and a headache, waiting in the wings. Rachel looks at me and throws her arms around me. Once again I cry on her shoulder, the emotion strangling at my throat and I sense her holding back sobs in sympathy.

On my couch, I sit and stare at my fingernails, clasped around a mug of hot, black coffee that Rachel has brought me. They offer me no solution, no clues to the situation I find myself in, but I can't look up at Rachel now. Instead, I study the tiny details of the nail clipper cuts, sometimes cutting into the skin around my nails, I wonder why it doesn't hurt, doesn't bleed?

Rachel is calm, trying to comfort me, offer reasons and advice, but I can only see my fingertips and hear the patter of the rain that has started to tap on my roof windows. I'm an idiot, or I'm insane, delusional? Did I hallucinate all those box-journeys? No, surely not, they were so vivid and real, I was THERE. But was I?

"Drink your coffee, dude. You'll feel better."

I watch my hand bring my cup up to my face, like I'm not in control. As if I'm behind myself. I sip at the sweet black liquid, and feel the heat run down my throat. Distant, but right here.

"I don't understand." I repeat the empty words, but nothing else comes to mind. I am lost for answers.

"I googled." I look up at her finally, she's perched on the coffee table in front of me. Her phone in her hand.

"Have you ever suffered from narcolepsy? Or depression?"

"Narcolepsy?"

"Yeah, when you randomly fall asleep."

"I know but… No, I don't think so?"

"Stress and lack of sleep and trauma can trigger it. You can have vivid hallucinations with it. Do you have any St John's Wort?"

"Any what?"

"I guess not." She looks up at me, smiling patiently.

"Do you feel okay?"

"I feel like a fucking idiot! I'm embarrassed, and possibly crazy!"

"No! It's fine! You just need to chill I think. Sleep properly, relax. I'll get you a herbal tea to drink every day."

Along with the embarrassment and headache, there's a massive sense of loss. I had a time-machine, now I just have a box of junk and a strange sleep condition. No matter what she says, Rachel must think I'm some kind of fool, how could I be so deceived? Something clicks in my head, and I think back to the tarot reading Rachel did.

"The Moon." I look up at her, she tilts her head, confused.

"The tarot cards, the Moon. You said it was deceit, confusion and stress, losing touch with reality."

"Yes."

"But I saw the writing, the cone spinning inside, the control knobs."

Rachel shrugs, trying to look sympathetic and comforting.

"The eyes show the brain what it needs to see."

"And the tower, the people jumping out from a fiery death. The redundancy?"

"Could be."

"Shit."

My knives are blunt now, after years of neglect. They used to be razor sharp. All of ours were, brand new, rolled up in a bundle of thick canvas. The same knives I bought for college, all those years ago, I now use to chop onions and garlic and freshly picked basil from a little plant. I should sharpen them.

I can hear the college tutors in my head, telling me if I'm going to cut myself, make sure I do it with a sharp knife, it will heal faster, cleaner. Scar less. My thumb instinctively goes to a tiny scar on my left ring-finger, where I almost cut the end off with a Japanese knife I was unfamiliar with, somehow the ridges of the scar reassure me, tie me down, ground me.

We still need to eat, and I have all the ingredients, so I got up off the couch eventually and started making dinner, because what else can I do? Life goes on.

Rachel is watching, leaning on the other side of the counter, sipping at a glass of red wine.

"Pour me a glass?"

"Really?"

"Yeah, fuck it." I realise that we were planning to go back to the hotel after dinner.

"Oh. Never mind. I have to drive us back later."

"You have a bed here, dude."

I look up, she's smiling, cute, running a finger up and down the glass in her hand. She stands up and goes over to the dresser and picks up another glass and fills it with my sauce wine.

"Mum always says that Chianti tastes like old pennies."

"It tastes like blood."

I pick up the beef packet and show her the drip of red liquid at the bottom.

"You want some of this?"

"Agh! You nasty! How long does the tub take to fill up?"

"Oh, well, the water has to heat first."

"How long does that take?"
"A couple of hours, give or take."
"Heat it then, dude!"

I flick on the water, and despite the emotions and fears still lingering in my mind, I smile at the evening ahead of me. Good food, good company, a hot bath and my bed.

Chapter Thirty-Eight

SUNDAY 30TH SEPTEMBER

Rachel found my store of storm candles and lit them all around the bathtub. She made some kind of concoction with coconut oil, sugar and lavender oil from her purse. She said my colourful bubble stuff was terrible for the skin, too harsh, this lotion scrub thing she made was much better. She sprinkled basil leaves into the tub as well.

It was wonderful. Bath skills levelled up three notches. As music drifted in from the bedroom speakers, and Rachel rubbed my back with her coconut scrub, while I sipped at the wine, I felt the tension of the day flow away. Rachel only drank one glass, I think I drank the rest of the bottle myself.

I woke up early, and as I sat up, it felt like I slammed my head into an invisible iron bar above the bed. Woolly and painful and my mouth tastes like I drank a gallon of unleaded petrol. I got a bottle of water from the fridge and dropped soluble painkillers into it, then laid on the couch, throbbing gently.

I open Twitter on my phone and post a random thought:

Time, For a Change

Life is like an Amazon review: "absolutely loved it, best thing ever." and then lower down "DO NOT BUY! Waste of money, terrible product!"

I'm angry at myself for being so deluded and blind about a box of junk. How could I have been so misled and confused? Could it all be down to stress, trauma, tiredness? I don't understand it.

What if it was all real, and just fulfilled its purpose, then turned into a box of junk? Did dad set it up to expire at a certain point? I'm clutching at straws here, but I just can't believe all those journeys were hallucinations. It was all too real.

I need coffee, I drag myself to the kitchen and put on the pot, following through the steps like a robot, automatic, disconnected from my limbs that seem to know what they are doing, so I leave them alone. In the kitchen I see the remnants and mess of dinner last night. Rachel said my lasagne was indeed the best she had ever tasted, I brushed invisible specs of dust from my shoulder, and she rolled her eyes. But she didn't eat much, she said it was very filling. There's loads of it left in the fridge. I still always make enough for a restaurant full of people.

The food and wine made me think of Italy and my family that I haven't seen for a long while. I will soon have some free time and some money. I should probably visit them. I wonder if Rachel would come along? The logistics of that would be complicated, plus she is undoubtedly expected back at work in Ohio soon.

As my head gradually calms and the dull ache fizzles away I send a group text to my family: 'I have some news…' I get back a stream of questions and exclamation marks as I explain the job situation, and they are already planning to clear out a spare room for me to stay in. I haven't even looked at flights or dates yet.

I didn't tell them about Rachel, and I never told them about the box.

I hear activity from the bedroom, then a toilet flush, and then Rachel appears in the living room wearing my T-Shirt and slippers. The floor is cold, big grey stone flags, worn smooth, and the occasional small rug. Slippers are cheaper than rugs.

Under the stone is mud, dirt, earth, whatever you want to call it. The occasional slug, or worm have been known to squeeze through the gaps from underground. But the slugs here are less of an issue than the slug-people at work.

"Hey." She yawns and stretches.

"Hey." I can barely make the sound come out of my mouth, I sip the water. The coffee-maker coughs out its last dregs into the pot, and I wander over to pour us a cup.

"Did you sleep okay?"

"I don't know. I was asleep." She gives me a look and comes over and wraps around me.

My phone continues to buzz in my dressing-gown pocket, the group message is wild with questions, when will you come? What will you do now? How much money did you get? Why did they sack you? What did you do?

I don't feel like answering anything now. I'll get back to them later.

"I think I'll go to see my family for a bit."

"Oh, in Italy?"

"Yeah."

"That would be nice."

"I don't suppose…. I mean, is there any way you could come?"

"Oh, wow. I dunno, I'm meant to be back at work soon. But…"

"Yeah, I thought so. But what?"

"Nothing, I would love to go, but I don't know how right now."

"I haven't made a plan yet, I was going to look at flights and stuff in a bit."

"I'll have a think."

"Okay. Do you want to do anything today? Go anywhere?"

"Not really. I'd rather just hang out."

"Hairy muff."

"What!"

"Fair enough. You hungry?"

I start to make some breakfast, scrambled eggs today for a change. Toast, bacon, sausages. The works. Rachel cleans off the table and sits down with her coffee.

"I had a crazy idea."

"Oh? What's that."

"About the box." She looks up and looks a bit concerned, but I smile, and she seems satisfied.

"Hear me out… I know this will sound crazy, but, what if the box-journeys were real. The box was a time-machine. But Dad set it to somehow cease to exist once it had served its purpose."

"You are right, that does sound crazy."

"No, listen… Time is a complicated beast. If you change

something tiny in the past, it can have massive repercussions in the future."

"I guess."

"The classic time-travel problem. What if you travel back in time and stop your parents from ever meeting? You would never exist, so how could you travel back in time. Or, what if a future me travelled back and stopped the box from ever being made."

"Why would you do that?"

"Good point. Maybe I fucked up something, changed something critical. Tried to go back and stop it from ever happening?"

Rachel ponders, and I bring our breakfast to the table.

"Or, maybe I was trying to prevent something else, and it didn't work. What if some things are inevitable? And no matter what you try, the universe has already made up its mind?"

"Cancer?"

"Yeah. So I went back and stopped it before it could torture me anymore. Something like that."

"Is there any way to find out?"

"I have no idea… Are you going to eat that?" Rachel picks at her toast but hasn't touched anything else on her plate.

"No, you can have it."

"Good, I'm wasting away here!"

"Yeah, I can see!"

"My skin feels soft." I hunt around the bedroom for my jeans from where I flung them last night.

"That's the coconut oil. It's good for you. Way better than that bubble shit."

"But I like bubbles."

"You like soft skin?"

"Okay, fair point. But the tub looks like we fried chips in it."

"Rinse it out, it will be fine."

"Shall we go for a walk down the lane? It looks clear out now, but my phone said it might rain later."

"Yeah, that would be nice."

People always moan about the cold, but I prefer it cool. If it's cold out you put a jacket on, walk faster, you'll soon be warm. But if it is too hot, what can you do?

I hate being sweaty, and my body simply shuts down with excessive heat.

Back in my cooking days, I had no problem with the heat of the kitchen but my body has changed somehow. If I won the lottery, I wouldn't be going to a hot climate. The only reason I feel like I can visit my family now, is it should be cooler at this time of year, halfway up a mountain outside Rome in October. I hope it is anyway?

There's a breeze, and Rachel zips up her jacket, stuffs her hands in her pockets. But she marches on, despite her hair blowing around her face.

We see a cow in the field, just behind the fence at the road. A big fucker, staring right at us, chewing slowly, contempt on its face, a big sloppy shit plops out behind onto the grass.

"Yup. The story of my life!"

"Ha!"

As we walk down the lane, the fence turns to a thick stone

wall, covered in hedges and gorse. Rachel takes some photos of the dangerous looking spiky plant. I've never really bothered to study it before, it's just a weed that grows everywhere, but the patterns and spikes are quite beautiful when you look with a different eye.

"It's so quiet here."

"Yeah. In the middle of the night, it can be even quieter. The only sound sometimes on a clear night is the ripping of grass as a cow chews. But the wind and rain can be brutal too."

"I believe you."

"You want to go back?"

"Please."

Back at the house, I heat up some lasagne for lunch, I put the rest in the freezer, no sense in wasting it.

"So, there were some other cards in the tarot reading."

"Yeah."

"What else might happen?"

"Hard to say, just be open to changes."

"More changes?"

"Maybe."

"I hope they are good ones."

"It probably depends on your point of view."

"How do you mean?" It seems like Rachel wants to say something more.

"Oh, I dunno, dude. These things are hard to interpret sometimes."

. . .

After we eat and clean up, we make our way back to the hotel. I want to check flights and things, and I left my laptop in the hotel, something I would never usually do, for fear of it being stolen or something. But everything was fine, and our room was nice and clean. The internet is faster here than at my house anyway.

I can fly to Rome very cheaply, but I have to go to Dublin first. Which is a pain in itself, but not insurmountable. So I book a three week trip to Italy, because - why not? If we figure out a way for Rachel to join me, then it won't be a problem to get another ticket.

Chapter Thirty-Nine

MONDAY 1ST OCTOBER

"Hey, buddy!"
"Hey, you old radge!"
Sean's ugly mug appears at my desk, as cheerful as a man who just invented blow-job underpants and sold the patent for a billion.
"Hey, Rachel." He peers over the cubical wall and waves.
"Coffee?"
"You buying? Only I'm out of a job here!" Sean looks confused.

In the canteen, I tell him about my employment situation, and he's stunned, pissed off, he says he'll go to my manager and complain. I tell him it's not worth it, the deal is done. The powers-that-be have made a decision based on 'who knows what' criteria and they won't give a single rats arse if anyone objects. In fact, saying anything could put his own job at risk. I'm sure there's a list somewhere of people who are troublemakers. They fucking sell it to Santa Claus in December, too.

. . .

"I'm really sorry, mate. Who's going to manage my projects now?"

"I don't know, but you know what? That is most definitely someone else's problem now."

"All the more reason for a slap up meal when this deal is done! We have to give you a good send off!"

I was going to object, tell him I didn't want a fuss, but fuck it, I think I deserve a fuss, I think the company can afford me one last epic feast.

The plan today is to have the first unit processed by the factory team and then Rachel will recheck it all. This will be the final proof we need that everything is good to go. Eoghan wasn't around earlier when I checked his desk. The fucker better not be out on a Monday-headache again.

I email the factory supervisor that we want to kick off a single unit for full processing. He sends me a message back almost immediately, they've already done it, Eoghan had already asked him to start it first thing this morning. The unit is already in our lab, ready for inspection. Eoghan must have contracted some kind of acute efficiency virus. Maybe that's why he's out today, lying in bed experiencing symptoms of actually doing everything he's meant to do on time. I'm impressed, and we head to the lab.

When we get there, I realise that none of us are actually allowed to touch the hardware, because of bullshit insurance reasons - I didn't do my static electricity course, because it's pointless and ridiculous, and I already know what I'm fucking doing. Sean wouldn't know one end of the server from the other, and Rachel doesn't work for us.

"Wait a minute!"

We look up at Sean who has lit up like he swallowed a lighthouse.

"This is invoiced now, technically it has left the factory. Rachel, this is yours now. Do as you please with it!"

"Fucking smooth, Sean! This is why you are on the big bucks!"

We help Rachel get the heavy server out of the box and set it up on a bench. I give her an anti-static wrist strap, and she pulls up all her notes again and begins her tedious inspection. Sean and I give her some space and wander over the other side of the lab.

"Fuckin' tidy wee one you got there, buddy!"

"Yup. I reckon she's a keeper. Don't know what I'm going to do now though. When she goes back, I don't know when I'll see her again."

"You interested in moving to Ohio? Pete was very impressed with the work you did."

"Oh, shit! Really? I hadn't even thought of anything like that."

"Might be worth a roll around the noggin. I'll put in a good word for you, no problem at all."

"But I'd need a green card, work permit, all that shite."

"I'm sure that could be sorted if they wanted to make it happen."

"Fuck… You've given me something to think about for sure."

"You know where I am if you need anything, mate."

"I'm taking a few weeks off anyway, going to visit my

family in Italy."

"Well deserved, get some pasta and ice cream into you!"

"Yeah, as you can see, I'm starving to death here!" I pat my expanding gut. I need to do something about that. More walks maybe, cut down on the bacon. My problem with exercise is; it doesn't produce anything tangible. The only purpose of running, for me, would be to escape an angry girl's father with a shotgun, or something along those lines.

Speaking of which, Rachel waves to get our attention then gives a 'thumbs up' sign. Nice one!

"That was quick!"

"I've done this like a million times now."

"Everything good to go then?"

"Yeah, but Pete wanted me to do some more random samples. To make sure quality was predictable and persistent or some shit."

"That makes sense. But now, must be lunchtime?"

I email the factory lad and tell him to proceed with fifty more units and to randomly choose five of them for us to do more tests with. Then we head out for food. Sean wanted to have a mini celebration. There's a fancy Chinese place near the office, so we drive over, in two cars, because we can't decide which one to go in, which is both ridiculous and wasteful, but I can't be arsed to argue.

It's open for lunch, but there's no one else here. There's a hint of bleach in the air as the door opens, which is precisely what I don't want to smell as I go into a restaurant. We are seated at a specific table by the waiter, way at the back, which seems unnecessary, but whatever.

Rachel is quiet, as expected since we have Sean as company. She seems content nibbling at her food and sipping her glass of water though. I don't want to make a fuss and embarrass her. Sean doesn't seem to mind anyway, we talk about work and the painful customers we've had, present company excepted of course! Poor girl is probably bored out of her mind hanging around with us old farts talking work.

"Where do you want to go for your leaving do?"

"Oh, I haven't thought about it. There's amazing smoked salmon in Reykjavik…"

"I was thinking more local!"

"Right, right." I ponder for a moment.

"What about a real medieval banquet? In a castle!"

"Sounds great!"

I send Sean a link to Bunratty castle, which is between here and the airport.

A real, old castle where they have dinner and a medieval show for tourists, I've been once before many years ago. I think Rachel will appreciate it.

"It's not cheap, but I don't care as I'm not paying!"

"Aye, don't worry about that. We are entertaining a valuable customer!" Sean winks at Rachel, who shyly smiles, blushing a little. I show her the castle website and photos, and she seems excited.

But once again, the feast celebration is just a prefix to the sadness that will follow when I take her back to the airport, and she leaves my life again. I will have to do some serious pondering about approaching Pete at FutureCloud to see if he has a job for me. I've already moved country once in my life, and it was only a short hop across from England. Going to America to live and work would be quite different. I have

Time, For a Change

thought about it before, when I've been on other work trips. I could deal with it, but the way of life would take some getting used to. I guess the first step would be finding out if they had a job available. I think I'll take Sean up on his offer to reach out to Pete. I'm sure some favours are owed there.

We amble back to the office and find some sample servers waiting in the lab for us. Rachel does her due diligence and finds no problems. We're flying it. Sean is delighted, and on the afternoon status call, Pete is full of praise for everyone. We may even ship all five-hundred units a day early if the factory continues at the rate they are going. Pete mentions on the call that he's looking forward to having his engineer back in his own factory. That stings a bit, I know it's going to happen, but I'd preferably not think about it. I've gotten quite fond of having Rachel around. She's changed many things in my life already, even stuff I thought I was expert at, like, how I make my eggs and even how I soak in the bath.

But there's no point in worrying about what will come. We still have some time together. Time to make memories worth remembering.

Sean is staying in an even fancier hotel, across town from us, he was bragging he had a view of the Shannon, but I know what he means is - he has a view of the scrap yard next to the Shannon. Fine if you like the colour of rust I guess.

He wanted to go for a drink this evening, out in town, we said no, neither Rachel or I had a desire to linger in a stinky pub. Rachel has gone off booze recently, in fact, I think I've drunk more than she has on this whole trip. Maybe my influence is wearing on her in the same way hers is on me.

In the end, we agreed to meet Sean in his hotel bar for a while before dinner, but dinner for us will be something simple. I'm serious about trying to lose some weight, but it isn't easy when almost every meal is takeaway or restaurant.

We get back to our hotel, and Rachel disappears into the bathroom to get ready. I start looking at house rental prices nearby to Columbus, just in case. I like to have as much information as possible before I make any choices. I haven't mentioned the idea yet to Rachel. There's no need to get her worked up if there's zero chance of it happening. I don't even know if she would want me to be in Ohio full time. I still have problems accepting that this beautiful young girl wants to be with me, of all the people in the world she could pick. A boring old nerd.

Having spent some time in Ohio, I know it isn't the worst place in the world, but it wouldn't ever be on my top ten list of places to up and move to, without the influence of Rachel. They do have a nice office upstairs at FutureCloud I guess, free coffee too…

"Hey." Rachel pops her head out of the bathroom.

"Dude, you go meet Sean on your own. I don't feel like going out."

"Oh, really?"

"Yeah, you guys can talk your boring shit. You don't need me around."

"Oh, well, I don't need to go…"

"No, it's okay. Go have fun with Sean."

"I'm not going to drink. One bottle of wine is enough for me for a year."

"Whatever, I'm fine just chilling here. I might call Mom."
"Well, okay if you are sure. I'll bring food back."
"Cool. Get burgers."

The walk is about twenty minutes, probably fifteen if I have the wind behind me. I don't want to move the car, and a taxi seems wasteful. I kiss Rachel and ask her seventeen more times if she's sure she doesn't want to come, and doesn't mind me going alone, she kicked me out of the room in the end. But kissed me goodbye and told me to be safe.

The walk is bracing, if a little painful on my feet, I think I'll probably get a taxi back once I have grabbed some food.

Sean is propping up the bar when I get to the hotel, he has a pint and a whiskey in front of him. If he wants to go and get arse-faced then he'll be going alone, I'm not interested in that. I told Rachel I'd be two hours max.

"Hey, hey! Get the man here a drink," he turns to the bartender.

"Sparkling water for me, please."

"Ahh, you need to lighten up, lad."

"Nah, not tonight."

"Where's your wee yin?"

"She didn't feel good, stayed back at the hotel. She's not into the drink at the moment either."

"She's a funny one for sure. Quiet as a mouse."

"She's not like that when we're alone. She's just a bit shy I think."

"Nothing wrong with that."

"No, she's fine, anyway she's young, and we're old and boring."

"That's true."

"I was thinking about what you said. About talking to Pete."

"Yeah?"

"Well, I mean, nothing may come of it. But it might be worth a go?"

"Yeah, of course, can't hurt to try."

I sip my water and Sean downs his two drinks and gets two more. I think I need to call it a night before this gets out of hand, and he starts chatting up the table full of pensioners that just came into the bar. It sounds like they are from New York. Probably looking for their heritage.

"You going into town?"

"I was going to, but I changed my mind." He nudges me, and motions towards the bartender with a wink. I hadn't even given her a second look, but now I think about it, she looks like Sean's type. Mid-thirties, short-cropped dark hair, distinctly eastern European, tits that you could 'bounce a fucking peanut off'. I think this is my cue to exit, stage left.

"I'll leave you to it, lad! See you in the morning, right?"

"Aye, mate, no bother at all."

I slope off leaving Sean in his natural habitat, in a bar, staring at cleavage, and I head up into town, to the burger venue of choice.

Chapter Forty

TUESDAY 2ND OCTOBER

Sean was in the office super-early this morning, in with the first factory shift around seven, he said. The efficiency virus must be spreading. I hope I don't catch it now.

He's organised another hundred and fifty units to be processed on the first shift of the factory, and another one-hundred tonight. That means we'll be over halfway done in only two days. It's quite depressing, actually, that my most successful project is my last one, but maybe it is best to go out with a bang?

On the subject of bangs, Sean told me he lucked out with Magda the bartender last night, despite his smoothest and most eloquent performance, apparently. She 'wisnae interested'. Some you win, some you lose, eh buddy!

Rachel has already tested five more units and found no problems at all. She's happy that things are going well, but there's a tinge of sadness in her too, I think. Perhaps because she's heading back soon? Maybe she misses her family? There's something on her mind, but she doesn't seem to want to discuss it, so I let her be. If she wants to talk I'm sure she will.

Eoghan graced us with his presence in the office today too, he's made a miraculous and full recovery from the death-bed illness he must have had yesterday. I introduced him to Sean, but he showed little interest and went back to whatever new thing he's working on, now that FutureCloud is done for him. By tomorrow he'll have forgotten every tiny detail of it. Sean invited him out for dinner on Thursday with us, for our medieval feast. Eoghan looked as uncomfortable as a shopping-mall marriage proposal that went badly, but he agreed after some coercion. He did do exceptional work for this deal, so he may as well take some credit and enjoy the mead and wenches.

Rachel and I sneak off for a sandwich picnic lunch by the river again. I think she is a bit overwhelmed by Sean and his ever-cheery demeanour. She said she wanted some peace and quiet.

"I have to book my flight back later."

"Oh, yeah." Suddenly my appetite has vanished, and I wrap my half-eaten sandwich back up.

"It's okay, dude. You are going to Italy anyway."

"Yeah, but then what?"

"I don't know. We'll talk every day anyway," she motions with her phone.

"I guess. But still."

"I know. The universe will figure it all out."

She smiles and squeezes up next to me, her arm through mine, her head on my shoulder. The intoxicating scent of her perfume is melting through my pain and stress as we watch the river drift by, high on the banks and powerful.

"Can we go back to the hotel? I don't feel like going back to the office now."

"You don't have to ask me twice!"

I send Sean a message that we're not coming back, to cover for me on the call later, and if anything strange happens.

Back in the hotel Rachel takes off her shoes and flops down on the bed, she looks tired, but she motions me to come over and lie down with her. She rests her head on my chest and I stroke her hair.

"If there was anything you could go back in time and change, what would it be?" That came out of the blue. I wonder what she's thinking.

"My time-machine is broken, remember?" She laughs and pinches my nipple through my shirt.

"Ow!"

"If it was working, and it let you change things."

"Wow, there are many things, I guess."

"But, do you have any big regrets?"

"Someone once said: 'as I grow older, I realise that the only things I regret are the things I didn't do' or something like that."

"That's neat, but okay, so what didn't you do?"

I want to say something like, 'I wish I had met you twenty years ago', but then I realise that she would have been a toddler twenty years ago, so that isn't going to work.

"Most people my age would have a wife and kids, two cars in the driveway, a pension, an annual holiday to Portugal, after-school activities, dinner parties, pub mates, evenings in front of the telly. They would have all their excrement centrally located. Or at least, they would think they did. But, I have none of those things. And honestly, I don't want most of them… But the one thing that hurts me the most, is that my dad never got to meet my potential offspring." She twists her head and looks up at me, sadness in her eyes.

"I never had a Grandfather. It seemed important to me that one day I would introduce a new baby-person to Mum and Dad. That my kid would be able to benefit from all their knowledge, like I did. We'd make things together in the workshop, discuss science and the nature of the universe. Learn about plumbing, metal-work, electronics and magnets. Then eat roast chicken and gravy around the big table." Rachel is sniffing. I think she's crying. "Are you okay?"

"Yeah, dude. Sorry."

"Don't be." I kiss her head gently and squeeze her tight to me.

"Are you saying you want kids?"

"Well, honestly, I never did, I have no idea how to look after kids, and anyway it was never possible before, not being a starfish."

"But now?"

"But now, I just lost my job, and I may be going slightly mad. Maybe now is not a good time either! What about you?"

"Me?"

"What do you regret? Or what would you change?"

"Oh boy, don't get me started. The whole college thing, I think it was a mistake now. This job, it's not great honestly. I mean, it's okay, but I don't think it's for me long term."

"What would you do if you could do anything?"

"Oh, that's easy. I'd have a camper van, driving round to all the craft fairs, selling crochet blankets, spells and charms. Then at home, I'd have a big garden, growing my own fruit and vegetables, beehives for honey. And I'd raise moths."

I laugh, "Seriously?"

"Yeah, I have a plan. I had a plan anyway. Things don't always turn out how you think."

"No, they sure don't."

I think we drifted to sleep, at least I did. I wake up on the bed, clothed, feeling like I've been trampled by an antelope. Rachel is at the desk on her laptop.

"Hey." I get up, slowly, moving towards the bathroom.

"Hey, sleepy-head."

"You okay?"

"Yeah. I just booked the flight. Saturday morning."

"Oh."

"Pete was up my ass to be back at work on Monday," she motions at her laptop screen and rolls her eyes.

"No rest for the conflicted, huh?"

"I've been thinking about quitting."

"Quitting? Really?"

"Yeah, I think I got what I needed from this whole deal."

"Hmm. Do you think FutureCloud would need an experienced project manager, who is already familiar with their products and technical requirements?"

"You?"

"No, Eoghan!" She slaps me on the arse and looks up at me.

"Yes, me!"

"Um, I dunno, I mean, maybe."

"Can you wait until I'm back from Italy before quitting?"

"Yeah, sure. Oh my god! You'd come live in Ohio?"

"Well, I guess, why the fuck not?"

"It's not exactly the centre of the universe."

"You've seen where I live."

"Okay, yeah."

"I will have some cash, something to get set up with. Maybe a massive change is a good thing?"

"Maybe it is…"

"Are you hungry?" I check my watch, six pm, I must have slept for hours.

"You want to go get chips?"

"Yeah, okay."

"Do you think I'm crazy?" She laughs as we walk back from the chipper, dipping into her bag of 'fries'.

"What? No. Why do you ask?"

"Because I think I had a time-machine in a wooden box in my shed."

"Oh, that. Well, maybe you did?"

"Or, I have some sleep disorder and hallucinations. I prefer the time-machine explanation."

"Either one is okay."

"I wish I had a way to find out the truth."

"Go to a therapist or something?"

"Oh, yeah, they'd love that," I scoff. "Hello, I'm Terry. A stressed out, sleep deprived, redundancy-cheque-holding, ex-project-manager, who thinks he had a time-machine in a box, that he found while clearing out his late Father's workshop. They'd see a big euro note walk into the door of their clinic.

No, I'll give that a miss. It's a box of junk now anyway. I have zero in the way of proof."

"Did you ever take a photo of it? When it was still a time-machine?"

"No, it never occurred to me. I was sort of keeping it secret. But that would have been a good idea…"

We get back to the hotel and go up to our room. "I forgot to do this last time." I take out my phone and grab Rachel and perform the 'selfie' action that I've seen other people do, but never once found a good reason to do myself.

"In case you turn out to be a figment of my imagination."

"I'm real, dude."

She pokes me in the ribs and then flicks my chest, proving her existence with pain and tickles.

"You wanna watch a movie or something?" She motions at the vast TV on the wall that we haven't yet switched on once.

"Oh, yeah, okay. I haven't done that in a while."

Chips and a movie with my girlfriend, I'm turning into a normal human!

Chapter Forty-One

WEDNESDAY 3RD OCTOBER

When I woke this morning, Rachel was still asleep. I popped out and tried to find a florist open, but of course, there weren't any yet. I ended up in the supermarket, looking for a bunch of roses. Today is four weeks since we met, I thought I would mark the occasion, since Rachel reminded me last week it was three.

I didn't think about a vase, and Rachel is still sleeping when I get back to the hotel, so I get the ice-bucket and put the roses in that. They don't stand up very straight though. Best I can do in the dark while tip-toeing around.

I put the pot on for coffee and head to the bathroom, and wonder who the old, grey-templed, pot-bellied dude is, lurking in the mirror. Why is he in a hotel room with a beautiful young girl, without significant money changing hands? Some mysteries are too complicated to solve, especially at this early hour.

. . .

Time, For a Change

Rachel has woken and is sipping a coffee. Fumbling in her purse, she pulls out her phone and takes a photo of the roses, languishing askew in the ice-bucket.

"You are so sweet!"

"Good morning, gorgeous. Happy four week anniversary!"

"Oh my god, I can't believe you went out and got flowers."

"Well, it was easier, and quicker, than growing them here."

"Shut up!"

She gives me a hug and a kiss and then runs off to the bathroom.

I'm not in any rush to go into the office this morning, I don't have much to do now anyway, Rachel will test and sign off a few more samples, but I'm just sitting around scratching my arse, unless something goes entirely pear-shaped, which is unlikely now. I call down to reception and get a big breakfast ordered up for room service and scroll the endless tweets for a bit while I wait.

Rachel is still in the bathroom when the food arrives. She sure knows how to lollygag in there!

When she finally emerges I'm already halfway through my breakfast. She sits down and nibbles at a piece of toast.

"I don't think we need to rush in today. There's not much left to do, right?"

"No, it's kinda boring really."

"No shit, imagine working there for ten years."

"Time for a change. Do you really think you could come to Ohio and get a job?"

"Well…" I pause while I chew a bite of sausage.

"There's a lot of unknowns. Visa issues, logistical complications. It almost sounds like a project that needs to be managed…"

She smiles and scoops some scrambled eggs onto her fork.

"Then there's my house here. What do I do with it? No one in their right mind would buy or even rent it. It's either a liability or an asset, or both, depending on how you look at it. And it's my house…"

A wave of nostalgic sadness hits me, at the thought of just leaving the 'pile of stones, vaguely house shaped' home I have lived in for a good chunk of my life. My blood, sweat, tears and any other bodily fluid you care to think about, has been spilt there. It's a part of me, no matter how nasty it may seem to anyone else. I need to keep it, even if I don't live in it. Maybe I can fix it up a bit with the redundancy money? I probably won't be able to make it a hundred-percent woman-friendly without dropping massive amounts of cash on it, but I can at least fix the door and maybe paint a bit, and get some more rugs. Despite what Rachel said, I know she was just being polite about it.

"If I can get a solid job, then I'm sure I can figure the rest out. If you want me around…"

"What? Yes! Why wouldn't I?"

"Well, honestly, why would you? I'm an old boring nerd in drastic need of a diet and exercise." I realise the irony as I take another bite of sausage wrapped in buttery toast.

"You are smart, funny, thoughtful. And the dad-bod is in right now." She smiles and reaches over and pats my tummy.

"Thanks… I think!"

"And the universe brought us together for a reason."

"Okay, but what reason?"

"Good question."

She takes another bite of eggs, and then pushes the plate away and gets up to do her makeup and hair.

"You gonna eat that?" as the words come out of my mouth I hear myself and I'm embarrassed.

"Oh, never mind. I need to diet, or at least, just try and eat less."

When we get to the office Sean is flapping around like a bird caught in a chimney. He's making a lot of noise, disturbing a lot of soot and dust, but not getting anywhere. Apparently, the factory only processed about half of what Sean had asked them to yesterday. Some other order was given a priority by a faceless Vice President, and the factory just blindly obeyed and dumped us. They didn't mention this to Sean, who was unaware until this morning that we are about a hundred units short of where we should be by now. So much for getting this out early!

Sean is now bending the ear of anyone he can think of to get his priority back, raising hell, calling in favours, getting managers off golf-courses, but the order came from the US head-office, so they won't even be awake for hours.

This is precisely the kind of shit I won't miss one single bit. We all worked hard to get this deal done, on time, to a critical deadline, under stress and pressure. Only to have the sugar-apple snatched out of our sweaty hands at the last second, by a prick who has no idea of the implications of his decision. Probably acting out of ball-swinging bravado, trying to prove something to his manager. Sucking the dick above him to get that extra five percent bonus.

Rachel is shocked, and I think she's embarrassed for us, this is going to look terrible to Pete. If this was any other customer, I would have hidden the truth away from them, made up some story about temporary factory downtime, while a crucial system is updated, but we'd plan a night-shift to get back on track. Anything to take the focus off the shitty truth, you got dumped for a shinier pile of gold.

"Cunts willnae budge!" Sean walks over to my desk, pulls up a chair from a nearby unoccupied cubicle and flops down. He looks exhausted, drained of colour, sweating like a turkey in December.

"He said he'll try and get some of it done on the evening shift. But he cannae make any promises."

"Sorry, dude. This is shit. Everyone busted their holes to get this done. So close, but no fucking cigar."

"Any ideas?"

"How many left to do?"

"Err, they did a hundred, plus the fifty before. So about three hundred and fifty units."

"Motherfucker."

"Aye."

An idea comes to me, but it's not a pleasant one. I walk over to Eoghan's desk, Sean follows. Rachel, curious, follows too.

"Hey. How many burn slots in the lab?"

"Twenty-five I think, why?" Eoghan looks up at the three of us, standing by his desk, ominous.

"Oh no! Forget it!"

"There's no other way. The factory won't help. We can't come this far and lose the deal."

"What's the plan, Terry?" Sean looks hopeful but worried.

"We bring the systems into our test lab. Fucking do it ourselves. I reckon we could maybe process eighty or a hundred units a day."

"Us?"

"Yep."

"But I haven't a clue what tae do!"

"Follow the work-instruction; it's written for muppets to understand. Trained monkeys could do it."

"There's other stuff in the burn racks," Eoghan complains.

"Temporary reassignment to the hold queue. I don't give a shit, they can't fire me any more than they already have."

"Let's do it!" Sean seems pumped again. I'm not sure if he knows what he's getting into, it's tough work, delicate with sharp edges, he's not used to actual physical work. Nor am I, of course, it's been a long time since I was hands-on.

I look over at Rachel and raise an eyebrow, she nods in favour. I lead the way to the factory to find a fork-lift trolley. Eoghan is notable by his absence. Fucker stayed at his desk, so I go back for him, no man left behind!

"The fuck, lad?"

"This is not my problem." He stares at the code on his screen, doesn't look up, doesn't make eye contact.

"Not mine either. But shit happens."

"I have other work to do now."

"Can it wait a couple of days?"

"No!"

"Look, I don't know if we can do this as it is, but I had to give Sean a glimmer of hope. Four of us will make more headway than three of us. I'll clear it with your manager. Make sure he knows how hard you worked on this deal. I'm sure he won't want it to fail now either."

Eoghan continues to ignore me.

"Come on dude, it'll be fun!" He sneers and finally turns to look at me.

"This is my last ever project." I try the sympathy card.

"It would be nice if this one didn't crash and burn like everything else."

"Ugh! Fine!"

"Nice one! I'll buy the coffee break biccies!" Aye, with Rachel's fucking credit card!

In the lab, we've stacked up a hundred boxes of servers, which take up a surprising amount of space, and were no fun at all to load up onto the forklift, then wheel over and unload. We're all sweaty now and the lab smells like a gym locker-room after the overweight and unfit olympic weightlifting team practice. Sean rolled up his sleeves and kept up the morale, back to his cheery self.

It took way longer than I estimated just to get the stock into the lab, and we haven't started any configuration yet.

I've commandeered every download rack and six benches too, just in case we can drum up some more help. The lab manager was moaning and whiney about us doing this, until I introduced him to the customer we have with us onsite. He shut-up very quickly once he saw Rachel, he even helped us empty the other crap out of the racks. Incredible the power a pretty girl has in an environment of mostly old dudes.

"Okay, lads, we have benches, racks, servers. I've printed out the full work instructions and put a set on each bench. There's a whiteboard by the rack, divided into four. When you complete the hardware setup and move a unit to the download rack, chalk up a point. When we are finished, the most points wins."

I don't encourage competition usually, in fact, I despise it, it can drive aggression and pointless patriotism, but I think in this situation it could be useful to keep up the pace.

"What do we win?" Eoghan pipes up, arms folded.

I was going to say, the satisfaction of doing a good job? But that won't fly here. I look over at Sean, as it will be his credit card funding this.

"Um, an all expenses paid trip to the supermarket to buy us all some chocolates?"

"Nah, I'll buy something decent for the winner. A brand new phone perhaps? Top of the range."

"Oh, that makes things interesting!" Eoghan looks impressed too, Rachel doesn't seem to care. I think she's less impressed by gadgets than us long-term-nerds! But that's my morale boosted. I'll wipe Eoghan off the board and get an extra leaving pressie!

Although I haven't done any of the physical configurations, I've watched Rachel and Eoghan do it over and over, so I'm okay with it. Sean will need to practice and start slowly though, I better run through it with him the first couple of times.

We disperse to our benches, where a shiny server is already set up, waiting to be filled with expensive equipment.

"Electrostatic discharge strap up! And may the best man - or woman - win!" I almost feel like adding 'Go team!' but there's no way I'd stoop to that level.

"Oh, and remember we are going for quality as well as quantity. Don't bend any pins or drop anything!"

. . .

The benches, the monitors on wheels, the keyboards and mice tangled up, hanging down by their cables, it all reminds me of when I started in the company. Doing the overnight deployments and testing. The whole effect tied up with the familiar smell of new computers, acrid and electrical.

I pop in some headphones and select a suitably rocking playlist and fire into it.

When we break for lunch, the scores are:

Sean - 4, Eoghan - 9, Rachel - 8, Terry - 7

I am not doing anywhere near as well as I had hoped, but we have made some good progress overall. I have been helping Sean quite a bit, but by the third system, he was pretty confident. After lunch, he's on his own and I'm going to tear into it!

Sean ordered pizza to be delivered to us, and we take it to the canteen to eat. If anyone complains they can lick my sweaty balls.

"We're doing it!" Sean claps his hands together. He's taken off his tie and jacket. Circles of sweat under his arms confirm my plan to leave him to work on his own for the afternoon shift.

"Yeah, even though we shouldn't have to.'

"I'll try hassling the VP again later. But we're doing great here anyway."

"Still a long way to go."

"Stay positive!"

"Yup, I plan to be winning the new phone by the end of this!"

"That's the spirit!"

Eoghan looks up from his pizza, a knowing grin on his mug, he may be ahead now but I plan on doing two at once later, using two benches at a time. This is like short order cooking. Time slows down in my head, and I see many steps ahead, I have been optimising a system, a more efficient method than the work instruction shows. I need a longer wrist strap cable though, so I can jump between benches easier. Also, it would help if all the cards and parts were already unboxed and ready, so I'll spend some time doing that up front. Maybe I did catch the efficiency virus the other day?

This is a challenge, something to exercise the mind and body, it requires concentration, dexterity, accuracy. It blocks out the need to scroll tweets, delete emails. It's freeing in a certain way, freeing my brain from its endless cycles of bullshit to keep it occupied. Now I have a real task to process.

Rachel is quiet, sitting next to me, nibbling at her pizza. I expect it now, she's not going to be comfortable around other people, what I don't understand is what is different about me? Why is she an entirely different person when we're alone? Perhaps her universe theory is correct, maybe we are meant for each other somehow? Soul mates? I don't know if I believe in souls, let alone soul mates. I have to admit, there is something spiritual about the whole thing.

. . .

We head back to the lab and the 'still-tall mountain' of servers yet to process. I start setting up for my afternoon shift, I reckon I can crank out sixteen more systems today if I stick to my plan.

Sean stops off at the vending machine and gets a load of cold drinks for us. He sets them up on a different table, far away from the servers and benches. The last thing we need is a can of drink emptied inside one of the expensive systems.

I pop in my headphones and level-up the heaviness a few notches. I need a rhythm to pace myself to.

Still unfit, still old, still overweight. By the time I get my sixteen units done it's six pm. This day that started out as a lazy one, ended up exhausting. We have completed eighty units in total. Eoghan chalked up another fourteen, meaning me and him are tied at twenty-three for the day.

Sean worked his arse off, in fairness to him. He's not cut out for this at all, but he's doing his bit. He promised to spend the evening on the phone, trying to get the factory to prioritise our orders again. But if he doesn't, then we'll be back at the grindstone again in the morning.

Tomorrow looms ahead, another stack of servers, another day of hot sweaty work. It seemed like it might be fun, but now I can barely walk to the car. Rachel looks okay, if a little tired. She has youth on her side.

When we get to the hotel, I collapse onto the bed, Rachel goes to shower and change. I order food on my phone and sink into the soft mattress. When I close my eyes I see the servers, the sharp aluminium edges, the needle pins and copper traces, I smell the electricity, the pungent taste of metal in my nose.

Chapter Forty-Two

THURSDAY 4TH OCTOBER

After we ate last night, I felt a bit better, energised, but aching everywhere. I stood in the shower for at least twenty minutes, letting the hot rain soothe my creaking joints. I fell on the bed after, and Rachel, feeling sorry for my old bones, massaged my back, her fingers squeezing out the stress of the day with her scented oil. I woke up slowly this morning, from a depth of sleep I haven't known for years.

I check my phone for messages and emails to see if Sean had any luck, but there's nothing. That means we're building systems again.

I assume we're still going out tonight to Bunratty Castle, for the banquet? But if I'm as tired tonight as I was last night, that will be hard to be enthusiastic about. Sean has arranged a big taxi to take all of us there and back again, so no one has to drive. Not that I plan to drink, but whatever.

. . .

We get to the office quite early, but Sean is already there. He's started loading up the fork-lift already. That confirms another day of hard labour!

I join in hefting boxes, but Rachel excuses herself from the lifting and goes to check her emails, which is okay, she's half our size.

"They did a few last night for us, so we're up to three-hundred units complete now."

"Oh, that's good. Still a lot to do."

"Aye, I know, but the factory lad said he'd try and do some more this evening too."

"Nice one."

Eoghan shows up just as we have a fork-lift full, and Sean and I are already sweaty and panting. I'm sure he timed that on purpose. Sean had the good sense to wear a T-Shirt and sweatpants today instead of the suit. He looks like he's trying to run a marathon on a drunken bet, but he's knackered just by walking to the starting line.

We congregate in the lab and unload all the boxes and then set up one on each bench. Here we go again!

I feel bad being so pathetic about doing this physical work, after all, there are plenty of people right now in our factory, doing precisely the same job. But they do it every day, all day. I think most of them are much younger than Sean and I though, and they probably haven't spent the last decade sitting on their arses at a desk. Back when I cooked for money I could have run circles around this task.

But now, the morale boost of possibly winning a new phone has worn off. I'll buy my own fucking phone! I'm going to pace myself today and not try any crazy stuff.

. . .

Rachel said she didn't tell Pete what was going on, there was no need to cause panic. After all, the work is getting done anyway. Sean was very grateful for that.

Lunch is delivered, sandwiches this time, on Sean's tab again. We've clocked up forty-seven units between us already, we got an earlier start than yesterday. Might make the hundred today if we have a good afternoon session. But we need to stop at five, so we all have time to go home and shower and change before we get the taxi to Bunratty.

"Looking forward to the feast tonight!" Sean tucks into his foot-long with aplomb. He's earned his lunch today, he's processed ten units already himself, no assistance needed.

"Yeah, should be a laugh. Go easy on the mead though. Factory work on a mead hangover won't be much fun!"

"Put hairs on yer chest that will!"

"What's mead?" Rachel asks me quietly.

"It's kind of like beer or wine, but made with honey."

"Oh boy, that sounds awesome."

"It goes down very nicely. But you have to take it easy, or you end up with no feeling in your face!"

"Yeah, I don't want to get wasted."

She reaches under the table and squeezes my leg, I look over at her, and she's smiling, pretty as a sunrise on a misty morning.

Sean checks his emails on his phone. He's been trying to get ahold of the VP who instructed the factory to process the other order before ours, but no luck so far. The fucker seems to have dropped a bomb and then done a vanishing act. At this rate, we'll have it all done before we get anywhere.

We head back to the mines and start smashing rocks again, with our pick-axes, like the prisoners we are. No rest for the convicted!

The work is repetitive now, boring, I don't bother looking at the work instruction anymore, I have a nice little pattern going here, and I'm in a groove. Eoghan might be doing more than me, but I am no longer able to donate any excrement to that cause. My mind drifts back to the mysterious box in my shed, the time-machine that was. I'm sure that it wasn't just a box of junk, the experiences were too real, too vivid. So if that's true, then something must have changed it into the junk that it is now. What happened? Or, what will happen? Does my future self find out how to communicate back into the past? Do I destroy the machine? Do I tell Dad not to make it in the first place? I may never find out. I live on a different time-line now. I have to assume that whatever it was that made this change was significant. Maybe something in Rachel's tarot reading can explain it? Or at least, shed some candlelight? So many questions, bugger-all answers. There's no Wikipedia for 'Am I going bat-shit crazy?'

"FUCK!"

I pull my hand up, and blood drips onto the server lid, I move away.

"Er, anyone know where the first-aid box is?"

Sean and Rachel come rushing over, but it isn't too bad. I just slid my finger along a sharp edge. Shit. This will slow me down now. We find the first-aid kit, me holding my arm up above my head, clasping the finger tight.

Rachel takes charge and sits me down.

"You asshole! You have to be careful!"

"Sorry."

"Okay, let me see it."

I unwrap my hands and look away as Rachel mops up the blood, and dabs at the cut, and then wipes my hands clean.

"It's not bad, just messy. But you'll have to rest for a minute and wrap up with a band-aid."

"Ugh."

She fixes me up, and Sean brings me a cold bottle of water, then he goes over to check the server I was working on. I don't think any blood went inside, and the lid is just sheet aluminium, so it will wipe clean. No harm was done, but I expect I'll have a wee scar from this. Physically and mentally.

Five-o-clock comes around eventually, and with it aching limbs and throbbing feet, not to mention a bloody finger. My war wound did slow me down considerably. Surprising how often you need a finger to be flexible, and not wrapped up in bandages.

Despite that hindrance, we finish the day having processed ninety-six units, not bad at all. Shame we didn't make the hundred, but I'm hopeful the factory can work on some tonight. We may not even need to do this again tomorrow if we're lucky.

Driving back to the hotel, I wince every time I change gear, my finger protruding like I'm drinking Earl Grey tea with the Queen of England. This is what happens when you let your mind slip away.

Which reminds me of the evening's events, guests of the Earl of Thomond in his castle at Bunratty. Now I think about it, I really would prefer pizza in bed, but Sean is excited about it, Eoghan reluctantly agreed, but made a fuss about it, Rachel seems to be looking forward to the experience.

"I'm gonna jump in the shower."

"That sounds dangerous. You could slip over."

"Shut up, Dad!"

"Oh my god, don't call me dad!"

"Don't make dad jokes then."

She smiles and sticks out her tongue, and vanishes into the bathroom. I take the opportunity to lie down for a while. I'm not as shagged out as I was yesterday, but I'm still tired. The overwhelming kind of tired, that puts the world in a shroud around me. Coffee doesn't help, only resting for a while lifts the heavy fug of somnolence from me.

When Rachel comes out of the bathroom I'm drifting along the thin line between conscious and unconscious, but she wakes me with the whip of wet hair on my face, followed quickly by a kiss.

"Wake up, sleepy-head."

"Ugh."

"Take a shower, and you'll feel better."

"Ugh."

I do as she says, and she's right of course, the hot water somehow washes away the lethargic torpor, and I emerge brighter and more able to function.

Rachel is still doing makeup. I'm used to her rituals now, next will come the hair straightening. She's wearing an outfit that somehow I haven't yet seen in the two weeks she's been here. A long black dress, seemingly torn at the edges, but probably not torn. Cleavage spills in abundance, and her black boots draw my eye to pale skin, meshed in fishnet. A shiver runs through me as I towel myself dry, and she delicately colours around her eyes with some kind of pencil.

"You look suitably medieval!"

"Thanks." She stands up and shows me the full effect, which is stunning, I feel like I'm not meant to touch the delicate art, but that's what I want to do. She has an aura of perfume that only drags me closer, but she bats me away, the portrait is still a work in progress, and she sits back down and resumes the pencil-work.

"You better hurry up. The taxi won't be long."

"Don't worry about me. I'll be ready in two minutes."

I pull clean clothes from my suitcase, a fresh pair of jeans, and an Iron Maiden T-shirt.

"A band shirt?"

"No, a medieval torture device!"

She rolls her eyes at me, and I scrape back my hair over her shoulder in the mirror.

"Ready!"

"Men are so lucky."

"I don't know about that. We have to go hunt and gather,

make fire, invent smart-phones, fly to the Moon and stuff… All before dinner."

"Shut up!" She plugs in her hair device that she'll probably leave with me when she goes home.

"We do, or you women would stray away to a fancier nest. Or something like that. It's all about the genes." I point to the groin area of the jeans I'm wearing, and attempt an Elvis style grind, but I fail, and look more like an arthritic Penguin trying to hail a taxi.

"Never do that again!" She laughs and swipes through her hair with her hot straightening device.

"I think you have good genes. Aside from the dancing ones."

"Thanks, I got them from Amazon on special offer."

"You know what I mean!"

We linger down around the front entrance of the hotel, waiting for the taxi-bus to the Castle. Sean messaged me they are on the way, so we hurried downstairs. There's a crisp bite to the evening air, a mist of breath dissipating on the sharp breeze. Rachel snuggles up against me, her perfume causing me distraction and thoughts of going back upstairs. But here we are, ready to go.

"Do I look okay?" She stands back so I can see.

"You look like songs were written about you, songs of heartbreak and pain."

"Is that good?"

"Yes."

The taxi-bus pulls up beside us, Sean pops open the sliding door, and we get in, he's changed and showered, but it smells like he showered in aftershave. The taxi stinks like a stag-night group, going through duty-free. I crack a window open, so we don't suffocate. Eoghan lurks quietly in the back seat, scrolling his phone, ignoring the world.

The journey isn't long, I've driven past the castle many thousands of times, to and from work every day. But taxis always seem slow. Sean has some banter with the driver, I can't make out what he's saying. Rachel is looking out the window, contemplatively it seems.

The castle looms next to the motorway, lit in sodium orange, impressive and daunting. We exit the taxi and step into the past.

There's a sound of distant bagpipes droning as we walk up to the tower, so much bigger now. Oppressive and cold. We climb the stone steps and cross a drawbridge. If it weren't stone cold real, it could be a dream or a fairytale. As we enter a massive hall, we're offered bread with salt, and a cup of mead by a lady in colourful medieval style clothes. A lone, kilted piper plays his morose tune. I've never been a fan of bagpipes, but the others seem to be enthralled. Rachel sips at her glass of mead, she smiles at me, but puts the cup down on a table. I haven't tried mine, but Sean has gulped his down, so I hand him my glass which he takes with a grin. Eoghan sips slowly and nibbles his bread and salt that they call a 'bite of friendship.'

Other dinner guests arrive, and the piper finishes his tune. We are ushered into the vast dining room, where a group of the staff are singing, and a lady plays the harp, another on a fiddle. You don't get this at the drive-through burger place!

We are seated at a long wooden bench table, Rachel sits at the edge and me next to her, Eoghan and Sean opposite. Presumably, strangers will be next to us shortly. That makes me uncomfortable. I'm not in the mood for empty small-talk with a tourist, desperate to find his roots. I'm never in that mood.

In my youth, I had a 'fuck-off zone' around me. An aura of blackness that meant people would avoid me on public transport, or in the street. But I think it has worn away with time. Strangers ask me directions in foreign lands, people sometimes talk to me in the supermarket. I'm not sure what happened, but perhaps I have softened over the years?

Still, I wish the table we are at was only going to be us. But we'll cross that drawbridge when we get to it. Sean flags down a serving wench and orders up a jug of mead for the table. Which means him and Eoghan. Rachel and I get water.

The menu is quite sparse, but looks nice. Wholesome and unpretentious, yet still presented well.

"This place is brilliant!" Sean gulps down a cup of mead and looks around at the vast dining hall.

"Think of all the Kings and Queens that have dined here."

"Oh aye, we're dining like royalty tonight!"

Sean fills his cup and then motions we all lift our glasses, which we do, somewhat awkwardly.

"A toast to an amazing partnership with FutureCloud!" He nods at Rachel who smiles shyly.

"And to Eoghan for his outstanding work getting the project working." Eoghan mutters a quiet 'thanks.'

"But also to Terry, for managing the details, for winning the deal, for his outstanding work over the last ten years. And for good luck in the future, mate, with whatever you end up doing."

He nods at me and clinks on my glass.

"Thanks, Sean." Everyone looks at me, expecting some kind of speech? I'm not set up for this.

"Err. I've had some fun times over the years. Worked with

some great people." I look around at the gathered throng of three.

"But sometimes, the universe offers up a new path to take. An unknown adventure is waiting to happen." I look at Rachel, next to me, and my future seems to be bound to hers.

"Uh, I don't know what else to say really!" My pathetic speech went off like a damp squib. But we all clink glasses and everyone seems happy.

"Anyway, the deal isn't done yet, we still might have to process some more servers tomorrow."

"I had a word with the factory lad. He's going to try and get the rest done for us somehow."

"Nice one!"

"Aye, we'll see what he says in the morning. But either way I have to leave for my flight back by one o'clock."

"Right. Go easy on the mead then, eh!"

"Aye, right!" Sean gives me a wink and drains his cup.

A group of medieval servers bring us soup, bread and more mead. The food of Kings! This is turning out to be a nice evening. I'm glad we came.

Chapter Forty-Three

FRIDAY 5TH OCTOBER

Rachel and I decided to sneak away last night, before things got too wild. Sean was made King for the night, Eoghan was taken to the dungeons. I'm thankful to whichever deity it was, that arranged for us to not be selected for audience participation!

Sean's 'Queen' was an American lady who was seated next to him. They were extricated and moved to the top table and given crowns. They ruled over the dinner feast from there. It was probably fun if you were drunk, but of course, Rachel and I weren't.

I don't think they really took Eoghan to the dungeons. I'm sure he was plied with more mead just outside the dining hall or something. In any case, everyone seemed to have a good time. Sean especially as he vigorously flirted with his Queen.

We got our own taxi back to the hotel and left them in their revelry. I'm sure we'll hear all about it when - or if - they arrive at the office. I checked with the factory when we got in this morning, they almost finished all the orders last night. We have just twenty units left to do now, so after our morning coffee we started the loading up. But it isn't going very well. My finger bandage fell off and had to be replaced, because the wound is still a bit delicate, plus my gout foot pain flared up during the night, despite my avoidance of booze and plenty of cherry tablets. Stress and hard work probably aggravated it, so I'm limping around until my painkillers kick in.

We need to leave early today, Rachel flies back tomorrow morning, and we still need to pack up and pay the disturbingly large hotel bill. Rachel seems a bit distracted and sad this morning. I'm not looking forward to saying goodbye either, so I'm almost glad we have work to take our minds off the inevitable.

"What happened to you last night?" Sean rolls into the lab, all smiles and good cheer. No sign of a hangover.

"Hey, nice of you to finally join us. We're almost finished here, only a few left to do."

"Had some things to take care of this morning." He gives me a wink. Say no more.

"We decided to go home early. We had things to do, too." I give Sean a wink back. We had sleeping to do, but he doesn't need to know the details.

"Where's Eoghan?"

"No idea. Maybe they kept him in the dungeons?"

"Ha, no, I saw him later, chatting with a woman."

"Really? That doesn't sound like Eoghan."

"Alcohol, buddy, loosens up the brain."

"Fair enough! You going to do some work then?"

. . .

Time, For a Change

Sean makes a show of going over to his bench and starting work on a system, and I go back to my area, without the limp now the painkillers are doing their job.

As we load up the last unit into the download racks, we celebrate with a high-five, and we decide to go out for lunch while the systems 'cook', and then Sean has to head off to Shannon for his flight back home.

There were no fireworks, no Champagne pops, but we're finally done. The deal worked out, and everything can now ship out later. Pete will be happy, Sean will get paid, Rachel will go home and probably quit her job soon, and I'll go to Italy and think about what I'm going to do with the rest of my life.

I have no more work to do here, but I still have to come in every day for the last week, so I get my redundancy money. It's going to be a boring week sitting on my arse.

Maybe I'll write the emails I've been wanting to for ten years, telling everyone what I really think of them? But probably not, the old saying rings in my head 'Living well is the best revenge.' Anyway, if I end up going to Ohio and working for FutureCloud, I'll probably still have to work with people here. From the other side of the fence. I'll still see Sean when he inevitably comes back to Ohio, for the next project and piss-up. Some things change, some things remain the same. I might even end up back in this very lab again one day, in the same capacity Rachel is here now. Best not to burn any bridges then.

. . .

"Any thoughts on what you want to do next?" Sean turns around in the line for the pub carvery we ended up in.

"Loads of thoughts, mate, but no conclusions. I might give you a shout next week about something."

"Do that. I have a feeling this isn't the last I'll see of you!"

"Yeah, maybe so."

Sean pays for our lunches, and we find a nice big seat in the spacious bar.

"You happy, Rachel?" Sean takes a bite of beef. She looks up, shocked to be addressed.

"Oh, yeah. I mean, everything is done on time. Pete will be happy."

"How about you, Sean? You'll get your new Mercedes after all?"

"Ha! I wish it were that simple. Aye, I'm very happy with the work we did, but it won't make me rich. Just keep the wolves at bay for a little longer."

"Someone is getting rich off this though."

"Oh yeah, the man at the top of the pile."

"Always the way, huh?"

"Aye."

I was sure Sean would be raking it in from this deal, so I'm a bit shocked to learn it isn't that much of a boost for him. I always assumed the sales people were rolling around in cash from all the work we did. Maybe I judged them too harshly? Perhaps we all do our little bit, and we all get shafted in the end, by the man at the top? We all get paid just enough to keep the bills at bay, and give us a tiny sense of freedom, but deep down we know we're slaves to the system.

The mortgages, the holidays to Portugal, the new furniture and big screen TVs, they all keep us chained to the production line.

I'm lucky to be escaping then, given a change of civilian clothes, a passport, a wallet full of cash, and the guards in the gun-towers look the other way while I run across the dirt fields. But do I run into another type of prison? Or find something better to do with my life?

"I better head off." Sean stands up and sticks out a hand, I get up too, and give him a firm shake.

"Safe flight, mate. I'll call you Monday."

"Bye Rachel, I'm sure I'll see you again, in Ohio soon enough."

She stands up and smiles, shakes his hand, but doesn't say anything. I don't think she will see Sean in Ohio. I think she'll be busy at a craft fair or something.

Sean exits, stage left.

"I guess we better go see if everything has finished?"

When we get back to the lab, Eoghan is hovering around the racks, logged in to one of the servers with a screen and keyboard on a little trolley.

"Are these the last ones?" He looks concerned and nervous.

"Er, yeah, nice of you to show up now everything is finished."

"Dude. I had a thought this morning. I needed to check something on the software." He motions to the screen he's standing in front of.

Oh holy fuck, now what? I look at Rachel, and she looks pale, worried.

"What have you done?"

"We've loaded the wrong software on all five hundred servers," he delivers the news with a calm, steady voice.

My mind races trying to process how this could have happened, my legs feel weak, adrenaline slams through my veins. I look around for a chair, but see nothing but a lab full of wrongly set-up servers, for a deal that has to ship today.

"What? How? Oh my fucking god."

Eoghan starts to smirk, and then breaks into a fit of giggles.

"Just kidding! They are all fine. That's for leaving me in the castle to rot in the dungeons!"

"You bastard!"

Rachel bursts into laughter when I look at her, my heart still racing, but the laughs are infectious, and I join in.

"You should be rotting in the dungeons you fucker! Are they done?"

"Yeah, all done, all fine. Let's get them moved over to shipping."

We load the servers back onto the forklift, and take them back through the factory to the shipping hold area. This is finally it. Everything is done. Anything else that goes wrong now is officially not my problem. We walk back to our desks and Rachel gets her bag and laptop, ready to leave.

"Hey, can we go for a drive somewhere before we go pack up in the hotel?"

"Oh, sure, if you like. Where do you want to go?"

"I don't know, just drive around? I don't feel like going back to the hotel just yet."

I point my car North and drive, over the Shannon river, past our picnic spot, out of the city, and along the motorway. Past

Time, For a Change

the Castle, grey and monolithic, past the exit for the airport that we'll take tomorrow early morning, and head toward my secret beach, that isn't so secret anymore. Rachel is quiet, no music, no singing, she just stares out of the window at the landscape passing by. I leave her to her thoughts and focus on the road. The dull pain in my foot makes me glad of the cruise control.

When we get to the little beach carpark, I stop and turn off the car. I turn to Rachel, and she smiles.

"Do you want to go for a walk?"

"Yeah, but not for long."

"We'll just go down to the beach and back."

I get a sense that Rachel wants to say something, but she's holding back for some reason. Is she going to tell me this is over? That she's going back to Ohio now and that's the last I'll see of her? Because she can't cope with a long distance thing, and there's no certainty that I'll be able to move country, and get a job?

Maybe she's waiting for the right moment, maybe she's just sad that she's going home, and this adventure is almost over? I don't know what is in her head, but I'll leave her to tell me whatever it is, when she's ready, because I wouldn't want to be pushed myself.

We walk down the narrow sandy path, through the golf course now owned by the U.S. President, and on down to the rocky dunes, then down onto the sand where the tide is out. We get to the edge of the water, where the sand becomes squishy.

"Well, here we are."

There's a cool breeze and an ominous looking sky out to sea, threatening rain. I turn to look at Rachel, and she's huddled in her jacket. The salty spray is causing her to squint.

"Okay, let's go back."

We walk back to the car, the wind on our backs.

"Where do you want to go now?"

"Is it far to your house?"

"No, not really, twenty minutes maybe. You want to go to my house?"

"We could get a coffee there, or something?"

"If you like."

I wonder if there's an ulterior motive for going back to my house, does she want to let me down in familiar surroundings? I can't get the notion out of my head that she wants to end this. It's painfully clear, she's got something to tell me, and she's trying to find a good place to do it. The beach was my choice, I always end up going there when something is off. But it was too windy to talk.

I think we can find a way to make things work, the universe will help, surely? Could I spend some of my redundancy to get set up in America? Or maybe she could stay here? I don't want this to end. A heaviness fills me as we head towards an inevitable closure. I don't think she really wants coffee at my house. But I need to piss anyway, so we may as well go.

I shoulder open the door and check for any post, but there isn't any. The air is musty and damp as it gets when no one is here, I should leave a window open to blow it out. Rachel sits down on the couch, and I prepare the coffee pot and switch it on. I run to the toilet while it brews.

As I piss, I remember the box in the shed and have an urge to go and take a look at it, just to be sure of things. You never know, time is a tricky beast to understand. I wouldn't be surprised if it was a time-machine again, because of some kind of cyclical feedback temporal anomaly, or something. Or maybe I just watch too much Star Trek? Either way, I need to find out.

"Hey, I'll be right back. Just going over to the shed for something. Pour the coffee if you want?"

I want to look on my own this time, in case the complication of Rachel in the room was the trigger for the strangeness.

The rain has hit now. Running over to the shed gets me soaking wet, as I fumble with the keys and open up the door. The box is where we left it, where I put it on the bench. There's no clicking sound now, no drone as I move closer. The words on the top of the lid read:

"General odds and sods !!"

And as I open up the lid, I see nothing but the promised 'odds and sods' inside. A box of junk. Tools, plumbing equipment, bits of copper pipe, a sheet of brass. Four black knobs in a small dusty bag.

I guess that's it then. The machine has gone, replaced by junk. I'm relieved and disappointed. I had one final hope left that there would be a spinning cone of brass inside the box, unnaturally defying the laws of physics, and, in-so-doing, causing some kind of temporal displacement field. I go back to the house, where Rachel is no doubt planning some more disappointment for me.

Two coffee cups sit on the table in front of the couch. Rachel is perched on the edge, and she beckons me over.

. . .

"Hey, Terry. I've been trying to tell you something for a while now."

Here we go, the prelude to the dumping. Do I cut in with reasons why she should reconsider before I've heard her story? Do I change the subject and avoid the whole conversation, and drive us back to the hotel for some last minute, mind-blowing sex, to convince her to stick with me? Do I let it wash over me, and just add it to the pile of massive life-changing events that are happening to me?

"Oh."

Or do I just sit here like a bacon sarnie in a synagogue?

"But the time was never right. There was the whole thing with your time-machine. And then the work stuff. Anyway, now I'm heading back home tomorrow, and I have to tell you now."

"Okay. Are we over?"

"What? No!"

No? I feel a wave of relief pulse through me, a knot in my throat melts away, she's not dumping me? Well, then, what is this?

"Oh! I just thought…"

"Shut up and listen! I've taken two tests now, and they are like, super-accurate."

"Tests?"

"I took one at three weeks and one at four weeks. So, there's no doubt now."

"Three and four weeks? From what?"

"When we first had sex! Terry! I'm pregnant!"

. . .

Time, For a Change

I hear the words, but they don't resolve in my mind for a moment, the room grows dark, I feel a wave of nausea…

A sudden change, a drop in temperature, the feeling of falling fast. Darkness, no weight. Silence, a rapid fade of all external senses.

... [please hold while we try to connect you] ...

Do me a favour?

I genuinely hope you enjoyed this story and I'd love to hear about it. So would other readers. I would be eternally grateful if you would leave a review on Amazon for me.

I don't have a big-name publisher or agent, or any marketing help. I rely on the kind words of readers to spread the word and help others find my books.

In a world of constant rating requests from everything you buy, I know it's a pain, but it does make a huge difference and it encourages me to keep writing.

Thanks!
Adam.

www.AdamEcclesBooks.com